P9-CDK-691

blue
rider
press

CATALINA EDDY

ALSO BY DANIEL PYNE

Fifty Mice
A Hole in the Ground Owned by a Liar
Twentynine Palms

CATALINA EDDY

EDDY

A Novel in Three Decades

DANIEL PYNE

BLUE RIDER PRESS
New York

Iosco-Arenac
District Library

blue
rider
press

An imprint of Penguin Random House LLC
375 Hudson Street
New York, New York 10014

Copyright © 2017 by Daniel Pyne
Penguin supports copyright. Copyright fuels creativity, encourages diverse voices,
promotes free speech, and creates a vibrant culture. Thank you for buying an authorized
edition of this book and for complying with copyright laws by not reproducing, scanning,
or distributing any part of it in any form without permission. You are supporting writers
and allowing Penguin to continue to publish books for every reader.

Blue Rider Press is a registered trademark and its colophon
is a trademark of Penguin Random House LLC

Library of Congress Cataloging-in-Publication Data

Names: Pyne, Daniel, author.
Title: Catalina eddy : a novel in three decades / Daniel Pyne.
Description: New York : Blue Rider Press, 2017.
Identifiers: LCCN 2016041986 (print) | LCCN 2016052645 (ebook) | ISBN
9780399171659 (hardcover) | ISBN 9780698168718 (epub)
Subjects: LCSH: Police—California, Southern—Fiction. | BISAC: FICTION / Crime. |
FICTION / Mystery & Detective / General. | GSAFD: Mystery fiction.
Classification: LCC PS3616.Y56 A6 2017 (print) | LCC PS3616.Y56 (ebook) |
DDC 813/.6—dc23
LC record available at https://lccn.loc.gov/2016041986
p.   cm.

Printed in the United States of America
1   3   5   7   9   10   8   6   4   2

BOOK DESIGN BY LUCIA BERNARD

This is a work of fiction. Names, characters, places, and incidents either are the product
of the author's imagination or are used fictitiously, and any resemblance to actual persons,
living or dead, businesses, companies, events, or locales is entirely coincidental.

For my mom and dad,
who took me to the church of
The Rockford Files, Harry O, and *Peter Gunn*

4c
Py

7/17 B+T 28.00

CATALINA
EDDY

THE BIG EMPTY

JUNE 1954

1

THIS NUCLEAR EXPLOSION was unlike anything anyone had ever seen before. Bigger than Fat Boy. More terrifying than Little Man. A dazzling flash of light, a bright-blooming fast-growing impossibly mushrooming billowing monster of dust and debris, larger and larger, rising, at first quaint on the horizon and simply surreal and then, somehow, taking on the quality of death itself; the proportion of scale so out of whack, the dumb-dawning understanding that what you are watching is a window into extinction, not the fucking apple in the fucking tree in the garden with the snake, but the thing that should never have happened, the doorway you didn't open.

His angular face a shimmering transparent reflection with Hollywood Boulevard rippling behind it, the detective stares through plate glass at newsreel footage of the Castle Bravo nuclear test on Bikini Atoll, crisply wrought on a brand-new Philco television; broadcast, as a matter of fact, on half a dozen new mahogany Philco console televisions stacked like crackerbox apartments in the Nicholson's Appliances sidewalk window display, the broadcaster's narration quavering gravely down from the sidewalk PA speaker.

Empty sky.

A pale sparkling sea.

Fingerlets of land in that water: dark, insubstantial smears on a mythomorphic multiform black-and-white Mark Rothko of a horizon.

Or something.

WHOOoom. There it goes.

Breathtaking.

". . . A thousand times more powerful than the A-bomb dropped on Hiroshima . . ."

Which is, what, supposed to be comforting?

And Behold I come quickly: to every man according as his work shall be.

It's beyond words—

Alpha and Omega, I am the beginning and the end, the first and the last. So you better get on the stick—

—The hellcloud's cataclysm keeps rolling, roiling, rising.

WHILE HE'S PLEASANT to look at, the detective is not in any way pretty; cool but not cold; youthful, but not callow; shrewd, but not smart enough to avoid the trouble that invariably will find him. Dove-gray drapes his narrow frame, hat, white cotton shirt, stark black tie: the kind of guy you want your daughter once to fall in love with. But not marry.

"What have they done?"

He turns his back on the televised atomic test and levels slate eyes on the young mother, a girl still, nineteen going on forty, bum-rushing an adult world she is not nearly prepared for. Pleated skirt and sensible saddle shoes, pushing a plump baby in a carriage, she has arrested her stroll and stares past him, transfixed, horrified by what she's just seen unfold on the cathode-ray screens. Tears stream down her cheeks.

"I just keep asking myself. What have they done to our world?"

"Even they don't know, ma'am." It's a mystery the detective won't be solving.

For without are dogs. He keeps recalling, for some reason, sermon fragments from sitting sleepy beside his mom at Sunday service, in the tumble to war, when he still was trying to believe it. *And sorcerers, and whoremongers, and murderers, and idolaters, and whosoever loveth and maketh a lie.*

In other words, pretty much everybody, the detective thinks. But oh well.

He offers the young woman his handkerchief: white cotton with embroidered initials, RL—Rylan Lovely. There's a stack of them, cleaned and pressed and folded in the top drawer of the bureau back in his room.

Lovely tips his hat and waits for a rattling Red Car line to pass before continuing on his way.

"HAVE YOU NOTICED how television makes everything the same size?"

The day glares with fiery high haze cloaking a dim dot of sun;

he left his car in the shade of the clock tower and came through the delivery alley, between Pace's newsstand and Humphrey Bakery, to find his usual stool empty and waiting at the counter of Hal's Coffee. The Farmer's Market squats like some strange clapboard gypsy village in the fast-growing flatlands west of downtown Los Angeles, on the corner of Third and Fairfax, a disheveled collection of green wood kiosks and canvas awnings, the new Television City studios rise midcentury pristine to the north, where the old Gilmore Stadium once reigned.

Front page of the *Daily News* spread out next to his coffee, black, he picks at the questionable glazed Danish.

Hal's stool is Lovely's office.

"Eisenhower and Howdy Doody," Lovely gripes. "Ed Sullivan and thermonuclear war."

Headlines: H-BOMB TEST ON BIKINI ATOLL 'A MILESTONE FOR WORLD PEACE,' SEN. McCARTHY CLAIMS ARMY GENERAL 'UNFIT' FOR UNIFORM, IKE TO NIXON: VIETNAM INTERVENTION A NO-GO.

Hal, quite round, blue-black Navy tattoos on both forearms and sporting the usual cook's cap and functional apron, refills Lovely's cup of joe. "What are you on about now?"

"I was watching a newsreel of the H-bomb test in the window at Nicholson's. Our newest doomsday weapon—as if doomsday needs be enhanced and improved—a thousand times more powerful than the one we dropped on Hiroshima . . . but on the TV? No different from the lather coming off two tablets of Alka-Seltzer during the commercial break."

Hal just stares at him.

"'Relief is just a swallow away.'"

"What are you gonna do?" Hal says, rote. He's inured to

Lovely's morning jeremiad, and Lovely worries, as he often does now, that maybe he's thinking too much out loud.

Lanky greengrocer Johnny Leong crosses from where his tiny wife is stacking Valley Fresh grapefruit, and drops several scraps of messages in front of Lovely, all scrawled in Chinese.

"Not many calls for you, Ry Lovely. You should advertise. Get on the stick."

Lovely smiles, bemused, smooths and stares at the notes. "Your wife has beautiful handwriting, Johnny, but I don't read Chinese." He holds up the first one. Leong puts on his glasses:

"Miss Lily Himes—"

Lovely tucks the message away, cuts him short. "—Okay. I know what that's about."

"Word from the bird," Hal cracks.

Leong reads the second. "Screen Gems. They have an actor who has got himself in a scrape—"

"No more movie studios. I made a new rule." Lovely crumples it up. "Next."

"Jimmy Del Rio called."

"The divorce lawyer? Categorically no." Lovely crumples it. Leong shows no reaction. Another:

"Lost cat. Some little girl's pet. You have rules for cats?"

"Any reward offered?"

Leong scowls, scolds. "Mercenary."

Lovely smiles, pockets this one. The last message is written in English. Beautiful cursive that Lovely can read.

"That one came here looking for you," Leong says. "I wrote down the information myself." When Lovely stays quiet, the grocer angles his head, expressionless. "Attractive lady. Long of leg."

Lovely stares at the address.

———

HIS BLACK MORRIS MINOR rumbles around a shady curve and slides to the curb in front of a Spanish courtyard sixplex overhung by fan palm and jacaranda in the Silver Lake hillocks on the city side of Griffith Park. Rusting wrought-iron cursive on a low stucco wall spells out: *Diablo Bonita Apartments.*

Lovely double-checks the address against Johnny Leong's note, then climbs out of the car to walk under an archway pegged with tangled pink bougainvillea, and up the flagstone steps.

Bubbling fountain, tropical planters.

A lithe, sulky wisp of Aspiring Actress has arranged itself on a lounger, platinum hair fanned out, two-piece sea-foam bathing suit with rocket-cone padding she doesn't really need, a perfect ass Lovely can't help but admire, and a winged foil sun reflector tucked up under her chin, trying to find a tan in the flat, chalky light.

Big rhinestone-studded, cat's-eye sunglasses follow Lovely speculatively as he walks to the apartment in the back, and she calls out in a low, throaty stage whisper culled from Liz Taylor by way of Lauren Bacall, "Hey, Fuller Brush man. Where's my gift?"

Lovely throws her an indifferent glance and stops before the door to apartment C. Thumb poised above the doorbell, he looks back at the actress again. She smiles, lots of teeth.

Behind the screen, the front door creaks in the breeze: unlocked, not completely closed. Lovely draws open the former and nudges the latter; it swings in, revealing a cool, dark flat done up in Deco, with a female bent. Everything is tidy, symmetrical, unnaturally well ordered. No knickknacks on the counters or tables. Furniture all squared up.

Strange.

He steps in and pulls the front door shut behind him. Listens to a soft flop of curtain over an open window in the bedroom he assumes is at the end of the short, dark hallway. To his left is the kitchen, checkerboard linoleum, white Formica counters, pastel-blue painted cabinets with chrome pulls glinting the spackled light that passes through a louvered window in the back door.

A gnawing dread draws him down the hall to the bedroom, where everything, again, is ordered and pristine.

Except for the bed: unmade, tangle of sheets.

And the woman who stares sightless up at him from the floor, arms and legs awkwardly disposed, shot through the chest.

Dead.

She's beautiful, Lovely thinks. A silvery haze, like the discarded shroud of a soul, has already begun to veil her turquoise eyes. Her lips are purpled with scarlet lipstick and the start of livor mortis.

Lovely is visibly shaken. It's not the dead body; he's well acquainted with death. It's her.

Overcome by her, stunned: The utter silence of this woman is surreal to him.

He gathers himself, finds a phone on the bed stand, reaches for his handkerchief to lift the receiver, careful of fingerprints—but then discovers his handkerchief gone and remembers that he gave it away. As if separated from his body, he sees his hand is shaking, ever so slightly. His legs feel numb. He moves to the bathroom door, thinking he'll use a washcloth for the phone, but when he opens the door he discovers three policemen and a blunt, bristle-haired detective he recognizes waiting in the middle of the small tile bathroom, staring back at him like a huddle of guilty children.

"'Lo, Henry."

"What are you doing here, Lovely?" Detective Sergeant Henry Paez, Los Angeles Police Department, is wily, cynical, a third-generation Angeleno—maybe he and Lovely used to be friends and maybe Lovely made the LAPD look unusually foolish and craven not so long ago and Paez took the heat, they don't talk about it, but it haunts them both.

"New departmental policy on urination, or you just got more equipment than one man can handle?"

Lovely steps back and the cops come out, sheepish, as Paez growls, "Don't be a wisenheimer. We got an anonymous call."

"Shots fired?"

"No. Just a tip," he says, deliberately vague. "We were barely getting started, heard you come up the steps and wondered who it could be. Did you know her?"

Lovely hesitates. "Prospective client. She left a message at my office, I came at the appointed time. I don't know what she wanted."

Paez hears the equivocation. "That's not what I asked. I asked, did you know her?"

In the pause that follows, Lovely has time to reflect on all the self-recriminations and unanswerable questions and bitter contradictions Paez's question sets in motion, like faded snapshots and archive footage from someone else's life: a landscape of pulp fiction and B movies, the butt of fatuous East Coast jokes; drifters, dreamers, starlets, schemers, fast money and fancy cars, improbable fauna under demented blue skies or unbearable secrets and unholy dreams—Queen of Angels, stripped naked and waiting, beckoning, lurid, yearning, daring you to take her, and fall.

"Yeah," Lovely admits finally, conditionally, and says what logically follows but which feels alien and somehow impossible, after all this time, even wrong, the minute it comes out of his mouth:

"She's my wife."

2

"YOU'D THINK you'd have told me you were married."

Front walkway of apartment C, Diablo Bonita, Lovely and Paez bake in the midday heat with a mute boot detective who just takes notes, his hat cocked back.

Cops going in and out like Union Station.

They've hashed through the basics already. Name: Isla Lovely, née Schollenberger. Age: twenty-nine. Only child. Hometown: Grand Junction, Colorado. Occupation—

—But there's a lot that Lovely simply doesn't know.

"How long?"

"Eleven years, in August."

Paez whistles. "Holy mackerel. How long since you'd seen her?"

"I don't know." In fact, he does. "Seven."

"Seven. Years?"

Lovely shrugs. "I got busy. Time flies."

"You didn't divorce her, she didn't ask for one?"

Lovely doesn't want to talk about it anymore. He doesn't want to think about it. He wants to rewind a couple hours and give Johnny back the note she wrote and maybe—"It's a long story, not . . . relevant."

"Relevant to what? This? Somebody shooting her? Well, guess what, my friend? You do not get to decide what is or is not relevant to a homicide."

Lovely looks at him, raw. "Just give me a little space, Henry, I got another appointment I need to attend—"

"No sir. I'munna need you to come downtown and—"

Lovely cuts him off: "What happened to you? You used to be a good guy, now you're a prick."

"I was always a prick," Paez says. "I just hadn't made sergeant yet."

"Okay, well, how about I save us both some time, here, *Detective*. You're gonna ask me if I have any idea who might want her dead, and I'm gonna tell you I don't even know who she is anymore—you'll imply I'm a suspect on account of maybe she threw me over and I got jealous, I can tell you how far up your ass to put that idea and then maybe we'll circle a few times like a couple of bantam roosters, but it won't get us anywhere, so eventually you'll tell me, 'Stay in town and out of my investigation, Lovely,' and I can swear to you—swear to you—that I have no interest in solving this one."

Paez studies him. "No interest in solving your own wife's murder."

"Nope."

"That's nuts."

"Is it?"

"Yeah." Paez starts to turn away—

"But if I was," Lovely says to the sergeant's back, "interested, I mean, in solving, or at least taking a stab at understanding what happened here"—waiting until Paez turns to face him again—"I'd start with the guy she was sleeping with."

Paez squints, like some kind of burrowing rodent emerging in daylight. "Thought you said you hadn't even seen her in—"

"Dents." Lovely lets this hang for a moment, petulant, he knows, but wanting to take some of the piss out of Paez. "On either side of the bed," he adds, finally, and advises, "Go check. I'll wait. But make it snappy, there's this thing I gotta do."

"Like I said, Love, I'munna need you downtown to get your official statement typed up—"

"I will. After my thing. Go. Check."

There follows a stubborn repose, in which Paez, not wanting to appear too eager to see if Lovely's right, studies some scuffing on the side of his wingtips.

In the bedroom, where the body is already covered with a coroner's sheet, Lovely knows Paez will find in the sheets and feather mattress padding, under the swirl of covers, two shallow human-sized depressions he noticed before he saw Isla's body. Dents, side by side.

The day's gray glare has Paez putting on sunglasses when he comes back out to Lovely and the note-taking junior detective left behind to make sure Lovely didn't leave.

"Now you're seeing dents."

"Or snow angels," Lovely says drily. "Take your pick."

"It never snows in L.A."

"Process of elimination, I guess."

"So who was she sleeping with?"

Lovely gestures: no idea. Jams his hands in his pockets and starts walking back to the street. "It never snows in L.A."

"Yeah, well . . . it sure gets cold enough." Then Paez calls after him, "Hey, what time should I expect you? Hey. Hey! Lovely—?!"

The actress is standing barefoot in the open doorway of her flat, chaste and demure now in a cotton swim cover-up due to all the leering cops and consternation, although the front's tied loose; she tilts her cat's-eye shades down and idly follows Lovely's retreat.

Back in his Morris—it smells like old baked leather and wool—he rolls the window down, puts the key in the ignition. But just sits, staring out at nothing, overcome.

It was during lunch, ninth grade, the first time he saw her, across a crowded cafeteria at Goddard Junior High. They'd been in school together since fourth, when her family moved west from Chicago, but this was the first time he saw her, really saw her, in that way a boy can see a girl; she took his breath away and, to be truthful, he never really got it back.

Three weeks, it took, to work up the courage to say something.

The first time he touched her face was electric.

The last time—he can still conjure the ache of her rejection. It doesn't seem possible that she is never to be touched again.

He closes his eyes. And breathes.

Opens them again as he becomes conscious of something he's seen but not registered: a two-tone Hudson Commodore, with a square-faced, good-looking man inside, confident chin, wheat-colored hair piled haystack high, hands hooked over the wheel and gazing out at all the activity spilling from apartment C of the Diablo Bonita.

After a while, Mr. Handsome swings his head to the Morris

and locks eyes with Lovely. Realizes he's been made. Starts his car, drops it into gear, guns the engine, and pulls quickly from the curb, cutting a sharp U-turn before heading away.

Lovely has his car already idling. He allows the Hudson half a block, then eases out after it, but a big black Buick sedan cuts him off from a side street. Screeches to a stop, blocking Lovely's right-of-way, and a white guy in a dark suit and aviator glasses angles his square, pink head out the driver's-side window like a turtle from its shell and shouts: "Why don'tcha watch where you're going?"

By the time they back up and untangle, the Hudson is gone. Lovely watches the Buick cruise past, the turtle man expressionless, not even giving him a second look, and in his rearview mirror Lovely sees the U.S. GOVERNMENT license plates that scream federal cop.

Hudson has a babysitter.

LOVELY HAD HOPED LILY HIMES was wrong about her nephew. He'd tailed him from the colored projects at Jordan Downs north through midcity and Chinatown to the wilds of Elysian Park, and then parked and followed on foot, taking the winding overgrown paths into the lengthening shadows of Sulphur Canyon, and the Mexican-American squatter towns in Chavez Ravine, where he understands, now, not only what business the kid is about to transact, but that it is not going to end well without some proactive interdiction.

At least it gives Lovely something to think about besides Isla for a while.

The young man with the ebony face answers to Oscar, and

the gabardine suit stands out starkly, as if surely a mistake against the pale dust of the Ravine. He waits near a ragged picket of abandoned mailboxes, mopping his face with a cotton handkerchief and sipping from a bottle of Coca-Cola. Two dirt roads intersect here, equidistant from the ramshackle ruins of vacant housing clusters built over the years by Calexican families from salvaged bricks and lumber, and emptied recently under eminent domain by the Los Angeles Housing Authority.

Only a few die-hard residents have resisted relocation, and two of them are leaning over the balcony of a clapboard house high on the southern hillside to look down at the colored man, pretty sure that he isn't there for the scenery.

Sure enough, a green Chevy coupe crests the rise from the Silver Lake side and rattles down the steep gravel slope toward the intersection, grinding gears.

Lovely comes out of the shade of a half-collapsed *carnecería* and starts to walk briskly up the road. The morning's brume didn't burn off; a dying, dyspeptic sun bakes out its last behind the low clouds that cloak the canyon, heat trapped between the hills wafts weird thermals devoid of any real breeze.

The gabardine delinquent is in deep discussion with a trio of Mexicans in shirtsleeves and felt hats. It's civil. There is a proffer of money and an exchange of what can only be a paper-wrapped brick of marijuana. Handshakes all around, some final small talk and an intent to conclude and depart, the free market at work, supply meets demand, everybody happy.

Lovely picks up his pace. Unfortunately, two big black Cadillac coupes blow past and dust him with their backwash, just what he's been worried about, skidding up and hard men spilling out of every door, some with guns, before Oscar Himes or his suppliers can manage a getaway.

Chavez Ravine is still Mickey Cohen territory, still the go-to spot these days for bootleggers and illicit transactions despite (or maybe the genius of it is because of) the Police Academy training grounds right next door, and now here is Mickey's muscle, no doubt all thinking that three brown faces and one black one will not, in the scheme of things, be missed if they simply disappear from God's green earth and are made an example of.

Plenty of unmarked graves to keep them company.

The Mexicans are put on their knees, their money thrown to scatter into the mustard weed, while Lily's nephew is stripped of the dope and struck with a crowbar swung by a Hollywood B-movie-gorgeous, curly-haired man who seems to be in charge of Mickey's crew.

"Johnny Stomp!" Lovely has recognized him: a former Marine and putative Brentwood gift shop owner who's become Mickey Cohen's enforcer since Cohen went to jail, and who harbors a secret crush on Lana Turner, for whom MGM recently hired Lovely to mediate.

The curly-haired man shades his eyes, straddling the fetal curl of the black man bleeding on the ground beneath him. "Lovely? Geez Louise. What brings you up here?"

A squat muscle monkey in an ill-fitting brown suit has cocked his pistol and put it to the back of the nearest Mexican's head. Lovely keeps coming, friendly. "Day care." He gestures to Lily's nephew. "Turn my back, he's got his track shoes on, hightailing it up here for some reefer madness with these mariachis."

Johnny Stompanato frowns as all this new information rattles through his reptile brain. He looks at the Mexicans doubtfully. *Mariachis?*

"They open every Tuesday and Thursday at the Fall-Out," Lovely lies, adding, "free tacos," and arriving, hands casual in his pockets, finding the trigger of the .38 on his right side, in case he needs it. "Kid is Lily Himes's sister's boy." He uses his chin to indicate the gabardine victim at Stompanato's feet.

"The singer?"

"That's her." Lovely looks down at the kid. "I hope that tire iron knocked some sense into you, Oscar."

Johnny Stomp's monkey snorts, impatient. He looks keen to put a bullet into something.

"They're on Mickey's turf," Stompanato says.

"True enough," says Lovely. "But that trumpet player"— meaning the man with the gun to his head, and Lovely goes all-in with the bluff—"he happens to live right up the hill there, one of the last families holding out against eviction—and that's his dad and his uncle looking down at us right now, so if you whack him, you're gonna have to go whack them, too, which won't be easy, as they have the high ground, not to mention that I doubt Mickey'll to be too thrilled to hear about you starting a war with the White Fence Gang."

The decision is slow coming. Lovely starts calculating the odds he can survive a close-quarter firefight against four armed men with his six-shot revolver, but Johnny Stomp steps back and waves for his monkey to put the pistol away. "I appreciate that you didn't queer things with Lana when I had that misunderstanding at Culver Studios," Stompanato murmurs low to Lovely, so that his crew won't hear it.

"Love is a lonely journey, Johnny."

"A-fucking-men." Stompanato, losing interest, glances down at Oscar Himes and points with the crowbar. "He'll be okay. I cracked him in the one place I couldn't hurt him."

It's meant to be a joke; Lovely has to work a bit to supply the laugh. Cohen's crew climbs back into their Hudsons and, as the cars jockey around to head back the way they came, Johnny Stomp leans out his window toward Lovely and confides, "She's got the hots for me, Lovely. Nobody believes it, but you and me, we know. Just a matter of time, baby. And I am a patient man." His Cheshire leer lingers in the dust clouds long after the cars are gone.

Lana Turner, Lovely muses, shaking his head. *In your dreams, Johnny Stomp. Only in your dreams.*

Lily's nephew is back on his feet. Glassy-eyed, thoughts all thickened, his bell rung, slick red blood lurid down the side of his face. But the paper brick of dope has made its way back into his pocket.

"You're welcome," Lovely says.

Oscar just licks the blood from his lips.

The Mexicans brush themselves off, rattling in Spanish as they bend and stoop to retrieve their money from the hillside weeds. Lovely doesn't know the language well enough, or he'd say something, warn them to keep their business east of the river, but as they return to their car, the one who'd had the gun pressed against his head turns to Lovely and asks, still pale, with no accent, not joking, "How did you know I played the trumpet?"

Now Lovely laughs for real. But there's no joy in it.

And only after they've driven off does he turn to discover

that Lily's nephew is already halfway to the ridge, running, too far and too fast to chase down, trailing a lean, lanky shadow, coattails and silk tie flapping back dismissively in a mocking contempt.

AT the Westwood Veterans Administration Hospital tucked tight to the runnels of the ragged Santa Monica Mountains half an hour's drive from downtown, Lovely's Morris exits Wilshire, climbs toward the Wadsworth Theatre, curls east on Eisenhower to Bonsall, and floats between the concrete-block buildings filled with forgotten casualties of war. The stolid marine layer has soughed back in over the West Side like a thin paste, ghosting the eucalyptus and live oak, giving the scatter of new Brentwood Arts and Crafts bungalows and Deco apartments that litter the near distance an aura of geometric dream.

Lovely's Florsheims click-clack on the freshly waxed tile of Building T-88. Light from a window on the opposite splits the hallway half in shadow, and against the wall, shrouded, sits a gangly Korean War vet in a wheelchair, short sleeves, arms amputated, a futile pack of cigarettes in his lap.

"Got ya knock-knock joke, Kilroy."

Lovely stops, comes back, picks up the veteran's crumpled pack of Chesterfields and shakes a cigarette out. He puts it in the man's mouth and flicks the chrome lighter he always has in his pocket, even though Lovely doesn't smoke, the one he got in the service and keeps for good luck.

"Nucular rib-tickler."

Lovely is game. "Go."

"Knock-knock."

"Who's there?"

The armless veteran says nothing. Just levels his eyes at Lovely and smokes. After a moment, deadpan: "Get it?"

Lovely nods. "Yeah, I get it. That's a good one." He first heard it in Baghdad, in '51. He puts the coffin nails on the vet's lap and keeps walking.

"Nuthin'!" The vet laughs, yellow teeth bared, hacking smoke. "No answer! Gonesville, baby . . ."

Room 123 contains a precisely tucked bed, a wooden dresser, no decorations, and, at a metal desk, pecking laboriously on a typewriter, his rounded back to the open doorway that Lovely has entered through, a man Lovely's age but those same years lived perhaps twice as hard.

"There's whole species that evolve faster than you can type, Buddy," Lovely says.

"A-a-and, tragically, you're not a m-member of any of them," the man at the desk rattles out, without turning. His typewriter is odd: six keys, a palm-sized space bar. The Perkins Brailler. A sheaf of blank pages with little dots pressed into them is neatly stacked beside it.

"Still favor your Heaven Hill rye?"

Buddy Dale turns to face Lovely, blind. A big crimson scar is slashed across his once-beautiful face, more or less horizontally. He wears the dark glasses, his hair is short, slicked back carefully, his shoulders broad, muscular once, his skin almost translucent. Just slightly off: "I stopped drinking in '49. They said it would help with my m-m-memory. Maybe it did, I can't remember." It's like Buddy's brain has a couple parts missing. The stutter, the loops.

Lovely stares sadly at his old friend, remembering the times in high school when all he wanted to be was half as cool as Buddy Dale. And Buddy smiles, crooked. As if he can feel Lovely thinking about him. The awkward silence aches. Lovely has already pulled halfway out of his inside coat pocket the bottle of whiskey he bought in Westwood; now he starts to push it back in, but—

"Go ahead, put that pint on the bureau, though. I'll try to b-bribe my nurse with it, maybe get an extra s-sponge bath."

Brush, comb, sundries all lined up so Buddy knows where they are. And, incongruously, a Rolleiflex. Lovely puts the Heaven Hill next to them, on the dresser.

"What's this? You got a camera?"

"I like taking pictures."

The contradiction of the blind man with the twin-lens Rollei automat poses its own question, but Buddy just shrugs, as if sensing what Lovely is thinking: Don't ask.

"We blew the Bikinis to kingdom come," Lovely says, stalling the reason he's come. He picks up the camera. There's film in it.

"Yeah. Three months ago. I heard, I still got ears," Buddy says. "H-bomb. Seven letters bigger than A."

"Bigger and better," Lovely riffs. "American ingenuity. Yankee know-how." Whatever rapport they once had is stale.

"And I heard you were back," Buddy says, cutting to the quick. "Three y-years ago. Guess you forgot how to g-g-get here."

Lovely takes a guilty breath, replacing the camera, staring at himself in the mirror, not at his friend. "Look, Buddy, I know—"

"—I heard you were a private dick, too," Buddy talks over him, his voice loud and forced, "which kind of makes sense, I s'pose, for a guy who never runs out of questions."

Turning back, Lovely catches sight of Buddy awkwardly stuffing something into the top drawer of the desk.

"What do you come wanting, is my question. Three years and nothing, then, all of a sudden here you are with a b-b-bottle of hooch. Gets a man wondering."

"Isla's dead."

The silence that follows this statement says everything. Buddy's face collapses. Lovely feels a weight pressing down all over again, same one he took on at the Diablo Bonita Apartments, when he looked at the body on the bedroom floor and understood who it was.

"Shot through the heart." And Lovely wonders: Was that his voice, saying it?

"Oh, God, when?"

"I don't know. Last night? I found her in her apartment this morning. Cops were already there."

"You?"

Lovely resents the implication. "Yeah."

Tears leak from Buddy's ruined eyes. He's overwhelmed, his voice frogged. "Why would somebody want to kill Isla? Why would somebody want to hurt Isla? She's a saint. God help me, she is a saint."

"Was."

"Goddamn it."

Outside the window, on the lawn, two old soldiers are playing catch. A sharp leather smack as a ball hits a mitt. Lovely watches Buddy twist in his chair and stand up, with nowhere to go. His hands flutter out from his sides, and settle. He searches for Lovely with sightless eyes. Wipes the end of his nose with his shirt cuff.

"She wanted to see me, Buddy, but I don't know what about. Do you?"

Buddy orients to Lovely's voice and crosses. His movements are exact: six steps to the bed, half a turn without touching it, and sit. His head angles at Lovely, his hands grip and ungrip the metal frame. "We split up, me and her. Six months ago. I haven't heard a hide nor hair since."

Buddy was always a good liar; Lovely studies his friend now and senses he's not telling the whole truth, but isn't ready to press it. He pushes away from the bureau and crosses to the desk, Buddy tracing the sound of his movement with dead eyes.

"Your idea or hers?"

Buddy hesitates. "Let's call it mutual consent."

"Let's not call it anything," Lovely snaps. "Let's tell it to me straight. Or does she just still keep her furniture all nice and lined up for old times' sake?"

Buddy shakes his head, back and forth, back and forth, a metronome. "She moved on, Ry. I'm damaged goods. She m-m-moved on from me, just like she did with you."

This silence cuts deep, honed on the tangled past.

Coldly, Lovely says, "No, I'm pretty sure what happened with me was a onetime deal." It's mean, and he knows it, but it's the first thing that comes to mind as he reaches down and silently eases the desk drawer open to see what Buddy stowed inside it. Buddy stands up again, agitated, still with nowhere to go.

"We didn't mean for it to happen," he protests. "And you could've—"

"—Why was she calling me?" Lovely asks again, with no interest in following Buddy down Bad Memory Lane.

"She loved you," Buddy says.

"She loved us both," says Lovely, and knows it's true. "Or whoever was in front of her. *Cherchez la femme.*"

"Knock off the frog talk, will ya?" Buddy lurches, walks, six quick steps, reaches, finds and slams the desk drawer shut, almost snapping Lovely's fingers in it. This brings him right in Lovely's face, sightlessly searching for Lovely's eyes, as if it would matter.

"I didn't come to argue about what did or did not happen seven years ago," Lovely says to him, contrite. He wants to mean it.

"Why are you here, then?"

"To tell you she's gone. I figured you'd want to know."

Silence.

Lovely adds, "I didn't want you to hear it from some cop coming to see if you have an alibi for last night."

"Blind ain't enough?"

"Or whatever. You know."

Another silence.

"Just that?"

"Yes."

Smackpop of the ball in the glove. The rattle of a lawn mower starting up. A nurse's rubber soles squeak down the corridor. Lovely feels like he can't get his breath. The air in Buddy's room has become thick, like the Arroyo Seco Parkway at morning rush, bitter and acid and foul. What is it they call it? Smog?

Or, Lovely thinks, the unrelenting regret.

"What's it like outside?"

"Oh, you know."

Buddy wipes at his eyes with the back of his hands, voice breaking: "You've got to f-find out what happened to her, Rylan."

Lovely shakes his head, testy. "Why's everybody so sure I'm interested?"

"Because," Buddy sparks right back at him, "th-that's who you are, isn't it?"

No, Lovely hears himself screaming, but he says nothing. No, not this time.

This silence hunkers down, stubborn. Softer, sadder. Angry or lost, Lovely can't tell anymore, Buddy repeats himself: "That's just who you are. White hat and everything."

Lovely wants to explain to his friend how wrong he is. Instead he walks out, hoping he won't have to come back.

3

A TRUMPET SCREAMS.

Ramshackle hip, hep, bright-shiny and raucous as the best of the jazz clubs packed tight along Central Avenue, the shoebox Fall-Out (its "Shelter" implied) is packed to overflowing even this early in the evening. Supple big-grilled cars are nosed into it like black and chrome fish feeding. Neon leers off all their arcs and angles, as the soft, luminous night crawls in over downtown Los Angeles.

Inside: cosmic kitchen, concrete and chrome—space-age mock-nuclear decor, dry-ice drinks that will peel paint, and tiny isolate islands of pale Anglo float in a vast sea of roiling, moiling brown and black. Foxy, angular Lily Himes, headliner, owner, siren, the rock on which many a metaphorical sailor has willingly crashed and drowned in vain, brings Cole Porter sluiced with Monk and Miles, her shimmering sequins and violet eyes and chiaroscuro curves backed by an airtight quintet, her voice a darting hummingbird, in and out of the instrumentation, weightless.

It's "Too Darn Hot." The dance floor jumps.

Squeezed to the end of the long, blunt bar, Lovely, one of those few white faces, hat on his knee and a regular from the way his glass is never empty, doesn't much like jazz but can't take his eyes off Lily.

Lily. Who has recently decided there was no point to their continuing, no future in their attachment, the world was wrong, but they were in it: *à la guerre, comme à la guerre.* Lily is as different from Isla as Lovely is from the boy Isla married.

When the set ends she finds him. Her body glows, slick with a sheen of perspiration, despite all the doors thrown open and the big overhead fans kicking on.

"You." She tries to throw him indifference, but her post-performance verve is intoxicating. Electrifying. Singing sets her on fire, and while his instinct is to move back from her, there's no place for him to go. Or that he wants to go.

"Nice set."

"Was it? Says the man who says jazz ain't his thing."

Lovely shrugs, they'll never agree. A bartender brings Lily tonic with a twist. She leans back against the bar, looking out at the crowd, her body making soft contact with Lovely not entirely by accident, Lovely notes, despite their supposed estrangement.

"I took care of that thing with your nephew."

"Mmm. I figured as much. Oscar come through here briefly, late this afternoon."

After running from me, Lovely thinks. "I tailed him. I scotched his score. He wasn't too happy about it."

"I'm right?" She says it sadly.

"Yes." Lovely shifts to give her body room, his thoughts interlaced with Isla guilt. "I kept Johnny Stompanato from braining him, I guess that counts for something."

"Send me the bill."

"On the house," Lovely says. "I doubt I more than delayed his fall, though."

"We'll have a fine talk, him and me."

Where Isla was a gentle, awkward beauty, everything about Lily is improvised and lyrical, even her toughness, and including the way she moves, turning back toward Lovely, close, all arc and flow. She crunches ice and they stare at each other blankly for a moment, black and white, improbable, Lovely thinks, and rife with problems—she's right. But in an H-bomb world, aren't all bets off?

"You okay?"

Caught short, he says, "Yeah," but it's unconvincing. "Just tired," he adds, trying to sell the lie.

"You don't want to talk about it," Lily interprets.

The truth is, he does, but only to her. "I saw my wife today." Lovely watches his words make her whole body tense, defensive. She doesn't know much about him. The existence of a missing wife never came up, he never had a reason to raise it.

"You better keep talking," she said.

"Her name is Isla. I saw her, she's dead." It's the best way he can think to tell it, but understands that it might be a little lacking in the details.

"Did you love her?"

It's an excellent question. Lovely is flooded with memory: eyes, lips, hands, the sharp inward curve of her waist, just above the hip. Her hard-won smile.

"Yes, I did." Nothing more or less.

Lily blinks, turns her back to the room, and leans on the bar, shaken. No tears, but a true sadness; one of the things Lovely most admires is her ability to feel: loss, love, outrage, betrayal. Sometimes all at once. So much of his last ten years have been spent with the calculated dispassion those of higher pay grades believe is required to bend the world's will.

Lily turns back to him and shakes her head again, touching his hand with hers, long perfect nails dusted with glitter. "You can't stop there, baby," she says softly. "She deserves better. So do I."

Lovely drains his drink, stalling to gather thoughts he'd hoped he wouldn't ever have to gather again. A couple of the guys from Lily's band are back onstage, tuning a guitar, thrumming a stand-up bass. The clatter of the crowd roils like a waterfall on rocks. "We were high school sweethearts. Colorado. Same town, same neighborhood, same schools, fourth to twelfth grade. Companions. Friends. You know. That small-town thing."

"I don't," Lily says. She's a city girl, West Coast, Baldwin Hills, working-class parents, a brother who died in the Pacific war.

"Fall of our junior year. It came out of nowhere, one night, I don't know. Stuffing tissue paper in the chicken wire of a homecoming float, I just looked at her and everything changed."

"You are romance with an exclamation point," Lily says, dry.

"I made her my war bride." Lovely's voice is raw. He remembers them: Isla, Buddy, so young. The half-assed wedding. And making love for the first time when that was a thing that people did that meant something.

Eighteen years old.

He stares at his knuckles. "Two days after, we shipped out to basic. Me and my best friend—who was also her best friend." Buddy, now so blind and bitter. "But . . ."

Grand Junction Station, they stood in uniform while the cameras flashed and goodbyes were said, light, airy, nobody looking into the certain darkness that waited to swallow them because to do so would have broken the fragile patriotic façade. Isla, his parents, festive, as if he and Buddy were off to great adventure on the Denver & Rio Grande, soon to return. Grinning, devil-may-care.

"Somewhere north of Anzio, on patrol, Buddy took a face full of shrapnel meant for me."

He takes a moment, remembering. Lily's fingers stay on his hand, warm. A cymbal brush sighs and the Fall-Out band, reassembled, begins a slow groove on Jule Styne and Sammy Cahn.

"I carried him ten miles back through enemy lines to the mobile surgery unit. To this day he thinks that I saved him." He stops again.

"You tell your personal stories," Lily says, "like LADWP rations water."

"His eyes were the price of his ticket home," Lovely says, ignoring her. "Isla came west on a Greyhound, found him in rehab at the VA, he gave her all my letters, broke down in tears, and Isla stayed to help his sightless transition."

"You ever come back into this?"

"I soldiered on, through V-E Day. Got extended. Or maybe extended myself. Worked some occupation, Berlin and Tokyo. Here and there."

A there and where that Rylan Lovely will not talk about, at all, Lily chides.

Lovely shrugs, his default with her, and rotates his empty glass to make the bevels flare. The bartender asks a question from a distance; Lovely faintly nods for a refill. Lily waits. She knows him well enough by now to wait.

He inhales the stale, smoky club air. "Came home after four years to find that my wife had fallen hard for my blind best friend." Captain's uniform and flowers, raw anticipation, no knock, walking in the door of her Lexington bungalow, the address he'd memorized, discovering Isla and Buddy on the divan, laughing, kissing—

—Lily lifts and brushes the soft of her hand across his cheek tenderly, bringing him back. "I am sorry." She's sorry. Everybody's always sorry, Lovely thinks absently.

"Vapor trails," Lovely says.

"Life," Lily counters. "You going to find who killed her?"

"We have cops who get paid for that."

Lily stares at him doubtfully. Lovely avoids her gaze. "I don't even know her anymore."

"Sure."

"Seven years."

"Yes, I see."

The snare drum snaps, the band picks up pace. Horns rise, bark like Griffith Park coyotes. Lovely finally looks into the violet eyes and says simply, truthfully, "Buddy needed her more. That's the kind of girl she was."

Lily considers this. "Sure. But what kind of guy does that make him?" Lovely has no ready answer for her. She leaves him and slips through the crowd and steps up onto the stage in perfect rhythm to start, *"I fall in love too easily . . ."*

By the time she gets to *"my heart,"* Lovely has gone.

———

WARM LIGHT GLOWS from the window of the flat opposite Isla's: the actress, inside, furniture pushed to the walls, leopard leotard, she's dancing with a lean, supple instructor and singing some show tune Lovely doesn't know; it bleeds soft and lonely over him in the shadows at Isla's front door, where he fumbles to pick the lock and wonders if this looks as amateurish as he feels.

Restless night Santa Anas rattle the palms that picket the Diablo Bonitas, flailing them into pointless frenzy. The city sky glows terra-cotta, cloud cover reflecting all the light back down.

He lets himself in and shuts the door with a gentle click. There whispers a squeeze of wind through the kitchen door louvers, and the pock pock pock of the Wedgewood stove's clock.

Never much of a black bag man in his service to democracy and a better world, he has also always been too impatient to be a solver of puzzles. He's not sure how to proceed. Mysteries confound him, he prefers problem solving: abduction, extraction, elimination, hammer to nail.

But he's read enough detective stories to take a stab at this, even if Lily teases him for always getting fooled by the twists at the end.

He can change; he was changed; he is, he's been told his whole life, obstinate to a fault.

In the bedroom, on the vanity, is a silver-framed wedding photograph he must have missed seeing when he was here before on account of the body that caught his eye; a posed portrait of Lovely, Isla, and their best man, Buddy Dale.

On the floor, taped crudely, is the outline of Isla's body, half on the Chinese rug, half on the bare, varnished oak. The dry stain of her blood. The lingering scent of her lavender soaps and the sweat of the cops and technicians who probably spent the whole hot day here spinning their wheels.

Under the bed Lovely finds an empty velvet-lined box that once held a soldier's standard-issue U.S. Army service revolver.

In the closet, Lovely goes right to the huge hanging shoe rack that covers one wall—he still knows where Isla hides her important things—checking the pumps and flats, discovering the jewelry she's hidden in them: bracelets, brooches, pearl strands, and the diamond ring Lovely gave her to get married with, but which she never wore, only kept. None of this is what he wants now.

Lined up, on the closet floor, are her boots, all empty . . . except an old pair of English riders that Lovely can, holding one of them in each hand, feel are different in weight. He takes up the heavier one to confirm it; turns the boot over and shakes it, hard—out tumbles a small, locked diary, a new passport, and a fat white envelope.

In the kitchen, light from a glass-shaded gooseneck spills across Lovely and the Formica breakfast table Isla has turned into a work desk: typewriter, stack of blank sheets, carbon paper, pencil holder, plenty of white correction fluid.

Lovely glances inside the envelope to confirm what he already suspects from the feel of it: three thick bundles of hundred-dollar bills. He puts it aside.

The passport is newly issued. Isla looks tired in her photograph. There are no customs entry stamps, but there's a fresh, folded-up visa for France.

It takes him a moment to jimmy the diary open with his pocketknife. She has always kept diaries as far as he knows; however, she didn't write so much as archive her days: cryptic fragments of prose in a cramped, barely legible cursive, newspaper and maga-zine clippings, snapshots, her childlike drawings, scraps of wrap-ping paper, canceled stamps, postcards, recipes, reminders, bar coasters, greeting cards, receipts, check stubs, pressed flowers, lost feathers, doctors' prescriptions, and fortune-cookie platitudes.

She filled most of the pages of the new book and it's only June. Lovely stalls, reluctant to read it. But he can't avoid the two yel-lowing news clippings taped inside the front cover: SEARCH CONTINUES FOR MISSING PACOIMA GIRL and PA-COIMA GIRL FOUND DEAD IN DESERT. Yearbook pic-ture of the victim, a fetching Sarah Blohm, seventeen, stares out at him, too happy.

He closes the diary and places it on the table in front of him. He runs the tips of his fingers across the typewriter keys his wife was recently touching, then thumbs through the carbon paper. All fresh, unused. But there's a folded handbill slipped in the stack. Lovely smooths it out:

CHURCH OF THE COSMIC EVOLUTION
FAITH IN THE FUTURE
at which altar
the HON. A. R. DRUMMOND presides

A crumpled collection of similar flyers fills half the wastebas-ket beneath the table.

Tumble of the front door lock. Voices. Men.

Lovely puts the handbill back where he found it, drops the diary into the toaster (and yanks the power plug from the wall socket), reaches for the gooseneck light switch, and then sees, for the first time, on the floor along the wall near the back door, easily missed: a long, thin smear of blood.

As if somebody dragged a body out, or in, that way.

The front door opens. Lovely kills the light.

In the resulting darkness, listening as a couple men enter blithely, Lovely rises and creeps to the kitchen entry and peers into the living room as a light comes on in there, illuminating two linebacker-sized men in dark suits they'll surely never get used to wearing.

"Twenty thousand bucks cash, she's not gonna carry it around in her ever-loving purse."

Stiff creak of their dress shoes. Too much aftershave cologne that Lovely can already smell from where he waits.

"My opinion, she's not gonna keep it in her apartment. Is all I'm saying." It's hard to tell them apart. Gauging the pros and cons of taking these two, Lovely draws back as they move deeper into the living room, feels the warm outside air on his neck too late, and can only twist and get an arm partway up in time to blunt the blow that sings down hard on the base of his neck, sparking shooting stars, like in a cartoon.

"Gotcha."

A third man, the angry Buick driver Lovely remembers from the traffic snafu out in the street earlier, has crept in the back door and struck with a crushing sap smack that sends Lovely stunned, staggering and sprawling into the living room, where he crashes into a lamp, then the wall, finds his balance, and drops into a defensive boxer's crouch, lashing out as Mr. Buick comes stalking in after him.

"Hey, look what the cat drug—"

Lovely flattens Buick's nose with two hard jabs, blood sprays—

the man's a bleeder—then pivots and wheels a stiff roundabout right into the ribs of one of the big mooks rushing in to help his friend.

His fist goes deep into extra flesh, his target doubles over, wheezing: "Hey hey hey hey!"

Lovely tucks in, feinting, punching. At four o'clock, with bravado, comes, "Big mistake, buddy—" and again Lovely pivots to tag the remaining big man under his left eye—but this one's got a badge out, he's flashing it as he staggers back—and now Buick is upright again and snotting blood, his wavering .38 pointed into Lovely's face.

"FBI! FBI! Get on the floor!"

Whereupon the wheezing big man wraps Lovely in a bear hug and they both go crashing to the carpet.

"Criminy. Who the hell-o are you?"

Steel cuffs cut into Lovely's wrists. The names sort out quickly: Agent Buddiger, with the new shiner, flops Lovely onto his back as Agent Johnson, more fat than muscle, finds his wind and straightens painfully to hand Agent Kapnik—of the Buick—a crusty handkerchief from an inside pocket. Kapnik has to think for a moment before committing to shove it against his already swelling nose.

The three Feds stare down at Lovely. Breathing hard.

"What is he doing here?" Kapnik asks his crew, evidently just to establish that he's in charge. "What are you doing here?"

He drops Isla's envelope of cash onto Lovely's chest.

"Yours? Where's the rest, huh?"

Kapnik toes Lovely in the ribs with his wingtip, but his heart's not in it. Buddiger roots out Lovely's wallet and holds up the California State PI license for all to see.

"Snooper. Snooping?" Kapnik seems to be the only one allowed to talk.

"Why do the Feds need to come tidy up a murder scene, I wonder?" Lovely says aloud. "Or run a moving pick for some dandy in a Hudson Commodore?"

Stronger than he looks, Buddiger hauls Lovely up by the shirt, frog-walks him back, and pins him against the wall as if to study him.

"Snooper," Kapnik cracks, the airways in his nose all swollen up now, and bleeding only a mucous thread. "He's a wise guy. Are you a wise guy?"

"Me?" Lovely shakes his head. "No. I'm dumb as dirt. I mean, look at the company I'm keeping."

Which prompts Johnson to haul off and hit Lovely as hard as he can. Which, when Lovely will think back on it later, was pretty fucking hard for such a soft man.

4

"WHAT WERE YOU DOING in her apartment?"

"She was my wife."

"You broke in."

"I lost my key."

For a couple hours Lovely has been handcuffed to the single chair in an FBI interrogation room in the U.S. Courthouse building downtown, the requisite harsh overhead light, sketchy air circulation, no other furniture, and all three Feds still present, with Kapnik still in charge.

Lovely contemplates Kapnik dispassionately. "You want to get some ice or raw steak for that beak, I'll wait."

Kapnik slaps him, openhanded, and nearly knocks Lovely out of the chair, but it rocks back in place.

This has been, Lovely decides, a very long, strange day.

"Don't play dumb with us. We know the score, 'kay? Blackmail, the rocket-fuel formula. We've had your wife under surveillance for the past two weeks. We recorded her ransom demand, we watched her pick up the first payment—"

"And you didn't see who killed her?" Lovely moves his jaw gingerly, grimaces, his skin burning numb. "You guys are unbelievable." And stupid, he realizes, in assuming that Lovely knows what they're talking about, which is likely classified, but oh, well.

"Maybe you were in on it, with her. Maybe you're a Red, too?" Kapnik circles him. "Maybe you killed her to shut her up. And take the plans and the dough for yourself."

"Maybe pigs will fly. Maybe the moon is made of cheese. Maybe the H-bomb is something we all just dreamed, a mass hallucination we'll wake up from tomorrow and the world'll be safe again—well, except for mustard gas and incendiaries—and little kids will have a future—maybe—and Ike and Khrushchev will pop a couple Eastside Old Taps and have a good hard laugh about it.

"I'm a Red? Sweet Jesus. Where is that coming from, Agent Kapnik? What are you—"

"—Local Fuze Project 602. Heard of it?"

Lovely hasn't. But he goes with the flow, like a true Angeleno, another lie in a long day of lies and half-truths and ever more discouraging developments: "Yeah." Something clicks, old skills shake the rust off and his tarnished intuition tells him that Kapnik has said too much. "Only now I think it's called Feasibility Study 567," Lovely riffs, but not entirely improvising, now, "and if you don't know that, anything else I tell you is gonna be way above your pay grade, and next thing we know you'll be sitting here in the hot chair answering one of those prickly 'are you now or have you ever been a member of' questions that's ruined more careers than it's unmasked communists."

Kapnik stares at Lovely with a worried look: *Who is this guy?*

The interrogation room door swings open and a crew-cut ex-Marine strides in, expensive two-vent suit and Buddy Holly glasses, and a natural prepossession that Agent Kapnik can only dream of ever having: "What's going on here, gents?"

Kapnik and the others have straightened up; clearly this is somebody they answer to.

Lovely can't resist. "Kappy here was just asking me about 567, that top-secret rocket program at—"

The senior agent says, "Shut up."

"Sir, this man was apprehen—"

"This man is a former OSS and CIA clandestine operative, Agent," the senior agent cuts Kapnik off, "and frankly you do not have the security clearance to be asking him for the time of day. Get out."

All the junior agents hesitate.

"Out! Go!"

Closest to the door, Kapnik does, quick. As his accomplice mooks try to slip past, the senior agent glares at Johnson and smacks Buddiger on the top of the head like he's a misbehaving fifth grader. He uncuffs Lovely from the chair as the men shuffle out. The door clicks but doesn't quite shut.

"You go ape on my man's nose?"

"He tried to break my fist with his face."

"Five sixty-seven. That's rich."

"I think it was French underground code for a hooker in Reims who had some unique, highly desirable breathing techniques."

The agent extends his hand. "Ed DeSpain. I ran Berlin Bureau while you were off, where, Operation Paperclip? Goosing Kraut V-2 rocket engineers away from the Russkies?"

Lovely grips the big mitt, wary: ". . . DeSpain. I remember that name. They say you went through the embassy typing pool like a racehorse put out to stud."

DeSpain laughs. "Yeah, well, one of 'em put a bit in my mouth, threw a saddle on me, and rode me home. We've got five half-heinie kids and I have to pretend to like schnitzel."

"Was it Brunhilde?"

"You don't know shit about Fuze 602, do you?"

"I could make an educated guess."

"God, no. Don't."

DeSpain turns, gestures, holds the door open for Lovely, and out in the corridor they brush right past the chagrined junior agents still waiting like whipped dogs, backs to the wall.

"So this is about stolen formulas?"

DeSpain ignores him, talking, overlapping: "Rumor is you went off-grid in Tehran, right before Operation Ajax, Lovely."

Lovely knows he should hold his tongue, but doesn't care anymore. "Yeah. Overthrowing a democratically elected government in Iran didn't seem American to me, somehow." But he goes right back. "Look, Ed, my wife—"

"Persia. The whole goddamn of Arabia," DeSpain shrugs, dismissive, still ignoring Lovely's tack. "Bunch of Bedouin horn-dogs in perpetual search of a stag party. They're no match for us. Ten years from now it'll be a division of Standard Oil and the ragheads'll be fat and rich as Texas wildcatters and nobody'll give a camel's butt about it."

"Or we'll all be reduced to bones and ash."

"You one of those nuclear negative Nellies now?"

"Alliteration makes me dizzy, sorry."

"Existential shit don't float my boat. Sorry."

The local bureau office is almost deserted, doors locked, windows dark. They edge past a night-shift man worrying a chrome canister floor-waxing machine.

"Guy in the Hudson today," Lovely presses, stubborn, "where does he fit into this?"

"You were never cut out for the spook life, Lovely. You know why? You asked too many questions. I heard the stories. Collected them, connected them. You're a legend. Russia, Saigon, Shanghai, Prague. Iraq and Iran. Always trying to find sense in what is, truth be told, a senseless world."

"I'm lousy with mysteries," Lovely allows.

DeSpain lets this pass.

"I just wanted to do the right thing," Lovely adds, subdued. He's uncomfortable with this Fed's selective trip down memory lane.

"As if there is such a thing."

"Eventually I'll want my hat back."

DeSpain's office has a big picture of Ike, and an American flag in the corner. He takes command of his desk chair and offers Lovely one of the two unremarkable armchairs facing it.

"My wife, Isla, thought 'pinko' was an eye condition. You're barking up the wrong tree."

Eyebrows lifted in mock surprise, DeSpain chuckles, "Wife? Ry, Ry, Ry, Ry. Cards on the table, Rylan: Yours was not the picture of connubial bliss."

"Communist? I think I would know."

DeSpain merely grunts.

"Okay. Supposing you're right," Lovely says. "Was she killed because of something she knew, something she had, or something she did?"

Nothing stirs, for a moment. They just trade practiced poker bluffs. "Sit."

Lovely doesn't. "Hat?"

"Coffee? Cola? Johnnie Walker Red?"

"It's late." Lovely waits.

DeSpain sighs. "That ten grand you found was ours. Extortion bait. Marked. There's another ten still missing. Last week she booked a flight to Europe. It's not a pretty picture for your wife, if that's what she still is, or was—not a pretty picture for your Isla, that's all I can say. Let it go at that. Much as I'd love to tell you the rest, I can't. Okay? I can't."

"Do you know who killed her?"

DeSpain wags his finger: no, no. "What we're gonna do, okay, is leave her murder to the cops, and the rest to the shadows. Pay no attention to the man behind the curtain. You know the drill."

"Yeah, I guess I do. But, see, I'm not getting paid anymore to swallow the bullshit." He turns to go.

"Oh, and Lovely?" DeSpain allows him time to stop and look back. "Her diary? Nothing in there but personal stuff, so. We left it where you hid it. Along with your hat."

"HE QUOTED THE WIZARD OF OZ?"

Back in her apartment, Lovely can't find anything he's come into Isla's bedroom to get and show Paez. "Gun box isn't under the bed anymore. Her passport's gone." He stands for a moment, motionless, frustrated, trying to connect the young women he knew with this older young woman he doesn't, then turns out the light and goes back down the hallway into the living room where, in darkness cut by a spill of kitchen light, Paez waits, shoulders square, hands stuffed in his pockets. "They've cleaned up."

"Federales." Paez says it skeptically.

"That's right."

"Big Red Scare cover-up."

Lovely doesn't have patience for the sardonic Paez patter just now. "You don't believe anything I've told you."

"I believe Feds might have roughed you up. You prolly deserved it. And I believe your wife coulda been a commie and you can't see it because you never got over her. Either way? Does not concern me."

Lovely is no longer sure why he called the cop. After DeSpain cut him loose from the federal realm, he felt a need to tell someone what had happened to him, sure, a knee-jerk reaction to any off-book government encounter by someone who'd been on the other side of the equation more than he wanted to remember. But Paez lives in a black-and-white world. Good guys, bad guys. No room for equivocation.

Lovely lived there once. In another life.

Now he's caught in an eddy of uncertainty.

His past flickers, a raw jumble. He shoves it back into the shadows and, irritated with himself and with Paez, shakes his head like it might clear something up, and walks in the kitchen for the light.

"You still owe me that signed statement," Paez throws after him, but without much enthusiasm.

The floor, of course, is spotless here. Newly mopped. He senses Paez come close behind him, no doubt curious what Lovely might be seeing that he can't.

"There was a blood skid near that back door. Like she was killed somewhere else and carried in."

"Tell me something I don't know, that you can *prove*," Paez yawns, "or I'm going home."

Lovely can't prove anything. The breakfast table has been searched by the Feds and slightly disarrayed. Toaster. Typewriter. Blank sheets of carbon paper. The wastebasket underneath is empty now.

And there's his hat.

"You remember a murder, last year, young lady named Sarah Blohm?" Lovely hits the lever on the unplugged toaster and the diary pops out.

"Vaguely." Paez is wearing smugness like a cardigan and Lovely realizes that the cop knows something Lovely doesn't, can't wait to tell it but waits nevertheless, drawing it out, almost bursting with anticipation of the imminent, triumphant spill. It's annoying.

"Last year, summer," Lovely continues, but Paez keeps talking.

"Look, much as I hate to admit it, Rylan, you've had this pegged from square one: It ain't about Reds or Feds, cuz get this—"

Clipping the cop off midsentence, Lovely repeats, "Last summer. Disappeared, they found her body out near Barstow—well, Isla kept clippings." He opens the diary. The yellowing news stories he saw inside have been removed. Faint furry trace of where the tape was. Shit.

"The coroner says she was pregnant." Paez rushes it, undermining its intended impact, but in case there was any doubt, doubles back: "Your wife, I mean."

It takes half a second for the words to land. Lovely looks up, truly surprised. And numb: "What?"

"Yeah. Bun in the oven. Twelve weeks."

Pregnant.

An abrupt silence driven by that hollow pock pock pock of the clock on the stove. Lovely stares at Paez, not really seeing him. He can't find words.

Pregnant.

The copper puffs up, grand, all Hercule Poirot. "From where I sit, this murder's about dents in a bed. And dollars to doughnuts, we find the man who made 'em, we'll find our killer." He waits again. "Baby was blood type O." And then, pointedly: "What's yours?"

Lovely surfaces, annoyed now, "You already know that, Henry, or you'd have run me in."

"Honest, I don't." Once more the cop waits.

"AB positive," Lovely says finally. "And I know from high school bio you can't get to O from there."

Paez, with the mirthless grin: "Yeah. What a shame."

WILSHIRE BOULEVARD MIDCITY gleams with the slick-silver light of night traffic. Lily's song lingers, stubborn, like a brushfire, smoldering sparks pinwheeling out hopeful into the darkness just when you think it's gone for good.

He sits on the bed, in his room in the Normandie Hotel. Thin trails of headlights limn the ceiling molding, ghost the curved plaster cornices, and bleed down on him. He's frowning, again, again having split open and begun to read Isla's diary.

She always recorded with diligence for the first couple weeks of a new year, then quickly devolved to shorter entries, then mere notes to complement the mosaic of scraps and keepsakes, after which the gaps would begin to appear, days, weeks, months. October, November were typical loss leaders, she once told him; December always saw a surge. She would laugh about it on New Year's Eve; curl up with Cold Duck and review her past year's cryptic record, sharing parts of it out loud, if she had company. A ritual. At midnight, she'd burn the diary and begin again fresh, new blank journal, on the new year's first day.

January 1. A twice-folded napkin from the Brown Derby, smudged with crimson lipstick. A quote from Tennyson, printed with an eyebrow pencil: Hope smiles from the threshold of the year to come, whispering, "It will be happier." *A matchbook from the Roosevelt Hotel. Fragments of a party favor popper, its rainbow tissue confetti threads gutted. Four tiny snapshots from a photo booth. Isla and Buddy. She sits on his lap; they're not smiling, not mugging; all their expressions blank, the same. Happy New Year.*

To say that Lovely's monthly room is Spartan implies that he has had a hand in its disposition; in truth, the only sign of occupancy is a suitcase in the corner and the dormant stick of a water-starved potted orchid on the dresser.

Purple and cyan neon pulse against the windowpane.

A siren keens.

January 2. Movie ticket stub for the Egyptian, eight-o'clock showing of How to Marry a Millionaire. *A receipt from The Broadway for a pair of felt gloves.*

Her hands were always cold.

He reads the scrawls and scraps and symbols and recalls his wife; hears the scrape of her voice across his heart. Memory fragments: perfume and baby powder and trusting looks, a rare smile. The hurt that came to live behind her eyes.

January 3. Her job is stressful, she "worries about the girls," but trusts that "a man of God" must have pure intentions, right? January 6 offers a single black-and-white photograph, soft focus, oddly framed, of Isla, dress lifted, ankle deep in the foaming surf at Will Rogers Beach. On January 14, Marilyn married Joltin' Joe, and Isla has the UPI photograph clipped, and a lot to say about it, in her tiny, cramped chickenscratch.

It's well past midnight when Lovely puts the diary down, rubs his eyes with the heels of his hands, and gazes blankly into the middle distance, remembering all of a sudden, in the darkness, the flyer from Isla's kitchen, under the carbon paper, the handbill advertising the outdoor church.

5

"WE ARE SPAWN *of the unknowable.*"

A blazing midmorning murk bakes the hard-pack clay of a new drive-in movie theater south of Jefferson, where the West Side commuter town of Culver City is quickly spreading. The lot is half filled with cars parked angled up on rolling berms. Lovely's Morris curls around the back row of the congregation and drives to a clapboard concession stand where worshippers have lined up to buy coffee and Cherry Cokes and Chili-Egg Fries. Out of his car, Lovely squints across the lot at the Hon. Rev. A. R. Drummond, Church of the Cosmic Evolution, who, dwarfed by the shimmering white movie screen, stands on a dais behind a simple mahogany lectern inlaid with a bleached maple cross comprised of a scaled-down vertical Viking rocket and a horizontal banana-neon lightning bolt, delivering his sermon:

"Under the sun and under the sky. Embraced by the eternal, at the mercy of the laws of the Universe. No more, no less."

His voice reedy and nasal and bleating, Dopplered, jittery, wafer-thin from speakers hanging on car windows, Drummond looks just like his picture on the flyer: tweed jacket with patches, bow tie, a trim beard. A rumpled professor. Male pattern baldness, his threadbare combover razzed by the breeze.

"Einstein says the religion of the future will be a cosmic religion. Transcending any personal God. And avoiding dogma and theology . . ."

Fresh-scrubbed young girls, virgin in spirit if not in fact, weave bicycles through the cars, taking up the collection, pastel sundresses rippling across slender tanned legs. Lovely's dad was an usher who served Communion at the Grace Presbyterian in Fruita. Sunday funeral-black suit, shoes gleaming. Grape juice and unsalted crackers. Bicycle girls would have been a real plus.

". . . based on a religious sense arising from the experience of all things natural and spiritual as a meaningful unity. Einstein. Who can argue with him? Amen. Truly, amen."

From many of the cars come honks of approval: Praise the Sky God, whoever or whatever she might be. Quavering music from a theremin worples from the tiny portable speakers as the congregation unhooks them from half-rolled windows to return them to their posts. Engines starting up. Drummond steps off the dais, his nubile ushers fall in line behind him like baby ducks in saddle shoes, and they parade toward a silver Airstream trailer tucked behind the screen, where Lovely is waiting for him.

"A. R. Drummond?"

A dismissive gesture of irritation. "If this is about poor Isla, I've already given my statement to the police."

"I'm not a cop. Or a newsman."

Lovely offers him a card and matches pace as Drummond begrudgingly glances at it. "Leong's Fresh Fruit and Produce?"

"It's where I get my messages."

Drummond gives the card back and keeps walking.

"Communist?" Lovely asks.

"Excuse me?"

"Or left-leaning. I heard she was a little pink."

"Isla?"

"You agree, then."

Drummond stops. Creased brow. "Who are you?"

"I'm nobody," Lovely says. "Just a guy asking questions."

Drummond studies him. The acolytes study him, chests out, hair back, chins high, hands knotted behind their backs or lost in the front pleats of their breezy frocks. "No, you're not," Drummond decides. "Okay, listen, Mr. Nobody. Isla typed for me, answered correspondence, kept my files in order. That's it. We didn't socialize. I didn't really know her that well. I can't tell you who would want to hurt her. I'm sorry that she—that what happened happened and—" He takes a breath. "Now, if you'll excuse me—"

"I've got a few more. Questions."

Drummond says, "I do not know who killed her." Two steps up and he disappears into the trailer and bangs the door shut.

"That was one of them," Lovely says to the door. "Good guess."

If Isla was pregnant, she had a collaborator: long-term, one-time, accidental—Lovely seriously doubts this space-age preacher is the man, but every trip has its starting point. He tries to take the emotion out of this, because emotions are just cloud cover, they gather and swirl and obscure. He sidesteps to a window, rises on his toes, and sees Drummond inside, talking on a telephone, agitated. Their eyes meet and Drummond snaps shut the louvered blinds. Lovely steps back, turns: the bicycle girls are still staring at him, suspicious, mistrusting.

"I liked his sermon," Lovely tells them. "'Spawn of the un-knowable.' Pretty much sums up my current condition."

The joke either lands flat or eludes comprehension; the girls drift off, a school of fish. Lovely gazes out thoughtfully at the drive-in lot, now almost empty of cars. Then takes his time, saunters slowly back toward the concession stand, kicking up dust, and eventually gets into his Morris.

The Airstream rocks on soft, shot springs as Drummond moves around in it. Someone in a smock and paper cap comes out of the concession shack and empties a huge bin of caramel corn into a galvanized trash can. Lovely starts his car. The Airstream blinds shuffle and part. In his rearview Lovely can see Drummond's dark eye peer out between slats from the trailer's shadow and hold vigil as Lovely's Morris joins the end of the queue of cars crawling out the gate.

Then they disappear.

In a few moments, like a jailbreak, Lovely expects Drummond will exit the Airstream, probably through the rear awning window just to be extra-careful, and he'll hightail it for his rag-top Ford. He won't drive to the exit, though, he'll steer back toward the drive-in's entrance instead, avoid the line of cars, and wave for the keeper to lift the wooden barrier gate just in time for Drummond's car to barrel through.

Just outside the drive-in Church of the Cosmic Evolution, a dusty black Morris will be waiting, idling on a side street. And after Drummond signals and merges into traffic, Lovely eases after him, laying back a few cars, but easily keeping the convertible in his sights.

He's spent the past decade learning that as long as he's in forward motion, whatever's past is held at bay.

FORTY-SEVEN MINUTES LATER, Lovely is parked high on a fire road that skirts the rim of the Arroyo Seco, peering down through a security fence on a fat old wooden barn that has been recently converted into what looks like a rocket fuel test facility lab. Drummond's car is parked outside, and the man himself is arguing angrily with a roguishly fine-looking, broad-shouldered man in an open lab coat.

Lovely recognizes him: it's the guy from the Hudson Commodore, who was camped like a vulture outside Isla's Diablo Bonita apartment courtyard the previous day.

Drummond is apoplectic. Shouting. Lab Coat Man is cool and indifferent. The arroyo air currents carry to Lovely only fragments of their dispute:

". . . what did you tell them?!"

Lab Coat says something dismissive, muffled, inaudible. Drummond lunges at him, and they begin to wrestle awkwardly, graceless, like, well, a scientist and a holy man, Lovely muses—Drummond climbing on the handsome man's back, they stumble and collapse in the dirt.

Blur of their limbs is punctuated by Drummond's yelps. Lovely considers the fence. Undoubtedly electric. He shrugs off his coat and throws it across the barbed wire, then goes up and over like somebody who knows what he's doing.

The Arroyo Seco is a seasonal floodwater gash through the rock and scrub of the Angeles Crest Forest east and north of Los Angeles proper, stretching from Red Box Saddle near Mount

Wilson down through the quaint towns of Altadena and La Ca-
ñada Flintridge, to the Devil's Gate Dam, under Pasadena's
Colorado Street Bridge, where it skirts the Rose Bowl and bi-
sects Brookside, trickles lazy through the already aging bungalow barrios of Highland, Montecito, and Cypress Parks before
dying just shy of Echo Park, in the dead concrete channel some
still call the Los Angeles River.

The bridge is popular with suicides and Mickey Cohen en-
forcers. Paez says Forest Lawn should open a branch office underneath it and offer package deals.

But above Flintridge, where the land opens up and the new
housing developments peter out, a razor-wire-topped chain-link
fence and skinny gatehouse mark a vast restricted property be-
longing to Aerojet Laboratories, part of Ike's military-industrial
complex that has grown like fungus in the moist shadows of the
Cold War. Lots of warning signs and some military guards who
nevertheless had waved the Reverend Drummond right through
when they recognized him. Lovely, who doubted he would get
the same friendly reception, had slowed his Morris at a gentle,
weedy curve to wait, concealed, and once he saw the Ford disappear through the gate, made a three-point turn and hurried back
to find the fire road up above, from which he presently slip-
slides down into the argument through the parched hillside
brush, ruining his slacks.

Drummond has a pistol. Something random: not a .38. Possibly a military sidearm the good reverend didn't turn in after
the war. He's up on his feet, stumbling backward and aiming it
at the man in the lab coat like somebody who just figured out
which end was the one to hold.

"You're not going to shoot me, Atlee," Lab Coat says, willing it to be true. But he's sweating, scared.

"No? No?" Drummond's hand shakes. "You don't think so?"

"No. Put it down."

"Fuck you, Lamoureux."

Lamoureux. Lovely arrives at the flats, finds his balance, and starts to calculate how much distance he can cross in the time it will take Drummond to find and pull the trigger.

"That's hostile."

"Fuck you and the horse you rode in on." There's no fire in Drummond's threats, though. Just fear of defeat.

"Put it down, huh?"

And just like that, Drummond lets the gun drop, limp, to his side.

Hidden in high weeds on the edge of the barn clearing, Lovely watches the scientist named Lamoureux take the gun, pocket it, and lead Drummond inside his lab. His arm goes over Drummond's shoulders, as if fondly, murmuring, low.

Lovely reassesses the two adversaries, if that's what they are. It's more complicated than it first looked. Nothing is ever simple.

As soon as the lab man and ersatz minister are inside the building, Lovely darts out of the brush, moves past the big parked Hudson, and presses his back to the barn wall under an open window.

The lab is an impressive clutter of expensive equipment: analytical instruments, armatures holding beakers and flasks and distillation stations, ventilated hoods over lab tables, portable blackboards filled with equations, huge combustion chambers, and racks and racks of chemicals. Lamoureux holds court at a workbench, lecturing Drummond, still low, still inaudible. Almost seductive. A treatise; a theorem.

Drummond has slumped on a stool, staring at the floor, like a scolded schoolboy. Nodding dully. Nodding. Nodding. And eventually, the disquisition done, he's up, out the door, without another word, licked. The rocket scientist just watches him go. Expressionless.

In a crouch, Lovely glides low and tight to the building, under the windows and along the barn, to witness Drummond's Ford fishtail away in a rising retreat of dust and exhaust.

Inside, Lamoureux stands at a jittering ventilator hood, wearing safety goggles and protective gloves, mixing solutions. He tenses, turns suddenly, looks right out the window where Lovely has come back to watch; Lovely times perfectly his step away from it, out of view, but right into a puddle under a leaking spigot with a noisy sploosh.

In the time it takes the scientist to cross the lab and peer out the window, Lovely is back behind the Hudson, safely concealed.

He waits until Lamoureux resumes his work. Then Lovely crawls around the car. He's got a handful of mud from the spigot bleed, and he packs it over one of the taillights before disappearing back into the high brush to scramble up the slope.

DUSK WHEN THE ROCKET SCIENTIST locks up the big barn and gets in his car.

Twilight when deep shadows blue the Aerojet gatehouse guards waving the Hudson through.

Like squat steel dancers, the Hudson and its stubbornly tailing English coupe snake away from the watershed, headlights sweeping synchronized through copses of live oak and eucalyptus, past winking houselights that ghost the narrow roads of Flintridge, and darkness drops like a scrim.

The Colorado Street Bridge spans the arroyo from the quiet neighborhoods of Pasadena, streetlight globes stretched like pearls through a stagnant mist. Lovely lets his Morris lag farther back into the gloaming just to be safe, the telltale mud-smudged Hudson taillight making his job easy. He's still telling himself he's not trying to solve Isla's murder, just following the threads of its unraveling in the hope of understanding why she's gone.

Down through South Pasadena, the grid streets, tumbledown Victorians and squat Craftsman houses lining them, and downtown Los Angeles glowing brightly to the southwest, a promise that the Hudson can't keep because it turns off finally into the driveway of a low-slung motel, the King's Kort, idling untended under the office awning as its driver registers at the desk inside.

From the curb across the street, Lovely watches the man called Lamoureux park and disappear inside unit 19, on the end. Then Lovely puts his car in gear and drives into an empty dry cleaner's lot for a better, head-on vantage point.

He doesn't have to wait long for the next act.

A light flicks on behind the curtained window of unit 19. The man's shadow passes back and forth, settles. The faint cast of a television blues the edges of the curtains.

Traffic passes, flows, a runnel of lights.

A taxi pulls into the parking lot and glides to the end.

Lovely takes his opera glasses from the dashboard of the Morris.

A young girl dressed to look legal gets out of the cab, pays the driver. Fire-red party dress and matching high-heeled shoes. She seems familiar, but in Los Angeles every pretty young girl is more or less like the next, an endless casting session, as if they were coming off an assembly line somewhere in Middle America, eager, willing, built to specs.

The man called Lamoureux opens the door. Stripped down to a sleeveless T-shirt and pants, no shoes. Stanley from *Streetcar*, but Brando only in his dreams. Cigarette holder. Some fragment flutter of Sid Caesar's *Your Show of Shows* blues every reflective surface behind him. The chatter of Philco audio. He takes the girl into his arms and kisses her, hard.

Lovely lowers his opera glasses and chooses not to watch the assignation disappear inside unit 19.

FEBRUARY 11. She writes, *"Love is something other people are gifted. Me, I got cursed with it, infected, twice laid low." There is another blurry photograph of Isla's torso in MacArthur Park, near the rippling water. A matchbook from the Magic Castle. A fortune cookie fortune, "The early bird gets the worm, but the second mouse gets the cheese." A handwritten invitation to a Pasadena dinner party in March, to benefit Hon. Rev. A. R. Drummond and the Church of the Cosmic Evolution.*

HOURS PASS, the motel window is dark. Only half of the neon KING'S KORT sign is working, and the VACANCY sign has a shattered panel. He's made his way through Isla's diary once and didn't understand much of it, it passed in a sad blur; the sound of her voice in his head dulled him, it was all he could hear, her voice, her words, her scattered thoughts reflected in the sundry archived bits and scraps and requiring translation. So much depending on a context he just did not know. So he goes through it again, in the pale cast of a streetlamp, looking for clues, he imagines, or answers, or intent:

Feb 15. I am the sum of my decisions. I make no apology for them. I have no regrets.

He doesn't believe it. But maybe she did. Or wanted to. He finds himself arguing with her, again, even in the cryptic guise of her journal. They had never talked about children when they were married, but normal people didn't, did they? It went without saying. Couples might talk about not having children, Lovely thinks; that made perfect sense to him. He hears a car door slam and looks up.

The Hudson's taillight glows red. The headlights switch on and the car comes tearing hell-bent out of the King's Kort parking lot, tires complaining, gears chattering, chassis throwing sparks when it bottoms out on a dip.

Lovely ducks down as bright lights cut across his windshield. The Hudson hurries west. Lovely turns his ignition key and the four-banger rattles to life.

Glendale.

Frogtown.

Silver Lake.

Los Feliz.

Skirting Griffith Park to Beachwood, and the black glassy Hollywood reservoir, across Cahuenga Pass, up onto Mulholland Highway, finally, and along the serpentine ridge road that splits the city proper from the San Fernando Valley. Los Angeles rolls out south, civilization almost as far as you can see; valley lights skitter north, gaped, haphazard, just thrown out there to choke out the old orange groves and be swallowed finally by a spooky darkness where it seems the world just ends.

The Hudson Commodore moves swiftly, but not nimbly, rocking on sagging springs. Lovely follows with headlights doused, straining to stay centered on the blacktop, grateful for brief glimpses of the mud-marked taillight dipping and twisting along and through coastal hills that ramble to the sea.

At a Franklin Canyon turnout, the Hudson slows, swerves onto the gravel shoulder, and crawls along, passenger door flung open as Lovely's Morris motors around the curve just in time to see the body tumble out, and the Hudson fishtail and roar away.

Headlights blaze jaundiced through scudded dust onto a crumpled young woman in a tattered fire-red dress, curled on the ground. Lovely brakes hard into the shoulder, stops and kills the lights.

She's even younger than he expects, fine-featured, pale, sobbing. She looks at him, eyes wild with fear.

Lovely says, very quietly: "I'm not going touch you if you don't want me to. Can you get up?"

Her head lolls around. Drugged. She can't stop crying. Her skinned legs and elbows bleed.

"I'm just gonna help you up and into the car, we'll get you to a doctor."

He gently gets his hands under her arms and starts to lift her, but she lurches against him and hangs on, desperate, sobbing. "I was nice to him. I was so nice to him. How could he do, how could he do this, I was so . . . sweet to him . . ."

Lovely has no answer for her, he's powerless, holding this crying girl, the city lights spread out below them like broken dreams.

6

SERGEANT COLE FROM VICE SQUAD shows his sensitivity right away: "You a pro, Judy?"

The girl doesn't lift her eyes. "I don't know what that means."

"Sure you don't." Cole believes he's got this all figured out. "You smell good. Lilac?"

Back downtown, at Police Headquarters, Lovely, Paez, Cole, and a few random swing-shift cops with nothing better to do than crowd one scared, shamed girl victim, Judy, Caucasian, not quite seventeen, wrapped and rocking back and forth in a fetid wool blanket, on a wooden chair beside Cole's desk.

"She told you what happened," Lovely grumbles.

Paez has a warning in his tone. "Lovely."

"Her version." Cole has bad teeth that he sucks at when he does what passes for thinking. "Situation like this, people sometimes, they see things . . . different. It's like, what's *his* version? Her date? Possibly, she led him on. Possibly, it was the both of them was frisky, and then things got a little rough, and she—"

"Who's the victim here?"

"Well it sure as shit ain't you." Cole's chin is the likely target Lovely considers tapping with a fist.

Judy glares dully at Cole. "You think I asked for this?" Her eye is bloody, her face purpled from open-hand abuse, her mouth swollen.

The Vice cop is unmoved. "You got the short red dress, the low-cut top. You're a looker, Judy. By your own admission you took a cab to this man's motel room all dolled up."

Judy's eyes go dead.

"This was a mistake," Lovely says. Then, to Judy, "You're wasting your time with these morons. I'll take you home."

Cole shoots an irritated look at Paez, so Paez yanks Lovely up out of his seat and shoves him across the room, suggesting, "Let's get some air, Ry—"

Judy, small, almost inaudible, insists, "I didn't do anything wrong."

Lovely barks back at the Vice cop, "I know what you're doing, and it stinks."

Cole ignores him, offering Judy a patronizing nod. "We're not saying you did, we're trying to protect you."

Lovely tries to twist away from Paez, hot. "Pick up the rocket scientist! I saw what I saw, Cole—"

Paez ushers Lovely out the door into the hallway, as Lovely continues to yell—"And while you're at it, ask why A. R., A as in Atlee R. Drummond—was waving a gun at him yesterday."

The door bangs closed.

Lovely shrugs Paez off and steps away, to the other side of the corridor, tired and punchy. He's been up all night.

"I saw what I saw, Henry."

"You don't know what you saw."

Through the glass door they can still see Cole: "Judy. Judy . . . should you decide to pursue this, and file charges, which is your right—as the details come out, all the details, well, it's just natural that people will start to think. About, you know, you. Lawyers and judges are probably going to ask some embarrassing, intimate questions."

Judy looks around, at the eyes of the other policemen, idly fixed on her. Measuring her. Judging her. They're not bad cops, just men of a certain perspective. Soldiers who serve under a self-righteous chief, with his tortured, rigid, crypto-fascist thesis of right and wrong.

"You really want to travel down this road?" Cole has put on his compassionate face.

Judy's voice, muffled: "I just want to go home."

Cole nods.

Lovely turns away and, low, intense, braces Paez, because who else is there? "He drugged her, he raped her, he beat her up, and he threw her out of his car."

"Or she jumped out," Paez counters. "Could be it wasn't even him in that car; did you see him? Can you say positive that you saw him? You can't. He could be back at the motel, you don't know. You don't even know his name."

"Lamoureux."

"You think. You overheard, during an argument, while you were trespassing on restricted government property."

"Who does the girl say drove?"

"You and I both know the girl isn't gonna be pressing charges."

Behind them, a matron has come into the squad room to help Judy up and walk her away from Cole and his desk.

"Who's pulling your strings, Henry? Feds? Aerojet? Is this guy marked 'special handling'? What was he doing outside my wife's apartment?"

"What is wrong with you? You think you can save this girl and make up for not saving your wife? Well, you can't."

Lovely is rocked. "Maybe not, but at least somebody gets saved. You know, there was a time when you guys actually believed in protecting the victims of crimes."

"Yeah, yeah. I got something to show you and something to tell you." Paez pulls Lovely away from the squad room, down the hall and through a doorway labeled PROPERTY.

Lovely has been in here before. The smell is rank: as if evidence carried the perfume of its crimes. Shelves of crime scene collections and confiscated property kept behind locked chain link. A low table where items not yet booked are spread out and tagged, with paperwork attached.

"While you were wasting your time harassing federal VIPs, we got a search warrant and tossed A. R. Drummond's apartment on account of apparently your wife worked for him and they were known to be friendly." Paez shows Lovely the gun box that was, when Lovely last saw it, under Isla's bed.

Now there's a pistol inside. Military-issue, showing rust and lots of miles. A strange nick on the handle, worn deep by repeated insult. Lovely tries to remember if it's the one he saw Drummond attempt to use.

"Ballistics makes it for the murder weapon," Paez says. "Drummond's prints are all over it."

Lovely is shaking his head. "How did you even know about Isla and . . ." Then it hits him. "What anonymous tipster?"

"Concerned citizen."

"Phone call. Or some Aerojet PR lackey?"

"Look, we get phone tips all the time."

"Pretty convenient, led you right to the dingle."

"You gonna argue with hard evidence?"

"Drummond barely knows which end of a gun to hold. And I saw the rocket scientist take that gat away from him today, and I didn't see him give it back."

"Will you forget the scientist? You're correct. He's off-limits. Okay? So. But more to the point? It was Drummond killed your wife. We're gonna find him, and we're gonna fry him. The end."

Paez bangs the box down and goes back into the corridor. Lovely takes one last look at the gun, then hurries to catch up.

"Maybe that's what he wants you to think."

"Who?"

"Why would Isla save news clippings of the Blohm girl in her diary?"

"Oh, for crying out loud—"

"Just let me look at the Sarah Blohm casebook," Lovely says, and Paez stops walking.

"What I think? Preacher knocked Isla up. Panicked. Bad press for the Church of the Cosmic Whatsit. She wouldn't get rid of it, so—bing bang. Drummond plugged her."

"Isla was a deliberate person. She wouldn't save something if it wasn't important." He thinks of the diary. He wonders if he's even right.

"Ninety percent of all murders are domestic in origin."

"Maybe there's a connection."

Paez loses it, face flushed: "NOT EVERYTHING IS CON-NECTED! Okay?" Henry's voice rattles up and down the empty corridor and back down to where the door labeled CHIEF OF DETECTIVES opens and Agent DeSpain steps out . . . followed by the rocket scientist Lovely knows as Lamoureux. They pretend to be oblivious to the hallway noise, pause to shake hands in the doorway with a well-fed Central Bureau captain. Everybody smiling like they're expecting a photo to get taken.

Lovely is not so much surprised as disappointed.

"Anyway, you got bigger fish to fry, my friend."

This chills him, and Lovely remembers that Paez had something else he wanted to tell. He glances, sidelong, curious, apprehensive.

"Central narcs raided the Fall-Out tonight, and Lily Himes was caught with a brick of Mexican loco weed hidden in her dressing room."

Oh, Jesus. "What?" Lovely is pretty sure he knows whose brick it is.

"Yeah. Chief Parker is over the moon. You know how much he loves celebrity busts."

Lovely, stunned, tells them that Lily doesn't use.

The cop shrugs, asks when that has ever mattered when dope turns up. "It's not good," Paez adds unnecessarily. "Given the volume, full disclosure, the charge is possession with intent to sell."

BRIGHT AND EARLY the next morning, the Commodore two-tone pulls in and parks in its space beside the Aerojet barn at the bottom of the Arroyo Seco. Lamoureux gets out, jingling keys, whistling, and unlocks the front door. Lovely allows it to open partway, then jams his foot against it, steps out, and punches Lamoureux in the face.

Lamoureux reels. Lovely hits him again. "How does it feel, Doc? To be on the receiving end?"

Defenseless, a punching bag, the scientist, flailing miserably, throws a feeble counter that Lovely slips, and then steps inside to nail Lamoureux so hard under the ribs the man's legs go rubbery and he pitches sidelong into a lab stand.

"Not so good, huh?"

Lamoureux is making a high-pitched noise, holding his bloody face, curled up, pathetic. There's no solace in this for Lovely; he spent half the night at the Hall of Justice getting the runaround on Lily's bail, until finally a churlish deputy in the women's wing informed him that "that hophead jazzbo won't be going any-where for a spell."

No visitors, no bail.

It's a free country, America, Lovely thought ruefully as the elevator spat him back out in the Hall's marble lobby and the slow bleed of dawn. A free country except when it isn't.

But, hey, at least now we have the bomb.

"Get up."

Lamoureux says no.

"Get up."

"No, you'll just hit me again."

Lovely stares at the trembling man, catching his breath, his hand tingling. He always forgets how much effort it takes to hit a man, even when he doesn't hit back. "You're right." He's cranky, having spent what remained of his night trying to nap in the Rover.

With a woozy flap of arms and legs Lamoureux manages to

get himself righted, sitting, back against the bench, legs stuck out straight like a cartoon. All kinds of ugliness leaking from his nose.

Lovely says, "I watched you toss a girl out of your car up on Mulholland."

"Did you know," Lamoureux snuffles blood, "that Oppenheimer is a communist sympathizer? Or 'fellow traveler' is the more delicate term. And yet. Not even Senator McCarthy can touch him."

"Father of the A-bomb. Don'tcha know." A blood-limned grin.

"You think you're that important to them?"

Lamoureux quips, "I don't know what you're talking about." His head must be starting to clear, because his eyes bear in on Lovely with real interest, putting pieces together. "You must be the fruits-and-nuts man who was asking the good reverend questions about Isla."

"That's right. The name is Lovely. Get up, I'm done hitting you."

Lovely steps back. His hand throbs. The knuckles will be swollen for a week. In the OSS they taught him never to hit a man in the head with a naked fist; the skull is rock hard. Use a blunt object, the instructors had said. Your palm or your elbow. Or aim for the throat.

Lamoureux rises and wobbles to a lab sink, where he runs water and splashes it on his face. Petulant: "You're not supposed to be in here." Lamoureux stuffs two rolled plugs of tissue up his nose. He looks like a wrongly drawn vampire. "Do you think he shot her?" Lovely says nothing, so Lamoureux turns and looks at him. "Drummond, I mean."

"I know who you mean."

Lamoureux just waits for an answer to his first question. Imperious, even in defeat.

"I don't know. Do you?"

"He says no." Lamoureux shrugs. "I believe him." Lovely decides not to argue. The rocket-science man towels away the blood and water, and tilts his head back as if with arrogance, which only amplifies, Lovely decides, the man's rancid stink of superiority. "If he was going to kill anyone, it would probably be me."

"And why's that?"

"I accused his girlfriend of stealing from me. Atlee has taken umbrage."

"Girlfriend."

"That's what I said. Isla. They knew each other . . . in the biblical sense."

"What'd she steal?"

"Atlee Drummond and I were at Caltech together. Roommates for three years. We took . . . well, slightly different career paths after graduation."

"I didn't even know Caltech had a religious studies department."

"Science is the future of everything, Mr. Lovely."

Lovely doesn't believe this, but wants to see where Lamoureaux will go with it. Immodesty in full bloom: "Did he tell you that his Church was made on a dare?"

"Didn't talk about religion, no."

"Atlee was an angry atheist, anti-papist, and downright Darwinian. Loved to gripe about how all the great religions were just moneymaking monopoly scams fostered by demagogues and fantasists. Phone companies, he'd say, staking out exclusive territories, taxing our personal dialogue with the unknowable. So one night, after a considerable amount of alcohol and cannabis, I said, 'You think you can do better?' He wagered me a thousand dollars that he could. And here we are."

"You get a piece of his action?"

"No. I don't have messianic yearnings. But while I'm not a holy man, I do have something of a following among the well-heeled cognoscenti. Occasionally I throw fundraisers for the Church. It's the least I can do for the man who got me through Calculus. Derivatives being my Achilles' heel."

Gathering things from the lab benches, Lamoureux heads for the back door out of the barn and gestures for Lovely to follow him. "In fact, it was the morning after my last soiree that I discovered that some extremely important papers were missing from my study. Where Isla had put the coats. QED."

"When was this?"

"April. Right around Passover. Or just after the Castle Bravo nuclear test. Depending on which God you worship. In Atlee's ever-evolving eschatology, the Great Confluence of '54."

"Sounds like it could have been anyone, stole your secrets."

"Could have been. Wasn't: I alerted security. Who alerted the federal authorities. Who intercepted a ransom demand from a certain aforementioned woman, which resulted in her getting hauled in for questioning. You can ask them how that went."

Behind the barn is a testing yard, perhaps twenty by thirty yards, the bare ground peppered with glittery sharp metal fragments that could only have come from things that have violently exploded. A giant aperture holds a fixed firing cylinder rigged inside a frost-laced refrigeration device powered by a chuffing compressor and wired with ignition and blast baffles, something out of *Buck Rogers* or *Strange Tales*.

"She evidently informed them," Lamoureux continues, all the while making adjustments and enhancements and corrections to the apparatus, "that my old school chum, A. R. Drummond, was the dirty commie who put her up to it. You can imagine how that made him feel."

"Stealing secret papers and selling them back to you."

"Or to the Russians. It wasn't clear. You might want to step back a bit."

Lovely does, just in time, because Lamoureux triggers the ignition and the blast cylinder erupts, spitting chartreuse flames and causing the whole rig to rock and shudder for five, ten, fifteen harrowing seconds, a hellfire of controlled combustion that finally sputters out anticlimactically, and vomits a clinging black exhaust that doesn't seem like it would be part of any successful trial.

"You didn't see that," Lamoureux mumbles irritably, stepping up with a chrome canister chemical extinguisher and furring out spot fires with clouds of suppressant, checking gauges, scrawling notes.

As Lovely watches, he flashes back to the wake of the war, and Operation Overcast, and all the so-called men of science he encountered while working for the Joint Intelligence Objectives Agency. "You ever cross paths with Strughold?"

Lamoureux freezes, turns, wary, "You know Hubertus?"

"I was the one who caught him trying to sneak off to Brazil under the ID of a blind German grocer we later found rotting under the floorboards of his shop."

"He's at Heidelberg," Lamoureux says. "Running the physiological institute and doing top-secret research for the Air Force." Lovely is pretty sure Lamoureux is lying when he adds, "I only know him in passing."

"Yeah. He said the same thing to me, once, about science. Future of everything. I guess not for all those Dachau human test subjects he crammed into air-pressure chambers and inflated and popped like cheap balloons. For science."

Bristling, Lamoureux reminds Lovely that Strughold was never charged with anything at Nuremberg.

"No, he wasn't," Lovely admits. "They hung his assistant, though, for war crimes. Guess that makes it okay, then. Lamoureux your real name?"

"Why wouldn't it be?"

"Were you Vichy, or just part of the Ruhr Valley crew that wound up working at Peenemünde?"

Lamoureux stops and regards Lovely like some kind of nasty skin rash. Takes a deep breath, looks up at the sodden clouds. "Do you know what an inversion is, Lovely?"

"When things are upside down?"

"A deviation from the normal, or the natural order of things."

"David and Goliath."

"I mean meteorologically." Gesturing to the sky. "All this stratocumulus. It never lasts. It burns off, bringing clarity."

"Is that what you think you have?"

"Something else you wanted to ask?"

Lovely wants to hit him again, but instead says, poker-faced, "Gee. No. Yours is a crackerjack story, Doc. Thanks. Normally I have to grind that kind of detail out of people, but you, you just had it all cued up for me like a goddamn dissertation."

A slow boil. "Do I detect sarcasm?" Lamoureux drifts back toward the open back door of the barn. "You bug me, Lovely." And now Lovely realizes he's made a miscalculation. Now it's evidently beginning to dawn on the scientist that Lovely may be considerably more intelligent than he supposed. And while this might have rattled him more than Lovely's fists ever will, it brings out the bully, too, the one with an inexhaustible legion of government goons standing loyal and patriotic right behind their golden boy so he can spit threats like "You know what? Security checks in on the half hour, they might take exception to a private dick tenderizing one of their prime assets. So why don't you just cop a breeze and we'll call it even."

Lovely chides himself for letting his pride manifest, but it's an honest mistake, and the blush of entitled rage on Lamoureux's cheekbones, the juvenile jut of chin cause him not to regret it. "Another girl tumbles out on Mulholland," Lovely says evenly, "next time I won't let you get up."

Lamoureux kicks the back barn door and slams it shut. Rattle of the deadbolt. The launch apparatus smolders and the smell of burned circuits lingers. There's the muffled murmur of Lamoureux's voice on the phone.

Time for Lovely to make his usual uphill getaway. His head hurts, from all this thinking.

7

MARCH 1. *With a pencil she's blackened the whole page. A lamentation for the Bikini Atoll?*

March 14. A recipe clipped from the Examiner:

SEAFOAM SALAD

1 box green Jell-O brand gelatin
1 6-oz. pkg. cream cheese
1 can pears, drained
Maraschino cherries
Whipped cream

March 19. The Pasadena dinner party. A dry, pressed carnation. A placeholder with Isla's name misspelled. Blank verse of her fragment observations: Mediterranean Mansion on Orange Grove. Fountain in the front hallway, tiny glowing fish. Waiters in white coats. Caviar! Men of science. A Huntington. A Chandler. The ex-governor. Deborah Kerr. The host has devil eyes. Girls from church collected checks. Atlee says "faith is a scientific procedure for successful living." Jazz trio outside by the pool. Negroes. Made to go around the side to leave. Caltech chemist assured me that nuclear war will be survivable. Host assured me that sex is a health-producing, life-changing, power-creating spirit lifter. Some girls stay after. Atlee says I'm a prude.

HUNDREDS OF TOWERING POTTED PALMS have been arranged along the banks of a speculatively Congolese river dug only recently, and Lovely would have guessed a new take on *Heart of Darkness* but for the three dozen African extras in grass skirts and bones through their noses—only two of whom are actually African in heritage. The others have pale skin lathered in various shades of brown and black body makeup drying and cracking and peeling in the broiler heat of the 10K lights simulating a tropical sun. Some kind of equatorial jungle cannibal situation seems to be the day's dominant movie narrative on the Paramount Ranch, so deep northwest into the San Fernando Valley it took Lovely ninety minutes to drive here from Pasadena, and he can smell ocean leaking over the treeless coastal bluffs.

Lily's nephew is one of the cannibals. His hair is Brylcreemed and parted in the middle, like one of the Bowery Boys, for some unknown reason. Lovely keeps an eye on the kid, staying safely out of eyeline behind the sound cart until someone shouts *Cut*. The putative star, who may or may not be Robert Taylor in a mustache and pith helmet, has several times rushed in swinging a prop machete and, as the jungle tribesmen cowered the way savages must when confronted by a matinee man, slashed the vine rope restraints off a spunky Studio Brunette steeping in the boiling vat of dry ice, and put his arms around her as if to lift her free.

Cut.

The master shot ends there, with any actual lifting evidently to be done by the stunt double who's been doing pull-ups on some scaffolding to make his oiled muscles pop.

Fifteen minutes are called to move the camera closer and re-light. With the 10Ks killed, the jungle escheats to the sorry score of potted plants, stagnant water, and green diffusion netting, its magic spell broken. Extras break and slouch toward the craft services table for something cold to drink, or a smoke. Lovely finds Lily's nephew at a cooler prying the cap off a grape NeHi.

"Your aunt's been arrested."

The kid jumps, sees Lovely and, if his eyes can be read correctly, not only knows that Lily's in jail, but knows what Lovely's about to ask next. "That weren't my dope," he says defiantly. But this time he doesn't run.

Lovely pushes his hat back off his forehead and wonders aloud, as if he really needs the answer, how Oscar knew it was dope she got popped for.

Oscar offers an adolescent shrug. "It were in her room, right? Possession is nine-tense of the law."

Lovely gives this a pass. "Where'd you stash that Mexican weed I helped you keep?"

"That were for a friend."

"Oh." Frowns. "All of it?"

"Man—"

"No. You went to see Lily yesterday afternoon."

Oscar tries the feeble lie that he just wanted to tell his aunt how he got a job on a movie. He pulls a wrinkled Lucky Strike from somewhere in the skirt grass, then seems to remember he has no match. Lovely flicks his chrome lighter.

"I am aware that you are a lowlife, Oscar. But, goodness gracious, come on. Not even a shitheel like you is gonna let your aunt do your time."

The nephew smokes, and talks through exhaust that wreathes his phony nose-bone, cool. "Look, man. This is my break. They gonna Taft-Hartley me. Wrote me some speaking lines, I'm gonna get a SAG card, the writer, he says I do good on this one he's got another pitcher, set the Civil War, I'd be perfect for."

"I bet. The writer."

"That's right."

Lovely just stares at him, wondering how this miserable jamook could be a blood relation to Lily Himes.

"Man, get real. I go tell the police it was my maryjane, they just gonna put us Negroes both in jail, me *and* Lils, two for one. And I know you know about what I'm talking." He hissed, "Bust us both. And what does that accomplish, hey? She *got* her career. Her club." Oscar's lids go half-mast. "Her white Man Friday." He enjoys his own joke; Lovely doesn't react. "It'll sit," Oscar continues, "but what about me? I'm just now standing at the opportunity door 'bout to open wide."

"You hid your grass in her dressing room."

"If I did? Well, shit, ordinarily, that'd be the safest place for it, sure, since she don't even smoke. You understand what I'm saying?"

Lovely's hands twitch and curl. "If I do I don't want to."

"You wasting your time, man."

"You won't help her?"

"Are you deaf?"

A second AD calls the extras back to the set for blocking. "First offense, she'll be fine," Oscar assures Lovely. "Eight months maybe, time off for good behavior. Prolly even be a career positive for her, you want my opinion on the matter. I mean. Reputation-wise. Little time in stir. People loves their colored chanteuse be a little dirty, you understand what I'm saying? I mean, man, lookit how it did for Lady Day.

"And anyway. Blues be all about pain," Oscar concludes, "and Auntie Lil's had it pretty easy peasy, so far, I'd say." He drops the stub of his cigarette and watches it smolder in the dry, matted ground before crushing it out with his bare foot. "It all good, man." He smiles, expansive. "Well. Showtime."

Lovely resists an urge to punch him, and tugs his hat down fretfully and lets the nephew take a couple strides back toward the safety of the Congo before he casts his line. "But where's the rest of it, Oscar?"

Oscar takes another step as this registers, then stops. The slow turn of his head, cocked, curious. "Rest of what?"

"You had a brick. They only copped your aunt for the two ounces you parked in her room. You sell the rest?"

As Lovely watches, Oscar goes from wide eyes with a smile of disbelief to the sly smirk of feigned indifference. His mind spins precisely the way Lovely wants it to, calculating. The hook sets, the line goes taut. "Yeah yeah," Oscar says. "Shit's gone, I moved it. Pretty good." That bone in his nose makes this lie especially unconvincing. Lovely notes. The big 10Ks surge on; a jungle is conjured, sharpens, and gleams again, wild, untamed. "But listen up. You get Aunt Lily a real good lawyer, shamus, you know, I be happy to chip in."

JOHNNY LEONG IS MISTING WATER over his bok choy and cabbage racks when Lovely passes by him, asking, not idly: "Is there a Chinese cure for moral indifference, Johnny?"

"Eggplant." The grocer tosses a measured, warning look to the counter where Reverend Atlee Drummond sits hunched over a cup of Hal's coffee. Lovely nods, sighs, this is pretty much how his day has been going, crosses the sidewalk, and slides onto his usual stool.

"Half of LAPD's looking for you, Reverend. Which gives you more than half a chance."

Drummond's voice is hoarse. Low, intense: "I didn't kill her."

"Okay. Except. Cops found the murder weapon at your apartment. Guess whose prints on it?"

Drummond says nothing, just looks into his coffee and stews.

A gruel of jaundiced morning sun drips through the Farmer's Market awnings; some TV comedy writers from CBS Studios, looking glum as if somebody died, as usual, are crowded around a single table at the waffle place that has no name. Hal brings Lovely's coffee. "You see where Ike says this new bomb will ensure a generation of peace?"

"I like Ike. I'd like to live in that world, where the H in H-bomb stands for 'Happy,' wouldn't you?"

Hal grunts, drifts away.

"He's setting me up."

Lovely asks who, just to keep the flow.

"Lamoureux." Drummond moves over, sliding his cup of coffee with him along the empty counter until it settles next to Lovely's. "Isla was just my typist." Drummond leans closer, his voice falls to a whisper. "He was the one who got her pregnant."

"Pregnant?" Lovely feigns surprise.

"You gotta help me."

"Go back a square, Atlee: who got who pregnant?"

"Lamoureux. Isla. He"—with his hands, unspecific—"got her—you know—in a family way."

Lovely offers him no real reaction, so Drummond plunges on. "Sexual congress. You see what I mean? And then he killed her because she wouldn't take care of the situation."

"Take care?"

"End it."

"Abort?"

Drummond makes a strangled noise and his eyes dart around the market worriedly, like they're trading state secrets.

"That's funny. I know a cop who's seen this same movie, only you're the star of his version. No top-secret stolen plans?"

"What? No." Drummond hisses, "Will you listen to me? Stolen plans is what he wants everyone to think. He's untouchable, Lamoureux. Cold War hero. But me, I helped him move the body back to her apartment, and I can prove he did it—"

"You helped him." Lovely cuts Drummond off, peevish, shaking his head, processing as he talks through it. "Helped him hide her murder?" For the third time this morning he wills himself not to lunge at somebody—Drummond, in this instance—with one of Hal's forks and a steak knife. Blind emotions flare nuclear behind the phlegmatic Lovely mask.

Drummond, oblivious, prattles, "Believe you me, our so-called friendship long ago crossed into the realm of assured mutual destruction."

What can Lovely say to that? "Oh."

A sturdy little boy in a coonskin cap darts through the market, fleeing a marginally bigger boy in a dime-store Indian headdress. Cap guns and rubber tomahawk, warbling war whoops and gunfire noises made in the back of the throat.

Johnny Leong's sons.

Sunken-eyed, Drummond watches them go, and repeats his claim that he can prove Lamoureux is guilty of Isla's murder.

Lovely says, "Turn yourself in. Tell it to the coppers. I'll go with you, right now."

"They won't believe me," Drummond protests. "We need proof."

"We?" *Here it comes.*

"I'm meeting the man tomorrow night." Drummond drains his coffee and puts the cup down, rattling. "At Aerojet Labs. The barn, so. Lamoureux. I get him talking, you'll be my witness. Eight o'clock."

"What if he doesn't say what you need?"

"Eight o'clock. He'll spill, trust me."

The reverend drops off his stool, makes a gesture of confederacy, and melts into the morning shoppers, furtive. *Just like that.* Lovely sniffs traces of a setup, but doesn't imagine it's anything he can't handle.

Hal clears their cups. "I guess you're payin' for your pal."

"I guess I am."

"He don't look worth it, you ask me."

Lovely shakes his head. "In the End Times, who can say, Hal? Who can say?"

IT TAKES A WHILE to convince Zeke Cazanov in Vice to waste his happy hour on Central Avenue humoring the possible resolution of Lovely's fishing trip to Lily's nephew. An acquaintance in

Paramount Studio security has relayed the release time of jungle extras from the set of *The Lost Expedition*, giving Lovely and the narc a reasonable window in which Oscar should arrive at the Fall-Out, if he's taken the bait, under the assumption that he'll want to get his stash quickly; today, Lovely tells Cazzie, today or not at all.

Cazanov has doubts. The arrest of singer Lily Himes was squeaky clean, the case is a winner, why mess with success? In fact, Cazzie would still be bitching about it while they sit and wait backstage in the darkened Fall-Out, if not for the providence of Cyrus the bartender, who has unlocked the doors and joined them, and who just happened to have a bottle of Old Overholt tucked away, and free hooch has mellowed the Vice cop out considerably.

"People think we're all about justice," Cazanov waxes, "but we're not. We're about winnable cases. Because, truth be told, everybody's guilty of something. Catholics got it right. Sacraments of penance and reconciliation: contrition, confession, absolution . . . and something else, I forget, don't tell the nuns." He holds his glass out for another splash of rye. "It's not our job to decide who's innocent or guilty. We just collect the evidence and haul in whatever unlucky sap is most likely to hang for it."

"Which, strangely, tends to noose the darker complected," Cyrus adds.

Cazanov frowns. "Excuse me?"

"Shh." The front door opens and closes, they hear footsteps across the concrete floor of the club, and then on the wide planks of the wooden stage. A shadow passes. From where they stand they can see down the back hallway and into Lily's private dressing room and office when the door is pulled open.

No light comes on, but the figure moves directly to a metal file cabinet and draws open the bottom drawer. A scrape of shoe when the shadow folds into itself to grope beneath the drawer for the expected hidden contraband.

When Oscar finally retrieves the brick—the whole brick, since Cazanov agreed to put it all back where they found it, admitting that, yes, anyone who knows where it's stashed would likely be its owner (although, "kid and the singer could be a team," the narc posited feebly, trying, Lovely figured, to salvage his original arrest)—when Oscar stands up with the brick in his hands, Lovely is blocking the office doorway and Cazanov has come all the way inside to flick the switch on the dressing room light that catches Lily's nephew cold.

Oscar sulks and gives the stink eye to Lovely while Cazanov cuffs him and relieves him of the pound of weed. A couple of times it looks like the nephew's going to say something, but he's led away by the uniforms who were waiting outside, without protest, without comment.

Back at Police Central, the negotiation on Lily's disposition from the colored wing of the women's jail takes most of the rest of the afternoon. And although Lovely drives to Lincoln Heights to pick her up and take her home, when she emerges from lockup, red-eyed and hair a disaster, she won't talk to him either.

She has a cab waiting outside.

MAY 5. *Just a carefully cropped scrap of typing paper with twelve lines of braille bumps.*

THE FAINTEST OF MEMORIES dust him: her eyes, her smile, the dents of dimples, the awkward—no, stubborn—innocence. Memories he carried across continents; that sustained him in the long shadows of his black-hearted missions. Memories from which he thought he'd become immune.

The house band has found a strange requiem dirge in "Sing, Sing, Sing." The tom-tom thumps like a death knell. The horns mourn. Lily, head down, eyes closed, grips the microphone stand and sways.

Skinny, pox-scarred Cyrus glides over for Lovely's refill. "How's that book?" And before Lovely can answer, "Miss Lily's been asking."

Lovely looks up at the bartender. Then to the Fall-Out stage, and Lily, scatting now, deliberately not looking in Lovely's direction, ever.

"She can ask," Lovely says.

"Miss Lily says that reading a dead lady's personal diary is bad form."

"Not just any lady, Cyrus."

"I know." Cyrus shrugs. "Gonna be hell to pay, is what Miss Lily says."

"Hell already took its cut." Lovely closes the book. With a whimper, not a bang, the drumming dims out, the song ends, and the applause makes the whole building shake. "And how, I wonder, would she know, Cyrus, what I'm over here reading in the first place?"

Cyrus blushes, eyes furtive, tops off Lovely's glass, and leans close, so he doesn't have to yell. "She's a bit tetchy that you put her nephew into the cooler, Mr. Lovely."

"I got her out."

"Sure."

"And, oh, by the way, Oscar's guilty."

"He's family, though. All the family she got."

Lovely can't really respond to that.

Cyrus's breath blows sour. His eyes rimmed yellow. "Two more songs in this set. Says she's pooped from her stint in stir. You gonna stick around, Mr. Lovely, face the inquisition?"

"It's none of her business," Lovely tells Cyrus, slipping the diary into his coat pocket, but casting a wider net.

"Yeah, you two just keep pretending that."

Lovely takes one big swallow of his drink, slides off his stool, and angles his hat. He hasn't learned anything about women, he thinks. When he does, if he does, will he still get wrecked on the rocks of them?

"Tell her she sounds real good tonight."

"Real good don't cut it, for her. You know."

"Tell her she sounds perfect, then."

"That gets it closer, sure. But she won't believe you, and she won't believe me saying it was you. How about I tell her you come down with a case of the cowards and had to skedaddle?"

"Whatever floats your boat, Cyrus."

Lily's band starts up with the angriest "Here's That Rainy Day" he's ever heard. Lovely feels Lily's icy stare on his back all the way out and, turning at the door, makes his best effort to deflect it; no reaction at all. Neither one of them giving an inch.

He will sleep without dreaming again tonight. It's been his requisite for survival so long he no longer knows of any other way.

8

STUFFED FULL with Du-par's biscuits and bacon, Lovely sits and threads the coiled roll of microfilm into the sprockets of the library's brand-spanking-new microfilm reader in the empty viewing room, clicks on the screen light, and manually spins through a year's worth of *L.A. Times* back issues while the fan comes up to speed.

The Los Angeles downtown Central Library news archive is a cellar gallery of narrow aisles lined with tall galvanized drawers filled with microfilm and floor-to-ceiling shelves thick with acid-free portfolios of yellowing newsprint going back half a century. It smells of printer's ink and dust and mold, and Lovely had to wait for a while at the check-in desk until the ancient clerk librarian, with his precious few threads of carefully oiled hair swerved up over a melon of skull, shuffled out with a box of film.

On the hooded screen, headlines blur. He leans in. Photos,

text, banner ads, comics, sports. A time machine. Lovely works the wheel, in no hurry, settling, reading, noting the dates, back and forth until he finds the crime story he's looking for, the one Isla had clipped and saved in her diary: the abduction of Sarah Blohm.

Time spins, words smear, weeks pass. A follow-up story. Still missing, no leads.

Spin.

One final item. A full page, banner headline, sidebar, and time itself frozen in grainy halftones, men standing awkward around a shape under a sheet in the Mojave.

"Gruesome discovery" . . . *"loving parents"* . . . *"her mother Agnes"* . . . *"grief-struck neighbors in Pacoima"* . . . *"she never had an unkind word for anyone."*

Lovely scans the story, not so much reading as absorbing. It's not very original, the ending is hopelessly clichéd, but that doesn't make it any less sorrowful.

CHICKENS IN THE YARD of a small, paint-desperate clapboard farmhouse scatter like refugees as the Morris pulls through the chain-link gate. A boy in short pants looks up from the puddle he's been slapping with a willow stick. His eyes are like two holes drilled in his angular face, watching Lovely climb out of his car.

"What kinda crate is that?" the boy brays, high and reedy. Lovely makes him for just shy of seven.

"It's called a Morris," Lovely says.

"That's English," the boy says. "The grille badge shows an ox fording the River Isis."

Lovely's impressed. "Is that right?"

"River Isis. That's in Oxford, England. World's best university. Someday I'm gonna go there and learn to row."

A bright-eyed, skeletal woman, younger than she looks, pink skin hanging in folds from her bones, comes through a screen door, wiping her hands on her apron. "You're going to go get cleaned up, boy."

"He's got a car from England."

"Gilbert Blohm . . ."

"Yes, ma'am." The boy stabs his stick in the puddle and runs inside.

The woman shades her eyes and squints. "You get lost?"

"Mrs. Blohm?"

"Agnes."

Touching the brim of his hat, "My name is Lovely. I'm sorry for the intrusion, but I guess you don't have a phone."

The woman laughs, without pleasure. "I guess we're not Rockefellers is what."

The woman and the boy live fifty minutes north of the city off a two-lane blacktop lined with almond trees and billboards advertising BEAUTIFUL NEW HOMES! that don't exist. Lovely's Morris had hustled past several scraped and graded grids of raw earth awaiting sewer and water, snaked through Kagel Canyon, and finally found the bumpy dirt-road driveway that wound into a dusty glen overhung with oak and Santa Lucia fir.

He explains that he's come to talk about Sarah. He tells her that she can say no and send him packing, but he notices she hasn't heard much after he said her daughter's name. It's like the wind has been knocked out of her. She turns her back on him, to thumb at something from the corners of her eyes, and takes a deep breath and then waves for Lovely to follow her unsteady gait inside.

"For an instant I thought you was here to tell me they found the monster who done it" is the first thing she says when she has him seated at the kitchen table, Lovely having politely declined an iced tea refreshment, thank you. He watches as Agnes seems determined to find something in the room to keep her busy, and distracted, finally settling on a single dish she washes up and then keeps drying, over and over, while they talk. "They never will, though, will they? That's what I think."

Lovely tells her, "Sometimes there's patterns to what these guys do. They have habits, rituals—police can connect the dots, and—"

"You mean he'll have to kill another girl."

"Or try."

"See, I wouldn't want that. Even if it meant . . . No, nobody else. Nobody else. When you lose someone you love . . ." She looks at him directly, earnestly, all the raw emotions bared by his visit, which he regrets now. "Do you know how that feels, to lose someone, Mr. Lovely?"

He does. Lovely says nothing. There's a long pause. The chickens. The wind. Tears want to gather in Agnes's eyes, but none come. Maybe there's none left. Lovely knows how that feels, too.

"It was wrong to let her go to Los Angeles. I couldn't ever say no to her. She was all goodness and light."

"Did she tell you about how things were going?"

"Called. Every Tuesday." She reads Lovely's confusion, "My neighbors, the Woolseys"—she gestures off in a direction that could be correct—"they have a two-party line with the Chapmans, and there was a pay phone where Sarah was staying."

"Did she talk about who she met, who she was seeing, friends—"

"She always made friends easily."

"She ever mention a friend named Isla?"

"I don't remember. No." Agnes sinks awkwardly into a chair across the table from Lovely, folds her palsied hands on the table in front of her, as if she's praying for him, and Lovely understands now: she's dying.

Agnes can see that he's figured it out. She smiles sadly, revealing yellow, broken teeth and swollen gums. "I got the cancer," she says without emotion. "Six months is my pill-pusher's best guess."

Lovely is silent for a moment. "I'm sorry."

With a wave of her hand she dismisses it. "You didn't have anything to do with it."

"Husband?"

"Bastard drank himself to death over our girl. No thought for our Bert. Son of a bitch."

For some reason Lovely asks what will happen to the boy, and Agnes shrugs, helpless. "I got no relatives. The Woolseys are, God, in their eighties or sure, they'd pitch in. Chapmans can't support the brood they have." She smooths her hair with both hands and sits back, chin up, looking down on Lovely like some deposed, exiled royal. "I don't know. County Home. I don't know. I can't bear to think it through just yet. Why?"

Lovely has burrowed so far into this he doesn't know how to turn around and get out. "Seems like a good kid, is all. I'm sorry." He shifts, uncomfortable.

"You keep saying that," Agnes observes. "Maybe if you told me why you're interested in Sarah we could move this along and you can go back where you're not so sorry."

"Missing persons," Lovely lies. "This woman named Isla, she

had news stories about Sarah clipped and folded in her personal journal; I thought maybe they'd met."

Agnes nods. "Maybe. Can't say yay or nay. Missing persons?"

Well. "Dead," Lovely admits, then. "Somebody killed her," he clarifies.

Tears flood Agnes's rheumy eyes. "Now I'm sorry," she says, and bursts out laughing, a dry heaving expulsion of air and bitter irony. Lovely lets her get calm and blot her eyes on her apron. "Oh, shoot," she says finally. "Shit. Shoot."

"Sarah have a job waiting? Or was it Hollywood that brought her to the city?"

"Oh, Lord. No. No. Sarah was very spiritual. She became enamored of this preacher on the television and went to Los Angeles to be a bicycle altar girl at the drive-in Church of the Cosmic Evolution."

The words hammer Lovely so hard he's not sure he even heard them. He looks away and accidentally locks eyes with the little boy hiding in the quiet of the hallway, just peering around a wall's edge. Green guileless eyes. He reminds Lovely of something he's lost on his long journey.

Hope?

"God." Agnes, her voice thin, husky, falters through the rest of a prepared speech, practiced, oft-delivered, but unsparing, "I thought God would protect her, but turns out it's an astral—no, how did Sarah explain it?—an astrophysics-based belief, science and numbers and such, I don't know. And so God was turned the other way when my little doll got taken, and . . ." No tears this time, but their absence somehow makes it worse. Whispering, "He wrote me a beautiful note, though."

"Who did?"

Clears her throat. She looks like she's slowly collapsing in on herself, second by second, a vanishing act. "The preacher." Again she's able to muster that unhappy, gracious smile. "Reverend Drummond. Just the most beautiful thing you've ever read, full of God's goodness, sorrow, and regret."

GRIM OVERCAST had chased him all the way back from the outer valley, but an incandescent sunset had momentarily erupted under the clouds and pinked the Angeles Crest when Lovely parked above the Arroyo Seco one more time, on the fire road. He had nosed off into the weeds, where, from the front seat of the Morris, he could peer down through the fence at the Aerojet barn.

Now night falls fast on the Colorado Street Bridge; the globes flick on and glow. Farther south, dreamlike at this distance, the peculiar Oz of downtown Los Angeles, scattering of Bunker Hill lights powdered by night mist, City Hall tower jutting blond, nothing taller, into a luminous mocha starless sky. Headlights strafe the bridge railings. Someone's big Bel Air wagon hurries into Pasadena on whispering whitewall tires.

The quiet is harshed by crickets. Drummond's Ford, parked out in front of the barn, has been there since Lovely arrived long before the appointed time. Lovely doesn't expect this to unfold the way Atlee Drummond has promised; in the spook life, his guiding principle had always been that there was the strategy you went in with, and then there was what actually would happen.

No light from the lab. But after a moment Drummond comes out, a shadow, and looks around. Nervous.

Lovely checks his watch.

It's time.

Drummond, anxiously pacing the car park, lifts his eyes as Lovely comes skating down out of the sage. Dust swirls. Security lights drop white curtains along the barn side.

"I was worried you wouldn't come."

Lovely assures the preacher he wouldn't miss this for all the world.

A primer of Drummond's plan: "He thinks we're meeting to talk about my surrendering to the authorities. You'll stay out of sight, but close enough to hear. I'll get him talking. He loves to hear himself talk." Drummond flicks on a flashlight and leads the way back inside the lab door he's left gaping. "There's a Dictaphone I can turn on, maybe it'll pick up our conversation.

"He shot her in here." By the time Lovely catches up with him, Drummond is crouching down, his flashlight beam aimed at the unfinished hardwood floor. He pushes back a scrap of rug. Faint stains, but this is a working lab, they could be from anything.

"Why?"

"She tried to get more money out of him," Drummond says.

More?

"He paid her ten grand to take care of the pregnancy, but she got greedy, came back, and asked him to expand the hush fund. Considerably."

Lovely can't let this go unchallenged. "Greed was not one of Isla's vices."

"How do you know?" The preacher flicks the flashlight beam into Lovely's face, suspiciously, momentarily blinding him, then darts it out the door, into the darkness. "He'll be here soon. You better hide."

"If you don't start telling me the truth," Lovely says, "I can't help you."

"Truth?" Drummond laughs. "What do any of us know about the truth? What does the truth even matter in a world where we can be vaporized in an eyeblink? The truth is, we are nothing. Atoms gathered temporarily, in space and time, destined to be released again, a scuff on the shine of eternity."

"It matters to me," Lovely says. "That's all I got. I can't answer for the universe. I don't want to."

Lights out. Click. Lovely can barely see. "Drummond?" He hears feet scuff across the floor. Tracks what he thinks is Drummond's shadow in the shadows, but it could be wishful thinking.

"I'm thirsty," Drummond says, unconvincingly, from nowhere near where Lovely is looking.

Then there is the sound of water running. Of footsteps scraping floor. But no disruption of that splatter of water streaming into the steel sink basin, no rustle of clothing as man hunches over the tap. No sharp intake of breath as he drinks. Lovely closes his eyes and then opens them again, trying to locate Drummond, pretty sure he knows where the preacher's going now. "I talked to Agnes Blohm today. She said you wrote her a very touching note, after the discovery of her daughter's body."

Nothing from Drummond. But there is a faint ticking sound: the clock? Lovely feels a dull buzz of adrenaline, but his mind is still catching up with his intuition.

"Sarah Blohm. Name ring a bell?"

Nothing from Drummond. Time slows: the ticking of the clock, slows. A rattle of metal. "She was one of your girls, Drummond. Did you kill her?" Lovely takes a quiet step backward, toward the door behind him. "Or was it Lamoureux? Was he backing your church so he'd have pick of the litter?"

Not a clock. A timer.

Now Lovely hears a palpable panic of clatter from the back of the lab. An eruption of light, in which: Drummond, at the rear door, his flashlight aimed at the deadbolt, fingers frantically throwing the latch back and forth, dumbfounded that the door doesn't—won't—open for him—

—tick tick—

—*Habakkuk 2:3. Though it tarry, wait for it; because it will surely come*—

—tick—

—Drummond glances back at Lovely with an expression of desperation, then utter surprise—and helplessness—horror—perhaps even contrition—

—*Daniel 11:27. The two kings, with their hearts bent on evil, will sit at the same table and lie to each other, but to no avail, because an end will still come at the appointed time*—

—tick tick—

—and Lovely pivots and plants and throws himself toward the front door, letting gravity carry him just that much faster through the gap, shouldering it open wide, stumbling out onto the gravel driveway, falling, curling, covering, hands over and behind his head, because—

—tick tick DING.

The flash of fire beats the first thundering concussion to Lovely by a fraction of a second. It doesn't seem likely that there could be anything louder; a dust of window glass spews, pulverized, a hot wind lifts and skids him pinwheeling farther out across the yard, thrown clear, while, inside, debris and the hellfire leap toward shattering beakers of chemicals and spilling vats of rocket test fuel, igniting all of it, everything, and causing the barn to explode in a hurricane of wood and metal and glass, and the pyrotechnics of secret fuels and molten metals cyclone around Lovely like mad Chinese fireworks.

Time stops. He can hear his heartbeat. He can hear his father's Sunday school scripture: *Zephaniah 3:8. The whole world will be consumed by the fire of my jealous anger.* He can hear the high-hat cymbal at the Fall-Out switch and scuff and Lily's high, clear voice singing the opening stanza of "C'est Si Bon," and it's in whatever key that fierce ringing in Lovely's ears is in, and, yes, he's still breathing, still intact, he's been here before, always in the wake of some dreadful nonsense in which he played the fool's role—Dresden, Berlin, Shandong, Damascus, Seoul, Tehran—watching the drift of civilization's crimson embers and impossible indigo spitfires from the smoldering rubble, and Lovely sits up in mustard weed and the smoke sifting stillness of the Arroyo Seco, brushing cinders off his shredded suit, dazed.

Lucky, as he's been told many times, to be alive.

9

"Cops got their man."

"I guess."

"That's what matters to them."

"Is it?"

"From where I sit. Always."

Four a.m. The Fall-Out has emptied except for Lovely and Lily Himes at the bar. Chairs upside down on tables like ramparts or troops in surrender, the sweet smell of whatever mopped the floor; Lily is still ashen from her overnight in the women's jail; eyes smoky, cheeks drawn.

He loves being with her at the end of the night after she's sung. There's something immutable in her that augurs a better day. Tonight, though, she's flinty and adrift, and Lovely's got bandages on his face and neck, cuts and nicks, both eyes blue-bruised and hollowed out.

"Meaning what?" Lovely wonders aloud. But he knows what

she means. She's not happy about what he's done to her nephew, but he'd do it again in a heartbeat.

"Cops got their man," Lily says again, stubborn, her refrain heavy with judgment. The difference between them is sometimes simply unbridgeable.

"They'll think so, sure," Lovely says, just as stubborn. "Paez is convinced the poor cosmic preacher was a jealous lover. De-Spain and the Feds think he was a commie spy."

Lovely hadn't cared to hang around the smoldering lab for the cops and FBI to arrive and get into the usual jurisdictional snitfit. He'd gimped his way sorely back up to his Morris and watched the first fire responders come wailing down the dirt road and then he slowly drove away, without headlights, skirting Aerojet's security fence to where the fire road opened out onto a local blacktop, and from there made his way back to the city. And Lily Himes.

He takes a sip of his cocktail. He doesn't know what she's mixed for him, but it soothes his throat, raw from soot and fear. A late bus rambles past on Central, rattling the fixtures. "So everybody's pretty pleased with themselves."

"Including," she says acidly, "you."

Lovely decides to go all in. His ears continue to ring from the blast. Frustration rises like bile. "Your nephew is a deadbeat punk."

"Is that what we're talking about?"

"I don't know. You tell me."

"He's family."

"That's what Cyrus keeps saying. What kind of family lets you take the rap for him?"

She has no answer.

"It didn't please me to do it," Lovely offers.

"I'll make a note of how bad you feel." Lily looks away,

evidently not quite ready to let go of her anger with him yet. "So what'd you get, Rylan? All these windmills you keep fighting. Besides more scars?"

"I got you out of a tangle," he says. "Everything else is vapor trails."

Slowly she turns her violet eyes back to him. He never tires of looking at her.

"What I have is puzzle pieces that don't fit," Lovely says. "Lost wives and rocket scientists. Babies, blackmail, and broken friendships. And a body out in the desert."

"That part is old news."

"Is it?"

"Yes. And maybe they're not pieces. Maybe they're notes. And you're just trying to find a key to play them in."

Lovely studies her. "That's kind of poetic, Lily."

"Nah," she tells him diffidently, "it's just bebop."

"Just," he repeats, putting the spin on it, "like you and me? 'Just' friends?"

"I want a hot shower." Lily sighs. "I gotta wash a whole layer of new indignity off of me and try to forget the last couple of days." But the venom is gone. She adds, searching his eyes for something, "If you'da told me you had a wife, I probably never would have given you a second glance. And we never would have got together."

"And you wouldn't have had to break my heart."

Lily seems unconvinced. "This world broke your heart, baby. If we didn't live in it—"

"—I know. I know."

In what crazy construct can love be called a crime?

It's possible they will get through this. It's probable they will not. Life takes weird turns, Lovely knows and, as long as you're alive to live it, sky's the limit.

Many men he's known didn't get that chance.

NEXT DAY, noon, there's an empty wheelchair where the Korean War vet had previously bivouacked with his knock-knock jokes, and Lovely makes another journey down the long VA hospital corridor toward Buddy's room.

The blind friend is not in situ, as Lovely's Operation Ajax point man, Chet Nelson, was fond of expounding after draining several dirty martinis in the Baghdad embassy bar. Chet was a Princeton egghead, president of the college rug society: an idea man, especially when the ideas edged toward regime change in the Middle East. Shocked, of course, when SAVAK decided to round up and execute alleged traitors afterward.

Nobody here, in other words. Room spotless. Camera gone.

Lovely goes to the desk, moves the chair, opens the drawer Buddy didn't want him snooping in and finds an impressive tumble of crazily framed square-format photographs that Buddy has taken of, it looks like, anything and everything, in focus and out, Los Angeles through a random lens. Blind man with a camera. But repeatedly the aperture found Isla, somehow. Her headless torso furry in the foreground, her shoulder edging into frame, half a face, the top of her head, an arm and a hip, the side of her head, with one clear eye staring out at Lovely, as if she knew he'd someday see them.

And nested among these pictures is a small reel-to-reel tape recorder spooled up and waiting to teach a sightless veteran his LEARN FRENCH EASY lessons, one through ten.

Fuck.

The trouble with mysteries is always their solution.

"Somebody in here?"

Buddy is in the doorway. Lovely freezes for some reason, and doesn't respond.

"Lovely?"

Can he know? Buddy comes in, confident, step step stop, the Rolleiflex jangling against his chest from a strap looped around his neck. "I smell you." Committing to his silence, Lovely dodges away like a silent movie boxer, dancing around his old friend, matching his footsteps to Buddy's.

"Just because I can't see you doesn't mean I can't tell you're—"

There's a clatter of metal and wood when Buddy collides with the desk chair that Lovely moved out of the way to get to the drawer. Buddy wasn't expecting it. But now he's sure that someone is in his room.

"What do you want?"

Lovely slowly tries to back out of the room. He doesn't want to have this conversation. He can't.

"Rylan?" Buddy twists and lunges and flails at air, almost stumbling into the bed.

And Lovely is out. Out in the corridor, up on his toes, trying not to make a sound, moving, already halfway down the hallway, a coward's momentum taking him back the way he came—always back the way he came—

"LOVELY!"

THE POSITION FOR PAEZ is wholly pragmatic: motive, opportunity, suicidal suspect, case cleared, move on. Even before

Lovely has finished telling him what he knows, and suspects, Paez is shaking his head, lips pursed like a scolding schoolmarm. "So, what? You suggesting Buddy killed her?"

Lovely insists he's not, but he knows he needs to tread lightly because it could easily take that turn.

"Then what? Cuz I'm pretty busy here." Paez indicates a cooling cup of coffee and a well-thumbed *Look* magazine with Grace Kelly on the cover, threatening to unbutton her shirt.

"The murder weapon was Buddy's gun."

Paez isn't really listening. "They want a new motto for the Police Academy."

"Army issue. The M1917 revolver."

Having scrawled some ideas on a pad of paper, Paez offers one up: "How about 'We Serve to Protect'?" Then, admitting, "I kinda stole that one from Joe Dorobeck. But his goes the other way around."

"Henry—"

"What with all the monkey business on your face, a better detective might be more curious about where you were last night when Drummond blew himself and that barn to kingdom come."

"Are you gonna just—"

"Criminy, Ry, there must've been a million of those M1917s issued during the war."

"With a nick on the handle? From this fast-draw thing Buddy used to practice on deck en route to Algiers? I didn't mention it before because I knew you'd take it and run the wrong way."

"Insulting me is really working for you."

"How did Buddy's gun get into Drummond's hand?"

If, Paez mumbles, it is Buddy's gun.

Lovely is undeterred. "You got two strange guys, college pals, one who made up a religion, one who likes the religious one to pimp him young altar girls to be pummeled like a speed bag. What if Isla knew that Drummond had set rocket man up with the Blohm girl? That kind of scandal would pretty much put an end to the Cosmic Church gravy train, and the rocket scientist's recreation. And what if that's what the blackmail was about?"

"Luckily, here in the LAPD, we use what's called evidence to solve cases."

"It's gotta add up for me, Henry. All of it."

"It adds up," Paez points out. He lifts the magazine and uncovers Hostess Twinkies. "You just don't like what the sum says about your girl. Everything doesn't connect all neat that way, it's more like a swirl."

"You're right. And in that swirl some things circle back and crash together. I don't buy that a guy who beats up a woman like Judy has never done it before. I don't buy that Isla had intimate relations with Drummond, or Lamoureux. Not her style. Neither was stealing secrets and selling them to communists. It's all just correlation without causation, and we're talking about Caltech eggheads who assume cops and Feds are dopes."

Paez starts to unwrap a Twinkie. "Did I tell you Drummond was blood type O? Same as Isla's baby?"

Lovely is getting fed up. "Sure, him and sixty percent of the world's population. But, hey, it fits with your story, right, so—"

"—it fits the FACTS. It fits the facts." He stuffs the industrial snack cake in his mouth and the white goo squeezes from the corners of his lips. "You hadn't seen her in seven years. A lot can change. Look at you."

"I'm the same. It's the world that's tilted."

Licking his fingers, Paez says, "Oh. Uh-huh. And, what, you, you're the guy's gonna level it up?"

Lovely, resolved and determined: "Yeah."

FACTS.

Shukri al-Quwatli didn't want the Trans-Arabian pipeline going through his country. Fourteen months later, he was no longer king of Syria. The public verdict? Spontaneous coup by an unhappy population.

And Bechtel, and the British, and their plucky Americans, like Lovely, who did all the shitty things that didn't get recorded in the factual record, packed up and hustled back to Berlin where the clarity of the red menace was a comfort.

There are facts, and there are facts.

Fact: The weekday double feature at the Egyptian offers *Hell and High Water* and *The Glenn Miller Story* for seventy-five cents. Fact: A gauzy magic hour light, as they say in the movie business, teasing real summer slants down flaxen through the walkway palms, Radio KLON twittering low on public address speakers as a cigarette girl in a flouncy dress works the milling courtyard crowd. Fact: Foundation and dark nylons can't quite mask the telltale scrapes and contusions of her unfortunate ride up the Mulholland Highway. "Cigarettes? Free Winston samples. Cigarettes?"

As if anticipating his approach, she pivots abruptly and recognizes Lovely after a fleeting frown.

"How much for the whole tray?" he asks her.

Judy's eyes struggle to keep what Lovely can tell is just a managed despair at bay. "Tell me he's dead. Tell me he tried it again, and the cops caught him and shot him dead."

"I can't."

Traffic spawning on Hollywood Boulevard, silverfish slipping past one another.

A trio of teenagers want to try the Winstons. The boys with their hair waxed high, the girl with lips the color of fresh viscera. Judy asks them if they're all eighteen, knows they're not, but gives them a promotional short pack each. "It's good for your complexion," she tells the girl. "Four out of five doctors agree."

Facts.

"What do you want?" she says, fragile, to Lovely after the teens saunter away.

"How much for the tray?"

"I don't want your charity. You can't save me. You were too late, you still are."

"I know that," Lovely admits.

"I came out here for the Rose Bowl," she says. "Michigan State. Boo-rah."

"You beat Cal."

"Did we? I never made it to the game." She shifts the tray and the straps leave soft furrows in her shoulders. "This would have been my sophomore year. But I was mostly there to get my MRS, to be honest. Came out of an East Lansing winter and it was so blue-sky beautiful here, I stayed. I just . . . stayed." She seems to lose herself in this thought for a moment. "You ever been to Michigan?"

Lovely allows that he has not. Western Colorado. Berlin,

Warsaw, Inchon, South Korea. He says he knows what cold can be, anyway.

"I thought I'd meet Mr. Right, and boom. Astrophysicist. How about them apples? And I met him at church. At church. How could that turn out so wrong?"

She has answered his question about Lamoureux before he could ask it. Lovely says, "Under the sun, under the sky. You were an altar girl. At the Church of the Cosmic Evolution." He would have been astonished if it had been any other explanation. *But still, what difference does it make?*

Judy nods, fights back tears. "I want to hire you to kill him."

Lovely says no.

Raw: "Please?"

"Not my area," he says, uncomfortable, because it might have been. "I'm sorry. How much for the whole tray?"

She presses him, "I've got over five hundred dollars in savings."

"You don't want to go down that road," Lovely tells her, and means it. "It's a dead end. There's nothing there for you."

Judy nods again, in the empty way of a broken person who doesn't agree but won't argue, looks out at all the people filing into the theater. Expectant faces. Ready to be transported out of this sorry world and into a better one. Ready for a good show.

"They have no idea," she says, downcast.

"No," Lovely agrees. "How much for the tray?" he asks one last time.

Judy looks crossed-up and frowns, "Well, the Winstons are a free promotion. The others, I don't even know. I'd have to . . ." She stares at the tray, then at Lovely. "Why?"

"You're going home," he says.

———

THE FIRST SET at the reopened Fall-Out is probably just settling in, Lovely muses: a packed house of angel city hepcats, a reenergized Lily stepping up to the microphone to open with the band's new signature, a hard bebop Cab Callawoy call-and-response:

Who's got fission?
(We got fission!)
Who's transmutin'?
(Gamma rootin' tootin'—)
Talkin' 'bout the nuclear blues . . .

He wishes he were there to see it, and not standing in Judy's bachelorette studio, watching her pack, and all his usual recriminations swirling like the Catalina eddy, bleak, gray, indefatigable, cycling through the same wretched human crimes and calamities over and over again.

The inescapable limbo of the Southern California Bight.

Judy's been boarding downtown in a gloomy Victorian tower doomed for demolition, halfway up Bunker Hill, rendering the Angel's Flight funicular pointless, so they walked up the long run of concrete steps from Hill Street, where Lovely has parked his car near Grand Central Market.

Judy can put everything she owns in a single suitcase. The flat smells of lavender and new paint. It's nothing like he expected. It's strangely warm and inviting, almost magical, lit up smoldering by the last issue of another gauzy muted sunset: hook rug, beveled mirror, matched blond bedroom set. There's no small talk between them, they've both said pretty much all they intend to. If he expected more static, between the mechanical movements of folding and packing and the empty way she looks at him, it seems clear that the fight is gone from her, and all she needed was a nudge to make her go.

Who's gonna drop it?
(Not me, not me!)
Then why you even need it?
(You got one! They got one!)

The walk down is always easier; Lovely hefts her big scuffed Samsonite into the trunk of his car and they drive the eight minutes to Union Station, where, as travelers drift abustle, under the majestic vaulted ceiling, Judy gazes up at the departure board while Lovely buys her a one-way ticket to East Lansing on the California Zephyr.

"I'm sorry it didn't work out for you here," Lovely says.

"What?" She looks at him oddly. "Oh." She thinks it through. "Well. I just lost one semester, right? My grams says when one door closes another one opens up, and you just walk through it to a better place."

Lovely nods. Lovely's grandmother was a teetotaling evangelical eccentric who once had the back door of her house screwed shut so that "people" couldn't get in and steal the pork chops from her icebox, raw cuts of which inevitably turned up, rotting, days later in her purse, where she had hidden and forgotten them.

Isla's grandmother was a runaway Mormon, who didn't want to be a Provo bishop's fourth wife.

Lily's grandmother was a slave.

One door closes, another opens up.

On the platform, he tips the porter who takes Judy's bag. Without saying anything, without even looking at him, she starts to follow her suitcase onto the train, but abruptly comes back down the three metal steps, wraps her arms around Lovely and silently squeezes him, leaving two blotted tearstains on his jacket, and then just as quickly disappears inside the car.

He walks away before her train pulls out.

Thermonuclear
electrostatic 'pulsion, baby
lemme see your critical mass . . .
[drum solo]

He's dodging taxicabs in the crosswalk on his way to the terminal's public short-term parking when the dime drops and Ry Lovely understands fully what he saw without seeing.

One door closes, another—

He backtracks to the station.

Finds a pay phone outside the entrance, dialing local:

"DeSpain?"

10

LOVELY KNEELS and digs through the detritus with his bare hands. Flashlight clenched in his mouth. Searching.

On the lip of the arroyo, an Aerojet Laboratories security Jeep has found, in the moonless Flintridge darkness, Lovely's Morris nosed into the fire road brush again. Down below, a solitary trespasser picks through the remains of Barn Number 5, white shaft of a flashlight stabbing down.

High beams coming fast up the access road pin Lovely to the rubble. He stands and shades his eyes as black federal sedans skid to a halt and agents hop out, lively with guns and rifles. The generation that just missed the war, Lovely notes: Buddiger, Johnson, Kapnik . . . and DeSpain, who was there and then some.

"What's buzzin', cousin?"

"Does it at all bother you," Lovely says to him, "that some rocket scientist's tall tale about stolen secret plans and the Red

Menace gets everyone in Justice aquiver, and it's you poor over-worked G-men who have to make it hold water?"

"Fidelity, bravery, integrity."

"Oh, uh-huh. And the *G* stands for gullibility."

DeSpain comes forward, his expression wary. "You don't know when to say when, do you?"

"I've got a thing about loose ends."

"Welp. Even though you called me, I can't give you a pass for this one, Rylan. It's a federal crime, your being here. Trespassing, secure facility. Not to mention poking through classified material."

Lovely is bemused. "This?" He aims his flashlight down at the shards of barn again, and resumes rummaging. There's the chilling sound of bullets chambered, guns cocked—

—and Kapnik screaming, "DO NOT MOVE!"

DeSpain shrugs. "They want any excuse to shoot you."

Lovely keeps working. "All this extra light helps, thanks."

Kapnik, brittle: "Sir?"

DeSpain waves them off and steps between his soldiers and Lovely, who grunts and yanks at something stuck in the ruins.

"What are we looking for? I hope it's that missing ten grand, I'm getting a lot of static from my section chief."

Lovely straightens and shakes his head. "A doorway."

"Literally, or figuratively?"

"Literally."

DeSpain wades in to help—braces himself, gets a grip, and they both tug and Lovely's find releases: the big, blasted wooden remainder of the barn's faded green back door, still in its rectangular doorframe. Together they drag it free, lift, and Lovely stands it up, crooked. Backlit, it takes on the character of a strange gallows. Lovely fingers a couple of crooked twelvepenny nails still embedded along the jamb to prevent the shattered door from opening.

"Your Paul Lamoureux's a monster," he says. "And a murderer."

"Mine? Funny. Pentagon, Joint Chiefs, Congress—Ike himself—think he's one of the most important American scientific assets of the Cold War."

"More important than Strughold?" Lovely wonders darkly.

"Okay right. Play the Nazi mad doctor trump card, go ahead, Lovely. Cheap shot."

"I didn't say he wasn't smart. Hell, he out-conned a con man sharp enough to start his own religion. Drummond. Convinced him to lure me to the barn and blow me up in a 'lab accident.' Walks me in the front and then intends to slip out the back"— Lovely bangs on the broken door; it won't budge from the frame— "only the back way . . . was uncooperative. And God's servant got to meet his maker."

Lovely lets it all clatter back into the jumble of barn remains.

DeSpain stares at it. "Okay, you've convinced me. Big deal. We can't touch him, Lovely"—he's irritated—"goddamn it, why did you show me this? You think showing me this will change anything?"

Lovely says, "A man can dream."

DeSpain fumes. "Who put the red *S* on your chest?! You can't prove it was Lamoureux! You can't prove a goddamn thing!" DeSpain's voice echoes through the arroyo.

"No, I can't." Lovely says it softly. "That is the bitch of it, Ed. Some men get blinded so others can see."

Nobody says anything for a while. Kapnik and the young

Feds let their weapons sag and their boots scrape the gravel. On the horizon, Hollywood searchlights sweep black cotton skies as if trying to find the stars.

DeSpain breaks the quiet, his voice bitter and sardonic. "Yeah, well. At least he's our monster, huh? Like you said."

"Did I?"

DeSpain sighs, jams his hands into his pockets, and starts to walk back to the cars, signaling for his men to follow, waving for the headlights to dim and give them all some measure of the comfort of shadows.

BEHIND HIS FARMER'S MARKET COUNTER, his apron smudged with doughnut jelly, Hal is surprisingly philosophical about the new H-bomb, once he's read up on all the Operation Castle tests, Bravo to Koon. "Knowledge makes us more dangerous. Always has, always will. Rocks, spears, broadswords, crossbow, catapult, cannon, rifle, and so on and so forth. The closer we get to our Creator, the closer we risk his final embrace." Lovely suspects Hal heard this on the radio, from Arthur Godfrey or Norman Vincent Peale. "I've been doing quite a bit of research on underground shelters," Hal admits. "There's a company in Lancaster can do you one in the backyard, deluxe, soup to nuts, for about five hundred bucks."

The fact that Hal doesn't have a backyard and lives in a Fairfax fourplex with his mother seems not to figure in. Two weeks have passed since Lovely found the door that Lamoureux used to murder Drummond. Summer has burned through the marine layer and sent it packing; bright, hot, rich blue cloudless skies as unreal as Technicolor. Fourth of July promises to be a scorcher.

"With proper air filtration and food management, a family of four can survive not just the initial attack but also the aftermath: fallout and radiation. What they call a nuclear winter."

"Yeah, but doesn't that last for, like, five hundred years?" From the other end of the counter a wag who Lovely has never seen before pipes up.

"Scientists tend to exaggerate," Hal says. "So they won't be caught with their pants around their ankles come a doomsday scenario. Plus, it plumps their funding."

Lovely sorts through the new messages Johnny Leong has collected for him while he and Lily went south to sort themselves and their relationship in Ensenada: more possible studio gigs, a teenage runaway, this philandering housewife that he's already caught in flagrante delicto once, and warned the poor forgiving spouse that she would be an unapologetic recidivist. A probate lawyer's call looks promising, surely boring and procedural, which is something Lovely would be craving just now if he could just get the foul taste of Lamoureux out of his mouth.

On the balcony of their Baja room at the Hotel Riviera del Pacífico, Lovely had shared Isla's diary with Lily. She flipped through it as if disinterested, found the blank braille scrap right away and lingered. Lovely had assumed it was a love note from Buddy. Lily, running her fingers over the bumps, closing her eyes, said, after a while, "No, baby, I think it's lyrics to a song."

There happened to be, in El Sauzal, a blind Mexican accordion player Lily had met when Django Reinhardt toured the States in the wake of the war. They brought him Isla's journal and a bottle of reposado, and he recognized both immediately, by touch.

"Ah. Brahms. Volkslieder," he said, grinning, touching the braille after they'd sampled the tequila. *"De un poema checo de filósofo Daumer."*

German love song. A composition by Johannes Brahms, Lily explained. With lyrics from a poem by some philosopher.

The Mexican sang:

Nicht mehr zu dir zu gehen,
Beschloß ich und beschwor ich,
Und gehe jeden Abend,
Denn jede Kraft und jeden Halt verlor ich.

"To visit you no longer," Lily translated, "did I resolve and swear. Yet I go to you each evening, for all strength and resolve have I lost."

Ich möchte nicht mehr leben,
Möcht' augenblicks verderben,
Und möchte doch auch leben
Für dich, mit dir, und nimmer, nimmer sterben.

"I long to live no longer, I long to perish instantly. And yet I also long to live for you, with you, and never, never die."

The Mexican shut his sightless eyes and sang the final verse softly, his voice high, quavering:

Ach, rede, sprich ein Wort nur,
Ein einziges, ein klares;
Gib Leben oder Tod mir,
Nur dein Gefühl enthülle mir, dein wahres!

And Lily half sang it, too, then, almost a whisper after he'd finished: "Ah, speak, say only one word, a single word, a clear one; give me life or death, only reveal your feelings to me—your true feelings!"

Lovely's throat grew thick, and his eyes were wet, and he didn't have the strength to tell her that he understood the German just fine, or that it was Buddy who had introduced him to the lieder of Brahms.

On the last night of their stay, with the lights of the harbored yachts shimmering on the sea swell and the rattle and thrum of bar-crawl traffic below them, they began to talk about the boy.

Lovely's point was that he couldn't do it alone.

Lily wondered if he was proposing.

He wasn't, in any conventional sense. "Where I've been the past ten years, what I've seen," he said. "We fought a war to get rid of evil, but it had already leached out, and we were covered with it. The world we knew, the one brave men in Europe and the Pacific died to come back to, it's gone, Lil. I've seen what's coming. Not just the bomb."

Lily pointed out how a country that still prevented people of a darker skin tone from sharing drinking fountains with their pale brothers and sisters was splitting hairs, where Evil was concerned. And that Lovely couldn't protect the world from itself, if that was what he was saying, she wasn't quite sure. She said his intentions sounded frighteningly similar to the rationale Ike and the Dulles brothers were using to go around the planet making trouble in the name of Freedom and the American Way.

He didn't want to admit to her he'd been a part of that effort. "No," he started to argue, then thought better of it. "Well, yeah.

But maybe I can hold it off for just those around me. Friends, family. And people who come to me for help."

"And boys about to be orphaned."

Lovely allowed that it was probably a fool's errand. But he was the perfect fool for it.

Lily had laughed and kissed him and stretched out long and lovely on the balcony recliner. The sky held that same terra-cotta glow they'd left behind in Los Angeles; no stars, a veiled crescent moon.

"What's his name?" she asked finally.

"Gilbert."

"FOR YEARS the problems of burning high-energy fuels in rocket engines has stymied us. At stake, quite literally, was the future of mankind . . ."

Blah blah blah. Standing, hatless, next to the chunky television news cameras aimed at a lectern under the replica Wright Brothers' biplane that hangs from the great room rafters in the Natural History Museum in Exposition Park, Lovely—grim, jaded, and intractable—should be able to just let this go, but when he read in the *Herald* that Dr. Paul Lamoureux, noted rocket scientist, was due to receive the city's Man of the Year Award, he couldn't stay away.

". . . This new Aerojet Zip Fuel means that our ICBMs can soar farther and higher, and our glorious B-29s will have greater ability to rule the skies and protect this great nation and its allies with a thermonuclear arsenal second to none."

This kind of jingoistic blather always gets enthusiastic applause, and Lamoureux, flanked by shit-grinned company executives, a few USC senior faculty, the usual local government suspects, and some well-fed Pentagon brass, takes a professional pause to allow the tribute to settle on his deserving shoulders.

"In the titanic clash with those who would enslave free men under the brute lies of socialism, it's not just Science that leads the way, but Science in the service of defending our American Way of Life, in which every man is allowed to pursue his dreams."

Even if they include casual rape and murder, Lovely observes. It goes on for a while, and ends with a standing ovation, the rocket scientist flashing a winning smile; a general pats him on the back, the governor shakes his hand. Flashbulbs pop. A reporter's shouted question: "Elis Mankiewicz of Caltech says this puts you on the short list for the Nobel Prize in Chemistry, Professor. Care to comment?"

One of Aerojet's PR flacks steps up, but Lamoureux is happy to respond. "I would never disagree with Dr. Mankiewicz on matters of pure scientific reasoning."

The admiring crowd laughs. A second ovation erupts and Lamoureux mimes "Thank you" and steps away from the lectern microphones. His federal escort materializes from the wings, DeSpain in a new pale summer-weight suit.

Lamoureux posing: with the generals, with Aerojet executives, with the mayor, with a pretty girl who drapes a ceremonial medal around his neck while his hand drifts down to her ass.

The whole entourage falls in behind as Lamoureux makes his exit like a king leaving court. DeSpain and his Feds clear an aisle through the lingering well-wishers pressing in. Touch of hands, vague smiles. A yellowing Tyrannosaurus fossil skeleton leers down at them.

DeSpain doesn't notice Lovely drift in and match stride, until he's asking, sharply, "What's the Zip Fuel death toll now, doc? Two? Three, if we count Sarah Blohm?"

"No need to make a scene." DeSpain slides between them.

Lovely ignores the Fed and shrugs off Lamoureux's glare. "Sarah Blohm, yeah—you remember her? Another one of your motor hotel trysts gone wrong."

DeSpain's last warning: "Rylan—"

Lovely feints, lags, slips back inside of the federal gauntlet, up against Lamoureux's shoulder, low, intense. "It took me a while to figure, because I'm no rocket genius, but that's what it was all about, right? Isla witnessed you recruiting from the ranks of Drummond's Cosmic altar girls. One of the perks for you of being a church rainmaker. Pristine gash."

Lovely is pressing for a reaction, and sure enough, Lamoureux slows and turns his face, eyes like ebony buttons, lifeless and dark. "Go away."

"Saw," Lovely continues, "Sarah Blohm pedaling around the drive-in. Then Isla saw her pictures in the papers: story of a murder-kidnap. And Isla, being smarter than me, puzzled it out a lot quicker. How'm I doing?"

Lamoureux glares at Lovely, but says to DeSpain, "Make him leave."

DeSpain slips his arm through Lovely's and finds the eyes of another Fed on perimeter detail and nods the man over. But Lovely keeps talking. "Isla hit you up for hush money. You told the Feds it was about secret documents, because the murder of a girl might be a hard pill for even them to swallow. No matter how many sweet bombs you build."

"Tall tales."

"Drummond helped you disappear Isla's body. Just like the last time. Sarah Blohm."

DeSpain says, "C'mon, Rylan. You've said your piece. Let's take a hike."

Lovely grabs Lamoureux's arm to keep him from getting any separation, "You killed Isla to shut her up."

"Rylan," DeSpain warns, "that's enough." He starts to tug Lovely away, but Lovely still has Lamoureux's arm in his grasp, so they all spin to an awkward halt.

"And killed Drummond, when he got all bent out of shape." Lovely's face is so close to Lamoureux's that they nearly touch foreheads. A whisper: "And you just missed with me."

"You're a pointless little man. A speck of dust in the vastness of known space."

"Yeah, so you keep telling me. Thanks."

It should be finished, the Man of the Year should walk away because Lovely has nothing but empty threats, but Lamoureux can't seem to stop himself now. "And even if your theory was true, what can you do about it, Mr. Lovely? We're in the Age of Science. Big men, big ideas. The rules don't apply to us."

DeSpain looks troubled. As if this is too much for him. "Sir, can we just—let's—"

Lamoureux's face goes ugly; surface calm stripped bare, his corrupted soul revealed. "You, my friend, your 'wife' . . . any number of pretty trifles I may suffer and cast in my considerable wake . . . just don't matter. Sorry."

Lovely knows better, but jumps at him anyway, takes a wild swing and, uncharacteristically, misses. All the Feds react. A scuffle ensues, no blows landed, but eventually DeSpain finds purchase on Lovely's shoulder and shoves him sideways against a display case, holding him there while Lamoureux backs away, smug, sneering, "I want to press charges. I want him arrested."

Lovely struggles to get back into the fray, but DeSpain stands his ground. "Let it go," he says to Lamoureux. "You, too, Lovely, let it go. You heard the man. We don't factor in this equation, we never have. It's about bigger weapons and better death. All we can do is duck and cover and pray."

Lovely sags, relents. They watch Lamoureux go out a side door into Exposition Park, his retinue momentarily losing track of him.

The door gapes and stays open on an air-piston closing mechanism. The formal gardens of Exposition Park line a stone sidewalk in the shadow of the building. Sculpted trees sway in a warm breeze. Lovely sees that Lamoureux has stopped to light a cigarette, and flicks the match away. The piston sighs and the door slowly begins to close on him, squinting up into another glorious day.

There is a pop like a firecracker.

His head twists, jerks, spasms.

A small-caliber bullet punches through Lamoureux's temple and exits in a puff of red mist just behind his ear, and he drops clumsy, like a stringless marionette.

Judy stands over him, numb, sobbing, with the smoking gun.

The crowd inside reacts and cowers, but Lovely and DeSpain rush outside by instinct or training, it no longer matters; Lovely strips the gun from the crying girl and takes her in his arms while DeSpain tends to his rocket man.

"I put you on a train."

"Track goes both ways," Judy says emptily.

DeSpain, ear to Lamoureux's gaping lips, just murmurs, "Holy cow." Dead.

Lovely raises his hand and—bangbangbangbang bang—empties the .22 revolver into the sky, causing anyone in the museum who might have been thinking of coming out the door to scramble again for cover and make their muffled calls for help.

"What the hell are you doing?!"

"Buying us ten seconds," Lovely says, and two of them tick by while the former spooks trade weary looks. "She won't get a fair shake, Ed. You know she won't."

Sirens wail, approaching. Footfall of cops coming through the garden, and voices from inside:

"Agent DeSpain! Status?"

DeSpain shakes his head, "Aw, Rylan, for the love of—"

Lovely counts down their margin. ". . . five, four, three . . ."

"You gonna always want your stories to have a happy ending now?"

Lovely shrugs. "Can't have a Cold War if the whole world is ice." He offers DeSpain the girl's gun, grip first, and the Fed takes it.

DeSpain's man, inside, calls again, "DeSpain?!"

"All clear," DeSpain shouts back. He considers the trifling mortal coil of what was once the Man of the Year and, to Lovely, wry as only an ex-spook can be, "Gee, I wonder who killed him."

Cops and Feds swarm the scene from inside and outside, a flood of law and order. DeSpain slips the .22 in his pocket and holds up his badge for the LAPD blues. "FBI, officers. Establish a perimeter, Fig to Vermont. The shooter is still at large."

Lovely hustles the girl away; gets lost in the chaos as reporters and rubberneckers press down the paths and out through the doors, causing the cops to be way too occupied with crowd control to be attendant to anyone casually moving away from the scene.

Refrain of flashbulbs and the dull roar of breaking news.

THE FOREST LAWN FUNERAL for Isla had been small and quiet, fanned by dry, hot desert wind that whirled and danced across the Griffith Park hills.

Buddy, in a folding chair, sat central, edge of the grave, restless. Surrounded by a few friends. Did he know that Lovely was in attendance? Lovely doubts it, seated now, here, days later, cooled by a fan in Isla's courtyard apartment, just a couple crow-flies miles away from where she's buried. He's listening to a Chico Hamilton LP that Lily gave to him for his birthday. He's drinking scotch. The diary is on the side table, within reach.

Last entry. *June 10. Write the things which thou hast seen, and the things which are, and the things which shall be hereafter . . .*

At the bottom of the page, skewed and rushed, like an afterthought, she's scribbled the phone number for Leong's Fresh Fruit and Produce.

All the furniture's been rearranged.

Buddy has been back to Forest Lawn every day, sweating so much it fogs his Ray-Bans; Lovely has followed the cab that takes him there, knows when he arrives and how long he stays. It won't be difficult for Lily to collect him today.

Lovely waits in the cool gloom of Isla's flat until a car horn honks. He pushes himself up from the chair and walks out into the slanting sunshine, letting the screen door close softly so as not to announce himself.

A convertible Cadillac has parked beyond the archway. Miss

Lily Himes is at the wheel, summer dress, floppy black hat and sequined sunglasses, Buddy just climbing out, with his white cane probing for obstacles.

He senses Lovely. "How many steps?"

"Five."

Buddy swings his stick, finds the stairs, and comes up into the courtyard, counting. Lovely meets him there and offers an arm, so close that he can smell on Buddy's breath the tinned mints Lily must have offered him on the way over.

"How's your French coming?"

"Okay, spit it out, Ry. Don't be a jerk."

"Was it gonna be Paris or just some protectorate like Algiers? Isla had a ticket and a passport and ten thousand bucks."

Something moves, eclipsed behind the screen door opposite. Lovely can just make out the gentle slopes of the actress, as if behind a stage scrim, watching them. Her fingers touch the screen door and bloom small pools of pink.

"You never broke up with her, Buddy."

They're at the open door to Isla's apartment. Lovely goes in first, and the door swings out all the way like an open arm, beckoning, but Buddy hesitates on the threshold, "I told you, she did to me what she did to you. Plus, I'm damaged goods. There was no future for us."

While Lovely draws back farther into the shadows, Buddy stays at the doorway, head cocked to one side. Listening to the click of the tonearm on the spent record's gutter.

"You're lying," Lovely says finally. "The baby was yours."

Buddy snaps, "You know what, you surrendered whatever high ground you think you had seven years ago! You ran away, Rylan! You ran away and left her here, lonely, instead of staying and fighting for her." Buddy steps into the apartment, not even bothering to use his cane, and—WHACK—immediately collides with a chair he clearly doesn't expect to be there; he reels back, startled, and topples the floor lamp behind him, and it goes crashing down.

"I didn't run, Buddy, I left. And this apartment was all set up for a blind man until I moved it around about an hour ago."

Buddy is quiet. He doesn't move; not so much afraid, it seems, as unmoored. Lovely can still see in his face that undersized sixteen-year-old Lovely taught to use a clutch, the ten-year-old who stole candies from Grand Junction's only Five and Dime, and then, so racked by guilt he got sick and couldn't sleep, brought them back untouched and confessed his crime.

"I got out of your way. So you could have what I had lost."

Buddy's head goes back and forth slowly. "But you wouldn't divorce her. She thought that meant something."

"No." Lovely thinks. "Or maybe it did." He didn't want the conversation to take this turn. "I'm stubborn. And I have feelings. I'm sorry." He lets a silence pass. "But the blackmail."

"What about it?"

"Isla's mind didn't work that way. If she thought Lamoureux had hurt a girl she would have gone right to the police."

"And the cops would have done nothing," Buddy says, bitterly.

"Probably not," Lovely concedes. "But the blackmail . . . that was your idea. Soup to nuts." As Hal would say.

Buddy just lets this go unchallenged. He uses his cane now, weaves with caution into the room, finds the sofa, sits. Lovely lifts the diary off the side table and puts it into Buddy's hands. This may be the hardest thing he will ever have to do.

"Isla's diary."

Pause. "I can't read it. Why—"

Lovely talks over him. "I thought it might give me a clue to what happened, you know . . . with me and her. It was just the year past but, like you say, we were still married and she never pushed for the divorce and I guess some part of me hoped, sure, that meant something. But no. No, sir, it's all major key, as Lily likes to say: upbeat, happy, eyes forward. On you," Lovely adds, sadly. "It's all on you." And he flashes on the last time they were all together. Isla's hand reaching out . . . to Buddy Dale's face.

A face that now, here, in her apartment, has tears slick streaming down it. "We had no m-m-money, and a family on the way. Look at me! The broken man! I made one bad decision, okay, but I didn't—"

"—you did."

"Don't. Hey, d-don't, don't say that."

"Her blood's on your hands. And I'm guessing you have the missing ten grand, so don't kid yourself." Lovely stares at the hunched shoulders of his oldest friend. His voice goes distant, cold. "Lamoureux balked. Isla got scared. She was calling me because now you had become part of the problem."

He puts his hat on, tilts it against the bloody, dying sun streaming through the window.

Buddy shudders in the room's deepening shadows, fingers unsettled on the journal's pebbled cover. "You here to pass judgment on me?"

"No. I came to say goodbye to my wife," Lovely confesses. "The cops have some questions, though."

Detective Henry Paez has taken a position on the flagstone,

respectfully hanging back, but peering in, curious, from outside in the Diablo Bonita courtyard. A couple LAPD patrol cops are just joining him, coming up the steps, gun belts squeaking.

Lily should be waiting in her car.

Lovely says, "Ready?"

LOSERTOWN

June 1987

1

ASSISTANT U.S. ATTORNEY GIL KIRBY. Something about him: casual, even rumpled, you'd never have made him for a lawyer, much less a federal prosecutor. Which is how he liked it. Guarded eyes, widow's peak, a swimmer's shoulders, the promise of a fair shake. Old-school.

"I come out of the private sector," he was telling the younger woman sitting next to him. Kirby was mid-career, mid-discourse, middle of an active operation.

"One of those hushed top-floor firms with dark wood and Berber carpets and fit men who still get their shirts starched and wrapped in paper, and the few women who pretend they can tolerate working with them. You know—litigating over enormous piles of money for rich suckholes who already have enormous piles of money, so what's the point? Moving wealth between two parties who already have more than they know what to do with. When I went into the law it was because I wanted to do good for society, my country, for the victims of crimes. I was glad to get out."

I had no choice, he added, rueful, to himself.

Beside him, big hair, faultless posture, cast cold porcelain pale in the muted light thrown from an IBM workstation screen: the delicate, almost-ingénue Sabrina Colter. Redolent of Chanel and hairspray, she'd been described to Kirby by Jack Djafar in Justice as somebody's kid sister crossed with a poisonous snake, but just now she was lovely and seemed harmless. Rapt, demure, attentive to him, as if Kirby were teaching an undergraduate seminar. And Kirby wondered idly, per Jack, if she was really a virgin.

"You know that old party game, Telephone? Where a message gets all garbled as it's passed from kid to kid?" Kirby cracked his chronically stiff neck and shifted in his chair. "That's what we're doing, here, in the federal system. Telephone. Played by desperate souls just trying to save their sorry asses." He shrugged. "We call 'em wobblies. And they're, like, 99.999 percent of the confidential informants we spawn. So a good half the job is trying to figure out if the snitch sitting across from me's got his message so garbled up somebody blameless's gonna get hurt."

"And the other half?" Colter asked as if interested, but was simply measuring him, as it turned out.

Kirby offered a melancholy grin. "The other half is three-card monte," he said, "and paperwork."

SAME TIME, western edge of Old Town, a shabby fugitive who called himself Tigger scampered bandy-legged and lickety-split, fast as he could, face flushed vermillion, arms pumping, running, his dusty, side-worn Jack Purcells running, spitting roof gravel, running zigzag to the edge of an apartment building rooftop, thirty feet up.

Where he leapt off.

Surrendered to gravity.

Arms gyrating wildly as if they could somehow slow his descent.

Down.

He landed hard in a dumpster below, cushioned by the cardboard and trash. The garbage leaked a heavy heat, the funky stench of rotting fruit and meat made Tigger's eyes water. He struggled to untangle himself, about to climb out, when—

—"Incoming!"

A violent impact rocked the bin, and Tigger's world got tossed. He went ass over elbow as DEA agent Hazel Fish, an unguided missile (here specifically, and in the course of life, generally), came hurtling down into the steel container from the roof above, the force of his arrival caroming the plucky fugitive into a grimy sidewall of the dumpster, hands clutching for the rim, desperate to keep himself from slipping into a sinkhole of black plastic garbage bags. And before Tigger could pull himself over the lip and get away, Fish bushwhacked him, shoulder to ribs, their combined shifting weight causing the dumpster to crash over on its side, where they spilled out into an alley and, quick as a calf roper, Fish had the fugitive handcuffed and flopped on his belly for the regulation pat down and reading of rights.

"Olé!"

Flashing lights jittered onto them from an arriving squad car.

A Baggie of drugs got liberated from the back pocket of Tigger's jeans.

"Wuh-oh," quipped Fish, smug, bone-dry.

"WE CALL IT a 'rolling bust,'" Kirby explained. It was Colter's first day. She'd come with a prodigy's résumé, White House pedigree, and the bright burnish of unexpected appointment; good Methodist upbringing, an undergraduate degree from Bob Jones University, and a juris doctorate from Trinity Law.

She seemed so green Kirby had rightly assumed that she'd never even prosecuted a criminal case.

Virgin on two counts.

The lights of Jack Murphy Stadium threw a sallow glowing halo behind the modest skyscrapers of America's Finest City, all cottoned in the sifting coastal gloaming and suggesting something magical to the north, but it was only the Padres and their small ball, breaking hearts and grounding into double plays.

Another night in paradise.

"Pop a street fiend for possession," said Kirby, staying on point, "remind him of the serious nature of his crime, flip him on the friend who gave him the gak, then go get *that* guy and flip *him*. And so on, and so on. Local and federal personnel. We do these interjurisdictional operations from time to time."

"Working your way up the food chain."

"Working our way up the food chain, yes, ma'am, fast as we can, all in one night, so as to prevent the alleged perpetrators from warning their colleagues in the drug distribution business that the jig is up."

Colter nodded expressionlessly.

Into the empty boxes of the boilerplate federal search warrant flickering on his monitor screen Kirby typed a rooftop rabbit's given name (just a moment before called in from a radio car), followed by the name of the arresting officer (H. Fish) and the authorization justification: "Found holding suspected schedule II controlled substance" . . . Paperwork was always a grind.

Colter issued one of those soft, barely audible noises that, in Kirby's experience, only very young women made: halfway between a sigh and a purr.

"Am I boring you?"

She claimed no.

AND THEN:

Some low-rent Chula Vista motel with a view of nothing.

El Perro Rojo.

It screamed of fluid exchanges and late-night misbehavior; if there were a *Zagat's Guide to Victimless Crime*, this place would have earned a perfect thirty. Lurid fluorescent signage softened by sea mist scrawled its nonsense in the night. A circling chopper's high beam slicked the pink door of an end unit with a bleach-white indictment.

Fish nodded for the local cop to kick it the fuck in.

"Police! Open up!"

Jamb splintering, Task Force agents bum-rushed past the owner of the offending foot, which was still stuck in the hollow-core door—a posse led by Fish (son of a kindergarten teacher and a Marine helicopter pilot, first in his academy class, top marksman, unmarried, but hopeful)—the baker's dozen free-basers inside late-reacting after the predictable cognitive delay, rousing, processing, freaking, yelling, flailing, rubber limbs refusing the screams of ruined neurons urging them *get out go get out get out get out*—

—too late.

Fish strode through like Patton. "Kiss carpet, tweakers! Down down down!"

They did, down, meek, defeated.

Fish loved his job.

FECUND.

"I'm curious, do you always have a target in mind? Or is it sometimes more of a speculative venture?" Colter pushed her Fawn Hall hair back with both hands, and her breasts, under the soft thin acrylic sweater, lifted and separated, Kirby thought, just like bra ads promised.

"Fecund" was the word for which Kirby, the past half hour, had been searching, heedless of his sorry past. A resumption of two-finger console keyboard typing, letters pixel-stitching across the CRT display: "methamphetamine" . . . "felony possession" . . . The familiar haiku.

"Always," Kirby answered her when he was done with the on-screen report. "Always a target, yeah. De rigueur for the blanket warrants. Leader of the pack. The head honcho. Tonight I'm calling him Crack King. Mucho Ding Dong."

"I detect heavy irony."

Kirby shrugged.

"You don't have faith in the president's War on Drugs?" she asked.

"Faith doesn't factor into it. Where we are . . . geographically . . . or let me put it this way: It's not insignificant that we live on the border." Kirby waited to see how this would settle with her. "Arbitrary lines of division. Us and them, here and there." He knew he was overexplaining, wanted to stop talking then, but he couldn't. "Nothing is ever as clear here as it should be."

"Here? In this country?"

"Right here. Physically."

"I'm always very clear on things," the young woman said. "You might say goal-oriented. I think it's important to know what you want, and not waver in your convictions."

Knock yourself out with that, Kirby thought. "Sounds right" was what Kirby said. "You're ready for the fog, is what you're saying."

"Fog?"

"Every day," Kirby said.

"But then the sun comes through."

"Yeah," Kirby said. "That bastard sun."

FISH HAD his half a dozen crackheads neatly arranged in the Perro Rojo breezeway, cuffed and sitting, heads bowed, backs against the wall, when Kirby and Colter arrived.

"Tonight," Kirby was telling her as they came through a shabby patio with the requisite empty pool filled with dry-rotted plywood and broken drywall, "we want the name of the man who's moving all this second-rate Mexican rock this side of the border. La Alianza de Sangre, the Sinaloa blood alliance, has lost its grip on Tijuana. Somebody's muscled the market. There's been rumors of an American. A mythical gringo they call *la fantasma*. DEA thinks it's bullshit, that it's a midlevel cartel scumbag named Juan Blanco making his move. Either way, on that side, it's not our problem. But on this side we're looking at almost forty percent more product on the street since last August. So."

He stopped and considered the bedraggled arrestees. Colter yawned, covering her mouth with a graceful, manicured hand, while the DEA man, Fish, finally took note and looked her carefully up and down and she pretended not to care.

"Hello. My name is Gil Kirby, I'll be your federal prosecutor tonight." Kirby's wit eluded his captive crowd. "Listen up. You're just sardines. Okay? Or maybe, smaller. Krill. Put you on a cracker, you're not even a full bite, so here's a onetime offer . . . give me the big tuna, and we throw you back. 'Kay?"

They stared at him in confusion. Kirby glanced at the DEA agent to see if he was brooding over all the fish metaphors: He was. Then, deliberate, as if to children, he elaborated, "We want the name of your supplier . . ." and waited for a moment, ". . . Anyone . . . ?"

One freebaser's veiny arm shot up like a first grader: *oh oh oh oh I know—me, me, me, me, pick me—*

THE HALF-NAKED, rail-thin hustler on whom the ratter at the Perro Rojo rolled—Flavian E. Bolero, AKA Danny Bolero, AKA Skinny B., AKA Dr. F. E. Bolo, AKA the Hedgehog— had dived out of the Oceanside double-wide trailer's louvered window in a shower of safety glass, and right into the open arms of agent Hazel Fish, who'd anticipated this alternate means of egress when the Task Force uniforms rang at Flavian's front door.

Dawn bladed the misty coastal hills, with their stumps of

manzanita and bleak promise of future subdivisions. Flavian, chest scraped raw, blackened eye and runny nose, shaking and twitching as he fell off the peak of some potent cocktail of uppers and downers, was presently shackled to a backseat security bar and staring dully out at AUSA Kirby.

"I'm not snitching."

Kirby nodded. "Nobody's asking you to snitch." He was hunkered down and squatting beside the San Diego County Sheriff's patrol car while, close behind him, Colter French-inhaled a long, thin Benson & Hedges and scuffed the toes of her pumps in the sandy soil.

"Good, yeah, well, I'm not doing it, so," Flavian said.

"I understand."

There was a pause.

"No, you don't," Flavian groused.

Kirby just stared at him, hands in his pockets. Patient.

He heard Fish's infectious laughter drift over from where the DEA agent was trading fond insults with some San Diego Sheriff's deputies. Flavian cut his reptilian eyes for a moment to Colter and asked Kirby, "Who's the slit? Is it Take Your Daughter to Work Day?"

Colter flicked ash off the cigarette and spoke to the back of Kirby's head. "This is how you work your CIs?"

"Did you know," Kirby said, without turning to look at her, "that confidential informants are the leading cause of wrongful convictions in capital cases? Forty-five-point-nine percent. You can look it up."

Colter yawned. "You sound like some whiny ACLU press flack."

Kirby had been waiting all night for the real Sabrina Colter to emerge. This was more what he'd expected; the eager schoolgirl bit, he thought, must have been hard for her to sustain. Their eyes met, a kind of poker being played. She seemed to realize she'd overexposed herself, and drew back in. "I hate snitches," Kirby told her. "I hate snitching. I hate these rolling busts."

"I'm not a snitch," Flavian reminded them.

Pursing her lips, curling her tongue between them, Colter sent silky smoke rings spinning and waited, staring at Kirby, expressionless.

"Informants lie," Kirby continued. "Juries believe 'em, we get lazy and rely on 'em. And the traditional safeguards of the criminal trial system are totally inadequate to protect the innocent against them."

"Uh-huh." Colter made a point of showing him how unimpressed she was. "Well, why are we here?"

He kept asking it. "Am I boring you?"

"Gosh, no. I'm riveted. Truly."

Kirby felt his temper flare and checked it. "You wanted to see what we do."

"I did. Carry on. Show me the magic."

"Oh, little lady, please, he ain't even got to the best part." Flavian flashed teeth marbled like blue cheese. "Go for it, Mr. Federal Fuckhead. C'mon. Scare me with the prison thing. Work my homophobic now'n tell me that tired old prison-shower-and-soap joke. Where I'm gonna be some life-without's new girlfriend."

"Sorry to disappoint you."

This surprised him. "No?"

"No. I hate those jokes, too," Kirby said, as if frankly, "which means this is it, my man. Dead end. Let's all go home and get some sleep." He stood up and stretched. "See, Flavian here, he's not gonna talk to us," he told Colter, but continued to stare absently at the shivering addict. "He's gonna nut up and do his hard time, and whoever sold him all that Sinaloa pure will, two to five years from now, when Flav eventually gets released, richly reward our boy for not snitching. Because they're like brothers, he and his source. Solid. Am I right, Flav? Solid as a rock. And the source, why, he'd do the same for Flavian." Kirby shrugged as if in surrender, and started to walk away. "So I guess we're wasting our time."

Flavian blinked, and blinked again, his tiny tweaked mind whirling.

Colter rolled her eyes as if to emphasize to Kirby how much she couldn't believe this ploy was actually going to work.

But Flavian, troubled now, just murmured, "What are you saying?"

Kirby kept walking. A violent shudder coursed through the thin frame of Flavian Bolero, and he started to tilt his head side to side as if there were bugs in it, stirring, crawling, and, "—Hey! Hey! Hey! Like hell!" Flavian shouted at Kirby's back. "Fuck him. Like hell he would! Like that Egyptian scumbag'd do squat for me!"

Colter did the honors and asked the obvious. "Egyptian?"

Kirby then stopped at the stumpy asphalt curb of the trailer park roadway. He took a pause, not quite ready to turn around yet, staring out at the silken misty darkness resolving itself into a western ocean horizon, barely a difference between sea and sky, wan glow of Coronado to the north. Another gray day rising. A melancholy clutched at him, as if he'd been half hoping that a snitch would surprise him just once and sack up.

THE EAST SAN DIEGO gentlemen's club currently operating under the name Hot Box featured twenty-four hours of "live" gyrating pole dancers on the round stage as well as on the multitude of bulky black TV monitors hung from the I-beam rafters of a converted Jiffy Lube warehouse. Everything—walls, ceiling, rafters, floors, bar, chairs, tables, stage—was painted a flat black that ate light. Prince bled from towering subwoofers out the exit doors as the night's Joint Task Force of Feds and local law enforcement frog-walked the straggle of hardcore, drunken, skew-eyed patrons who, in the gnawing daylight, wanted only to be invisible and go home.

It's silly, no? When a rocket ship explodes and everybody still wants to fly.

Eventually Fish emerged from the front entrance with the middleman Flavian had fingered: a painfully young and proud San Diego State postgrad whose passport declaimed was Saad Fanous, and who the DEA man had found in a private room entertaining some semiprofessional silicone-enriched ladies with his Byzantine charm and a jeroboam of California sparkling rosé.

Time.

Time.

Kirby and Colter were waiting at the suspect's riot-red Corvette in the parking lot, the plates already run to confirm it was Saad's, doors flung wide, a couple city cops searching it as Fish brought the frightened-but-still-smiling Egyptian across the pavement in handcuffs.

"This'll be our last roundup," Kirby had told Colter while they were waiting.

"How do you figure?"

"Some of the knuckleheads we popped earlier tonight have called attorneys by now, and as soon as word hits the street, the river goes dry."

"To mix several metaphors."

Kirby was struggling to convince himself that he couldn't decide whether he would try to sleep with Colter. It was an impolitic and misogynistic calculation, but he didn't care to be progressive or enlightened, he had long ago surrendered to a rationale that this was just his basic biology, and why fight it? He didn't have to like her. She seemed acceptably smart, decidedly fit, and cunning, which, he thought, would make it a challenge, at least.

When Saad was brought close enough, and saw his car, and what was happening to it, his dark eyes went dead. Still, Kirby noted, the Egyptian sustained the empty, obstinate immigrant's smile.

"Nice ride," Fish said.

Saad caved, craven. "I can get you a sweet deal on one, my chalky brother. I have connections at Del Rio Motors, I will duke you in."

Fish wasn't listening, he was briefing Kirby about a broken pager Saad had that appeared to be mostly for show, but, "The Egyptian had an ounce of controlled substance on him, divvied into eight balls, and seven-hundred-some dollars in cash. Couple of the Hot Box strippers were also holding, and named our boy as having sold it to them."

Only to his friends, Saad insisted. "Only to my friends, and only for what I pay for it!"

"He's a nonprofit," Fish cracked wise. "Saad Fanous, meet

Gil Kirby, Assistant United States Attorney for the Greater San Diego—"

"How do you do, sir. This is not what it looks like," Saad promised, but Fish wasn't finished.

"—And . . . his . . . I dunno." Fish frowned at Sabrina Colter. "Sister? Intern? Prom date?" Fish grinned at her lopsided and then tried to give what Kirby could only guess was a look that said, *Isn't she a little young?* And then, flirting, "Hi. Hazel. Fish. DEA."

Colter lit another cigarette and ignored him.

Saad, intent on Kirby, let his smile wick out. "Please. I understand how this works. You want the name of my supplier. I am happy to cooperate. Just tell me. Who would you like me to say it is?"

"What?"

Saad's eyes darted among Kirby, Fish, Colter, his Corvette. "If you can please inform me of the name of the individual you wish me to accuse. I will swear on the Bible."

"Hey. You're a Muslim," Fish reminded him.

"Some truths are truer than others, the prophet has said."

Kirby felt his spirit sag. This was where it always went, they always got transactional. Whatever you needed they just happened to have. "That's not how it works," Kirby said. "I want the name of the person who actually in fact sells you the rock."

Saad gave him a conspiratorial look. "Ho. Yes, yes, I understand."

"I don't think you do."

"Yes," Saad insisted. "It is ever the same."

"It's not."

Saad's smile rekindled, polite, smug.

Kirby shook his head. "No sale. Get this guy out of here, Hazel."

One of the local cops sweeping the car called out: "Fish?"

She was holding out a little fat leather notebook, thumb marking a page in the address section. "Suspect's Filofax. From the glove box. Look at who's right there under 'friends and family.'"

Fish took the book from her and split it open where she'd marked it. "Nick Mahrez," he read aloud.

Colter perked up. "Mahrez?"

"Oh, man," Fish said. He handed the Filofax to Kirby, and looked at Saad for a moment, in disbelief. "You know Stix?"

"Of course yes," Saad said readily. "Mr. Mahrez is my employer."

Fish made a whistling sound and Kirby stared at the name in the book, marveling at the odds of it turning up in a routine night of rolling arrests, and he only surfaced when Colter asked Saad, "Are we talking about the Mahrez who was partners with Victor Arnold?" and Kirby became acutely aware of her growing interest in the proceedings.

"Let's not jump ahead of ourselves," he said to Colter, but she pretended not to hear him.

"Point of clarification," Colter pressed Saad. "You're working for Nick Mahrez?"

A dusty federal Ford sedan screamed into the parking lot, portable flashing bubble light on the dashboard, high beams momentarily blinding them.

"Big Stix. Yes, indeed."

"Is that a nickname?"

"Nickname. Trademark. Reputation. All of this."

Kirby chewed on his lip. He could see where this was going,

Colter's hunger, the eager doglike shine in the Egyptian's eyes: Saad would give Colter whatever she wanted, and, clearly, she wanted Mahrez—a name that came out of nowhere and, given her age, she really should not even have recognized. But now Colter's evidently hair-trigger ambition combined with her overt ambivalence about, not to mention inexperience with, the raw realities of criminal prosecution, was a potentially catastrophic complication. "Stop. Wait a second. Can we back up?"

Colter and Saad both looked at him irritably, as if he'd interrupted something intimate; she made a vague, dismissive gesture.

Fortunately, from the arriving federal car, a curvy, unnatural blonde in well-filled jeans, a taut black T-shirt, and careless makeup strode to them, visibly pissed off, her shiny FBI shield swinging from a lanyard around her neck, ponytail stuck through the backside of her Padres cap. "What do you assholes think you're doing?" Kirby thought she looked awesome.

"Tina Z."

The blond Fed recognized, "Fish. Jesus—"

"How they hanging, girl?"

"—And Kirby?" She dismissed him with a flick of her dark eyes and, "Figures," then zeroed back in on Fish. "Dammit, don't you guys read the interagency reports?"

"Read? Who has time?" Fish leered, teasing her, and wiggled his tongue. "We're pulling a train of local and exotic cocaine cowboys as you speak. Wanna grease up?"

The Fed rolled her eyes and glared back at him.

Colter glanced impatiently to Kirby. "Who is she?" Kirby had to pause. Where to start?

"She's FBI," Tina Z. answered. "And she thinks this is bullshit."

Fish got defensive: "What are you all bent about?"

Kirby began to explain to Colter, "Christina Zappacosta. Special agent, special projects, San Diego subregion," but it wasn't so much a conversation now as it was a jumble of overlapping attitudes and agendas, making Kirby feel like a group gripe counselor.

Tina pointed at Saad. "You can't have him, Hazel. He's mine. Whatever he's done—"

"Felony possession. With intent to sell," Fish barked back.

"—I can pull jurisdiction."

"And, oh, let's see . . . we just now discovered maybe he can deliver us the legendary Nick Mahrez for trafficking in the Mexican crunchy."

This stopped the blond agent short. Saad smiled with polite supplication and interjected, friendly, "Hello, Christina. How do you do?" Kirby signaled for a uniform to escort Saad away to wait in a patrol car.

"Who?"

Colter was studying Fish. "You really think you can make it happen?"

Kirby saw there was no recognition of Mahrez by the FBI agent, which didn't surprise him—she was deep into domestic terrorism, weapons trafficking, and the resurgent White Power movement that had become an ugly by-product of the Reagan Revolution. Domestic drug dealing had never been on her radar.

"Time out." Tina Z. got Colter's attention. "What the fuck are you talking about?"

"Leverage," Colter said to Tina, and it sounded like she was trying the word on for size.

"Deliver Mahrez?" Kirby was still trying to put the brakes on Fish's overeagerness to serve Colter's cryptic agenda but knew that the forward momentum was already too great. "No," he said, "no no no. That's a circus sideshow, and gets us no closer to our local cartel Crack King plus, P.S., Mr. Fanous is not exactly a reliable—"

"—Unless *he's* the Crack King," Colter offered.

"Mahrez? He's not." Kirby heard himself sounding like a second grader.

"Well, anyway, you can't have Saad," Tina Z. told them. "I'll call in my goddamn ADIC up in Los Angeles if I need to." Kirby wanted to let her know he agreed with her, but she didn't even look at him. "The Egyptian is my primary for something I've been humping on for like six weeks. I'm this close, and if you pop him, he's gonna be useless to me."

"He's useless because you gave him too much leash and he's dealing drugs," Colter summarized. "Who's your ADIC? Boyce Johnson?"

"Excuse me. Who the fuck are you?"

A chilled silence dropped on them. Tina Z. had made a slow pivot to glare at Kirby's young ride-along, who didn't flinch, didn't care, and delegated, brisk now, imperious, all-business, to Kirby, "I want Mahrez. I want him cooperative. Do whatever it takes." She turned to Fish. "You may need to get us some factual corroboration for your"—she used the term, Kirby observed ruefully, as if she'd invented it—"wobbly snitch."

Then she glanced insincerely at Agent Zappacosta, dismissive, almost an afterthought, "I'm sorry."

"Sorry?" Kirby had never seen Tina Z. so flummoxed. She blinked, and blinked again; she looked to him, then Fish, then back to him, for some kind of clarification. "She's *sorry*? Who is she? Sorry? Who the fuck are you?" Tina asked Colter again.

"My new boss," Kirby admitted, regretfully, before Colter could answer.

Now Fish and Tina Z. looked stunned. This girl of a woman, five-foot-three in heels, impossibly young. Disbelief. *What?* Boss? Later, they both told Kirby they had been thinking she was some new equal-opportunity hire he'd been saddled with breaking in.

"Agent Hazel Fish, Agent Christina Zappacosta," Kirby made the official introduction, "meet your new United States Attorney for the San Diego region."

Colter favored them with a practiced, soulless, popular-girl smile that Kirby had seen only once, briefly, when he met her, and in so doing she aged ten years and assumed the full cold authority of her office. "Sabrina Colter," she replied. "I'm so pleased to meet both of you, I know we're going to do great things on the South Coast."

Then she touched Kirby's arm lightly. Flirting? Or cutting him off at the knees? Maybe both, Kirby worried. A calculated gesture charged with entitlement and dominion.

"This was neat," she said sweetly. "Thanks a bunch, Gilly, for showing me around."

2

"Nick 'Big Stix' Mahrez?"

"Mmm."

". . . Is a local legend." Kirby loved to talk while they made love.

"Oh. Oh. Shit. Oh."

Watching Tina Z. try to steer her way through the blizzard of primal, tactile feedback her body insisted on sparking off was a glorious adventure.

"Beach volleyball god and competitive surfer and pot dealer who made his millions back in the day—when dope was still quaint—and then got out, clean. There isn't a cop or a judge or federal prosecutor of a certain vintage here wouldn't give his left nut to bring him to trial."

"Oh. Ow. There." A shifting of hips. "She called you Gilly."

The quick turn of topic threw him. "Wait, what?" Then he made the connection, and her implication was clear enough, but Kirby just said, "That is technically a version of my name."

"Yeah. Your name. Which you"—holding her breath—"won't yes won't let anybody yes call you."

IN THE SILTED LIGHT of the new day, under the press of low-lying coastal clouds, a phalanx of SDPD patrol cars and colorless federal sedans swooped down the macadam driveway and into a low-slung Kearny Mesa Industrial Park complex studded with lavender-blooming jacarandas. The vehicles stacked up helter-skelter near the office and warehouse entrance emblazoned with some rainbow STIX SURFBOARDS signage, cops spilled out and Hazel Fish led his Task Force sweeping through the factory on fresh warrants, work stopping as the Feds and local law enforcement shouted and swarmed and secured the premises.

"NEVER CAUGHT, never charged."
  "Mahrez?"
  "Yeah."
  "Ah."

WHILE SUSPECT AND SNITCH SAAD FANOUS watched, docile, but contriving to appear undone, Fish gloved up and waited for another agent to pop open the metal locker bearing a hand-scrawled FANOUS masking tape label; they removed the filthy gray hooded sweatshirt balled in the locker's upper basket, the Members Only windbreaker hung from a hook, half a dozen Stix Surfboards promotional caps, paint masks, coveralls, work gloves, pronation-worn running shoes, a forgotten lunch, and a couple of shoeboxes stacked at the bottom under a pile of *Playboys* and yellowing *San Diego Trib*s.

Everything got opened, photographed, tagged, and the boxes, as expected, were found to be filled with glassine Baggies of crack cocaine.

In a formality of pure theater, the Egyptian had been read his Miranda rights again, in front of everyone.

"HE WALKED AWAY happily ever after," Kirby said. "Philanthropist and patron. Glassing his boards, giving to charity, celebrity volleyball, surf camps for ghetto kids. Pillar of the community. The whole nine yards."

"Okay okay okay okay, now just—"

"Of course, all those nut-giving cops and Feds are convinced he's still in the game, biggest drug distribution network on the West Coast—a claim for which they have never had a shred of proof—and that he's all cozied up to the Mexican cartels and protected by layers and layers of local corruption."

Rising tones, her squeak of completion, the release of held breath. "Good. God. Kirby, don't move," Tina whispered. "Don't move, okay?"

"Okay." Kirby stayed still, hands parked on her bare hips. Her body coiled, tightened. Eyes squeezed closed, her chin dropped, her hair touched his chest. After a moment she took another deep breath and exhaled and said, "So that's why your new boss is so keen on him?" She sank, trembling, sweaty, sour, naked, her head against his heart.

"Honestly, I'm still surprised she even knew who he was," Kirby said.

His apartment was hot and stuffy. Kirby's hands roamed, traced the massive tiger tattoo that curved from Tina's shoulder to the small of her back. "God, am I gonna need a shower before I go home."

"I don't know," he said, a little rattled, referring to pretty much everything.

Passing the open doorway of the new U.S. attorney's private office the previous afternoon, Kirby had pretended to be slowed and distracted by a case file in order to watch Sabrina Colter unpack her personal things from a couple cardboard moving boxes. She looked so young, slender blue-pale arms and legs, a freshman moving into her college dorm room.

"*Could* he be your Crack King?" Tina murmured.

Kirby's foot cramped. He joggled his toes.

"Kirby?"

"Yes?"

"Where'd you just go?"

The things she brought: Stuffed tiger. Silver pencil cup. Snow globe from SeaWorld. A small carved wooden crucifix.

"Kirby."

"I'm here."

"What are you thinking?"

"She's come with marching orders," Kirby said. "White House wants to seed the ranks of Justice with believers. Onward Christian soldiers. They've sent her here on a crusade."

"Who?" Tina had to ask, although she well knew.

A New World Plain Language Bible. A well-thumbed copy of *The Fountainhead*. Miniature scales of justice. Photographs of family, friends, of Sabrina Colter with a who's who of conservative politics: Deukmejian, Cheney, Bork, Wilson, Meese, Jerry Falwell and the President of the United States, Ronald Wilson Reagan. Kirby had lingered to watch Sabrina check her lipstick in a reflection, plump them, nick away an imperfection with a manicured fingernail and then look up to see that he was watching her, and she didn't look away, stared back, said nothing, unabashed, inscrutable and, for one terrifying moment, he was certain that she could read his mind.

"To what end?"

Kirby shook his head. "I don't know, Z."

"War on Drugs," Tina guessed.

"Let's hope it's that straightforward. Because now?" Kirby rolled Tina over and pushed himself up to look at her, going full cynical. "They've got themselves a High Priest of Snitchdom."

She said, "Saad? My Saad?"

Kirby nodded and thought of Saad, sitting presently in some bleak DEA interrogation room, eagerly waiting to be deposed, anxious, animated, and so, so determined to please.

"Everybody's Saad Fanous," Kirby said. "He's preaching to the choir."

Tina pulled him down. "Amen."

A STUMPY GUATEMALAN BODYGUARD squared his shoulders and from behind the heavy, carved oak door peered out at Fish and his badge held high.

"I'm with the DEA," Fish said. "I have a federal warrant here for Nicholas Mahrez, please step aside."

The bodyguard spoke without an accent. "I'll get him—"

But Fish pushed past, into the yawning foyer of the Spanish mission mansion—

"I said I'll get him." The Guatemalan, failing to register the serious and sanctioned intent of the federal interloper, tentatively put his hand on Fish and suddenly three uniformed county deputies on loan to the Southern District Interagency Task Force were surging in on Hazel Fish's heels, lifting the bodyguard and slamming him into a wall, where he made a flat-tire noise.

Fish said, "No, I'll get him."

A thrumming drew his eyes down the hallway, where a slender, astonishingly beautiful woman stood reacting oddly to the commotion, stumbling backward and pounding on the walls with the heels of her hands, her mouth open in a panicked strangled scream, a thin shriek, like a frightened rabbit Fish had witnessed, once, trapped by two coyotes outside Borrego Springs. A big diamond flashed on her finger as she turned and lost balance, her hands fluttering out to catch herself.

Fish reflexively pulled his sidearm and started after her. "Ma'am—ma'am, STAY WHERE YOU ARE."

But she didn't stop, she stumbled on, down the hallway, hands groping for the walls, as if drunk. She crashed against a table. A huge handblown glass bowl lurched and shattered on the floor, and she went down with it, onto the lacerating shards of glass. Hands and knees. Shrieking. Blood painted her dress, smearing the tile as she struggled to get up.

Gun caught up with her. Her blood was everywhere.

"Jesus. Okay, okay, okay—stop. Lady, don't move—" He felt the stupidity of the gun in his hand. The bodyguard yelled something and struggled, but couldn't get free from the deputies who held him.

The woman kept crawling.

"Lady, please."

Fish was trying to find his holster, to stow his ridiculously unwieldy .44 and minimize the damage the woman was doing to herself, when a tall, lean man came running out of a room at the end of the long hallway, a Bren automatic outstretched in the onrushing man's hand.

"She can't hear you!"

A deputy yelled, "Gun!"

Fish recognized Stix Mahrez. Forty going on twenty and improbably tall for a surfer. The silky thinning scatter of white-blond hair trailed his head like motion lines, the easy good looks, gentle Anglo-Saxon features, kind eyes: a California dream boy, eternally young.

His Bren pointed directly at Fish's head. "Who are you?"

"DEA! DROP THE WEAPON!"

Now both deputies had drawn their sidearms. It was a badly choreographed chop-socky film standoff. Fish almost laughed.

"She's deaf," Mahrez said. "Her name is Rose, and she can't hear you."

"Put the weapon DOWN, sir."

The weeping woman crawled to Mahrez, her arm bleeding, nestled into his protective crouch, and Fish saw the mad melt of vermillion scarring across one eye and everything behind it, skin melted so perfectly it looked phony, some horrible joke played on that otherwise perfect face and form. Moved to tears, Fish's eyes flooded. He looked away, self-conscious, blinking, blotting his cheeks with the sleeve of his shirt.

"She's deaf," Mahrez kept saying, and he let his gun drop to his side, and then placed it on the floor, and signed something to her with his hands, taking the woman in his arms before the local cops swarmed them.

"THIS IS SUCH INTERAGENCY HORSESHIT. I really was onto something. With my hate-crime sting," Tina said gloomily, pulling her chipped nails through tangles in her hair. "Now I'm nowhere. Talk about a total waste of six months."

The liminal cerulean twilight held Kirby's bedroom in its limbo. A faint wash of moonglow smeared the whorled western sky. They lay limbs overlapping in loose knots of comforter and sheets and pillows that had fallen off the bed with them on their second go.

"You can't replace him?"

A voice cut through, from a turntable, the raw pain of a torch song tempered by the strange remove of modern jazz. Notes held, cherished, bent, and released.

"I'm dealing with apocalyptic, Second Amendment crazies who think we're under threat from Sinister Swarthy People Everywhere. No, love, Saad was my ticket, without him I'm shit out of luck."

Skeptically: "An Egyptian car salesman?"

"It's all part of a gathering storm, Kirby. I mean, the whole Iran hostage thing was just the preamble. As the Cold War fizzles out, all this mischief we keep pulling in the Fertile Crescent? Or the mujahideen with the Soviets in Afghanistan? Someday those chickens will come home to roost."

"At least we're talking about getting rid of the nukes."

"Smoke screen. Never happen." Tina got up, wrapping the comforter around her, her bare feet squeaking across the hardwood floor. "And don't even get me started with Salvador and Nicaragua. Ollie North and his so-called Freedom Fighters." She found the can of beer and drained half of it, abruptly changing gears again. "But seriously, your new boss doesn't even look old enough to drive."

Kirby found a pillow and shoved it under his head. He loved watching her wind up. "Yeah, well. Supposedly her appointment was some quid-pro-quo thing between a certain sitting senator and the White House. And no, I know what you're thinking, but she did not trade moist and delicate favors for the job."

"What then?"

"Demonstrable piety, a glorious Moral Majority bloodline, and a wink to the evangelical base—I believe she even worked directly for Weyrich, right out of college—did a short stint with Justice, couple of years clerking for Burger on the Supreme Court. Rumor is she wrote his dissent on *Wallace v. Jaffree*, the silent-school-prayer thing."

"Piety. Fuck me." Tina sat on the edge of the bed, wouldn't look at Kirby. She finished the beer. "Before you sleep with her, ask to see photo ID. That's all I'm saying."

"She's not stupid, is *my* point, I guess."

Tina made no comment.

Kirby touched her ankle lightly with his finger. "I'm not going to sleep with her."

Tina made a doubtful noise.

"I'm gonna have to play along on Mahrez, yes, which I'm hoping will be mostly a fool's errand," Kirby explained. "Meantime, I keep working my cross-border crack case, find the Kingpin dope slinger, and show my new U.S. attorney how this job is done."

"As if you know."

She was teasing him. Kirby just smiled.

"I bet those old SCOTUS goats loved her briefs." A new song began on the turntable. Sadder. Tina looked sidelong at him. "What is up with this noise?" She meant the music.

"Lily Himes."

"You don't seem like a hepcat, Kirby, no offense. Jazz? I took you for a *Flock of Seagulls, Men At Work* kinda guy."

"Gay?"

She giggled. "New romantic."

"I only listen to this jazz," Kirby said, over the rolling sorrow of a stand-up bass lead. "Himes, Lily. Japan sessions, 1961. It's an import rerelease on Blue Note."

"Japan." Tina frowned. "You're buying imports and reading the liner notes?"

Kirby said, "Long story." He didn't want to talk about it anymore.

"Oh." Tina stood studying him, pale and pink and fetching, in the faint light—well, fetching for a Fed, Kirby thought.

"Does Ms. Colter's schoolgirl act give you a stiffy, baby?"

He grimaced, "Don't start."

"Because I can probably still squeeze into my Marymount pleated skirt if you want." It was a good riff.

"Stop."

"The nuns had tape measures. Two inches above the knee. So we'd roll them up at the waist after school and troll for college boys." She skipped back and dropped heavily into his arms, cool and damp, shedding the comforter. "You're going to sleep with her." Tina kissed him sloppily, silky tongue and beer breath, trying too hard, but Kirby thought he understood.

"I promise you I'm not."

"You will. It's who you are. It's how you say hello."

He knew she was right. "No."

"Your kryptonite." He couldn't argue with that, either. "And mine is you," she added sadly, pushing away from him to get showered and go.

3

SAN DIEGO FEDERAL BUILDING, downtown, Sixth Street, seventh floor, a functional beige interrogation room with blank walls and plastic-clad metal table and chair where it was just Kirby and Stix Mahrez, suffering the winking red LED eyes of security cameras mounted high in opposite corners; video capture, for the permanent record. Mahrez's mustard-colored jailhouse jumpsuit was short at the wrists and ankles; Kirby wore chinos, no tie, sport coat draped over the back of his chair.

"We found drugs in Saad's locker. In your factory. Drugs that he says you gave him to sell."

Mahrez regarded Kirby with disappointment. "Are you that lazy? 'He says'? Saad says? What'd you promise him? What'd you threaten him with? This is a guy who comes from a country where, if you get arrested, you can kiss your fingernails goodbye. He's expecting the guy with the pliers any minute. Saying whatever you want to hear to delay the arrival of Dr. Pain."

"He gave a sworn statement," Kirby said.

"Of course he did." And then, in a way that caused Kirby to pause: "I am innocent of these charges, you know it. You know it."

Innocent of *these* charges, Kirby thought cynically. Mahrez's long list of alleged crimes engendered a presumption of guilt on these new ones, and, moving forward, who knows? Jury trials were always a crapshoot, and if Mahrez opted to let a judge decide his fate—a white, right-leaning, Orange County Reagan Republican federal bench lifer—there was a very good chance he'd get hard time quid pro quo for all the bad behavior he was assumed to have gotten away with. And even if he prevailed, an indictment would be a massive, and expensive, inconvenience.

On one hand, Colter's interest in the man was so inscrutable, so unknowable, that Kirby should have felt obligated to protect Stix from whatever mad hijinks were lurking in the partisan jet stream that swirled above their heads. But on the other, as much as he hated the blatant miscarriage of justice in which Kirby was now playing the lead, it served a crude purpose in his own concrete pursuit of the elusive domestic cocaine dealer he had been chasing for over a year.

"Do you know Juan Blanco?" Kirby said, after a while.

Again, Mahrez said nothing.

"The wannabe narco-kingpin weasel from TJ. Shaved head and a diamond-crusted Rolex watch."

"Guadalajara Cartel?"

"That's right," Kirby said.

"Rafael Quintero's cousin."

"They're all cousins, aren't they?"

Mahrez shook his head. "No, they're not."

"Well, twenty years ago Juan Blanco was a scrawny little sociopath selling stems and seeds to American college kids on Ro-sarito Beach," Kirby said. "I thought you might have run across him." Crickets from Mahrez. "Now? He's a *presidente municipal* who runs the Tijuana branch of Félix Gallardo's operation, bur-ies young girls in the desert and claims to have half of the Baja California judiciary in his pocket. Or so I hear."

Mahrez said, "I don't know Blanco." He added, "But if I did, I would doubt the little shit is anything more than a straw-man fall-guy stooge for the Arellano-Félix boys, who actually run Ti-juana for Gallardo.

"And, oh—they're calling themselves the Sinaloa Cartel now. You should update your files."

Kirby smiled and leaned across the table on his arms. Mahrez may be long out of that sea, he thought, but the surfer in him still knew where all the shallows were. "Well, stooge or no, Blan-co's made a big move into the local rock and weasel dust busi-ness, and if we could just locate the American on this side who's making that happen, we can shut down the pipeline."

"Oh." Mahrez made a mock-serious face. "And what? People on this side will stop using? Game over, rainbows and unicorns, we all live happily after?"

Because it was (a) accurate and (b) only underlined the Sis-yphean nature of his job, Kirby never liked the line of this rea-soning. "Probably not," he admitted. "But maybe we could get an indictment on Blanco, ask for extradition, flip him on Guzmán Loera—with the potential to even bring down Gal-lardo. You do what you can."

Mahrez considered it. "If it's not Blanco who's calling the shots?"

Kirby frowned. "Who would it be?"

"Don't know. Just speculating."

"You don't know." Kirby remembered something dimly, rumors of a third, silent partner in Nick and Vic's infamous controlled-substance import business, and wondered if Mahrez, out of practice, had just slipped.

"And anyway, you're not just a dreamer, you're out of your mind." Mahrez turned glib. "You can't touch Gallardo. You can't touch Guzmán Loera. You can't even touch Blanco. Because they own the police down there. They own the politicians. All the way to Mexico City. You have no idea what you're up against. Ten, twenty years from now? They'll own Mexico itself. Unless Americans stop doing dope."

Kirby pressed on, stubborn. "If you know who that guy on this side is, or can give me any information that helps take us another step closer to discovering who he is, I can have you back home in half an hour, Stix."

"No shit."

"No shit."

Mahrez shook his head, said nothing.

"Conversely," Kirby continued, "you have two felony priors from back in the day, no doubt youthful indiscretions that would be easily overlooked except, my goodness, according to the Sentencing Reform Act of 1984, this would be strike three and require you getting twenty to life, mandatory, if convicted, no early release."

It took a moment for Mahrez to process this. "Not in the federal system," he countered, although he didn't sound sure of it, adding, as if to show he wasn't going to be bullied, "Besides, haven't you heard about the startling disparity between sentences for white, nonviolent offenders and their African-American counterparts?"

"No, but, see, I'd be happy to ship you over to the San Diego DA and let the state exercise those more restrictive sentencing guidelines." Kirby was bluffing, but he was playing with house money; Mahrez had nothing to call with but his liberty.

Mahrez fell quiet. Kirby had him on his heels.

"I'm noting for the audio record that you do not have an attorney present."

"I waived the privilege, yeah. If that's what you want me to say. For the record."

"And you understand that's unusual."

"Why?"

"I don't know. It just is. Everybody loves to lawyer up."

A pensive moment passed, then another, then it was Mahrez leaning in, a different expression, open, solicitous. "Look. Counselor. I'm clean. You know that I am. There was another time, another life, and, okay, I get that you'd like to balance the scales of justice, from my alleged misbehavior, way back when. But that's not how it works, is it? You do that, and the whole house of cards, everything you stand for, nation of laws, comes crashing down. You can't pick and choose, you can't play God. And in this case, this bullshit thing with Saad . . ." He stopped himself. Kirby was again fascinated by the veil that, however briefly, had been pulled back. Revealing what?

Mahrez restarted, "What I mean is, I understand that you think you're helping me, but—and you really should have thought of this before you ever hauled me in here to offer some kind of half-assed deal for my cooperation in something you will never, ever succeed in accomplishing—you think you're helping me, but as a consequence of those questionable decisions I may or may not have made when I was younger, there are individuals and organizations who would love to know I'm in detention, Mr. Kirby. Because if they have any cause to believe I may be cooperating with you—naming names, or like that—I am a dead man. Thanks for asking."

It was Kirby's turn to take a moment to let this sink in. "What are you saying? You don't trust your own lawyer not to rat you out to your old friends and enemies?"

"Same difference, but . . ." Mahrez shrugged again, his wrists rattling the shackles. "Would you?"

SABRINA COLTER WAS SITTING still-life, all settled in, behind her vast, clean, Deco desk when Kirby came to report on his interview with Stix Mahrez.

"He won't cooperate."

Kirby did not fail to note the stark contrast between the new U.S. attorney's previous night's guileless schoolgirl act and her utter sangfroid now. Seeing how easily she shouldered the considerable mantle of Justice Department power was jarring. Her lipstick matched the stripes on the American flag in the corner behind her, and lent a disquieting, naughty undercurrent to their debriefing.

"Won't cooperate," she said, as if struggling with a foreign language.

"Yeah," Kirby said, "and, oh, on a side note, he's not the guy we fucking want."

"Language."

"What?"

"Ephesians 4:29. *Do not let any unwholesome talk come out of your mouths, but only what is helpful for building others up according to their needs, that it may benefit those who listen."*

Kirby stared at her.

She smiled, little perfect teeth. "We have a witness who says he is. The man we want, I mean. So."

"He's not who I want. And I don't believe he can help me get there."

"I guess I wasn't aware that we were here to serve your personal agenda."

"We have an Egyptian illegal," Kirby said, trying not to show his impatience, "who thinks he's back in Cairo, and that he's got to parrot whatever we want to hear in order to prevent us from cutting out his kidney and then shipping him to some secret CIA prison to be tortured."

"Americans don't do that."

"Try to convince him otherwise, though. Any half-baked defense attorney who graduated from even a second-tier law school will chew Saad up on the stand. And meanwhile, cocaine continues to flood across the border, because we're wasting our time trying to bust an innocent man and flip him on a coke distributor he surely doesn't know, he's been out of the game so long."

"Who said anything about making him a drug informant?" Colter rose and walked around her desk and sat on the end of it, legs crossed, one shoe dangling on upturned toes. She felt for the tiny cross on the chain around her neck, affecting a Catholic schoolgirl vibe that made Kirby shift uneasily in his chair. He'd gone to Catholic school. With girls like this. It chafed him, still, and set his palms sweating.

"The ultimate determinant," the U.S. attorney said, reciting something she'd memorized, "in the struggle that's now going on for the world will not be bombs and rockets but a test of wills and ideas, a trial of spiritual resolve, the values we hold, the beliefs we cherish, and the ideals to which we are dedicated."

She paused, as if expecting Kirby to identify the source of the quote. He couldn't. "President Reagan," she said.

He tried not to look confused. "Okay."

"He said that to the British Parliament."

"I'll take your word for it."

Her dark eyes bored into him. "Is this how you always dress for work?"

"I'm not sure I understand the question."

"Casual," she said. "Like, hmm, I don't know. A community college writing instructor or something."

Kirby, growing more and more irritable, told her, yeah, this was how he dressed. "Okay, well, whatever, but," he said, trying to get the conversation back on point, "even if our snitch is telling the truth, and survives some half-assed cross, the evidence against Mahrez is paper-thin, and he knows it. Sure, we can argue he's tied to the drugs found at his board factory, but factually it was the Egyptian's stash. An employer can't be expected to absolutely control what employees keep in their private lockers, an employer isn't legally liable for it, and I can't make the charges stick unless you give me more time to build a real case, and either way—"

Colter cut him off and said she'd be more persuaded if he were wearing something Italian. Silk. Silk suits this climate, didn't he agree? Assessing him: "Dove gray, and a power tie would rock on you."

Kirby frowned. Is she serious? Or just nutty? Colter slipped off the desk and strolled around him like a dog show judge.

"So . . . you'd suggest we just let Stix Mahrez go?" she asked with a theatrical incredulity. "And then what?"

"And then . . . tap his phones," Kirby told her. "And audit his books, and dog his friends and work the street. You know. Build a case. *Do our job.* If Big Stix is, by some bizarre synchronicity, dealing drugs from his surfboard outfit, he'll slip. He'll stumble. And we will nail him. And then you'll have the leverage to get him to do whatever it is you need him to do."

Colter thought about it. "Nobody's 'got' him for twenty years," she said simply.

"Because he quit the game," Kirby said again. "But hey."

His opinion didn't interest her. "You must have some nice suits."

Kirby told her he saved them for trial, then suggested she could just tell him what it was she wanted, instead of playing this game.

"I want you wearing your nice suits all the time," Colter replied. "New office policy."

Kirby grinned and nodded and struggled not to lose his shit. Words tangled just behind his tongue. Stalled out. "Can I let the guy go?" he mumbled.

Colter, entertaining a smile, smoothed her dress and stretched her spine. "I think—well, why don't I just talk to Mr. Mahrez myself?"

A LITTLE BOXY SURVEILLANCE CAMERA leered down at them.

"You grew up with the mayor."

It was late and the Federal Building held the silence of its emptying, the hustle of the day's business always seemed, to

Kirby, to echo ghostly in the vacant hallways long after everyone was gone. Since Kirby's last session with Mahrez, somebody had left an empty Coke can on the interview room table, and the ashtray was full. Colter sat across from Kirby, who was puzzled by the question and wondering what the hell the mayor had to do with anything. The suspect was unshackled, on his feet, in a far corner, restive, arms folded and leaning against the wall.

"Poole?"

"Yes."

"In Chula Vista. I did," Mahrez agreed. "I grew up with the mayor, yes."

"And after?"

A pause. "After what?"

"After you grew up."

"We went different ways."

"You have some kind of falling-out?"

"Look. Ask me questions you really want answered, or I'm going to stop cooperating. I'm tired."

"What was his relationship with your old partner?"

"You'd have to ask Vic, but he's dead, so."

"You like Mayor Poole?"

"I guess."

"Personally and politically."

"I don't think much about politics."

"You backed his first run for City Council."

"Did I?"

"In a major way."

"Are you asking, or telling me?" Then he shook his head. "Fifteen years ago. Why is that—"

"Did he know it was drug money?"

Mahrez smiled. "You might want to rephrase that."

Kirby tried to get things on track. "Ms. Colter, maybe we should stick to—"

Colter talked over him. "Did he ever ask you to stop giving him campaign funds, once he realized you were, you know, dealing—or, sorry, had got this reputation for dealing—"

"You understand that I'm not going to dignify that with an answer, ma'am?"

"Fair enough." She thought for a moment. "Still keep in touch?"

There was a long silence. Kirby watched Mahrez walk from one facing wall to the other, making some kind of considered calculation before he said that he didn't keep in touch, no. Colter waited. Mahrez measured his words. "We cross paths, sure. We see each other, you know, socially, certain public functions, here and there. Why?"

Colter leaned on the table and folded her hands. "What if you called him up and said you wanted to talk to him?"

"He'd be surprised." Mahrez studied her. "And curious."

"What if I told you that we want you to go visit your friend, Mayor Poole, wearing a body wire? You won't be snitching; we'll give you a series of scripted questions, you can work them into your conversation in any manner you choose, and once you've done so, no matter what his answers are, I'll put it in writing if you want and you can bring your lawyer or other representative to witness it—you do this and we'll drop all charges relating to—"

Kirby had to interrupt this, "Hold on a second—"

"—the allegations of our informant that you employed him to peddle drugs." The U.S. attorney's dark eyes followed Mahrez intently as he turned his back to her and walked across the room to reacquaint himself with the corner.

Kirby reached across the table and put his hand lightly on Colter's shoulder, making her jump. "Can we talk? In private?"

Her hand jerked up to where he touched her, as if she'd been burned. "Don't do that."

Kirby glanced away, uneasy, and found Mahrez staring at him. Deadpan.

"I don't like to be touched," she said.

Mahrez shifted his gaze to Colter, and looked almost bemused. She got up quickly and went out the door. Kirby started to follow her into the hallway, but before he left the room:

"I'll wear a wire for you, sure," Mahrez called after them, weirdly cheerful.

"WHAT ARE YOU DOING?" Kirby asked.

They were alone outside the interview room, but Kirby and Colter nevertheless kept their voices low. The door was closed. The guard who had escorted Mahrez over from County had retreated all the way down to the elevators, and stood smoking beside a standing ashtray, blowing fat rings and watching them float away.

"Doing? Well, I think I just made a deal with a suspect you said was uncooperative," Colter said. Mahrez, visible through the window in the door, slouched and stretched his legs out and waited for them to come back.

"No no no. Wire him for a talk with the mayor? When did that become an option?"

"Excuse me, I thought I was in charge here. Do I have to clear everything with staff?"

Kirby let the sarcasm slide. "And what does the mayor have to do with anything? I thought this was about crack cocaine and the drug pipeline from Mexico to the States." But as he said it, he already understood that it wasn't.

Colter measured her words as she might trying to explain something complicated to a child: "Mayor Poole is one target of a federal anticorruption investigation being coordinated out of the Justice Department. As part of my assignment here, I've been tasked, by Ed Meese himself, one of several priorities I received with my marching orders, to help facilitate that investigation by gathering evidence and testimony about Mr. Poole's alleged hijinks during his turn in City Hall—and, apropos of your question, in so doing, help clean up our local government, which, in turn, should make it more difficult for drug dealers like Mr. Mahrez to operate with impunity in this community."

"Alleged drug dealer."

Colter smiled dismissively. "You're an advocate, Mr. Kirby. Not an arbiter. And your client is the American people. Never forget that."

"Don't you think that was a little too easy, though? I mean. He jumped at your offer. Like a trout. Which he isn't."

Colter tilted her head, cute, condescending. "By informing on his friend to squirm out from under a three-strike beef? He's jumping to exactly what I want, I'm not sure I follow your logic, Mr. Kirby."

Kirby wasn't sure he had any. He just had a feeling, born of too many prosecutions gone sideways, or too many cases, period; too many lies and compromises and devil's bargains in which justice was a dream somebody had once and forgotten when they woke up. He wanted to say to her: You're young, you see the world in primary colors and assume that your simple, self-serving dictums are unimpeachable, when the truth is that everything's confusing, real life is a swirling vortex of a million colliding aspirations and intentions over which we have no real control, we can only hope to endure them, and try not to be crushed by them, or do irreparable harm. Instead, he said, "I just think you are in way over your head with this guy. He's smart. He's playing you. He's a survivor."

Colter brushed it away like lint from her blouse. "I admire that about him. Call your girlfriend at the FBI," she said. "Let's not give him a chance to change his mind, shall we?"

"I don't have a girlfriend."

Something in the sidelong way she looked at him made Kirby unsettled. Did she know about Tina? What else did she know about him? He felt like some poor bug flittering to its doom against a humming patio electronic discharge device.

He felt a current go through him.

"Add Agent Zappacosta to the Task Force, tell her we've got a body wire surveillance she can run point on," the U.S. attorney continued. "It'll look good, come performance-review time."

Kirby made one more lifeless run at it: "He's playing you."

"Well, I don't play. So."

They said nothing for a moment, then she went back inside the room to finish up her deal with Mahrez, and Kirby stayed in the hallway, in the faint wake of her perfume, in the stolid institutional quiet, ignoring the static, trying to focus on controlling the body count in this new unwinnable war, and resign himself to his foot soldier's role in it.

THE SECRETARY WHO ANSWERED the phone at City Hall sounded baked. A raspy, high, hollow voice: "Office of the mayor." Mahrez pictured a mousy young college grad who'd gone door to door getting out votes and maybe engaged in some oral extracurricular with the bachelor candidate a couple times—hennaed hair pulled back lopsided, delicate, doper-deliberate, professional, betrayed only by pupils gaped a little too wide and sclera still faintly bloodshot pink despite repeated baths of Visine—and then realized that he was actually conjuring up Poole's high school girlfriend, Cheryl, who drowned off Todos Santos one stoned, hot night in '75.

"Hi. This is Nick Mahrez. Is he in?"

The polite pause of nonrecognition, but hedging her bets, because it could be Someone Important. "What was the name again?"

"Nick Mahrez. M-A-H-R-E-Z. But pronounced like the home-run hitter."

"I don't know him. Does he play for the Padres?"

"No."

The slightly annoyed hesitation. "Can I ask what this is regarding?"

An ambush, Mahrez thought. But he said, "I'm an old friend. It's personal." Then he added, "Tell him it's about a fin key."

In the office with him, where they'd prepped him and rigged him up, the FBI agent named Tina and U.S. Attorney Colter listened in on a common line, recording the call, trading a baffled look: *fin key?* Mahrez winked at them.

Now the secretary was confused. "Oh. Okay."

Mahrez said, "It's just I need to get the fins off my stick, and he's got my only key."

"One moment, please."

The hold music was Roxy Music. Poole's stubborn commitment to Bryan Ferry, Mahrez mused. He looked down at the typed page of questions in front of him. Stared at them blankly, wondering if the Feds, watching from across the room, expected him to memorize them.

The secretary clicked back on. "He's just getting off the other line. Can you hold?"

"All day," Mahrez said. "All day."

DRIVING THROUGH STOP-AND-GO downtown traffic in his Aston Martin, Mahrez kept wiping the palms of his hands on his jeans. In his rearview mirror: the federal sedan containing Agent Tina Z. and her associate—what was his name? Bingham or Ingram or something. With the mullet and soul patch.

STILL PHOTOGRAPHS and surveillance video would afterward show him hurrying up the steps and into City Hall. Tina Z. had a slick little listening rig through which she could hear the filtered rustling of Mahrez's clothing, the hard rattling echo of overlapping voices in the main hallways, his footsteps clipping on tile. A door opening and closing. Faint whisper of his breathing. "Hello. Nicholas Mahrez. I have an appointment with the mayor?"

"I'll let him know. Please take a seat."

Mahrez could be heard sitting down, and, after a moment, turning the pages of a magazine.

FBI surveillance specialists had set up, in addition to the body wire, directional audio capture, plus SLR and VHS cameras in an empty office across the street from and more or less level with the mayor's office windows in City Hall, well suited for a telephoto lens. The video capture was continuous but suffered from autofocus problems exacerbated by the high contrast between the bright sunny day and the cool recesses of Poole's inner sanctum. The still photographs were crisp, however, and would clearly show the mayor get up from his desk—the mayor opening the door—Mahrez entering—smiles all around—a friendly embrace; this soft collision of bodies would muffle the initial audio feed:

"Stix! It's great to see you, man!"

Tina Z. patched in from her car, parked on a side street, couldn't tell without corresponding visuals if any of this was heartfelt or just cheerful political habit. She couldn't ask Binghamton, he was dozing. There was an irritating high-frequency squeal of interference that would need to be filtered out.

"HOW LONG'S IT BEEN? Ten years?"

"Longer. Vic's wake."

"Unbelievable."

"Yeah."

Mahrez was not surprised by Poole's modest, workaday office. His childhood friend seemed smaller, telegenic, incredibly hyperkinetic and intense, also older, which was no surprise, and unhappy, despite the smile.

"Man, what kind of screwed-up world do we live in where two longtime friends can't get together because—"

"Well, it was Vic, was the friend, you and me we kinda—"

Stubborn: "—friends can't get together because—"

"—one of them's toxic?"

"—that's not what I—"

"—doesn't matter, sorry—"

"—there was never, on my end, any—"

"—I know."

"Well, then."

"Is what it is."

"I guess."

Mahrez said, "Dicky?"

"What."

"Look at me." Still photographs and the soft-focus video would both show Mahrez—he didn't care—opening his shirt at this point and revealing to the surveillance subject, Richard Poole, the thin dark threads of insulated wire that veined his torso, and terminated in micro-microphones.

"Good God, what's that?"

"What does it look like? U.S. attorney's got me rigged for sound, Dicky. I'm sorry. Apparently they're coming after you for graft and whatnot, part of some big federal corruption sting."

IN HER CAR, Tina Z. nearly choked on her Diet Pepsi.

"Oh, no. Oh, shit. What is he doing?"

Her associate awoke with a throaty snort.

Voices crackled on her comm. She couldn't sort them out.

"We're blown."

"Wire's out—"

"—totally blown."

"Fuck this guy."

"—Opened his whole goddamn shirt."

"Damn, he's fit, though."

Binghamton sat up and wiped his mouth. "What?"

Mahrez's voice ran on, brighter, cleaner without the filter of his shirt over the body wire, "I've gotten a little tangled up in something myself, Dicky, got myself over a barrel and they bartered with me to come in here wearing this rig to ask some pretty pointed questions about your campaign finances and associations with certain foreign nationals and their narco-dollars, but I came to warn you instead because, you know me, that kind of shit doesn't fly, it's politics, it's sour grapes because you're a flaming liberal Democrat who won an election in the heart of the Elephant Graveyard, so, yeah, well . . ."

". . . Yeah."

In his office, struck motionless, staring oddly at Mahrez, the color had drained from Poole's face. He opened his mouth to say something, but Mahrez saved him the trouble.

"No, man. Don't talk. They're listening right now." An awkward silence settled. "Bottom line, I decided before I agreed to do it that if they've got questions they should tell you to your face. Call me old-fashioned"—Mahrez wiped his hands on his jeans again—"or naïve." This made his smile genuine; he felt as good as he had in a couple days. "You know, Vic always made a big deal of how you were a straight shooter. It got up his ass, for sure, but it didn't ever surprise me even after, you know, everything that went down with us."

"Vic's dead, though. Isn't he?"

"Yeah. Long time."

"What kind of trouble?" was what Poole had been trying to get from Mahrez since he flashed the wire.

Big Stix shook his head and started to rebutton his shirt. "You got a bright future, Dicky. Do good. Stay clean and watch your back. This will pass." Mahrez turned to leave, had his hand on the doorknob, when he remembered something and turned back to say, "Oh, but—yeah, trouble, it's mostly mine and I doubt I've helped my cause much here, but—if you got any bright ideas on how I can shake these pesky Federales, I'd be ever so grateful."

It couldn't, Mahrez thought to himself, then, have gone any better.

TIMECODE BURNED into the surveillance stills later would show that less than five minutes had passed. Artfully framed in the office window, stills and video showed Mahrez walk out. Showed Mayor Richard Poole turning toward the window, numb, and staring right into cameras, as if sensing them there. He moved stiffly, with the illusion of gliding, to the window itself, and gazed emptily out at his city.

The marine layer was burning off. Twenty minutes to another perfect day in paradise.

Zoom in. Refocus. Searing haze-smeared sun reflections glinted angular off the glass.

In the head-and-shoulders shot, foreshortened by the full-stop 500mm lens: Mayor Poole looked very tired, and very worried.

4

KIRBY WAS IN HIS BEDROOM, boxers and socks, closet door slid open, the rack hung heavy with his so-called junior college teacher's wardrobe, when Colter phoned, spitting fire:

"He screwed us!"

"Yeah, well. We're screwing him with a bad snitch." Kirby was indifferent, almost serene. "What did you expect?" He'd received a heads-up from Tina Z. on what had happened in City Hall. He couldn't say he was surprised by Mahrez's pyrrhic insurrection. Some part of him hoped that this would cause Colter to dial things down, but most of him had understood this would only calcify her resolve.

"DO NOT LECTURE ME!" The full measure of her anger manifested mostly in phone receiver distortion; it rang out, then she came through calmer, icy and clipped. "Set a trial date for Mr. Big Stix on the drug traffic beef."

"We won't win, we barely can show cause to file."

"I don't care. You'll think of something. Take him back into custody, the deal is off."

Kirby stared at himself in the mirror on the closet's front sliding panel. Farmer's tan, love handles, and pale, hairy legs. Jesus H. Christ, he was turning into somebody's creepy uncle. "I think he knows that," he said softly.

Colter, seething: "Get me an indictment."

"Even if he's innocent?"

Colter hung up on him. Dial tone.

Kirby tossed the whole phone on the bed, and the handset unracked and tumbled to the carpet, where a dial tone purred. He ignored it, reversed the closet doors, hiding the mirror and exposing, like a cheap magic trick, two dozen bespoke handmade suits in clear plastic protective sleeves. Tailored shirts on narrow shelves, silk ties, Italian shoes.

From another life. For an unmet future.

Kirby sighed. The dove-gray Armani pinstripe was as good a place to start as any, he decided.

HIS VEGAS LOUNGE ACT. Earnest, ingenuous, and open-faced. Saad Fanous worked the interrogation room. Only a whiff of desperation, Tina thought. Desiring to please:

"I understand how this goes. My cousin fell in love with a girl in Cairo. But her family was rich, so. And very, you know, well connected. It was not a good situation. Consequently, he tried to run away with her, but he was arrested and put in prison and tortured until finally he told them that his best friend was a Zionist spy, and they set him free."

A surprisingly subdued Kirby (resplendent in a handsome Armani suit she'd never seen before) sat with Tina Z. and the federal public defender, Bob Khorshandi, an effervescent Iranian-American (with scruffy Sonny Crockett stubble) for whom Saad Fanous was the last of two dozen clients he'd seen in a single day.

"Not to worry, my cousin's friend had police as relatives, so he also was safe, insha'Allah."

Big yawn, Bob's eyelids fluttered with fatigue. Kirby sighed. "I need you to tell the truth."

"My cousin? He married a French girl and moved to Tangiers. She is a gnarly bitch, but terribly fertile."

"No, Saad—"

"Truth? How can you, or me, or anyone but the Creator know what that is?" Saad snapped. "Truth? Please." Saad Fanous had told Tina he was convinced that the outcome of his case had already been determined by these government functionaries, as it always was, always would be, so he had nothing to lose. She tried not to think about her scuttled domestic terror case. Her section chief had told her not to worry over what clearly was a jurisdictional clusterfuck, but when her next performance review came up, she knew this whole thing would look bad.

"In our country, a jury decides," Kirby was saying. "They have to believe you. And I have to believe that they'll believe you, or I won't put you on the stand and I can't help you with your indictment."

Saad's laughter was bitter. "Believe. Me? The Muslim selling drugs? Tell me how this is even possible."

ONE BLOCK EAST of the Federal Building, Stix Mahrez perched uneasily on the edge of his hard-mattress Metropolitan Detention Center bed, listening to the dull roar of the cell block. Back in the day, a healthy fear of prison had been what drove him to be pathologically attentive to every detail of his illicit life. Now here he was locked up, his legitimate life proving to be no protection from the wryly subtitled surrealist black comedy he'd tumbled into.

He was worried about Rose.

A warning buzzer split the din and the lights went off. Curfew.

In a darkness leached with faint fluorescence from the guard station at one end of E-block, Mahrez felt a queasy disquiet overtake him.

Maybe it was the footsteps.

Or the abrupt absence of them.

A loud, two-part metal clack as the door of his cell slid open automatically, triggered from the control panel beyond the outer security door. Followed by the spooky quiet.

Mahrez rose and walked to the opening. Footsteps, closer, quickening. He peered into the darkness and two shadows blindsided him. Violently drove him back into the cell so fast Mahrez couldn't react, he was off-balance, there was a quicksilver flash of angled metal, and his breath left him as something punched and seared the soft flesh under his ribs.

And ripped him open.

"YOU THINK YOUR COUNTRY is so different. That's just arrogance," Saad grandstanded.

Tina watched Kirby shake his head at the federal public defender. "This isn't going to work, Bobby."

Khorshandi made a nebulous gesture of agreement. There was no gamesmanship between these two, Tina knew; they had a history and a shorthand. The goal was to get a good result, posturing just got in the way. The public defender faced Tina. "What about his cooperation on your other thing, with the haters?"

"I'm afraid the drug bust trumps that."

"I am spoiled meat," Saad whined.

"They popped him for distribution, he has zero value to me as a CI, and so my hate crimes case is history. No deals."

Saad slumped in his chair, pouty. Khorshandi murmured something in Farsi, Saad griped back at him bitterly in Egyptian, and suddenly they were arguing, then shouting at each other, vehement, in competing languages it was unclear the other even understood. Kirby and Tina exchanged weary professional looks, and she marveled at how effortlessly they both dissembled when in public, and though she thought she saw a glimmer of something new, raw and vulnerable, in Kirby's eyes, she attributed it to the immediate unreliability of this snitch.

The door to the room then swung open and Hazel Fish stuck his burred head in. He was out of breath from running there. "We've got a fucking problem."

MAHREZ WAS NOT ALONE in the isolation ward of the MDC hospital infirmary: two U.S. Marshals idled near the door, and his tragically beautiful, scarred girlfriend, Rose, had coiled next to him on the bed. Kirby and Tina Z. had already toured the scene of the crime with Fish, a fussy, ass-covering prison subwarden having led them swiftly past the line of locked-down cells with blank convicts staring out, all the E-block lights blazing and the subwarden, Fish noted, jacked up into full-bore damage control: "It was one of the mandatory trusties, hadda be. Black on white. Or the goddamned Mexicans. Judge Gibson and her court-ordered desegregation bullshit. Somebody with access unlocked his cell door after curfew. We think it was two guys, one to hold him, one to do the deed."

The implication was they'd never catch the perpetrators. Jail was funny that way. Unless you caught the assailant in the act, or found somebody with a grudge to bear, it was Darwinian in its blindness to justice. And, Fish thought coldly, useful when officious assholes like this guy fucked up.

Blood had splashed the floor near the back wall of the cell, and above it, crudely finger-painted: a bloody circle with a slash struck through the word SNITCH scrawled inside with Big Stix's blood.

"He was lucky," the subwarden had opined.

"Sure" was what Tina Z. had responded. "Yeah, that's what I'd call this. Luck."

Fish was pretty sure the subwarden hadn't clocked the Fed's high irony.

They found Mahrez sitting up, pale, chest bandaged, girlfriend with the ruined part of her face pressed against his shoulder, her hair spread out like a photo shoot. He had the faraway stare of a man whose life had been turned inside out. Fish knew the look, didn't care; this man had gamed the system, and karma is a bitch.

Kirby settled on the edge of a vinyl chair facing the bed, fingers jittering, restless. Tina Z. stayed in the doorway behind him, Fish found a spot against the wall.

"You think this was a warning?"

"Nobody sends guys with a shiv to give you a warning," Mahrez said.

"Okay. Who wants you dead?" Kirby asked.

Nothing from Mahrez.

"C'mon, Stix. We can get these guys. Make you safe," Fish said.

"I used to be safe. And then you guys asked me to help you, and, what a surprise. Here we are."

Tina Z. said, "The leak didn't come from our end."

Mahrez ignored her and studied Kirby's suit. "Did you get all fancied up for me?" He touched Rose, and signed as he spoke, hands dancing. "He's wearing, what is that, Armani? Silk. It's killer."

Whatever Rose responded, unsmiling, ill-humored, stayed between them, because Mahrez didn't interpret it. Her fingers fluttered like poetry. Mahrez shook his head and shrugged.

Tina Z. pressed her point, "Less than half a dozen of my people knew you were wired. It was a closed system."

"Until you showed your friend, the mayor," Fish pointed out. They'd rehearsed this; Tina had stressed the importance of remembering to say *your friend*.

The room was quiet.

Nick Mahrez never looked at Fish, just stared at Tina Z. strangely, blankly, the inference slow-dawning. Fish registered the change of temperature: Mahrez realizing that they were thinking the mayor could have been the leak. His friend.

"Nick. Talk to me," Kirby said after a while.

Mahrez said nothing.

"I'm not pursuing the charges against you," Kirby said. "Our information was bad. I'm sorry, it happens."

Both Tina Z. and Fish looked at Kirby in surprise. This was not in the script. Fish doubted the new U.S. attorney knew what her lead prosecutor was doing. Mahrez mattered to him. And not for the first time, Fish had the thought that Kirby, who, no question, was one of the best lawyers he'd ever encountered, shouldn't be doing this job.

"Your information, or your informant?" Mahrez asked.

Rose's hands took flight from the blankets, and she vocalized as she signed, some alien tongue, her voice quaking a sharpness that betrayed her beauty, all vowels and fractured modulation in the monotone of the deaf. Mahrez translated. "She says I'll need protection now, twenty-four-seven three-sixty-five. That you need to protect me. She says I'm a marked man."

Kirby began to say he'd see what he could do, but Fish cut him off, unable to hold back his irritation with all the righteous posturing from this lucky old drug peddler. "Help us, help yourself, my brother. No free rides."

Mahrez exploded. "You did this to me! I was off the grid, and you put me back on it! This is bullshit! My blood, you might as well have cut me open yourselves!" Everyone was stunned by the outburst, including Mahrez, his face flushed, his breath came quicker. He was evidently in a lot more pain than he was showing.

Rose rubbed her boyfriend's back. Calmed him. Her hands traced the air with what could only have been words of love. Fish felt a pang of regret that he'd ragged on the man.

The room fell silent.

"Visiting hours are over," Mahrez said, and turned away from them.

—THEN AT DAWN, *when her alarm chimes, Sabrina Colter slips sleepy-eyed from a downy, white poster bed; wearing baggy flannel*

pajamas, she yawns and stretches, improbably young and un-
spoiled, she takes from her bed stand an NCIC rap of juvy arrests
and prosecutions

complete with a two-decades-old mug shot of teenaged Stix Mahrez

and pads on tiny pink bare feet into the walk-in dressing room-
slash-closet where a gleaming white StairMaster awaits her, facing
a wall-sized full-length mirror and a compact TV tuned to the morn-
ing news:

. . . blah blah blah—

she mutes the television, and sheds her PJs, and climbs naked as
an angel onto the stair machine, spreading the Mahrez rap sheet over
the control panel, to study it as she works out, but glancing up now
and then to admire herself, what God hath wrought: the bloom of her
perfect skin, the cant of her tapered thighs, the firmness of chest, slow
blossoming sheen of sweat like a million diamonds gilding a goddess

stepping her way naked to heaven and—

Kirby awoke violently, as if from a nightmare, wide-eyed, disoriented, shuddering. "Fuck."

Alone in his bed. Another gray summer day pressing down,
radio alarm clock bleeding a traffic report, tangled in the bed-
sheets and sticky with an addict's cold sweat of craving sweet
destruction.

"Bah bah bah BAH."

Tina Z. tried, when she was home, to push everything away
and focus only on Willa. Her ability to compartmentalize had
always been her strength, and she had a lot to keep separate.

Parallel universes that threatened to come apart if they ever
crossed.

Parents. Men. Her child.

But as she shook out Cheerios into the high-chair tray and did vowel vocalizations the way she'd learned from one of the child-rearing books Gracie in White-Collar Crime had given her during pregnancy, she couldn't stop peering out through the beveled windows to the driveway splashed with early-morning sun, where Bert was talking to the husky guy who'd shown up before the baby even woke; shown up in the grotesque wannabe monster truck with the gun rack and the *Hustler* decals and "Duke" Deukmejian bumper stickers and the ridiculous blue-chrome roll bar that practically screamed its date-rape advisory. Who was this guy? The cut glass distorted him like a circus mirror. She tried not to judge.

Albert Zappacosta was her long-term investment, the safe bet, first love, and father of record if not biological certainty (that one time with Kirby, unprotected—one time, what were the odds?). They'd met at Quantico, Bert was in logistics and supply, she was a female agent enigma who'd dropped out of high school, run away from home, put herself through junior college, aced the SATs, cum laude at Case Western, and then somehow talked her way into the FBI Academy, one of seven women who made the cut, much fanfare and prestige, but a lonely journey. Before Bert, she'd never had a boyfriend, never had felt the urge to brook the vulnerability a serious relationship would require or face the withering judgment of the helicopter parents who swooped in and out of her life like a chronic condition, but, boom, Bert, he flipped her switch, and for six months she was as happy as she'd ever be.

Then came the special assignments with LEGAT, long deployments to Nicaragua and Jordan (while Bert quietly unraveled), promotions, a full-on gender role reversal for which her husband was sorely unprepared (one droll military therapist had called it occupational emasculation), which led Bert to transfer to Pendleton and Tina to seek stateside posting in San Diego, but the move seemed to just make everything that much worse.

And then the baby.

Gil Kirby's baby, Tina was sure of it.

Neither man knew.

The baby was supposed to heal them. That had been Bert's rationale for persuading her to go off the pill and try. He'd hoped it would reestablish their God-given roles, mommy and daddy, man and wife; she even bought sexy pink lace thong underwear from Portugal that gave her a rash and rode up when she ran after bad guys. But her husband, still at Pendleton, still an NCO, a lifer, shot blanks, whereas Kirby did not, and now Bert had all but stopped talking.

To her.

But evidently not to fat fucks in jacked macho Chevy half-tons she could only see distorted through the fancy glass at six in the morning when, most days, it was all Bert could do to drag his lazy rear end out of bed before she left for work, to give Willa a kiss and a hug and ask Tina could she pick him up a couple sleeves of Copenhagen long cut, even though he could get them dirt cheap at the PX.

"Ma ma ma MOMMY."

Willa squawked and spat Cheerio mash into Tina's hair. How stupid, how pointless, how sad that out of nowhere Tina circled back, unprompted, again, to this fundamental indefatigable insistent question of paternity—happy, pale, pink, practically Irish, blue-eyed Willa—Kirby would never change, there was no future for them, whatever they had was a swirling eddy of emotion, and when things come back around and repeat the way she and Kirby did it was easy to assume there must be a resolution in the offing, a deeper connection . . . but it was just today's fog, it would burn off and be forgotten. Tina had to keep reminding herself it didn't, wouldn't, signify at the end of the day.

The big truck roared and backed out of the drive.

Bert came in, distracted, and told her the fat guy was interested in buying the dirt bike he hadn't ridden for two years. When she pointed out that Bert and his so-called buyer hadn't gone into the garage to look at it, Bert's eyes dulled and he went to take a shower, and he was still in the bathroom singing "Rock the Casbah" when Tina left to take her daughter to day care.

5

IT WAS SHOT from a cigarette boat cockpit, a grainy, handheld, amateur color 16mm film-to-video transfer that showed a distant surfer shredding the glassy green-blue near-vertical wall of a huge Northern California wave; something the Feds had found in a cache of VHS tapes when they searched the suspect's house.

"Have you seen this?" Colter had added a big Proton television to the bookcase in her office since the last time Kirby had been in there. She aimed the remote and froze the image on the screen as a frightening wave began to curl over the pixelated smear of its interloper. A lower-screen chyron read: MAN VS. WAVE. STIX MAHREZ AT MAVERICKS, 9/6/1969. "Look at that. Was he kind of amazing or what?"

Kirby, fronting her desk with the requisition documents, gave the television a cursory look. "I need your signature to provide him with a police presence at his property after he makes bail. Whoever came after him won't stop."

"I thought we were asking that bail be revoked."

"We tested the waters. The judge is unreceptive."

"Judge Clark?"

"Yes."

"Democrat. Figures." Colter stared at the paused, twitching frame of Stix Mahrez, crouched on his longboard, about to duck into the glistening blue tunnel of breaking surf. "Why should the People pay to protect someone who's so openly hostile to the pursuit of criminals and corruption?"

Kirby didn't offer an answer. He knew more was coming.

"You need to play hardball," she said.

"I'm sorry. What?"

"He may never be a useful witness, but Mr. Mahrez can still be a useful informant. You need to give him the proper incentives."

Kirby shook his head. "You're unbelievable."

"I like to think so." Colter smiled at him, perfect white teeth. "I can take that as a compliment?"

Kirby had to ask, "Have you ever even actually tried a case? In federal court . . . or anywhere else?"

She was unfazed. "What are you saying? I'm young? I'm inexperienced? Or are you wondering who I blew to get promoted to U.S. attorney at the age where most girls are feeling the pull of the ovaries and subscribing to *Modern Bride*?"

Kirby didn't know how to respond to this.

"I don't blow," she said. "Or whatever. I find the thought of it repulsive." She said this so matter-of-factly Kirby had to run it through his head again to understand what she was talking about; meanwhile, she continued, "Cut him loose, fine, but I say no to protection."

"You can't do that."

"I can, yes. Unless he helps us—"

"—We're the reason he needs protection."

"And, P.S."—Colter talked over him—"a little bird at the San Diego District Attorney's Office tells me the girlfriend, with the flower name? Was a high-priced hooker. Back in the day. Pled nolo to a couple felonies, which, gosh, makes her a possible candidate for deportation as an unwanted alien, does it not?"

Kirby stared.

As if innocently, Colter mused then, "How high would Mr. Big Stix jump for her, I wonder?"

WHEN THE EBONY TOWN CAR purred, curling down the driveway of Stix Mahrez's big house, trailed by a San Diego police patrol car, both gave wide berth to the Wash-Tech car detailing van from Del Rio Motors and its water trailer skewed strategically alongside Mahrez's Porsche and Aston Martin. Detail men scurried out of the limo's way, pulled their hoses in so they wouldn't get crimped by the passing vehicles, and killed their power washers out of professional courtesy for the homecoming parade.

All except a sunburned, hydrant-shaped white man working on the Aston Martin's interior, head down, oblivious, as if he didn't hear the two cars go by. But after the limo passed and everyone else went back to work, he rocked out from the front seat and looked, his eyes like currants in the doughy face, dark, grim, unapologetic.

Mahrez got out of the limo first, moving gingerly, a searing pain resulting from any sudden shift of weight; he nevertheless reached back to help Rose. Their Guatemalan bodyguard emerged from the house, in huaraches and a festive guayabera shirt, and said, "*Hola*. Welcome home."

The cops in the patrol car gave a courtesy honk and continued around the driveway's gentle arc, no intention of stopping, heading out the other gate.

"Where are they going?" Mahrez took a few weary steps and shouted after them. "Hey. Hey!"

Mahrez watched the cops go with mixed emotions. He didn't really want them around. But he found himself laid bare by their not staying. A big portable compressor kicked in, the Wash-Tech workers resumed power-hosing the cars, the patrol eased out into the street, no rush, but gone. The sunburned man squinted up at the fried egg of midday sun that hung in overcast, and went back to his vacuuming.

Rose signed: *The police are leaving?*

"Yeah." Mahrez nodded to his bodyguard, grim. "You're gonna have to hire some more security people, Emilio." He linked arms with Rose and she steered him up the walk. Under his breath, disgusted, or maybe more disappointed, he muttered, "Give me grace to accept with serenity the things that cannot be changed."

Rose's hands danced: *Say the rest of it.*

Mahrez shook his head and signed back at her: *That's all there is anymore.*

KIRBY FELT A QUEASY URGENCY to straighten out the Mahrez mess as soon as he could. Letting it fester would only increase the likelihood that a rot would follow, and the rot, Kirby knew, would eventually make its way back to him in some even worse form of Holy Hell. It was just him and Fish in Kirby's cramped office, files from the rolling arrests with mug shots of each suspect clipped to the front of a folder were tiled across an already overloaded desk, wing table, guest chairs, and the floor.

"His name was in the Filofax."

"It's not a crime to have your boss's phone number written down."

"Shoeboxes filled with crack."

"In a personal work locker. And nothing to link Mahrez to the drugs."

"'Cept the Egyptian."

"Who is about as toxic as Chernobyl. You want to rest your entire case on Saad Fanous, Hazel?"

Fish sighed. "Okay, so if Nick Mahrez is just an innocent bystander to this, can I just emphasize, for the record," Fish said, "how much that would suck, big-time, because I've been getting serious props from my DEA brothers for my historic bust of the man nobody thought could be got."

"I appreciated your candor. Let's work backward through our night and see where it went sideways."

"I was maybe even looking at a promotion."

Kirby decided to just wait this out.

"Fine. Let's recap." Fish walked through it: "My happy hooker gave us the street fiends who gave us the roof jumper, Tigger. Tigger, he gave us the motel tweakers. Solid ground, yes? Said tweakers rolled over on Flavian, car salesman extraordinaire, who, again, we can totally prove was selling the bump to them."

"Good so far. Saad?"

Kirby let Fish think about it. "Saad Fanous? Personally, I don't even think he indulges in the monkey dust. He's too twitchy all by his own self, he doesn't require any chemical additives. I think Saad Fanous was telling us the truth, he just bought cocaine to impress his girlfriends at the Hot Box."

"I agree with you," Kirby said. "But bought it where? Not from Mahrez."

Fish considered this. "Okay, so walk it back one." He found and picked up the Flavian folder, referencing it, and said, "In your version, Flavian isn't just a street dealer, he's a wholesaler with some retail outlets?"

"Keep going."

Fish talked it through. "Flav turned reality upside down, what a surprise: *he* was the one selling to *Saad*. Not the other way around. In your scenario, Flavian gave us a bum steer—ratted out Saad to protect his supplier. Counted on Saad to go crazy-helpful and confuse everything."

"Which he did."

Fish seemed unmoved. "None of this holds up in court any better than Saad's version, the one where Stix Mahrez is at the top of his food chain."

They both fell quiet. Fish put the paperwork down and looked for his cup of coffee, which was lost. Kirby said, "How does Flavian know Saad?"

Distracted, Fish gestured to the Fanous file. "The Egyptian leased that righteous red Vette from Flavian seven months ago . . ." Kirby knew where the coffee was, but liked to watch Fish do a slow burn, looking for it. Lifting files, pushing paper piles around, Fish found his Styrofoam cup next to the wastebasket, on the floor, under the desk, where he'd put it so it wouldn't get tipped.

". . . he could have made the drug connection sometime after, I guess."

"Okay. Different angle: Who's Flavian protecting?"

"I don't know."

Kirby wanted Fish to catch up with what he just said out loud, but the DEA man took a sip of his coffee, made a face: bitter and cold.

"He make bail?"

"I think it was fifty grand."

"Do we believe Flavian had fifty grand lying around?"

"I don't think his double-wide qualifies as collateral," Fish said, and then, having thought it all through again, saw where Kirby had led him. "Somebody put up the bond."

"Somebody who didn't want Flavian ratting *him* out."

Fish drained his cup and started out the door. "Well, hell, let's ask the little snitch."

THE INCREDIBLE VIEW was why Mahrez had bought the land, years ago, and staked a big Bedouin tent on it, thinking, this was it, this was the shit. Back in the day Vic had razzed him mercilessly for putting down roots, common wisdom being in their line of work fungibility equated directly with survival. Vic had a sailboat that he moved every few months to a new berth in a new marina, up and down the coast, Gaviota to Chula Vista. Which is why, while Vic was in Oxnard—having three bullets put into the back of his head by a couple of hired men when Vic jack-in-the-boxed up the main hatch from belowdecks, starting to tell a dirty joke to his fiancée that he never got to finish—Stix was romancing two La Jolla High School surf bunnies with a ball of

Lebanese hash and a bottle of mescal in the sultry half-light of his goat hair *bayt*. He'd gone off the grid and hence survived the first of the Sinaloa Cartel's bloody territorial purges, 1981: cashed out, put some seed money into the gifted hands of the legendary Dana Point board shaper Primo Santini, and went legit.

RIP Vic. Theirs was a friendship grounded in commerce, Mahrez didn't so much grieve him as miss the certainty of their bond and word. Not friends, partners, whose unquestioned trust in each other was, ironically because they were drug dealers, so fundamentally American, rule of law, absolute. The fiancée, a hatchet-faced anorexic who called herself Bunny because no one else would, was an early freebaser who fed Vic's paranoia and spent all his money and probably fingered him to the cartel's assassins. She had the body cremated and scattered Vic's ashes in the parking lot at Zuma Beach, where she'd first set eyes on him. Took the sailboat north, intending to go to Portland, but nobody ever saw or heard from her again.

"It's Stix Mahrez, yeah. I've left a couple of messages for him already . . ." Struggling to will his tension headache away, Mahrez listened impatiently to the City Hall side of his call, and watched Rose, out on the grass, playing with her new teacup poodle puppies. They danced away from her arms, barking. She was laughing, and her laugh, unleashed, guttural, raw, always made him smile.

"I understand. Just tell him—" The receptionist on the other end wouldn't stop talking: meetings, schedule, ground-breaking ceremony in San Ysidro, yadda yadda, Mahrez finally just saying his piece over her, "—sure, sure, I understand, if you could just tell the mayor to call me back soon as he can, yeah. It's pretty important. Nick—no, Stix—yeah, that's right, Mahrez. Like the ballplayer, you remembered. Thank you."

Click.

Steel-gray ocean bled to steel-gray sky.

Viscid stratus clouds hung shallow over water and shore. The Channel Islands loomed like phantasms in the far gloaming, and Coronado Bay was pimpled with the white sails. It was past noon. The bled-out sun wasn't going to burn through this dozy haze, Mahrez thought, and then wondered how long it would take him to drive to the border.

TWO SLOE-EYED GIRLS in halter tops blew bubbles from the steps of a neighboring Winnebago on blocks, listening to Wham! on a boom box and watching Fish pound on the trailer door, and ring the bell, and knock again. Nothing.

"Hey, Johnny Law," the girls sang at him.

Fish ignored them. "Flavian?" He listened for movement inside the double-wide, and heard only the faint, thrumming tone of water running in a leaky toilet.

Fish's government ride was parked in front of the familiar, shaded, rust-streaked house trailer at the end of a cul-de-sac. The hot gray day did nothing to improve the neighborhood. Fat, salt-rusted Detroit iron was parked in nearly every carport, excepting the occasional Toyota Camry with a coat hanger where the aerial should be. A big blue dumpster reeked of spoiled meat and grass clippings.

Behind the trailer he found that a piece of flattened cardboard box had been duct-taped over the bathroom window through which Flavian had come crashing into Fish's arms the other night. Tape intact. No escape or forced entry evident.

A fingertip pull-up on the sill got him eye-level with the back living room window. He could see an unmade sofa bed, a television atop a laminated faux-cherrywood eight-track stereo console, a pile of pornographic magazines spilt across a split leatherette recliner, and a framed, shimmering foil art print of *The Last Supper*, but with San Diego Chargers instead of the apostles, and Don Coryell sitting in for Jesus Christ.

Fish dropped down and moved through overgrown grass back along the trailer to the bedroom window, repeating his pull-up. There he saw the naked body facedown on the bed's bare mattress.

Flavian.

Executed.

Hands duct-taped behind his paper-white buttocks, shot twice in the back, neat little entry wounds, bubbled and blue. Blood had spritzed the headboard and the wall and leaked all over, dry now, almost black. Flav's clothes were balled on a plastic, stackable chair in the corner, and his Air Jordans neatly lined up below it.

Fish said, "Oh, man," and let go of the sill.

6

THE SHARP SHADOW of the serial billboards hawking to border arrivals and departures gave shade to the small herd of news
crews and spectators at the ground-breaking for a new immigration center that was the centerpiece of Mayor Richard Poole's eco-
nomic redevelopment plan for south San Diego. Just an empty
scrape of San Ysidro commercial land, its few acres tufted with
half-buried garbage and goatgrass and smother weed, within
walking distance of the Tijuana border crossing and a long spit
from the permanent gridlock of traffic crawling through customs. At the back of the gathering, where two local news mobile
vans were cabled up to Betacams on tripods, was Stix Mahrez
with tiny twisted reflections of the smiling mayor twinned in his
Ray-Bans.

His side still ached, where the blade had done its crazing. He
didn't want to be here, but so much control of his existence,

since the Feds showed up at his door, had been slipping like sand through his fingers, he had to do something. Anything. To keep hold of what remained.

Strategically fenced by an SDPD uniformed security detail, Poole gave a short speech, thanking the sundry politicians and businessmen who made this possible, including a few Mexican nationals, one of whom Mahrez recognized as Juan Blanco. Those mirror Revos, that big arrogant smile, Blanco was surrounded by his own honor guard consisting of tattooed, shaved-head, leather-clad steroid freaks suggesting a quorum of B-list *Luchadores* backstage at intermission.

That the Mexican narco was attending Poole's dog-and-pony show was not the surprise; it was how he was thanked for attending that struck Mahrez as odd, possibly worrisome. Rumors sifting across the border like the stories of the Greek gods had it that after the recent arrests of Quintero and Carrillo, God of Gods cartel *jefe* Félix Gallardo had gone into seclusion and apportioned his empire to a collective of relatively unknown subsidiaries: Juárez to the Carrillo Fuentes family, the Sonoran corridor to Miguel Quintero, Tijuana to the Arellano-Félix brothers, the Gulf territories would stand pat with Abrego, and Joaquín Guzmán and Ismael García would take over the Pacific Coast routes, henceforth to be called the Sinaloa Cartel.

Blanco, a midlevel suck-up not known for having more than single-syllable thoughts, was generally considered to be barely another brick in the wall, but his presence here might mean he was soon to be more than that. Mahrez mused darkly that if Richard Poole knew this, it was bad—and if he didn't, it was worse.

KIRBY WAS, at that same time, having a wrestling match, dueling Armani suits, with Mahrez's attorney in Kirby's Federal Building office, which he'd made a self-conscious half-assed effort to clean up by stacking all his case files precariously on the minifridge in the corner.

Several of them had already avalanched back onto the floor.

"Don't do this, Kirby." Damien Belasco decided not to sit, well aware that the guest chairs often also served as food trays for various high-risk burritos brought back from roach coaches that prowled the streets around City Hall.

"It's not my call." Kirby, hating himself, toed the company line. "My boss wants your client's help."

"Your boss. Your new boss?"

"Yes."

"I heard she's a piece." A roguish delay. "Of work."

Kirby said without mirth, "Ha ha."

"Look, man, the girlfriend, Rose, is deaf and disfigured, for Chrissakes. I mean. Kirby. C'mon."

Kirby made a vague, helpless gesture. His phone line lit up, got answered. The receptionist's interoffice message ID scrolled: GUNN. Kirby tapped the CALL BACK key.

"This is so beneath you."

"I am just glad Mr. Mahrez finally contacted his attorney," Kirby said.

"Yeah, now that everybody and his uncle thinks he's your informant." Belasco was the best criminal lawyer south of San Francisco, and still refused to take any cases in L.A., which took balls. Kirby admired him. Kirby admired anybody who wasn't AUSA Kirby, these days. Belasco had noted the wardrobe uptick. "I bet you haven't worn a suit like that since you were at Gibson and Dale."

Kirby shrugged. "New dress code."

"Only for you, I guess. Lipstadt's still wearing that J. C. Penney polyester two-piece his mom bought for his bar mitzvah."

"Maybe he didn't get the memo."

"Do you even know the story? Of Rose and Stix?" Belasco put his hands in his pockets, casual, the way he did when he gave his summations; he had a faint Denzel Washington vibe, right down to the contagious smile. "She's a former Paris runway model who found a little trouble with the junk. Her heroin dealer got her a green card, brought her to America, and then pimped her out to his wealthiest clients."

"I don't want to know. I don't want to know. Your stories always make me want to start drinking at, like, ten in the morning."

"She spirals down, you can only imagine, conventions and shore leave, but crawls back out, meets Nick at an AA meeting, tells him she wants to quit the life, so he gets her some catalog work with Hang Ten. Pimp finds out and attacks her with battery acid." Belasco said it simply, but took a pause to let the full weight of this sink in. "Ruined her face, pain so intense it shorted out her auditory nerves. But Stix took her in, man. That night. To his own house, hired security. Found her specialists, nursed her himself. He fell in love with her *after* she was maimed. He saved her life."

Kirby started to say something cynical, but stopped himself. Belasco wasn't just working him. There was real feeling in this. And yet— "What happened to that pimp?" Belasco started to answer, but Kirby beat him to it, "Lemme guess: Somebody pounded two feet of rebar through his head, and his body washed up on the beach. Or, no—no, a hiker found him rotting on the banks of the Salton Sea, sans hands, teeth, and feet. Or maybe he just vanished one day. Never to be seen again?"

Belasco said something under his breath.

"This isn't the movies, Damien. Whores don't have a heart of gold, bad guys don't see God and get grace. Our version of a happy ending is where Jack the Ripper gets taken out by Charlie Manson."

So much for avoiding the cynical.

Kirby laid it out. "All your client has to do is apologize for the stunt in the mayor's office and talk shop with us. Fill in some blanks; advise and consent. It's not really snitching, per se, it's . . ." Kirby couldn't find the words, because the whole thing was such bullshit, his side, their side, an endless circle, ". . . more like consulting." His shoulders sagged. Shit.

"Consulting." Belasco stared at him. Kirby felt dumb.

"It is what it is," Kirby said after a while.

"Unless it isn't," Belasco pointed out.

Kirby let his palms flutter out, helpless. Exposed.

Nothing.

Belasco seemed genuinely disappointed. "Don't do this. Don't do this, man. Just say no."

SAAD FANOUS WAS SURE he'd figured it out. The FBI agent Tina Zappacosta, lovely today, he noted appreciatively, in her sharp black skirt and coat, sat on the other side of the visiting booth glass, waiting for him to explain why he'd summoned her, but the truth was he didn't understand why he'd needed to summon her, he'd given everybody what they wanted, so, okay, maybe she was the problem since their case together appeared to have been derailed by his arrest and detention, potentially exposing him to the very suspects he and she, Tina, had been attempting to ensnare.

"I want you to get me out of here," Saad said.

"I can't do that."

She seemed truthful. Perhaps, he thought, because she was a woman. "Get the government prosecutor to arrange it for us," Saad advised.

"You're in on a felony possession charge," Tina said to him. "Your case will have to work through the system."

"I have a deal."

"You have an understanding that they'll put in a good word for you at sentencing."

This was where, for Saad, it all became a bit of a fog. But he had figured out his work-around. "I will make it possible for you to arrest a cell of Shia terrorists."

"A she-what?"

"Yes. Let me elaborate." Through a very lithe Moroccan stripper he'd met at the Hot Box, Saad had been introduced to some U.C. San Diego graduate exchange students, mostly Jordanian, he insisted, from very wealthy families and typically clueless; he was confident that he could persuade these earnest young Arabs to donate a portion of their allowance to give to the Hezbollah resistance in Lebanon without realizing that they would, in fact, be agreeing to the direct purchase of weapons and explosives for domestic mischief and, Saad believed, upon delivery to their apartment of the same, give Tina Zappacosta the local terror cell she needed to replace the local terror cell she'd lost. "Islamic jihadists."

"You're making this up."

"No. The Shia are a violent group. You can't imagine." Saad tried not to blush. "It's a dangerous situation, for sure. But, of course, I cannot do it from inside of a jail."

He didn't see how an American federal agent could refuse this. What was one harmless Egyptian when put on the scale with an entire group of radical fundamentalists?

"This cell is supported directly by the ayatollah."

"Khomeini? Guy in Iran?"

"You are very well read, Tina."

She smiled. "You gotta give me something more solid, Saad. So far this is all pretty sketchy."

"They wish to purchase explosives and weapons."

"From you?"

"Who else? I am told there is a man on the Marine base at Pendleton who can arrange for such things."

He watched her tense up. "Who?"

"I knew you would be interested."

"I need a name."

"When I am released," Saad said, annoyed that she didn't understand the bargain.

"No." Tina stared at him, thinking, and Saad started to lose confidence. To make a good sale you never let the buyer think. "The cell is something you made up," she said, as if reaching into his thoughts. "But the Pendleton thing is real."

Saad mumbled that he had no idea what she was implying. Women should not be asked to do these kinds of jobs.

"You think you have access to military surplus. We've had

rumors of a weapons black market for a while now. You were going to set up some poor Arab stiffs, but you know it wouldn't stick unless there was actual hardware to change hands. You wouldn't bring me over here if the Pendleton of it wasn't real."

While Saad didn't know what Tina was talking about, he felt confident he'd made progress.

"This embark officer. Give me a name. Then we can talk."

"When I am released," Saad said.

"No."

Saad shrugged, bluffing. Tina got up to leave.

"Albert." Desperation made Saad blurt it out, and after he'd done so he worried that she'd ask him for a last name, which he didn't know, but Tina just stood and looked at him for a long time, saying nothing, her eyes emptying as he waited.

"All I have is this name," Saad admitted, just to break the uncomfortable silence. "There. You have everything. I am at your mercy."

"You're lying," she said, finally. "You're wrong."

Saad knew he could be. But about which part?

EMILIO, THE BODYGUARD, was watching a Mexican-league soccer game and clipping his toenails when Rose breezed past him, hands and fingers moving. He understood enough to know that she couldn't find something, she was going outside to look for it. In the cars? His ten-year-old daughter had helped him learn a few of the deaf signs.

Rose tended to glide through the house, her body so fluid, the slight vertigo she suffered causing her hips and shoulders to do a strange samba, all woman, and Emilio never tired of watching her. As long as he kept his eyes off her disfigurement, it was like an ever-giving gift from God. In and out of the room once, twice, and Emilio finally understood that she was searching for the experimental device his boss had brought home for her: a compact square polished silver microcassette player that, if she held it against her skull, under her ear, at the back of her jaw, allowed her feel the music that pulsed through it at a special frequency. She loved David Bowie.

Emilio recalled the first week after Señor Nick brought the ruined woman home: the black rages, the shrieking, the bloody fingernail marks on Mahrez's arms and neck. The only blessing was she couldn't see herself, because they'd carefully removed every reflective surface before she returned. This went on for six, seven weeks, but slowly Nick had tamed her, rebuilt her, sculpted with his odd, relentless unconditional love a new world and new girl she could live in silence with and learn to love, too.

It was slick work, Emilio thought. He himself probably would have romanced her until it became tedious, then sent her back to whatever cold, bleak, Scandinavian climate had spawned her.

But Emilio was a practical man. Señor Stix Mahrez was a fantasist.

A couple moments after Rose breezed through the room one more time, still signing and now vocally chirping about the device, he heard the security system chime, indicating an outside entry door that was opening, and she was going outside.

Shit.

"Señora Rose?"

Of course, she couldn't hear him.

He heaved himself up, hoping Pachuca wouldn't score while he was bringing the beautiful, broken *diosa* back inside.

HIS BORDER GROUND-BREAKING ceremony and photo op concluded, Mayor Richard Poole was shaking hands that his aide had strategically selected for him when a voice over his shoulder murmured, "You've been ducking my calls," and Poole flinched. He finished a pleasantry he couldn't even remember as he was saying it, and, still smiling professionally, pivoted into Nick Mahrez as if that was what he was expecting to do, next, all along.

"You've left messages?" Poole's lie was unconvincing. "Sorry, Nick. Gee. Dammit. My staff must be screening my—"

"*Grande* Stix Mahrez*! Hola, amigo!*"—and there was Blanco, pushing imperiously through a restive, disappointed constituency hoping to glad-hand the mayor and buy a few seconds of his time to plead a cause; the Mexican's big cold evil smile leered and his dead mirror Revo eyes fixed on Mahrez like a shark's.

"—Long time."

Mahrez said, "Not long enough."

Only Blanco's chin registered the insult. Poole and his aide traded panicked looks for different reasons. The aide touched his watch. The mayor mimed helplessness and let his eyes drift back to worry about Mahrez as the Mexican talked shit; he wasn't sure if his old friend recognized how much the world had changed.

"Just the other day, I was asking, whatever happened to him? And then I remembered: Me! I happened! I took your business, yeah? You had to, what, go make like toys or something." There was nothing but violence behind Blanco's feigned good nature.

"Surfboards."

"¿*Qué?*" Blanco tipped his Revos down for effect.

"Surfboards was always my business, Juanito," Mahrez said.

Blanco winked. "Oh. *Sí, sí.* Of course. That and collecting melted whores."

"Your memory's fuzzy." Mahrez refused to be rattled by this thug. "Must be all the paint and glue you were huffing, between the fifty-cent blow jobs in *La Zona*, back in the day."

Blanco's face flushed purple and his manner lost all its cheap bravado. Poole remembered how Vic had always pegged Blanco for success, even as he mocked him to his face for what Vic called Blanco's "natural gifts of reptilian stupidity." Mahrez never liked him, or trusted him, and thought that Blanco was the weakest link in their distribution chain, an unavoidable risk factor emboldened by his inexplicable ties to Gallardo, who gave Blanco carte blanche over the marijuana trade with Southern California, this peasant who could barely count to ten. Mahrez made Vic deal with him. Vic assured Poole it was like heeling a dog. And while Vic would return from Tijuana and Baja with fantastical tales of bacchanalian Cabo orgies, Mahrez was fairly convinced that Blanco had double-crossed Vic on a two-truck shipment of pot that got interdicted at the Mexicali border crossing, and which subsequently put Vic on a short list to be taken out by the Sinaloans.

Poole pulled Mahrez away: "Would you excuse us, Señor?" They crossed the empty lot until Poole thought they were safely distant, and muttered, "Nice work. Christ on a cracker, Nick. Why don't you just piss on him?"

"You wouldn't mind?" Mahrez made as if to start back toward Blanco, but the mayor grabbed his arm.

"Enough."

"What is a scumbag like Blanco even doing here? What has happened to you?" Mahrez had to ask, and Poole didn't really know how to answer, except officially:

"He's part of their delegation, Tijuana sends who they want, I can't—why are you so—"

Mahrez cut him off. "Somebody tried to kill me, Dicky. Because word leaked that I came in to you wired. I guess the full story didn't translate, the part where I warned you Feds were on your ass."

Poole had heard about the stabbing. "And you think I was the leak? Me?" He still couldn't tell how much Mahrez actually knew, or what Vic might have told him in a stoned blear of candor, back when everything was boxes within boxes.

The stubborn quilt of inland clouds scudded, horizon to horizon, blemishing a vault of turquoise sky. Mahrez said nothing, patient to see how Poole would react, and Poole's eyes slid this way and that as people circled them, making eye contact, closing the distance on the mayor again with their endless agendas, and he had to have his mechanical politician's reassuring smile in overdrive.

"Tell me that you don't know what Blanco does for a living."

"I'd be lying," Poole said. "But I'm not stupid, Nick. He's also a Mexican government official. Someday he could be useful. He found us some private foundation money for the center. And nobody of import over there is clean."

"The leak was you, or the Feds." Mahrez kept his voice conversational. "And the Feds have too many reasons to keep me safe and happy, most of which relate to what they think I know about you."

A new silence not born of awkwardness. Poole felt an acid rise in his throat, the way it had in his office. He rubbed the back of his neck and rolled his shoulders to release some anxious tension. Blanco was still staring darkly at them from across the lot.

"What did you tell them?"

"Nothing," Mahrez said. "Yet." He walked away.

Poole barked after him, more a hope than a warning, "Because you don't know anything, man. You don't."

Mahrez didn't look back.

BY THE TIME EMILIO REACHED the open front door, Rose was halfway down the front walkway pavers. Two of the newly hired private security guys were up at the driveway entrance, standing sentry behind the electric gate, big handguns strapped to their hips, backs turned to the street, watching Rose make her way to the car just like any man should watch her, not so much wishing he could have her as appreciating, like Emilio, that such a thing, even sadly damaged, could exist.

The Guatemalan called out, "Let me get it for you, Miss Rose," and quickened to catch up with her because he knew she couldn't hear him, but his feet were bare and the walkway was peppered with painful stubs of broken acorns from the huge evergreen oaks that overhung the house.

She was in the driveway, threading awkwardly through the small fleet of cars to the newly detailed, gleaming 928, finally turning, looking back at Emilio, smiling, eyes alive, hands up, signing: *It's in the Porsche.* Emilio glanced guiltily to the guards at the gate and hoped they wouldn't say anything later; Señor

Nick's constant fear was that the men who had disfigured the girl would come back to finish the job, and that was why he insisted that Emilio never let her leave the house alone.

The alarm on the Carrera chirped, and Rose had the driver's-side door open before Emilio could finish gingerly navigating the walk, dust off his tender soles, and catch up with her.

He touched her lightly. "Miss Rose, please, let me get it for you."

She ignored him, stubborn. Vocalizing and signing, "I can do it." Climbing in, she reached down the front of the passenger seat and found her music box wedged against the seat frame. Holding it up:

"See?"

She climbed out again, using Emilio for leverage. Her hand was like a child's. She brushed against him, angular and soft, flush with soap and cotton.

She signed: *Thank you, Emilio.*

He couldn't help but smile at her. In another life, he thought wistfully, I'd have to make her turn her face. Once she found her balance and slipped past him, he closed the door, gently, and the car exploded in a fireball.

7

"I DON'T HAVE any illusions about what we're doing. People get crushed, lives are destroyed." Kirby tried to shake images of the long grim afternoon from his head.

The smell.

Mahrez's face.

Emergency personnel milled like an opera's chorus, the driveway taped off. A hushed, dutiful, disorganized jitter of pointless efficiency had passed in front of Mahrez as he stood apart, numb, and watched from the front yard of his house. Arms folded and pressed against his chest, legs planted, motionless, he looked hollowed out. No one spoke with or approached him.

Bottomless grief. Inconsolable.

"But to use the guy like a ladder, set him up, hold him, and climb him to try and get up where you want . . ."

C-4 explosives, military grade, had been rigged under the driver's seat, primed when the door opened, to detonate when the door closed. The Guatemalan bodyguard was blown to pieces, practically vaporized. Rose had been tossed a hundred feet, but mercifully killed instantly by the concussive force of the bomb.

Now, hours later, Kirby was at the window in Colter's office considering the skewed geometric grids of downtown lights, his hands shoved in the pockets of another nice suit. He was wishing that the night would erase him. That he might go back and start over. But how far?

Time travels in one direction. The eddy corkscrews, a maelstrom, counterclockwise.

"I feel dirty and complicit and helpless and duped. We're supposed to be the good guys. Or at least the smart guys. We—me—you—should be ashamed of ourselves. We should have given him and his girl protection."

Behind her desk, Colter swiveled back and forth, back and forth, in the chair that looked too big for her, sucking on a hard candy to complete the picture of the petulant precocious child; she leaned forward finally on hands folded as if to say grace and observed with a truly callous cold indifference that "Stix Mahrez is a drug dealer. Or was." And then, pretending to be thoughtful, added, "Maybe it was God's will."

Kirby just gazed out into America's Finest Darkness.

THE FRACTURED FAST-FORWARD SHUFFLE through surveillance videotape from Stix Mahrez's extensive security system went on and on. Multiple screens, multiple views: front door, back door, driveway, backyard, figures jerking and smearing through their day in fast motion, mundane, a scenario pathetic in its unremarkability, tragic in its failure to foreshadow the pandemonium and carnage soon to come.

Dregs of morning coffee were congealing in the Krups carafe; the assorted pastries Kirby had brought reduced to crumbs.

Having spent his night studying the tapes, one of Tina Z.'s colleagues, an agent they called JoJo, the local bureau's security cam specialist who, as far as Tina knew, had never qualified for fieldwork because he was, in a word, obese, loomed over their shoulders, hers and Kirby's, smelling of Egg McMuffin and unwashed chinos, and narrated, "Mahrez came home from jail about ten-thirty, he went out again, by himself, around three."

The visuals on all the screens had been captured in step-motion, at progressive ten-second intervals, meaning Mahrez presented as a streaking, blurring apparition, here, there, gone.

"No deliveries, no visitors, except for the private security detail that showed up midday, and took instructions from the bodyguard, after which a team of two stayed on. But these guys—" JoJo punched a button and froze the screen: the Wash-Tech car detailing van had magically been conjured in the driveway. "This crew was already there in the morning when Mahrez came home from county lockup."

Tina Z. studied the image. Something (or someone) in it had begun to make her queasy, a bitter jolt of déjà vu. "Working on both cars. You got a line on them?"

"Not yet." JoJo resumed the quick-scan. Images skittered past. Kirby leaned in and studied the video. Wash-Tech. Arriving. Attending the cars. Leaving. Tina tried to locate the source of her disquiet. It wasn't just what Saad had said about Bert. This was something else.

"Stop," Kirby said. JoJo complied. "Now, can you enlarge that?"

"It'll get grainy."

"JoJo."

"Ho-kay." Mouth breathing, adding a hint of sour institutional coffee to his fast food and pheromone array, the fat federal photo tech manipulated the image and magnified the frame for Kirby. Everything went soft and blurry as the VHS picture zoomed. On the back doors of the van, the small cursive hand-painted lettering was purely promotional; slanted looping dark letters that made for a smeary abstract in the enlargement, almost impossible to decipher. But after a moment, Kirby read it out aloud:

"'Another Courtesy Cleaning . . .'"

And Tina finished for him, "'. . . from Del Rio Motors.'"

THE PARKING LOT was deserted at the Stix Surfboards factory when Kirby's car pulled up and ticked quiet. The leaden day pressed down, languid, viscous.

Inside, the building was still literally lifeless when Kirby came through the front and into the main factory floor. It was a giant warehouse space containing God only knew how many hazardous chemicals, hopefully ventilated by an air-filtration system that was not presently in operation, with specialized stations for shaping, glassing, and finishing.

Light-headed, Kirby wondered if he should be breathing the funk he felt lacquering his lungs.

He walked past orphaned upright racks of snow-white foam blanks.

Nobody around.

A collection of solvents sat open and reeking of methyls and benzenes and aromatic hydrocarbon isomers near a paint gun someone had left abandoned in the middle of the floor when the bust went down. Serpentine hoses coiled back to a fat, mute compressor. Three wildly colored custom Honda Element trucks were parked side by side just inside the delivery bay doors. DEL RIO MOTORS embossed on the license plate holders.

"I gave everybody the day off."

Kirby turned as Mahrez came out of an office. Funeral-black suit, broken sloe eyes sunk back in their sockets, opaque.

"Orders for new boards are drying up, anyway," he said. "It's amazing how radioactive you can become when your luck turns. Clients go into review, suppliers go out of stock, friends disappear, suddenly nobody returns your calls."

Kirby said, "I'm really sorry."

Mahrez nodded out of habit. There was, Kirby realized, no reason for him to believe it.

"If you could tell us who you think is targeting you," Kirby soldiered on anyway, "if we could get the guy who actually is importing this high-grade Mexican product everyone thinks you're dealing—"

"—Rose would still be dead," Mahrez said, hollow. "My life would still be a shambles."

Yes, it would, Kirby thought, and said as much.

Mahrez frowned. "It's not the dealing they hate me for, is it? It's the getting out, the not getting caught."

"They?"

"You. Cops, courts. Everybody who worked so hard to get me to this moment." He stared at Kirby bleakly. The compressor kicked on, startling both of them. It clattered and moaned, topping off the pressure that had leached from the main tank while everything was idle.

"No, it's grimmer than that." Mahrez wanted Kirby to continue. "Nobody hates you—you're a loose end to be tied up. A stepping stone, if we're really lucky. A footnote in an unfinished case report if we're not. None of this was personal." Kirby thought about it, and added, "Whoever came after you was from your side of the equation."

"You had to know that, going in," Mahrez said. "What else aren't you telling me?"

Kirby didn't want to lie, so he changed subjects. "I knew this guy, once," Kirby said, as the compressor shut down again, leaving an uneasy kind of quiet. "Corporate attorney. Had it all going gangbusters—the righteous job, the righteous house, membership at Rancho Santa Fe, trophy wife, summers in Maine . . . it all came apart because he took the high ground over something stupid, during the biggest case of his career. Something great and brave and noble and futile that he could never even tell anybody, afterward, that he had done."

"Noting that the wife came listed after the golf," Mahrez observed drily. "But go ahead."

"Crushed him. I mean, completely. Divorce, depression, bankruptcy, goodbye job, ex got the house, Maine was a memory. Everything he had, everything he knew, was over."

Mahrez was impatient. "Go right to the moral of the story, I don't mind."

Kirby spread his hands out. "That's all. No moral, no redemption, no happily ever after. At first he blamed everybody else. But after a while he came to understand: there are no victims, only volunteers." Kirby said, "You can blame me for what's happened, and I can blame myself—God help me, I do—but you, you've got to think you wrote most of this epic tragedy yourself, man. However many years ago. When you *were* breaking rules and living large.

"Gotta pay to play," Kirby added. "Isn't that what they say?"

"They say that, and it's trite," Mahrez said.

"It's all trite," Kirby bit back.

If Mahrez had expected warm words, crafted sympathy, an appeal to his want for justice, Kirby just bled bitter and raw. "Get out," Mahrez said softly. "I'm done talking to you people."

"I don't blame you," Kirby allowed, chastened, and as he turned to go his eyes strayed to the delivery cars again, and the name on their complimentary dealer promotional license plate brackets abruptly slotted into his incomplete theory of the crime: Del Rio Motors.

Same as on the Wash-Tech vans.

"We get a fleet rate," Mahrez explained, after Kirby asked.

Carefully thinking it through: "And free car-washing service?"

"I guess." Mahrez shrugged. "My foreman makes the arrangements, I just sign the checks."

"At Del Rio. Is your fleet salesman named Flavian?"

Mahrez said that sounded right, and wondered aloud how Kirby knew.

"Things tend to connect," Kirby said. "In the swirl of a case."

"Or collide," Mahrez added.

DEL RIO MOTORS was a pimp-my-ride heaven, performance cars and custom builds, but fleet sales were the dealership's cash cow, especially to boutique local businesses like Nick's Stix Surfboards.

In the fishbowl showroom, Tina Z. had corralled and grilled a trio of nervous, commission-only salesmen for several minutes, and they answered all her questions to the best of their abilities, nodded, gestured to the back, and finally the small one with the sweater vest led her through the double doors to the service bays.

Work stopped as mechanics watched the curvy federal chick thank the salesman and stroll out to a tin-roofed station against the cyclone fence, where a couple young Latino men were washing and detailing cars ready for pickup. Parked alongside the metal canopy was the familiar Wash-Tech van, back doors gaping to reveal a cargo bed filled with buckets, rags, chamois and shelved solvents, cleaners and Armor All. Weatherproof video cameras were trained down on the area from the lot light stanchions, probably more to monitor employee behavior than for security. Tina made a mental note to get a warrant for the archived output, hoping it would go back at least a week's worth.

She smiled and lobbed some high school Spanish at the men, one of them ignored her, the other, compact, his broad freckled shoulders hung with a grimy wifebeater, worried a headlight lens with his sponge but met her gaze.

Tina Z. said, *"Sí, sí*—I *soy un policía. No,* I *no estoy aquí* to bust you, *siempre y cuando mantenga contestar mis preguntas."* She wasn't sure she'd said that right, so she added, in English, "As long as you answer my questions."

Now she had both men's attention. She showed them an ID packet of eight-by-ten black-and-white photographs of their crew in the Mahrez driveway.

"A stranger took a ride with you yesterday." They regarded her cautiously. *"Un desconocido.* Stranger? *Ayer."* She'd reached the limits of her middle school *Español* and faltered. *"Tomó un paseo . . .* um, he asked to go with you . . . *contigo."*

"Hey!" A big florid white man in a spotless shop shirt stitched with "Boyce," a man who looked like he hadn't picked up a tool in years and when he had was at odds with it—his promotions probably due more to canny politics than ability, or aptitude, Tina mused—came charging out of the service manager's office on soft, shined penny loafers. "Can I help you?" came out as a growling accusation.

Tina Z. badged him, unimpressed. She'd spent her career suffering and managing men like this one; pale white baby boomers forged in the fires of Vietnam draft evasion and tempered by a bitter resentment that the whole sixties free-love thing had never panned out for them. "Zappacosta. FBI. Do these men work for you?"

As she'd expected, Boyce leapt to the assumption Tina was here for an immigration bust, and he wanted no part of it. Backpedaling as fast as he could, he stuttered, "Um. No, no ma'am. They, um, they're . . . no, independent . . . contractors. Look, I—we—"

Tina Z. let him flounder, and returned her attention to the sturdier of the two detailers, who seemed afraid to say anything more in front of the man who signed his checks. She asked for his name. "Arnulfo," the man said, tentatively.

"He's Mexican," Boyce blurted. The pager clipped to his belt kept humming.

Without looking at the service manager, Tina said, *"¿Es este tu jefe, Arnulfo?"*

Arnulfo nodded.

"What's he telling you?" Boyce asked, but he'd already figured it out. "They don't tell me their legal status, I don't ask. You can't get Americans to do these jobs," he added, defensively. "I know that's no excuse, but it's the truth, and these guys do great work. I don't want any trouble."

Tina turned to Boyce, smiling. "Obviously." Then she played him, hard, and fast: "I don't, either. So. Listen up. Is it Boyd?" She knew what his name was.

"Boyce."

"Boyce, I need to ask these gentlemen a few questions in private and if I find out after I've left you've called the border patrol on Arnulfo or his buddy, here, and had them deported so as to cover your backside—particularly before next payday—I'm going to come back with a warrant and close you down." The service manager started raising his hands to protest his innocence, but before he could say anything, Tina continued, "Matter of fact? I'd like you to get them H-1B visas. Make it legal. I'll check back in with you about it next week."

Boyce closed his eyes. "You know what a hassle that is?"

"Yeah, I do, not to mention a couple grand up front and you'll have to pay them minimum wage and so forth, but hey. What a shame." She stared at him. Boyce sulked, thought about making a comment, then gave up on that, his shoulders dropped, he glared at Arnulfo and eventually shuffled back toward his office, checking his pager for all the messages he'd missed.

Tina was still waiting on Arnulfo. Her original question hanging.

"This man you want. This stranger. Yes: He took a ride with us, but we don't know him, so," Arnulfo told her. "And he never said his name."

"Who told you to take him?" Arnulfo's face flushed red, and Tina guessed why. "How much did he pay you to take him on?"

Arnulfo hesitated, which was all the answer she wanted—yes he paid them—so she put up her hands to indicate the amount wasn't really all that important, and shuffled through the pictures again: "Which one is he?"

"Five hundred dollars," Arnulfo said.

"Okay."

Arnulfo traded cautious looks with his colleague, then thumbed the lone, fat, thick-necked Anglo in the photograph and Tina's heart sank as she suddenly realized where she'd seen this guy before. Dark eyes, doughy face.

Just the other day, he'd been out in her driveway, with Bert. Not looking at a motorcycle.

"His name is Ellis Van Houten. Owns a gun store out in Hemet. Unimpressive rap sheet, to be honest, mostly misdemeanors and skinhead scofflawing, but documented association with the Hells Angels and White Aryan Resistance. For a while he may have worked security for RJM labs and our own Mr. Meth, Robert Miskinis. San Diego Sheriff's got him on their watch-and-worry list as a probable murder-for-hire guy. But so far nothing's stuck."

Kirby and Fish were in one of the small conference rooms at the Federal Building on Kearny Mesa, listening to Tina Z. and studying her still photos excerpted from the Del Rio Motors security cameras, as well as stills from the Mahrez security tapes, spread out across the table.

Tina looked oddly discomposed, preoccupied, Fish thought, but she soldiered through it. "Arnulfo alleges Van Houten paid the auto detail outfit five hundred bucks to let him tag along on the appointment to Mahrez's house yesterday morning." Tina found and slid prominent the image of the burly white man wielding the upholstery vacuum, hunched like a coal miner in the cramped Aston Martin.

Fish said, "Two hours later, kaboom."

Tina gave a distracted affirmation.

"What's wrong?"

She glanced at Kirby, poker-faced, shrugged. "What?"

"You seem—"

"—nothing. No, I'm—it's just—"

Fish watched them, curious. Tina shrugged again. Kirby, suddenly aware of Fish watching, nodded and seemed to decide to back off, "—okay."

"Anyway," she continued, voice brittle now, "I called ATF. They can confirm Van Houten has access to military-grade C-4 and detonators through his store."

Fish watched as Kirby moved the photos around like puzzle pieces. The husky sunburned man, his hair wrought almost wheat chaff by the sun, his tiny rat's eyes bored into the flat of his face, had worked inside all of Mahrez's cars. His scuffed boots' run-down heels gave him a bowlegged cant. He looked, Fish thought, like a bad guy.

Kirby sat down. "We could have stopped this."

Fish said, "Don't go there, man."

Tina Z. agreed too quickly, "We didn't know. Couldn't have known. Hazel's right." She started to clean up, shuffling and stacking and restacking the surveillance stills and faxes in the OCD way she did when something was weighing on her. Fish could recognize her moods, but generally didn't understand them.

His mother liked to remind him that Tina Z. was married. Fish's standard response was that she was just a friend.

Kirby started to ask her another question, but Tina beat him to the punch, deflecting, "Why are you always all dressed up now?" in reference to Kirby's latest fancy suit.

"I'm not."

"Yes."

"No."

"You are. Yes. That fucking suit."

Kirby looked down at what he was wearing, as if he just had noticed it, too.

"That's the one," Tina agreed.

Fish felt like a guy watching a tennis match. Kirby changed subjects; now he was the one deflecting. "Do we know who paid Flavian's bail?"

"Flavian himself," Fish said. "Believe it or not. From a Mexican bank account he had with over a quarter-million bucks in it."

Tina's brow creased. This didn't seem to compute for her. "Flavian's our local distributor?"

"No. Flavian's a pawn in a bigger game," Kirby insisted.

Fish had more, though, he'd been saving it. "Another wire transfer from the same account same day he got sprung: ten thousand bucks, to Gun Heaven. Van Houten's shop out in Hemet." He figured that settled it.

"Flavian was dead before the hit on Mahrez's wife even happened. We need to arrest Van Houten. He's key. If we can tie him to the—"

"—if we can tie him to the bomb," Tina overlapped Kirby, "we can try to flip him on whoever hired him."

Fish struggled to catch up. "Wait. I just told you it was *Flavian* that hired him—"

Kirby interrupted, "Hazel, think: Is it credible that Flavian Bolero is managing the movement of twenty to fifty kilos of cocaine over the border every month? Or that Juan Blanco would trust him to do so?"

Fish didn't much enjoy the free-floating speculation that Kirby and Tina thrived on. "Well. No. But—"

"I bet he never even knew he had a Mexican bank account. Because if he did, he wouldn't have been selling cars and living in a trailer park."

Fish's head hurt.

"You got a date?" Tina Z. asked Kirby pointedly, back on the suit.

"No."

Frustrated, Fish didn't want them going down this road again, "Kids, can we please not get sidetracked—"

"I do not," Kirby told Tina again, because she just kept staring at him, "have a date with anyone."

"You're going out with her," Tina said.

"New policy. We have to dress for work."

"Oh." Fish thought Tina looked disappointed that Kirby couldn't have made up a better excuse.

He tried again, "Can I just ask: If Flavian is the pawn, and Blanco is the chess master—"

"Grand master," Tina corrected.

"What?"

"Staying on the chess theme."

"I'm saying, we leap the local guy and get Blanco. Let him tell us who his partner is," Kirby said.

Had Kirby lost his mind? Blanco was in Mexico, Blanco was Mexican, they—none of them—had any jurisdiction there. The local was their only play. Fish sighed. "Aw, geez. Kirby—c'mon—don't, don't don't. Blanco? That is a dog that don't hunt."

"Always a first time, Hazel."

And a last one, Fish thought grimly. But, well, at least they had a plan, a direction. Forward movement.

"You taking her somewhere fancy?" Tina asked, still on it.

Kirby ignored her. "I'll arrange warrants for Van Houten, his shop, and his house. Still Task Force, we'll get extra bodies, but you guys ride point."

"Go slow. Be gentle," Tina trolled. She was up and moving. "I'll go clear this with the boss. Hazel? Call me in thirty?"

"There is no date," Kirby said.

"Sure. Keep telling yourself that."

Fish asked Kirby if they should put Mahrez back under some kind of protection.

"If he'll agree to it," Kirby said.

"Why wouldn't he agree?" Tina wondered from the doorway, even though they all knew the answer.

TEACUP POODLES TUMBLED and growled on the grass.

Backyard of his property skimmed with twilight, Mahrez stood, no expression, looking out at the tailings of a quiet sunset that had broken for one glorious moment beneath the regathering clouds, and the slate sea's ragged whitecap tessellation.

He didn't know what to do with Rose's dogs.

In fact, he'd forgotten all about them until, while he was moving swiftly through his house, sloshing the solvent he'd brought from the factory over floor and furniture, dousing everything, the dogs had come skittering out of her room, snuffling, sneezing, barking, determined to get as far away from the foul smell as they could. They darted out the open back door, and he followed them, forgetting that she was gone, worried that they'd run away and she'd be heartbroken.

He'd had no life before he met her, just the all-consuming illegal enterprise (or, later, the all-consuming effort to walk away from it) and his understanding with Vic and the endless parade of related incidents and adventures linked only by their chronology and his participation in them. No ex-wives, no bastard children; he'd lied and used, taken liberties and ruined reputations, broken hearts, dropped friends and become irreconcilably estranged from his extended family, missed both parents' funerals, burrowed deep into a corrupted version of bodhisattva in which nothing mattered but the moment and that he could justify his nihilism.

Rose had swept that all away. Reconnected him with the exquisite suffering of existence and gave him back his soul.

He fought back tears.

A chill wind blew in from the ocean, and the yard lights came on automatically. The little dogs grew tired, or bored with their ear-grab, and circled closer to him, scratching at the lawn and shaking their fur full.

He scooped them up; he could hold them both in one arm, snug against his side, their breath quick and their bodies trembling as he walked back inside, through the house he'd built and had expected to live in for the rest of his rescued life.

Mahrez found a canvas sports bag in a closet and folded a

towel in it, and put the poodles in the bag. They calmed right down, as if being carried around was their point and purpose. Staring up at him with empty brown eyes. He left the front door open when he walked out with the dogs. Flicked the chrome lighter he'd been given by his father, the lighter etched with an OSS insignia that his father said a quiet regular customer had left on the bar at Musso & Frank's up in Hollywood, where his father had worked for thirty years. A quiet regular who, his father said, had come in one time with a black woman jazz singer of modest fame. This guy'd been some kind of spook during World War Two and Korea and was headed that same night to Vietnam as an adviser after working as a gumshoe and problem solver for Paramount, Metro, and Fox. A quiet regular whose flight to Saigon, his father learned a few days later in the *Times*, had gone down in the South China Sea, no survivors. Mahrez's dad had kept the lighter under the register in case the jazz singer ever came back for it, because he was convinced they were in love—doomed, though, he said, because, black and white. When Mahrez later told his partner Vic of the strange radix of the lighter, Vic was of the opinion it was a flat-out lie. But it was a story his father liked to tell, because it involved mystery and romance and took place far from the beautiful, balmy, languid lassitude of San Diego.

Which his father had come to call Losertown.

God, how Mahrez hated it now.

The lighter had an excellent flame.

Mahrez turned and tossed it back through the front doorway, and it ignited the solvents and the hallway filled with flame. He backed away with the bag of dogs, watching the fire bloom.

The headlights of the Aston Martin curled out of the driveway, Mahrez at the wheel, leaving his burning house behind. He was two blocks away when two cop cars came flying around the corner, bubbles ablaze. The Aston Martin pulled dutifully to the curb, and the police blew past, drawn to the end of the street by the surging smoke and flames of his self-erasure.

8

"LEBANON. That's where I got scared for the first time." Tina Z. was confessing to Fish. "The crazy Stone Age villages in the shadow of skyscrapers and all these chic, Eurotrash beachfront hotels. Skinny, wide-eyed young studs jacked on nicotine and religion. All these women covered up in those crazy tent dresses, whatayacallum, chadors, head to toe. Floating down the streets like black ghosts."

She knew Fish had little interest in things thousands of miles away, but talking kept her mind off Bert.

"The fuck were you doing in Lebanon?"

"Legal attaché thing. Investigating the embassy bombing." She said, "Lemme just tell you, Hazel, the Middle East, what we're doing there? Is not a sustainable thing. This whole Iran-Contra mess? It's wrong. We're in over our heads. And you know what? Sooner or later a hard rain's gonna fall."

"Here or there?"

Tina just shook her head: *wherever*. Maybe Bert's meeting with Van Houten was just some crazy coincidence.

"I don't know," Fish said. "Reagan got the hostages back. I gotta believe he knows what he's doing."

Tina Z. was well aware of how Fish stood on the subject, and didn't care. "I was billeted right next door to the Marine barracks when they blew. Did I tell you that?"

"No way."

"Yeah. They put me and this other girl up separate from the guys because, you know: woman."

Fish nodded, mostly missing her sarcasm. "That must've been insane."

"Knocked us out of our beds," said Tina. "We ran out into this storm of dust and smoke. A couple snipers were shooting down from the tops of buildings, luckily they were shitty marksmen, we kept hearing the pop of the missed shots, and the chipped cement spitting around us. And then this weird roaring hush. It went on for a while, before we figured out what it was: hundreds of voices, yelling for help."

She stopped.

Tina stared out the window at the sunbaked sweep of high desert, and the bleached cinder-block- and clapboard-clad shop that was Gun Heaven, two hundred yards distant. Fish didn't say anything. The car broiled, despite the air-conditioning, forming little thermals where the cool air swerved and settled at their feet, while the tops of their heads felt like they were in an oven.

"You have nightmares about it?" Fish asked after a while.

"I started meditating on the number forty thousand. Which

is how many children die every day from easily preventable ill-nesses," Tina said. "Forty thousand. Recognizing reality leads you away from the self-centered into a more, you know, tran-scendent realm." She glanced at Fish; he nodded soberly but probably had no idea what in the world she was talking about.

"Where going with the flow is the only option," Tina added, helpfully.

"How's the baby?"

Tina didn't like thinking about Willa while she was working. "Good. Fun."

Luckily, Fish was terrible with small talk that didn't involve off-roading, football, or porn stars. They fell quiet. Tina drowsed, sleepy, and wondered if she could risk taking a quick nap. But Fish finally found the courage to ask the question that for the past couple of hours she'd been worried he'd ask. "Hey. So. Are you and Kirby . . ."

Tina Z. looked at him. He was looking straight ahead, out of the car, his face a little red. "No," she lied.

"Oh." Fish kept staring out the windshield. "Good. I mean, I didn't think so. It's just sometimes, when we're all together. All that shit with the suit."

"No," she lied again. "Jesus, Hazel."

"Yeah. Sorry. I . . ."

It was awkward. Tina's eyes softened. Fish had a crush on her, she knew it; she couldn't reciprocate. Couldn't, or wouldn't, or both, it didn't matter. Life was weird and complicated, and ulti-mately, she had decided, long ago, a matter of managed disap-pointment. She wished Hazel could just be a friend, she needed friends.

Gun Heaven was closed. No cars parked out front. Windows

empty, door double-bolted with a security gate pulled across it. Nothing moving.

Dust devils gyred through a yard of rusting barrels.

Their police scanner crackled: "Stand by."

Fish squirmed in his seat and tugged at his jeans. Tina mused: Standing by was the organizing principle of her career.

"YOU LOST HIM?" U.S. Attorney Colter's face warped with irritation, and Kirby got a glimpse of how hard she'd look middle-aged: "You lost him. I don't understand. How could you lose him?"

Air-conditioning blew stale waves of respite over Kirby and Colter in the Federal Building cafeteria, with the furniture that looked like some second-rate Danish designer had unloaded all his bad ideas for teak laminate. They sat across from each other at a little table surrounded by twenty matching empty table-and-chairs sets.

"He burned his house down," Kirby explained to Colter, slow and deliberate, as if she hadn't heard him before. "We found his car abandoned on a side street in La Jolla."

"And where were *we*? You didn't have eyes on him?"

Kirby stared at her, dumbfounded. "You wouldn't approve it," he said.

"I wouldn't approve protection. I didn't say you couldn't have somebody watching him."

This was said with a mother's scolding tone and there was no irony in it; Kirby was beginning to wonder if she had a sense of humor at all. He looked away and let a silence rise. A lone craft service employee was counting cash from the register drawer and putting it in the bank deposit pouch for later.

This was the room where Kirby had first made love with Tina Z. On this very Danish modern table, after hours, dark, the door locked, her lean, strong legs up over his shoulders like bolsters.

And now the evil queen.

"I want him back," Colter insisted.

"We don't need him."

"You're not listening to me."

"He's broken. We broke him."

"I don't care."

"Probably going to ground."

"What?"

"Seclusion. Hiding."

"I don't care."

"The bomb was meant for him; people from his past want to kill him for fear he'll rat them out, thanks to us. Or Poole, take your pick. But both, really." Kirby stood up, agitated, and walked away from the table, and came back. He put his hands flat and leaned down. "Everything he cared about is gone, you haven't got any leverage over him anymore."

"Not me, we." Sabrina Colter scoffed, "And he's still a material witness in a major Justice Department investigation—"

"I'm thinking the gun dealer, Van Houten, is gonna give us our Mexican drug connection. I'm focusing on that."

"I will not run this department on hunches and guesses."

"You're not running anything, you're an errand girl for a bunch of Washington ideologues."

She narrowed her eyes and showed teeth. "Gilbert, don't push me. I can have you transferred to the fraud desk, you'll wither and die under an avalanche of actuarial tables before you see another criminal case."

"It's not a hunch. We get Van Houten, we can roll him on whoever ordered the hit on Mahrez, find out who is flooding our region with weasel dust, and call it a very good day. You'll probably get your first citation for meritorious work."

"And Mahrez?"

"You mean Poole, don't you?" Before she could answer, Kirby said to her, as if to a child: "This case is about cocaine coming across the Mexican border to some unknown in-country whole-saler. And murder-for-hire."

"People who do drugs deserve their fate. We're at war. I want Mahrez," Colter said petulantly.

"No. You and your cronies want to upend a rising progressive Democrat who's threatening the conservative hegemony in San Diego County."

She was unruffled. "It's all of a piece: your part, my part. Why can't we both have what we want?"

"What you want has already caused the death of an innocent woman and her bodyguard."

"Nobody is innocent!" she exploded. "Not her! Not the Gua-temalan rent-a-cop! Not this morally corrupt, leftist, welfare-spreading mayor who tells people whatever they want to hear!" She took a beat, calming. "Not Mahrez." And then, looking fiercely, accusingly, at Kirby. "Not you."

Kirby thought: You have no idea.

But then, as he stared at her longer, and she said nothing, just stared back, he understood, and it scared him: Oh, shit. Maybe she does.

"I GUESS MY POINT IS, you spend a little time out in the real world, it makes you appreciate coming back to a civilized society."

"Middle East is the real world?"

Tina said that it was, now. She was sweating like a warthog, felt warm rivulets of perspiration running under her tactical vest.

"What about the Soviet fucking Union?" Fish said, and she could tell he was still raw from asking her about Kirby. "Or China. Stirring all that shit up in Salvador, right on our fucking doorstep? Middle East is a bunch of camel jockeys a million miles away, I mean, tents and carpets, right? And oil, but. Meanwhile a thousand nukes are pointed our way by a population of raging, first-world communists just itching to blister our free-loving butts the minute we take our eye off the ball. Thank God for Ronald fucking Reagan."

He was serious. Tina burst out laughing. She couldn't help it.

"What?"

Eyes watering, her bladder aching from warm Diet Pepsi, she tilted against the armrest and laughed. Fish wasn't smiling. He looked hurt.

"What?"

The radio crackled, a spotter barked "Suspect incoming," and moments afterward a high-water Chevy pickup truck with huge tires and decals and a blue-chrome roll bar came thundering into the dusty gun shop parking lot, made a wide circle like a dog settling down, and parked facing out.

The gun dealer, Van Houten, dropped two-footed out of the cab like a little kid dismounting a high swing. For a moment Tina thought of Bert again, and the potential shitstorm coming, then pushed it from her mind. It was a coincidence, she wanted to keep telling herself. She watched as the fat man hitched up his jeans, unfurled a jangling snarl of keys, and started to unlock the door.

Fish had already turned the ignition and dropped the car into gear when Tina Z. put a hand on his because the radio crackled again with "Stand by." Sure enough, a filthy Land Rover had followed the pickup into the Gun Heaven yard and now slotted in beside it. Two sturdy white women in high-collared, ankle-length prairie dresses and Marie Osmond hairdos emerged, the younger one, a teenager, visibly pregnant. Van Houten barked at them from the shop doorway, then disappeared inside.

Tina sighed. "Dammit."

"Well, this just got complicated," the radio concurred with her. "Over."

A third car rumbled in: Japanese four-door, Accord or Acura, Tina noted, or something equally generic, even Fish couldn't tell the difference from distance. It eased up directly behind the truck, and a pair of spry sixty-somethings climbed stiffly out and stretched, a bronzed silver fox and his pinkish wife, tennis shorts and sundress, respectively, twitching nervous energy as they watched Van Houten's women get to work. The hot wind off the Anza-Borrego badlands barely trembled the teased mullets of lacquered tresses made more hat than hair; the pregnant one climbed up into the truck bed and fired up an air compressor while the older woman popped the trunk of their car, then collected an air wrench the teen handed down to her and started powering off bolts holding the sedan's rear quarter-panel in place.

"Surreal," Fish remarked.

Van Houten reemerged from Gun Heaven with an armload of automatic weapons cocooned in Bubble Wrap.

"What are those," Tina wondered, "M16s?"

"No, it's that Soviet commie AK piece of shit."

The quarter-panel was off the sedan. Van Houten and the pregnant teen packed and duct-taped the guns into some dead space above one wheel well, then moved to the other side to do the same with more Kalashnikovs while the older woman began to power-bolt the first fender back in place. The retirees just waited, chattering like it was a church picnic.

"Snowbirds are looking at eighteen months in Lompoc," Fish said.

"Do these old people even think?"

"Not to defend them, but it ain't easy living on a fixed income. Inflation. Social Security and a maybe pension that got skeezed in the savings and loan scandal. Someone tells them you can make easy money driving a car across the border, don't ask questions. Couple thousand bucks for a few hours, maybe time even to stop at a dog track, two-dollar frozen strawberry margaritas and a boxed trifecta."

"Still."

Fish was gesturing. "Well, hey, lucky day: Here's your weapons case all wrapped up with a bow, Tina Z."

The radio hissed, "Agent Z., you want to bust the snowbirds, too? Over."

Tina took the radio mic out of its cradle, toggled the button.

"Negative. Not here, okay? Let them drive away. Tail 'em and take 'em down at the border. Over."

"Copy that."

"I'm going to feel like I'm arresting Gramma and Grampa," she said to Fish.

All done, the trunk slammed shut, Van Houten handed to the old man in the tennis shorts a fat white envelope of what could only be cash, they shook hands, and the geriatric mules got back in their car.

"Guys, let's also try to isolate the target from the women," Tina said on the radio. "I don't want the pregger teen subject to any potential Second Amendment nonsense when the primary realizes what's coming down on him. Over."

The radio just clicked its affirmative.

The Japanese sedan pulled out and hurried away, raising dust. Van Houten struck a pose, hands on hips, watching it go, engaged in some kind of discussion with the two women. He kissed them both on the mouth.

Tina winced. "Ew."

Fish grinned. "Yeah, baby."

Van Houten's women opened the doors of the Land Rover to let the interior heat clear, and the gun dealer strode back to the shop door to lock up.

"Okay, showtime."

Fish punched the accelerator to join a cavalry charge on Gun Heaven, half a dozen police and federal vehicles bearing down on the suspects in a pincer move.

Their Rover trapped, the two women tried to make a run to the building, but law enforcement was on them too fast, splitting them from Van Houten, who, defiant, had lurched into his shop and was struggling to bolt the door when Tina Z. and Fish, out of their car, hard on his heels, approached yelling, "FBI! Keep your hands away from your body! Get down on the ground! Get down on the ground!"

The pregnant teen screamed and spat when Tina raced past her. State Troopers pulled both women back to cover as Fish shouldered through the door after Van Houten and into the shop before Tina could stop him.

"Fish, wait!"

It was a typical Hazel Fish concrete cowboy move, and dumb; Fish didn't know who or what else was inside, or how it laid out, protocol demanded a tactical approach. Besides, they had the gun dealer trapped, surrounded. Contain and control. Yeah, yeah, Fish would later say to Tina, semiapologetic, "and enough firepower in that fucking cinder-block bunker to blow us apart and hold off half a division."

Van Houten hustled through the maze of high shelves in his shop and Fish lost track of him. Impetuous but not completely stupid, the DEA agent flopped forward and rolled to the cover of an aisle stacked with survivalist MREs, yelling back, "I've lost visual." Tina came scrambling in the door behind him, staying low. "FBI! We're FBI! Ellis Van Houten, we have a warrant for your arrest!"

She didn't really expect a response. The world went weirdly silent. Outside, Van Houten's shrill women were reciting all kinds of Old Testament at whoever had the misfortune of handcuffing them. Two Task Force plainclothesmen with shotguns crowded up to either side of the open door, and just as they slipped inside automatic-weapon fire began to shred the room, wild. Shelves of freeze-dried food above Fish were pulverized, a fine aromatic silt of edible nothing swirled in the shop like smoke.

Fish could see Van Houten's reflection in a glass display case, he was hunkered in the back room doorway, pale belly flopped over his pants, wedged behind the sales counter and jamming another extended banana magazine into an AR-15 rifle. Fish popped up and laid down a pattern fire, driving the bearish man into the back room for cover.

"Hazel, we can wait him out," Tina hissed. But Fish, who she knew would be pretty ticked off now by getting shot at, went forward, he had no other gear, a quick crabwalk on his hands and toes.

More automatic gunfire ripped the shop apart, Van Houten swinging out into the doorway and unloading half his clip. One of the shotgun cops dropped, just outside, with an astonished intake of air. His partner grabbed him and dragged him away.

Another burst from the assault rifle. Bullets sawing at the shelf cover behind which Tina had flattened herself, hoping that there was enough mass and matter between her and the shooter.

She lifted her head and looked for Fish. He was still scrambling forward. Particles glinted and swirled in sunbeams through the barred windows like whirling galaxies of stars. Van Houten put another clip into the AR and tried to locate Fish, but Tina Z. rose and squeezed off careful, measured shots that caused the fat man to flop backward again, and now she was pissed: "Hazel! C'mon. Mellow the fuck out! We don't have to rush this."

"Language? And the hell we don't. No. We need to get him now. Don't give him time to think."

Tina said, wry, "As if thinking is going to be his strong suit."

Fish laughed, letting off tension. With a faint "Fuck you," Van Houten threw two aimless bursts at them, then kicked the back-room door shut so they couldn't see him. There was the sound of his boots scuffing on the floor, the sound of cardboard tearing, the ragged wheezing of an overweight weekend warrior in full funk. Tina tried to imagine him, panicked, turning in circles. Security bars over all the windows, cops and Feds waiting outside; there was no way out.

But a trapped animal is a desperate adversary. And desperate, she knew, is deadly.

COLTER WAS ON him now, now, predatory, no more pretense of politeness: "You were a bad boy, Mr. Kirby, back in your private practice days."

"Those files were sealed."

"I don't know what's worse. That you settled so cheap, or that you really believe in the concept of sealing."

"If you've looked at them, it's actionable prosecutorial misconduct—"

"—A slam-dunk civil class-action case suddenly, poof, settled, just like that? With attendant murmurings of attorney misbehavior of a, well, sexual nature." She studied him. Eyes liquid, deep enough to drown in. "Sleeping with opposing counsel? Just guessing."

Kirby said nothing.

"I admit that I'm impressed, though, sort of. Brave man falls on his sword to shield an innocent third party, you lost your wife, you lost your job, and you got exiled to the public sector—"

"—those files are sealed" was all he could keep saying. And, yes, it scared him that she'd seen them.

"They were," she agreed. "And you were thoroughly vetted for this job by the NSA and the FBI, and they're trustworthy and discreet, right? So what could I possibly be talking about?"

The threat explicit.

Colter stood up and came around the table and pulled another chair uncomfortably close to him. Her knees angled over. He smelled a surge of her perfume fueled by the heat of her body.

"What spawned you?"

She ignored him, head canted, smiling. Lipstick tinted her teeth. "Two of the senior partners in your old law firm were at Yale with Senator Lindy. They like to talk. Especially they like to talk to pretty girls who work for senators, because it makes them feel potent and young. They invite you to morning prayer group and touch you lightly on the inside of your arm so the backs of their hands might brush the side of your boob, and they think for that moment they are the center of your universe and they tell you all sorts of things that might help you accomplish the tasks their friend the attorney general has given you along with the appointment that has fast-tracked your run to a federal appeals bench. Is it possible I even know the name of the third party you so heroically sacrificed yourself to protect?" She waited. Kirby's reservoir of easy wit was empty and he had no glib answer for this. "You were a snitch," she said, then. "That's why you hate them."

There was nothing he could say now to defend what he'd done, except that he didn't regret it. He hated it, but didn't regret it. He stayed silent.

"Would you say women are your weakness?" she asked. Colter was close enough to kiss him.

Kirby said, "I don't know, maybe. What's your analysis?" He thought he knew where the conversation was going.

"I've heard it's a black thing."

Kirby blinked. This was not in his file, or anywhere. *How could she know?*

She continued, low, intimate. "You don't look it. You're what, one-third? One-quarter? Octoroon? Do you even know? And"— she leaned toward him, distorted by her ambition, grotesque—"is that why . . . I mean, when it comes time to check the box on the forms, wouldn't it have been to your advantage to check the one that comes with affirmative action? I'm . . . curious."

If he hadn't been so disturbed that she had this most private, intimate detail about him, he would have laughed out loud. Instead, he wanted to be anywhere but in this dull institutional cafeteria with Sabrina Colter. His breath came shallow, he felt the room recede. *How did she know?* It wasn't what she was saying, and how wrong she'd gotten it, it was the violation. *Nobody knew.* Suddenly all he could see was her sharp little teeth and the scarlet lipstick that circled them.

In a whisper, smiling, "You want to be inside me." Not a question.

He did, still, even with everything he now could see about her, distorted, grotesque, it didn't matter, that much was true. It was his default. He shuddered, ashamed, and looked down at his hands.

"Is it true, what they say about black men?"

He found his voice, finally. "You're . . . unbelievable."

"Yeah." She thought it was a compliment, she was unfazed. "Don't worry, I'm color-blind. But it's not going to happen, Gilbert, trust me on this," she purred. "And trust that I will throw your innocent third party under the bus, unless you get me what I want."

Kirby forced himself to look up again, to meet her cold gaze. "And you, you want . . . what?"

Her voice cut, punched, steely, into him. "Hard justice. True love. To make my mentors proud, to save myself for marriage and those mind-bending orgasms I read about in *Fear of Flying*. At least a couple of sweet pink babies eventually, after I make judge. A personal relationship with my Savior. And Mr. Nicholas 'Stix' Mahrez under our thumb, back in the fold as a reliable and ongoing confidential informant for our office in the active fraud and public corruption investigation of San Diego Mayor Richard Poole." She took a deep breath and smiled. Her mouth that hellish mire of carnal red and bone white.

"However you choose to accomplish it," she said, touching and sending a cold shock through him. She stood, she stretched, she sauntered out, ass rocking, tick tock, tick tock.

Kirby sat, motionless, for a couple moments, watching the empty space that she'd left in her wake; sat with hands in his pockets, legs actually trembling, then he got up, spun, screamed, and put his fist right through the glass door of the beverage refrigerator, causing the terrified counter guy to scatter his cash like confetti.

LISTENING TO THE MUFFLED RIPPING of cardboard and scraping footfall coming from the Gun Heaven storeroom where Van Houten had holed up, Tina Z. and Fish reloaded.

"Maybe he's making a fort," Tina quipped.

Fish made some minor adjustments to his legs and his body, twisting, stretching out, trying to find a more comfortable long-term solution on the floor behind the blown-out displays. "We're giving him too much time."

Tina called out, "Ellis? Buddy, c'mon, be realistic. Even if you make it past us, there's a whole squad of SWAT guys outside with big guns I don't even know the name of that they'd gladly put you down with for making them drive all the way from the city, where it's gloomy but nice and temperate, to sweat this shadeless day out in the hot high goddamn desert."

The back room had gone quiet. There was just a flutter of loose shot-up paper on the shelves around them when a breeze came through.

With a hand signal Tina didn't understand, Fish hopped over the counter and slammed hard up against a cabinet near the cash register, a dozen feet from the door into the storeroom.

A SWAT sharpshooter had edged visible in the front door of the shop, with some hellacious variant of an automatic rifle rigged with every add-on his department could afford. Another SWAT cop leaned around the barred front window and smiled faintly at Tina Z., revealing braces. Red beams of their sighting lasers criss-crossed and settled on the storage room door, head high.

"Ellis?"

Tina had just begun to move forward in support of Fish when the storage room door yawned open and Van Houten filled it, wearing a Kevlar helmet and full body armor, sales tags dangling like Christmas ornaments on a moving, misshapen tree. Raising a shotgun in his gloved hands, he caused the sharpshooters to open fire, their bullets burrowing harmlessly into his protective gear, staggering him, but not before a flash bloomed from one barrel and Van Houten's shotgun's blast hit Tina dead center, lifted her and threw her backward onto the floor, where she puzzled over why she still hadn't heard its deafening report, and decided she was probably dead.

9

TINA Z. WAS DOWN. As still as a drowning pool. Her handgun had spilled away from her, out into the open where there was no way she could retrieve it, even if Fish had believed she was capable of doing so, which, in the mayhem of the moment, he didn't.

He was pissed at himself for letting it happen.

He saw the second muzzle flash of the shotgun shell that chewed apart the side window wood and caused that SWAT sharpshooter to disappear in a blur of debris. The SWAT gunman in the front doorway emptied a whole magazine, but still Van Houten stayed upright, dropping the shotgun and swinging a short-stock Kalashnikov up on its strap, into the crook of his arm, and raking the front wall, sending the doorway shooter stumbling back out into the dust of the yard.

The air reeked of cordite and burned wood and drywall dust

and oily smoke. Fish lunged out into the ether from his cabinet cover and fired point-blank, the cumulative impact of the bullets striking Kevlar and tilting the fat man back into a shattered gun cabinet, where he braced himself and began to turn his automatic on Fish, now fully exposed, still five feet short of his destination, surely to kill him.

And Fish thought: *Tina is right about me.*

But Tina Z. was up on her feet, and moving, Fishlike; he watched, amazed, as she leapt unarmed onto Van Houten's back and locked her arms together around his shoulders and neck in a choke hold and would not let go.

Bullets from the Kalashnikov sprayed everywhere: Fish was able to drop, burrow, disappear under a collapsing shelf, a punctured water pipe spewing fountains of mist up through the shredded floorboard, the Feds and cops outside the shop running for cover as bullets popped through the clapboard walls and peppered the surrounding vehicles like hailstones.

The gun dealer whirled, roaring, and slammed Tina Z. back into the wall, pinning her there, groping breathless for a silvery shaft of KA-BAR combat knife he conjured from the folds of his body armor, clutched with thick-fingered gloved hands, and clumsily began to stab wildly back at Tina. Her grasp slipped, he gulped air. Fish, hands and knees, groped for his weapon, and saw through the smoke and water mist Tina clawing at Van Houten's face as the fat man kept thrusting the knife at her— saw her hands find his forehead, grip and tip it back from the Velcro neck guard of his armored suit—

—to expose the pink unprotected flesh of his neck.

Fish aimed and pulled the trigger of his gun.

The barrel spat fire and it kicked hard.

Van Houten's head jerked once as a bullet went in through his chin and up through his skull and smacked against the Kevlar helmet's underside and all the distorted bits and pieces of it rebounded back down through his brain, whereupon he toppled over and onto Tina Z., already dead before the two of them found the floor.

"Get him off me! Get him off me!"

It took Fish and two SWAT guys to dislodge the huge body so she could wriggle free from under it.

"Ow," Tina complained, coughing. Her eyes betrayed a terror to which she would never admit.

"Fuck," Fish said.

Tina blinked back hot tears.

The others were pouring in now, SWAT and Feds, their weapons rattling, shoes and boots beating a dirge on the floor. Fish helped Tina up.

Admiringly: "You are a crazy-ass chick." But he was shaking.

"Fish. You okay?"

"Yeah. Why wouldn't I be?" She looked in his eyes and saw through the bravado to the man who had just taken a life.

"First time?" she asked quietly. But they were surrounded now, men pounding Hazel Fish on the back and admiring the kill. He smiled strangely.

She let it go and gathered. "Hey. Do you know how much paperwork this is gonna mean?" Tina Z. said, pretending to be exasperated, and not wanting to think, even for a moment, about what she'd just been through.

Fish, jacked in his adrenaline daze, drank the ensuing carnival in: Tina Z., the dead gun dealer, the shot-up store, the smell of spent weapons, the comforting blur of his brothers in arms, din of voices, fountain of tap water spraying, puddling.

The exhilaration of being alive.

"Sorry," he said to her finally, meaning it, but unable to dim his grin. It felt unseemly; it felt earned. Much later, after the OIS team arrived to take his gun and his statement and drive him back to the city for all the required officer-involved-shooting protocols, the full weight of taking a life would press down on him. And, alone, he would cry.

Miraculously, none of the SWAT team or support personnel had been hurt; the one sharpshooter had taken a round in his vest, Tina Z. felt like she'd been kicked by an elephant, a few others suffered minor cuts from flying glass and debris.

They searched the body and found keys, ChapStick, loose change, a money roll instead of a wallet, the ubiquitous pager, some loose pills, a thin little flip-top pocket tin containing a driver's license, NRA membership, ATM and some business cards that Fish fanned out to discover, among them, leathered and well-thumbed, one with the U.S. Marines insignia embossed and a contact name and phone number for Sgt. Albert Zappacosta.

On the back were figures and serial numbers scrawled in Bert's childish cursive. Prices and product.

Tina Z. reached for it. Her worried gaze found Fish. He didn't stop her from taking the card and slipping it into the pocket of her jeans, and he didn't bring it up when they were tallying the gun dealer's personal inventory, or, the next day, in the detailed recounting of the attempted arrest, the shooting, and its aftermath.

It would be a secret they shared. Not quite the one he wanted, but enough, she guessed.

KIRBY HAD TO MAKE the high desert drive during rush hour, with a swollen hand and the bandaged knuckles tender, but the X-ray was negative and he hadn't needed stitches. Nobody asked why he'd punched a fridge. By the time he got to the crime scene it was crawling with news vans and on-air talent, and his jaw was sore from having clenched it for the duration of the grinding gridlock he'd endured.

First thing when she saw him, Tina Z. told Kirby she had a bruise on her chest that she swore in quiet confidence had turned the inside of her breasts sickly Easter-egg colors already, "purple and yellow and pink striating right to the nipple," and she offered to show him but he demurred, for now, although it did strangely stir him. ("I'm impressed," he teased, "you even know what 'striating' means.") But the whole exchange felt forced, her eyes were empty, distant, as if she were in two places at once, and he was still reeling from Sabrina Colter.

Kirby deflected when she asked about his hand, skirted Fish's lively and already embellished retelling of the takedown for anyone who was foolish enough to listen, and went instead into the ruined gun shop where the body of Van Houten was being zipped into a vinyl bag by the coroner's crew, and an underfed criminalist wearing flip-down magnifying glasses was attempting with little success to breach the floor safe in the back room.

Arrows of evening sunlight stabbed through the ragged bullet holes in the walls of the building and left odd shadows and hot spots on the mad shambles of ruin inside. A moth-eaten old

California Republic bear flag covered one wall, there was a shattered, framed dime-store copy of the Declaration of Independence and an high school GED certificate and snapshots and Polaroids of well-fed white men like Van Houten dolled up in camo and shooting guns. A cardboard range target, with a nicely clustered firing pattern grouped in the silhouettes of two running figures wearing sombreros (man and boy), had fallen to the floor.

A strange shroud of defeat was trying to settle on Kirby. Even if his drug sting didn't dead-end with the gun dealer, the encounter with Colter had so unnerved and unraveled him, he was going through the motions now, gutted, all his talk of making a difference and getting the bad guys, of serving the People, soured. He didn't want to give up, but also didn't want to face that maybe he'd lost the fight before it ever began, that maybe his whole career as a prosecutor was a Promethean joke: whack-a-mole: catch one bad guy, another one popped up. Flip one informant and he gives you another, flip that one and on to the next, over and over and over, the little lies compounding, everybody desperate to protect themselves, all the way up to the top, where, depending on which way the political winds blow, something happens or something doesn't, but Kirby had no say in it, just a foot soldier, a fucking foot soldier, following orders, fooled by the patriotic patter of sophomore civics class, the illusion of rule of law. The world had slipped out from under him while he wasn't looking, and he was standing on nothing but air, Wile E. Coyote, about to plummet into the chasm and make his angry puff of existential dust.

After a while, Kirby went back out to confer with Tina and Fish about how they might best deal with Van Houten's women, who were presently handcuffed and glaring at them from the back of a patrol car, their high hair somewhat deflated, the gravity-defying bangs flayed and down in their eyes.

"Wives," Fish said.

"His? Both of them?"

"That is an affirmative."

"They belong to some kind of eccentric apocalyptic survivalist church," Tina Z. elaborated. "Cosmic something. They just keep spewing gospel at us."

"And, word to the wise," Fish chimed in, "they don't use deodorant and they don't shave their pits."

"Guns—owning, oiling, buying, selling, stealing if necessary, and, oh, yeah, shooting—seems to be central to their beliefs," Tina continued. "Hating government. Driving around the desert in ATVs. They won't be much help," she added. "I've tried to turn these religious types before. They all want to be martyred."

Kirby nodded. *"A false witness will not go unpunished, and he who tells lies will not escape,"* he said. Off the agents' puzzled frowns: "Proverbs."

"You're an atheist," Tina Z. reminded him.

"Lying lips are an abomination to the Lord, but those who deal faithfully are His delight."

"Sweet Jesus."

"No, Proverbs again. There was this one semester in college when I flirted with the idea of becoming an Episcopal minister."

Fish asked what had changed Kirby's mind.

"I got a C on the final. Only C I've ever gotten," Kirby admitted. "It was a sign from God." He looked to what was left of the sun, bleeding out over the western horizon.

"You okay?" He said it to both of them, meant it for Tina Z.

She didn't look at him. Fish squared shoulders, spat, and continued to pretend it'd been nothing.

"How come OIS hasn't sequestered you?" Kirby asked.

"They got lost. Still twenty minutes away."

Kirby looked at Tina. "Somebody here should have put him in a car and sat with him. He's not supposed to talk to anybody until he gives his statement." He knew he didn't need to tell them this, and Tina and Fish each made insincere gestures of resignation: *Oh well.*

"We tagged and bagged his gun."

"Suits concerned with covering Uncle Sam's fat ass."

Kirby nodded. "Let's get these sinners back to our sanctuary."

Another ninety-minute drive to the Federal Building. Kirby planned to just let his mind go blank.

"WHEN'D YOU GET married?"

They'd split the suspects, put them in adjacent interview rooms, and flipped a coin. Tina Z. took tails, lost, and got the younger one, the ferret-faced seventeen-year-old who kept spitting on anyone within range. She refused to tell them her name; they were running her prints.

"I got a vinyl Chargers rain poncho in my trunk," Fish had offered before the suits took him away. "And a can of Bactine."

"That's not funny. Shut up," Tina Z. had said. She was thinking, again, about Bert.

So the exhausted FBI agent and the defiant, pregnant teen faced each other across a scratched metal table in the Federal Building. Tina had put more than an average expectorating distance between them. There was a mirrored window behind which

Tina could feel Kirby's eyes, watching. She repeated her question about marriage, trying to ease her way into the tougher ones, but the girl hissed:

"That's between me and my Lord."

"Okay."

"You're violating my First Amendment."

Tina just ignored this and went straight at it: "Who hired your husband to blow up Nick Mahrez?"

"The Ventriloquist," the girl said.

"Excuse me?"

"That's what they call him. I dunno. My husband don't speak to me about his work."

"Oh. They?"

"It is better to live in a desert land than with a contentious and vexing woman."

"Ah. Hmm."

"I'm not to speak in church."

Tina felt adrift. "The woman we arrested with you—"

"Wife. Also, yes." She looked darkly at Tina Z. *"Judge not lest ye be judged."* The teen forced a laugh. Her teeth were brown and broken, ravaged by what Tina assumed to be a crack addiction. Shivering, tweaking, and defiant. "Everything's in the Bible," she said.

"Having two wives?"

"Yes."

"Where?" Tina asked, sincerely interested.

The young girl blinked. Maybe she didn't know.

"Never mind, I can check with the assistant U.S. attorney, Mr. Kirby seems to be fluent in your language."

The pregnant teen tensed and straightened her spine to spit, but Tina Z. had already flipped her notepad up to shield herself, annoyed mostly by the fact that this meant later she'd have to transcribe all her notes into a clean one.

"SOMEBODY GAVE YOUR HUSBAND a contract to kill Nick Mahrez," a ruddy, plump FBI desk jockey with crumbs on his meager beard was prompting the other wife, in the other room, when Kirby came in, ID lanyard slung crooked over his loosened tie like a checkmark.

"I want a lawyer. Don't I get a lawyer?"

The agent and this older woman were side by side in chairs, like old friends. Her eyes were red from crying, her hands twisted in her lap. Her dirt-blackened chapped feet were strapped into sandals and swollen like old salmon.

"I want a lawyer."

"You're in luck," the agent said. "Here's a lawyer right now. Assistant U.S. Attorney Kirby, meet . . ." The agent didn't know her name, but Kirby couldn't recall the G-man's, either, and marveled that the bearded agent had found a doughnut in the Federal Building at this hour. Maybe he kept some in his desk.

Nothing from the wife. Her face blank. Kirby pulled a chair around and opened his file.

"Barbara Van Houten. Spouse. No priors."

"I meant a lawyer for me," the woman said.

The federal agent nodded. "I'm sorry, I misunderstood."

The wife ignored him. "I don't have to talk to you," she said to Kirby.

"No, you don't. But, me, I can talk all I want. You need anything? Coffee? Water?" He looked at the agent and the agent looked back at him and Kirby added, "Doughnut?" while giving a silent signal that now would be a good time for the bearded Fed to take a break.

Nothing from the wife. Kirby waited.

The agent sighed and heaved up out of his chair and shuffled out mumbling as if he was pissed off by something.

"The pregnant girl—" Kirby began.

"—Sister-wife."

Kirby grinned, bemused. "You really call her that?"

"Yes."

"You got your own children somewhere we should be worrying about?"

The wife tensed, tangled her fingers. Kirby took this to mean not just "no" but "not possible." The Lord giveth, he thought to himself, and then sometimes he doesn't.

"Bedtime's gotta be awkward. I mean—"

"We share him. It's in the scriptures."

"Oh, uh-huh, well, that solves everything." And Kirby observed that pretty much anything was in the Bible, if you looked hard enough.

"It's in the Bible," Barbara Van Houten repeated sharply. This seemed to be the default position for both wives.

"But not, technically, legal," he said. "In the State of California. Plus there's the statutory rape thing, to which you would appear to be an accessory."

"There are man's laws, and God's laws."

Kirby processed this. "Who paid Ellis to kill Mahrez? Man or God?"

"Man who thinks he's God," she murmured. "Putting words in other people's mouths."

"Juan Blanco?"

The wife stared at her hands, jaw tight. "I don't have to talk to you."

For a long time she didn't. Kirby waited, patient. He wasn't much interested in arresting her, and whatever crimes she was guilty of—by her own accounting—she'd answer for in the next life, so the legality of his lingering after she asked for counsel didn't worry him.

"Did your husband tell you that he fucked up and killed a woman? Blew her into pieces."

The FBI agent came back with a bottle of water, a cup of coffee, and, yes, two sugar doughnuts. "Sister-wife's got a freebasing problem," the agent quipped. "She's down the hall doing jumping jacks without even getting up."

Barbara Van Houten rolled her eyes. "You think?"

Kirby saw the opening and bored down on her: "Let me guess. She came to church to score some white salvation from your husband, Ellis, high desert lay minister and gun guru and crack procurer—fell behind on her payments, she was easy on the eyes, Ellis took it out in trade. Certain vestments removed. Holy fluids exchanged. All those freedom-loving sperm swimming on. Knocked her up. You yourself can't have children, but: Polygamy! Hallelujah! God's will be done. A win-win-win."

The wife began crying again, pulling her clenched hands to her lips.

"How am I doing?"

"I want a lawyer."

Having hit the nerve, Kirby pressed harder. "Here's the deal,

Barbara: The girl's a crack addict, possible accessory to murder, they'll take the baby away from her the minute it's born. Social Services will find a foster home for it, but unless we have a witness to tell us how involved she might have been, sister-wife will do but a couple quick years in juvie, clean herself up, get out, request custody, take her little baby back on the street with her, and God help—"

"SHUT UP!" Everything went quiet. "Shut up." The wife sobbed.

Kirby felt nothing; he needed a snitch, this was the easier turn. "You loved him."

No response.

"*You're* Ellis's wife. Of legal standing, I mean. And it's his biological child. You could petition for and probably get custody . . . if you're not sitting in jail, too, while we slow-boat your case through the federal courts."

Again, he waited. He had all the time in the world. The deal implicit. Eventually the wife looked up. He was sure she was going to. Feeling generous because the man had shared doughnuts, Kirby tilted his head toward the bearded agent, allowing him to have the privilege.

And the agent asked, "Who hired your husband to kill Mahrez?"

Once Barbara started talking, they discovered, it was hard to get her to shut up.

"IT WAS JUAN BLANCO. Both wives have made sworn statements."

The Gun Heaven safe had contained money and documents—more than twenty grand, Kirby told Colter—along with, he added, a lot of half-assed federal gun law paperwork, evidence of tax evasion encouraged by antigovernment nativist groups, a commendation from the John Birch Society, neo-Nazi pamphlets, and a plastic flip-top container filled with floppy disks that contained enough names, dates, and transactions to indict and extradite Juan Blanco from Tijuana for contract killing, extortion, drug trafficking, and several dozen RICO violations.

He had walked into her office fifteen minutes short of midnight, not surprised to find her still working, soft-lit by the desk lamp, using large-framed reading glasses he'd never seen before and which she removed and put away and pretended she hadn't been wearing.

"But the hit man himself is dead."

"Van Houten? Pretty much. It was a clean shoot. Agent Fish has already been processed and sent home." He dropped the file on her desk and pinned it there with the box of floppies. "However, this, along with the witness depositions, should be plenty."

She just looked at the case file blankly. "We can't touch Blanco," she said simply. Lamplight bounced off her desk, glazed her eyes, like a cat, and made them incandescent when she looked up at him again. "What about your local facilitator? I thought that was the whole focus of this investigation."

Comparing notes after the interview, Tina told Kirby what the pregnant tweaker had said, about a ventriloquist. Putting it together with Barbara's rambling, elliptical statements, Kirby assumed this was a sly reference to Blanco running a puppet on the American side of the border. He had a ready answer:

"We'll get him from Blanco. Or a search of Blanco's files and records."

Now she was dismissive. "He's a foreign national, an elected official. You know that. The politics of it are impossible. But congratulations on solving two murders."

"Yeah, yeah, happy endings all around." He allowed a pause, full of irony, he hoped, because: "Except, let's see, Stix Mahrez . . . and his girlfriend . . . and the bodyguard, Emilio, whose nibbles and bits our lab crims are still picking up from a three-block radius, but hey. Wages of war, right? Congratulations to you, 'sir.' Don't forget to mention the close cooperation between local law enforcement, the DEA, and the FBI in your press conference tomorrow."

Colter was utterly unmoved.

"What I've always loved," Kirby said, unable to contain his bitterness, "about this job is how, every day, I could count on pursuing my case using my best judgment without having to get the approval of or listen to the opinion of some calculating individual with hidden agendas. I mean, the United States is my client. It never contradicts me or tries to force me to do things that do not have its best interests at heart." There was emotion in his voice that surprised even him. Colter rocked back in her chair, away from the desk lamp, her face suddenly lost in shadows, her hands in her lap.

Kirby said, still wanting to believe it, "This is what we do— we catch bad guys. We find them, we catch them, we put them away. And we're good at it. And that's the job I signed up for and that's all I'm asking from you now—"

"—And you call me naïve."

There was nothing more to say then, and they just studied

each other, from opposite, shadowed sides of the bright pool of light.

And Colter touched the nape of her neck. Brought it down over her breasts lightly as her hand fell to the desk.

She exhaled slowly, as if spent. "That was good for me. How about you?"

10

BERT LOVED HIS LITTLE GIRL. This was the gist of it. From the moment he saw her slip out of Tina, bloody and alien, squalling, helpless, he knew that, if nothing else, his life was now worth something, this something, this miracle-harvested bitter fruit of the killer bitch and the worthless layabout. Only Willa mattered. And he was good to her, unconditionally devoted to her, asking nothing in return because her very existence triumphantly justified his.

He was drunk. Tequila shooters with some of his noncom amigos down at a grimy waterfront dive in the shadow of the Coronado Bridge, no windows, the walls lacquered yellow by smoke. If he'd been single he would have gone home with the Thai chick his lance corporal Kimo was probably spilling into right about now. Instead he took snaking back roads to his own home, alone, buzzing. He knew them by heart, and was pretty sure the city cops would cut him slack when they saw he was

Marines, even if he was only a fucking shipping clerk, when you came right down to it. Semper fi.

Tina would be waiting.

He lowered his window to get some fresh sea air and take a little edge off the *añejo* he knew he reeked of, and that his wife would rag on him for, but not too much because the baby'd be asleep and what could she say to him that she hadn't said before?

The truck bounced up into the driveway harder than he'd intended and the tires chirped when he stopped it short, and the engine just died.

It wasn't his fault that he'd gotten shipwrecked in supply. And why should it diminish him? Every man matters, isn't that what they say? And they'd both thought, when she transferred with him to San Diego, that he'd eventually be the sole provider, medical and pension, she could quit the Feds and be a stay-at-home mom, but then the babies didn't happen, and she got stir-crazy and stayed with the Bureau and, consequently, started back with field operations and made herself indispensable again and here he was, again, some kind of back-row castrato with his wife singing the lead.

Willa will have it different, he thought, as he climbed from the cab. With the money he was socking away, his baby would be able to do anything, or nothing, be a girl, not a warrior, not a cop, not a stone-cold bitch; learn to dance, wear chic clothes, meet some Mission Viejo USC frat guy with a bright future in finance and a Porsche and beach house and Willa could let him carry the load. Even Tina couldn't argue with that. Could she?

When he came in the door and she hit him, at first Bert didn't even feel it.

The hallway was dark, he smelled perfume, her perfume, cut with sweat and something else, gunpowder or dust, and then light exploded on him and he couldn't keep his balance and his ears were ringing, and, distant, very distantly, he heard a voice calling him a stupid fucking bastard and then she hit him again and it was like a switch got flipped and he felt the shock and the pain and the blood streaming down his chin—Jesus, she could punch, for such a little thing, what was it, footwork? Weight transfer? He'd never been good at fighting in basic, the first of his many failures, spending most of his time on his ass hoping they wouldn't break his nose, which, he was reasonably proud to say, nobody had, until now.

He swung wildly and clipped her; he should win this, he thought, because she gave away fifty pounds at least, and ten inches (well, seven) (six and a half)—or at least be able to get his arms around her and hold her until she calmed the heck down, but Tina bounced off the wall and back into him and she hit him again right under the ribs, and again, and again until he couldn't get his breath and his legs went wobbly and he fell on his side, wondering what this was all about, thinking she'd never done this before, never ever raised a hand against him, even that time, after she came back from Cairo and told him about the embassy guard who'd died, Bert couldn't remember his name, a guy who Bert was convinced she'd been fucking so he'd pulled the gun and waved it at her and she'd stripped it out of his hand so fast he didn't know what had happened.

But she didn't hit him that time. She just cried.

Women.

"You're selling surplus ordnance to contract killers, Bert," she was hissing at him between tears, sitting on him, thumping on him and her leg with the side of her hand, and crying, sobbing. What was wrong with his arms that he couldn't just knock her away?

"What have you done?" she wailed. "Oh, Bert, what have you done?" She took something from her pocket and flipped it onto his belly and he fumbled for it and saw that it was the business card he'd given to that fat fuck gun dealer who'd told Bert he was looking to buy some hardware wholesale for his patriot militia group.

Bert's lips were thick, already swollen, and slick with blood or mucus, he couldn't tell the difference, and when he ran his tongue across his teeth one of the front ones felt loose. "It's nothing," he said, more meekly than he intended. "It's stuff we're supposed to decommission anyway. Bust up and throw away."

"C-4," she said.

"Crap. Old shit," he told her. "And I'm putting all the money into a college fund for the baby," he explained.

"The sunburned guy with the monster truck—"

"Yeah, he's just some right-wing kook. Survivalists. They buy stuff, they go out in the desert and shoot bottles and blow holes in the ground and pretend the world is ending."

"You stupid bastard," she said, crying, but no longer hitting anything, which was a plus.

"I won't see him again," Bert promised.

"No, you won't," Tina said. "You're stopping this, now."

"Okay," he said.

The baby was crying.

"Swear to me, Bert. I mean all of it. Selling."

"I swear."

She sat back and peeled her T-shirt off and pushed it against his face and nose. "Hold this. Pressure." He didn't hurt, really, everything was just numb. There was a massive bruise on his wife's chest that Bert had never seen before, but he hadn't seen her with a shirt off in a while. He wanted to ask about it, but she was already up and in the kitchen. He closed his eyes and heard ice going into a plastic bag, and then felt it, cold against his chest as she lifted and placed one of his hands on it and then rose and walked back into the house to deal with Willa.

"Read her a story," Bert called out. "She loves the one about the hungry worm."

There was no response.

It wasn't bad, lying down, on the floor. It felt, was so solid. You really couldn't fall any farther down.

KEY IN THE DOOR, it opened, but the chain held. Kirby, puzzled, outside, called through the gap. "Tina? Baby, the door's bolted."

Footsteps, light, shoes. Not Tina's: The door swung shut, there was a rattle of the chain unhooked, then Kirby took a step in and found himself tilted off-balance, shoved violently forward and down, catching himself with his hands before he slammed to the floor. A glint of metal and the cold blunt scrape of a gun barrel against the side of his face, his head pressed into the carpet and a knee in his back and a free hand frisking him, patting him down, while Kirby barked at the interloper, scared, "We don't carry guns! We don't carry guns!"

"Oh."

Nick Mahrez rocked back and rolled Kirby over but left the gun barrel resting between Kirby's eyes like an accusation. "Why not?"

"We're armed with the law."

Mahrez stared at him, unamused. "I'm tired." Mahrez looked it.

"We got the guy who killed your girl. Died in a shoot-out this afternoon."

Mahrez nodded, disinterested. "Who told him to kill me?"

Kirby chose his words carefully. "Flavian. It was Flavian hired him for the hit. Ten grand."

Kirby picked up on the hesitation: "Flavian."

"Yes. Your—"

"—I'm aware who he is. Was. Who whacked Flavian?"

Kirby didn't know. He thought maybe it was Blanco, but wanted to see where Mahrez would take this. "Who do you think whacked him?"

Mahrez yawned. He hadn't shaved, and smelled faintly of seaweed and salvia, like he'd been living outside. "I didn't know Flavian. I had no idea Flavian was dealing drugs, so I wasn't a threat to Flavian. Flavian had no reason to fear me, or try to kill me. You know this."

There was a cool offshore breeze from the balcony. The sliding doors were open; somehow Mahrez had breached the lock and come in that way.

"So I ask again, who told Flavian to hire a guy to kill me?"

Kirby said, "Let it go, man. Don't make this into—"

Mahrez continued talking over him. "—I've been out of the business for so long, I've had to take a crash course the last couple days in what's going on, what's current, you know, latest trends, retail, wholesale, new faces, lotta research, lotta recon. Colombians have raised the bar, huh? Back in the day, what we did was so, I don't know, romantic. Me and Vic, we were rebels. Ministers of the great enlightenment, it was . . ." His words trailed off. He looked lost. "Now it's just ugly out there, isn't it? War on Drugs. Sad and desperate and violent and ugly."

"Back in the day?" Kirby said, "What: Ten, twelve years ago? You talk like it was another lifetime. No. Blink of an eye. And don't kid yourself, Stix, it was ugly then, you were just on the party-hearty side of it."

Mahrez appeared to think about this. "Vic always used to say, in a properly managed drug deal there was no risk of arrest. Because, in order to catch you, the cops—or Feds, or Joint Task Force, take your pick—needed to know the place and the time of the exchange. That was where trust figured in. Trust was the most important thing. Because if two people knew the place and time, and they trusted each other, no one else would ever know."

"But that's just it," Kirby said. "Trust. Who can build a world on trust?"

Mahrez fell quiet.

"Walk away. You can still walk away. Take what's left."

"Nothing's left."

"I don't believe you, but—"

"—It was Blanco, ordered the hit, wasn't it?" was how Mahrez cut Kirby off, and he said it as if he already knew the answer, and didn't seem to care if Kirby confirmed it. There was something else he was looking for. "That's what everybody's thinking."

"There is no everybody. There's just you and me, we're the only ones who give a shit."

A longer hesitation. Again, Kirby measured his words. "Even if it was, we . . ."

". . . You can't touch him. The end."

Kirby shrugged apologetically.

Mahrez nodded. "Blanco," Mahrez said finally, "isn't nearly

smart enough to be Blanco. Do you hear what I'm saying? This is what nobody understands, or has ever understood, but that's just par for the course, isn't it? In the drug biz. Where we wage war on an enemy that is ultimately ourselves."

Kirby stared at him, unsettled suddenly. He had come to like the other Mahrez, the one who still had Rose. This one was changed. Or changed back, he thought. "I'm not sure I understand."

"No," Mahrez agreed, then asked, "You a Padres fan?"

Kirby had no idea what Mahrez was talking about. "No. Chargers. Kind of. If I had to choose."

"Chargers, kind of. Perfect. San Diego native?"

"No, I was—my parents weren't—I lived all over, but originally L.A."

"Originally anywhere," Mahrez said. "Also perfect."

Still confused: "I don't—?"

"—This place, this city. Everyone's an import. Military, aerospace, or just floated in on one of those yachts nobody ever uses and drank the Kool-Aid. Mutant spawn of Jarheads and Shredders. Losers. No commitment. Everybody always in a 'kinda' mood." And then, as if reading Kirby's bewildered look, explained: "This Arcadia. Where we live. San Diego."

"No, I got that, it's just," Kirby said, "four years ago weren't the Padres in the World Series?"

"Get up." Mahrez hauled Kirby to his feet, surprisingly strong, the gun still a vague threat.

"What is it you want?"

"Walk into the bedroom. Don't look back at me."

Kirby did so, moving gingerly, feeling a hitch in his hip where Mahrez had landed on him; held his hands shoulder-high, like a stickup victim. "Think. Think it through, man. Right now, there's no case against you—you're clear, clean—all the charges were dropped. Stay that way, let it go. Start over. You did it once. I know it's hard, I know you're hurting, but, I mean, life is—" *Life is what?*

He stopped.

Felt an emptiness behind him, turned.

Mahrez was gone. The balcony door open, drapery blowing. A soft mist had tucked in against the coastline. The front door wheezed in, unlatched.

He felt the chill.

KIRBY WAS IN HIS OFFICE early the next morning, stacking books, packing up his stuff, emptying his desk drawers, putting it all into a box on his desk. Diplomas, citations, the one photograph of Kirby and his ex-wife, happy, a tropical vacation somewhere he barely remembered. He'd put a call in to Damien Belasco, although he still wasn't sure what he'd say if Belasco proved interested in helping Kirby make the move to the other side. But he was done with this one.

"What in the world are you doing?" Colter breezed in like some pep-squad captain, coffee mug trailing steam.

"I put my resignation letter on your desk," he said simply.

"Yeah. Hmm. I didn't find it, though," she sang. "Strangely." But there was his letter, in her hand, in fact, and she made a production out of dropping it into the wastebasket before she sank down in his desk chair, swiveling this way and that. "Your chair. Is choice." *Choice.* It sounded like she'd been practicing saying it, and waiting for the right moment.

"Herman Miller."

"Who?"

"The designer. You can have it now, I got it five-finger discount from the city attorney's office one slow night, carried it up seven flights. They ordered a whole bunch of them for staff. Ergonomic. Ours are terrible."

She twisted her mouth, coy, assessing him. "Now, that suit I like a lot. Prada?"

Kirby just stared at her. "I can't work for you. I can't work with you. I'm through. I've contacted a couple people, see what my options are in on the client side. Worse case, I can do federal public defense, pro bono."

"Yeah," she said slyly, unable to resist the dig, "I guess going corporate is out of the question."

Kirby didn't take the bait.

"It's the weather," she decided then.

"What is?"

"This June gray. It's got you down."

"June gloom," Kirby corrected. "May gray."

"Whatever. It makes everybody so mopey."

Kirby assured her it wasn't the weather, he'd been thinking about this for a long time.

"Since I took over," Colter guessed. "So not really."

Crossing with the loaded box to leave near the door, Kirby reached into the trash can on his way and fished out his resignation letter and dropped it into Colter's lap.

She ran a finger along the envelope's edge. "I'll wait a couple of days in case you change your mind."

"I won't."

Kirby let an awkward pause grow until Colter relented and

gathered to leave before he did. "I will miss our little chats." Kirby didn't answer, and she took it as encouragement. "We have a certain chemistry," she said. Kirby couldn't deny it.

"If I'd agreed to let you go after Blanco, would you have stayed?" she asked.

Kirby said, "Yes."

She laughed. "Okay." It was a tired variation on a very old joke, but she seemed to revel in it: "Now we've established what you are, so, really, as they say, we're just negotiating a price."

She walked out.

11

LEATHER, MAHOGANY, AND POTTED PLANTS; the requisite manicured receptionist burritoed in dark silk and linen was parked behind the desk with a hands-free headphone, murmuring the firm's name, over and over, "Flynn Swift," like a spell. Kirby waited, poised, knees burning, stubbornly refusing to sink back into the low lobby sofa, his feet flat on the parquet.

He wasn't sure that she'd see him. He hadn't called ahead.

"Mr. Kirby?"

The receptionist was gazing over her big CRT at him.

"She'll be right out."

And she was: trim, tall, no hips, high waist accentuated by the black suit, white blouse, and power heels. Perfectly appointed, the imperfect eyes that flashed unreadable, the thin, pale pink lips that he wouldn't ever shake completely, approximating a smile that he knew was just nerves.

"What's it like outside?" she asked him.

"Oh, you know."

Air kiss. Her small hands on his arms, gently squeezing, suggesting that he follow her down the corridor. He couldn't process what she was saying because all he could think about was the exquisite trace of her nails on his back as he rode to ruin in the vise of her legs, more than a lifetime ago.

She had a power office, now: a wing of windows gaping out at the gray bay, barely acknowledging the decaying waterfront district far below. Arc of blue bridge, ramparts of Del Coronado, and the afternoon sun trying to burn through the brume. Mock-Mission furniture, dark, substantial, impersonal, a California cliché. A modest personal presence: diploma, snapshots, some collectibles he didn't recognize. A crystal vase with a single rose.

"This is awkward," she said, standing by the desk, neither offering him a chair nor the promise of one in the future.

"How have you been?" he asked, rote.

"What could he possibly want? I asked myself."

"Nothing." Kirby hesitated. "I don't want anything."

"Okay." She knew that wasn't all of it.

"I have a new boss," he said.

"I read about it."

"She knows."

Her hesitation was expected, but it didn't last as long as he'd imagined it would. He wanted them to sit and relax for this, but she just asked, quietly, "How?"

"I don't know." He lied. She was a lawyer, and if the U.S. attorney was opening sealed files it was a civil suit she could righteously pursue, and no doubt would, but she'd lose, as they had lost everything, before. The deck was already stacked against them, add to that Sabrina Colter, and the hard truth was that right didn't matter, in certain matters of wrong.

She folded her arms and waited. He could smell her hair, and her resistance, even from where he stood, unwelcome, still only a couple of steps inside the open office door. He was hypervigilant to her, and the way she worked on him: unique, a superpower that vanquished all pretenders and had doomed Kirby in the wake of her, more than once, to the skeezy gigolo's embarrassment upon accidentally meeting a woman he'd slept with and not being able to remember her name.

He felt the drift of someone walking past in the corridor behind him; her eyes tracked them, then came back to his.

"She's using it as leverage."

"Your boss."

"Yes."

"Why would she want that, I wonder?"

He broke eye contact. A schooner was tacking across the white-capped water in the bay, sails razor-stiff and bright. "To bring me to heel."

She burst out laughing, but there was no good humor in it: tough and sad and knowing. "Right."

"I quit. I gave my resignation."

She took a moment, as if to see if he was serious. "This is what you came here to tell me?"

Kirby said it was. He said he wanted her to know that their hard history had surfaced again, but that he had it under control. That he would continue to protect her. And she laughed again, and he wondered, ruefully, if he would ever love anyone as much as he had loved this woman, and it was not a rhetorical question, and, no, he didn't have an answer.

"If you've really got it under control, (a) why quit? And (b) shouldn't you have kept this to yourself? Saved me the worry?"

Kirby didn't like where this was going.

"Or is this just about you reminding me what a stand-up guy you are?"

"Do you remember," he said, not really answering, "when you told me you wanted to have kids?" Her eyes flickered with something. It was a sore point, the one time she'd shown vulnerability during the whole torrid affair, when she had opened up and he'd seen what she wanted from him: Tell the wife, marry me, commitment, a future. "You said it's all we have. People, human beings. Our brush with immortality, a promise of a better world, the one pure hopeful thing we can leave behind. All the cases, the settlements, the convictions, the bum-rush for money and power, all that is evanescent, you said, shadows on the walls of the cave."

"You remember all that?"

"Yes."

She said, fondly, so softly he could hardly hear her, "I said a lot of batshit crazy while under the influence of you."

For a moment it looked to him like she was transported back, lost in remembering, comfortable with him, saying nothing. Or maybe that was just wishful thinking; he broke the spell:

"You think you'll ever have kids?"

"What the fuck, Kirby? No. I won't, and you shouldn't," she said, trying to make a joke of it, he thought, and failing. "And anyway, the whole immortality thing is overrated. Just more time to repeat the same mistakes."

"Right."

"Don't look at me like that," she said. "Please don't."

He shrugged.

A soft buzzing drew her around the desk, where she looked at the message from her secretary on the narrow LED text display of the office intercom and keyed something back and then looked up at him with what he took to be as much apology as she could gather, though it was also clear that she wanted him to go. "I have a conference call in five minutes."

He made a slight, weird, formal bow, and started out the door.

"Kirby." On his look back at her: "Was it worth it?" she asked.

"No," he lied.

FOR THE ENTIRE TIME he was giving his first statement, Nick Mahrez's face held no expression, betrayed no emotion. The light in his eyes was dimmed, but he was resolute, almost serene, and for four hours he spoke deliberately, and precisely, as if reading from cue cards in front of him.

It had taken thirty-six hours to strike a deal with Damien Belasco (who would never know that the reason Kirby had left messages for him was to talk about leaving Justice for the dark side) and another eight hours to arrange a convenient time for Mahrez to come in. His client was still, Belasco reported nebulously, trying to find a safe place to stay.

"In November of 1984, at a party on a boat in Ensenada Bay, the boat belonged to my then partner Vic—"

"—Victor Arnold?"

"Yes. I introduced my childhood friend Richard Poole to Juan Blanco, a Mexican businessman who was always interested in connecting with young, ambitious American politicians."

Kirby had lasted all of three days in self-imposed exile. Colter had found him in shorts and flip-flops getting some pink on his pale legs at a Mission Beach brunch place he liked only because it wasn't crowded, and the mimosas were tolerable.

"Guess who just showed up in my office," she had announced without preamble, "alone, no counsel, ready to roll up his sleeves and go to work for us?" Kirby didn't want to engage, so she had answered herself, "Stix Mahrez." Colter was smug, sunglasses tipped back into her hair, smartly dressed, pantyhose picking up glints of muddled sunlight like somebody had gilded her legs. "I know: Shut up, Sabrina. You don't care anymore. Well, he says he'll agree to be our CI, and help us bring down the mayor to clean up City Hall. Boom.

"He only had one condition," she had added, when Kirby still didn't respond.

He had been only half listening, wondering how the hell she had found him, but now he had anticipated what she was going to say before she said it:

"Me."

"He wants you to run the show. That's right. You could have knocked me over with a feather." She had been completely earnest, delighted. For the first time, she had smiled like a human being. And it was, Kirby had to admit, a beautiful smile.

"Poole was in the California State Assembly at the time you made the introduction," Kirby remembered and, because Mahrez was talking so quietly, nudged the Naugra gain again, watching the sound meter needles waggle.

"First term," Mahrez confirmed. "That's right." He looked rested, but still changed, like a man who'd undergone a religious conversion. A faraway, closed-for-renovations look. Kirby wanted to ask him about it, but they weren't, technically, alone in the room.

"And what was Blanco's business?"

Up in her office, Colter had a soundless cable feed from the dysfunctional video camera in the interview room, and she absently observed Mahrez's deposition as she attacked a mountain of paperwork she told Kirby she'd been neglecting in her first week on the job. "I trust you completely," she'd said.

"Restaurants, bars, Tijuana real estate. God, I think he even had a Ford dealership back then," Mahrez recounted.

"But principally?"

"Principally, marijuana and cocaine."

"And to your knowledge, did Richard Poole continue to be in contact with Juan Blanco, after that introduction?"

As Mahrez thought about his answer, Kirby couldn't deny that he had missed this. Like a junkie craves the needle, for what it promises, and rarely delivers.

"To my knowledge, yes," Mahrez said. But something in the way he said it made Kirby suspect his snitch was skipping something crucial.

The door opened and Hazel Fish's head angled in, his eyes drawing Kirby out into the hallway, where he waited for the door to fully close after Kirby emerged.

"Blanco is dead," Fish said softly.

Kirby canted his head and wasn't sure he'd heard it clearly. "What?"

"Shot last night, in TJ." And knowing Kirby's next question, he said, "Some swanky disco where all the Mexican cool kids go."

Kirby glanced back through the door window at Mahrez. Fish followed Kirby's eyes, but kept talking. "Shooter reportedly fled on foot in, you know, the usual hail of gunfire and so forth, which usually translates to 'nobody lifted a finger to stop him.' Two dozen witnesses who all went blind in the moment. There's a long line of little Caesars ready to step in for Blanco, and Tijuana cops, what do they care? La-dee-dah, life goes on."

Kirby kept watching Mahrez, looking for a tell he sensed he wouldn't get; eventually Stix seemed to feel Kirby's gaze and looked up to meet it, making Kirby look away, back blankly at Fish, who hadn't stopped his tale.

"A second victim, Anglo, possibly American, was killed in the backseat, but the TJ cops aren't releasing any information on him. Somewhere between none and many innocent spectators got hit by the bodyguards' useless return fire, but everyone else is still alive. So far." Shakes his head: "Gonna be turf war, for sure, and for a good bit, yeah?"

"Yeah." Kirby was silent for a moment. "Possibly American?"

"Well, specifically not Mexican—we're the international shorthand for white guys, is all." Fish studied Kirby. "What."

"Nothing," Kirby said.

TINA Z. FELL AWAY postcoital, flushed and fumbling for her purse on the bed stand, as she continued the story she'd been telling, "—And when he pulled the trigger—when the flash of the shotgun happened and I felt impact and wind go out of me, I forgot I was wearing a vest and I thought I was a goner." Her hands trembled as she shook from its package and stabbed a slender Virginia Slims in her mouth without lighting it. Her knuckles were red and lumpy from punching Bert, but Kirby didn't remark on them; he still hadn't explained to her his own bandaged hand.

She became suddenly aware of the soft click click click of a needle across the end grooves in Kirby's spent Lily Himes record, which Tina had decided she was starting to love. Jazz. Who knew?

"Since when do you smoke?"

"I'm thinking of starting."

"Nobody starts smoking at, what—how old are you?"

"Don't judge."

"Okay."

"It's lame," she admitted. "I know. I'm not lighting up yet, though."

"Uh-huh." Kirby traced the Texas-shaped bruise between her breasts with his finger and she shivered.

"I was dead," she said, after a moment. She rolled up onto him again and found a comfortable fit, hips and pelvis. "And do you want to know what—who—my last thoughts were of?"

A long beat. If he answered right, she said to herself, she would tell him about Willa.

But he said, "No."

Her heart tripped, she nodded, brave smile, hiding her disappointment and pretending she was expecting him to say just that all along. They had discrete boundaries. Her mouth went slack, lips dry, chapped; she feared she was hard-featured in the unforgiving last of the day's light. Kirby smiled, distracted, but holding her gaze. She wouldn't cry, she'd taught herself at Quantico to never cry. But there was emotion in her voice she couldn't conceal, "What are we doing here, Kirby? What . . . is all this? I mean . . ."

"I don't know, Z. I don't know," he said.

For a while they stayed that way, skin to skin, not moving, without judgment, without sentiment. His neck hot against her cheek, and she could feel his pulse, steady. Until it got so dark there was only the memory of the other, and the weight of him, under her.

Tina rose and moved to the edge of the bed, and began to pull her clothes back on. Sidelong, she saw the soft slope of him sit up in some ambient outside light.

"Lily Himes raised me," he said, picking up a conversation she thought he was done with.

"Wait. Your jazz singer Lily Himes?"

"Yeah. The long story."

She sorted it out. Thought of Willa. Stared at him, in shock plus maybe, if she was willing to admit to it, panic. "She's black."

"Well, she was what she liked to call, in those days, high yellow."

Trying to comprehend it. "Lily Himes is your mother."

"No. I said she raised me. Kind of a foster thing."

Tina's mind swirled, but at least she could breathe again. And then some part of her was troubled by why it mattered, and the question would keep coming back, again and again, for a long time, and she would have no answer.

But right then Kirby was talking. Confessing. "It's not really as confusing as it sounds. And my foster dad was white as Wonder Bread, so. But. You know. Love is color-blind."

"Love?"

"Or what passes for it."

"The fuck do you know about love," she said. It wasn't a question. For a moment there was nothing either one of them could think to say. But Kirby, evidently misreading her silence as frustration, uncomfortably resumed:

"My real mom died and Lily took me. Himes was a stage

name, she was born Eula Kirby. Then she left me with her nephew Oscar and went to Tokyo to sing when the West Coast club scene fell apart. I was twelve-ish . . . and, well, she kind of forgot to come back." He took a pause. He sounded odd.

"But you had a foster dad."

"They weren't married. They didn't live together. And he was on a military charter plane that went down en route to Saigon, 1962. Flying Tiger 739. One of two Flying Tigers that went down that day, you can only imagine the conspiracy theories." He stopped again, then said, "I know. Pretty fucking tangled. Anyway. Did I say too much?"

Tina wasn't looking at him, wasn't looking at anything, she was motionless, soft, suspended in the darkness.

"It wasn't as sad as it all sounds," he added, discomfited by her quiet. "She left me her songs."

Tina felt ashamed, suddenly, and overwhelmed, and even in the darkness kept her head turned away so that Kirby couldn't see her face.

"I never tell anyone. But maybe it explains something. I don't know. I so grew up in the gray."

Another fragile silence settled and Tina took her watch and saw the time. "I gotta go. The baby'll be hungry again."

"Isn't your husband home?"

"He is," she said softly, "but." Leaning clumsy, eyes averted, she kissed him, sadly, too quickly and, dropping the unsmoked cigarette back loose in her purse, took out a compact to check her makeup and hair in the mirror.

"Losertown dusk is a saffron shower of soft, warm deceit, promising heaven and delivering darkness," Kirby recited from memory.

She wasn't really listening anymore. "Who said that?"

"Stix Mahrez. He waxed kinda poetic, toward the end of his interview today."

"Mmm."

KIRBY ONLY HEARD, couldn't see, Tina Z. walk out. It never occurred to him that it might be the last time she would ever be in his apartment.

Ninety minutes later he was on a gravel road in the hills above Tijuana, standing outside the private dance club where Juan Blanco had died, Café Mayahuel, his guided tour courtesy of a well-fed, acne-scarred local *policía* captain named DiMaria, who claimed his uncle was an ex–Los Angeleno cop who made bank from a civil rights suit against the LAPD in '68 and retired to Todos Santos, where he was a major player, now, in commercial real estate.

"Note the classy velvet awning," DiMaria said, gesturing as if directing a remake. "Cocaine King Juan Blanco swaggers out, late, red-carpet-like with his posse of hired *muchachas* and local hard guys. There's a crowd at the valet stand, but the *jefe* has his ride waiting, steps past the roped-off gauntlet of customers queued to get in, slaps a roll of *pesos* into the quaking palm of the valet captain—an individual who must've seen it all, no?, yet nobody can find him today—and gets behind the wheel of his Land Rover *ébano*, his retinue of jamooks about to join him, but this shadow separates from the shadows—*gringo, muy pálido*, according to witnesses who may or may not have been there. Suddenly? A pistol conjured from his clothing—"

"—And blows Blanco away."

"*Sí,* Señor. The Land Rover, she was here"—the captain walked it off—"and the killer, he comes quick up from over here. Nobody pays no attention to him until, boom boom, *vidrio quebrado,* it's everywhere, you know, and people ducking and scattering and the women screaming.

"Boom boom. *Dos mordeduras de la manzana,* isn't that how you say it?"

Two bites of the apple? "No," Kirby told him, "nobody says that about a shooting."

"Well, anyway. Two bullets, two bodies. Professional hit."

"Or just efficient." Kirby stood where the captain said the shooter had stood, and stretched his arm out, making a gun with his hand. Even he couldn't have missed from that close.

Gap Band bumped out of the club like the whole building had a heartbeat.

"Did he shoot the Anglo first?"

"*¿Qué?*"

"The gunman." Kirby turned back to the Mexican policeman and lied. "I was told the gunman shot the Anglo in the backseat, before he shot Juan Blanco."

Captain DiMaria seemed surprised that Kirby would know this, but pursed his lips and slowly nodded. "That is true. Strange, unless: Some say this backseat *Yanqui* was *El Ventrilocuo.* And Blanco merely his dummy."

"Ventriloquist?" Kirby remembered where he first heard it. "Was he American?"

"We assumed. We only assumed."

"Did he have another name, this Anglo?"

"*El Ventrilocuo* has been in Tijuana for a long, long time. Nobody knows how long. He had no papers, they say, just a *permiso* from an official in Mexico City, we left him alone," Captain Nostro explained. "I, personally, never crossed paths with him."

"Every man has a name," Kirby said stubbornly.

"Juan Blanco called him *Mi Fantasma*," the cop said. "Ghost."

The night was clear and dry. The dawn would bring another muddled gray shroud of imbroglio. Kirby looked back down the hill, across the jumbled crazy-quilt lights of Tijuana, to the luminous, orderly grid of his own country, stretching north into the big empty.

STIX MAHREZ'S HOUSE was destroyed: charred lumps of rubble, broken walls, with the blackened exclamation point of a chimney.

A black Lincoln Town Car with city plates glided down the driveway and stopped, headlights raking these ruins. Mayor Richard Poole got out from the back. A deputy on security detail emerged from the front seat to join him, but Poole murmured for the man to stay with the car, and walked across the burned-brown lawn, around the ruins.

The still, dark water of the infinity pool shimmered and a skim of ash shifted away from the glistering edge. This ocean view was, the mayor thought, spectacular, and he stepped up on the raised decking of the Jacuzzi to look down at the beach, searching, finally finding the figure he expected sitting, far below, knees folded up, arms braced, staring out at the roiling white surf.

Mahrez didn't turn even as Poole got close, bare feet squeaking on the damp, low-tide sand. Carrying his dress shoes. He came up alongside, took out a typed, folded note, and offered it to Mahrez, who finally looked, but didn't move.

"What's this?"

"Guy at that number works in the California Attorney General's Office," Poole said. "Liaison to Justice. He's going to get the Feds off your back."

Mahrez took the note. Slotted it between his fingers.

"Sorry it took so long, I . . . well, city to run. You know."

"What'll it cost me?"

Poole smiled like a friend. "One autographed Tom Curren tri-fin Red Beauty."

Mahrez didn't reply. The dark weighed on them. The ocean thrummed. Poole sat down.

"You hear about Blanco?"

Mahrez said, "I did, yes." He shifted the note from one hand to the other, to brace himself with a different arm. "And about Vic."

Poole played dumb.

"I knew he was down there, somewhere," Mahrez said. "You helped him disappear."

"Vic?" Trying to sound convincing.

"I just didn't—"

"I didn't help anyone, I—"

"—I just didn't know where."

"No, no, man, you're wrong. Vic died back in—"

"He's dead, all right. Yeah. Was it you?"

Poole was all off-balance, suddenly sorry that he'd come. "What? God, no. Jesus. No." He stared through the darkness at Mahrez, trying to read him, unable to stop the tumble of his thoughts out loud: "I thought maybe it was you." He laughed, hollow, as if it made saying it okay.

Mahrez offered no reaction. "Good. Stay clean, Dicky."

But Poole was spooked now. "The leak didn't come from my office, Stix. I would never do that to you."

That thrum of surf.

Mahrez nodded vaguely; he was done talking, Poole knew.

Another moment passed—was it a minute? Ten? Poole lost track—but at length he stood, brushed his slacks with blind hands and felt windblown grit swirl up in his face, then backed away, slowly distancing himself from his friend. He trudged reverse-course up the beach through the unhelpful soft sand and tufted salt grasses, troubled but, in the way of all politicians, able to gradually convince himself that everything was cool, crisis averted; he had the wind with him, up the long, steep wooden switchback staircase, back to his waiting car.

And Mahrez?

Stix crumpled Poole's note.

Dropped it.

The north wind caught it, took it, tumbled it on down the beach.

Into the inviolable gathering of shadow.

PORTUGUESE BEND

JUNE 2016

1

IT MATTERED TO HIM that his cameras still made the old reflex noise. Flash and click. The romance of negatives and red-light darkrooms was gone, image itself had become fungible, but even in this digital world, the mechanical and the illuminative were forever bound.

What he saw through his viewfinder: the body of an adult male murder victim, facedown, legs split, arms thrown out, splayed awkwardly on polished travertine tile.

Steady. Light. Speed. Focus.

Flashclick.

Blood pooling, black.

Flashclick.

What he saw through his viewfinder: the usual horror show. Close-ups, medium, wide, details, disconnected, all but stripped of their meaning: hands, fingernails, feet, head, entry and exit wounds.

A rictus grin on the dead man, as if the joke was not on him. One unseeing eye, canted sideways, peering into the void.

Loose-limbed, oddly graceful, the forensic photographer was freelance, a contract employee assigned to Long Beach Police Department's Forensic Science Division, and he circled the victim, stepping carefully around the working crime scene technicians, circling tasteful furniture and taking his pictures with his brand-spanking-new retro-body Nikon Df and trying to avoid upending the quickly accruing evidence markers sprouting on the hardwood floor. Late twenties, restless, hair unruly, he had dark blue eyes his first girlfriend complained "saw too much," and this had marked him and confused him because, to be completely candid about it, Finn Miller was always worried that he never saw enough.

Especially here, on scene, on task.

Late light through the big western windows washed liquid saffron through the minimalist Long Beach condominium; a desperate bleed of dying sun over the crazy quilt of rooftops that rambled to the sea.

In the living room shadows the police had in handcuffs, slumped against the wall, a small, stoic, square-shouldered woman who looked to be in her early twenties, wearing saggy desert camos, a blood-smudged Camp Pendleton T-shirt, and faded pink Converse high-tops. The cops believed she'd killed her husband with the service sidearm a crime technician was presently tagging and bagging as evidence. But of course nobody was saying that, they'd only just read her her rights.

"Victim is Charlie Ko, twenty-six-year-old male Korean-American. Some kind of salesman," a big buzz-cut plainclothes cop whose LBPD lanyard said MEXICO was briefing the lead detective who'd found the gun. The name LENNOX graced the detective's ID; he looked much better than the mug shot on it, imposing, pushing forty, hero's jaw, and built like a tailback.

Finn had shadowed him down the hallway a few minutes earlier, past a children's room with twin beds, neatly made, fluffy pastel throw rugs, drawings tacked helter-skelter on the walls, lots of stuffed animals. The little girls who lived here were loved.

In the master bedroom, Finn's photographs would confirm the detective's later written report that there was no sign of a struggle here, that half of the California king was unmade in such a way as to suggest only one person had slept in it, not two. Lennox had stood in the doorway and scanned the room and had noticed a smudge on the bottom drawer of the bureau against the far wall, a perfect blood-red thumbprint made by a small hand. And that was where he'd found, in the drawer, the military-issue Beretta 9mm that had been, it appeared, hastily and unsuccessfully tucked under a sweatshirt that Lennox, without acknowledging Finn was even there, had lifted so that Finn's camera could verify the hiding place.

In other words, good detective work.

"Appears to have been shot twice in the chest at close range." Mexico read from his notepad, stolidly, like a third grader. "His wife"—he gestured behind them—"Willa Ko, Marine Corps, active duty, she's a gunnery sergeant, says she came home and found the body around quarter to five."

Flashclick.

Bloody handprints: small, some smeared. Same size handprint as on the shirt of the deceased.

Lennox looked over and studied the suspect with professional indifference.

"Front entrance surveillance camera is nonfunctioning."

"Mm-hmm."

The sergeant finished, closed his book. Lennox nodded, and started toward his suspect, forcing Finn Miller to step aside as the detective crossed his path. Mexico then remembered one other thing he'd neglected to mention: "Neighbors heard gunshots, saw nothing."

Lennox nodded imperceptibly, leaned against the wall, and let himself squat down next to Willa. His shoe leather creaked. "You need anything?"

A clipped soldier's voice. "No, sir."

For a moment, they both watched the forensics crew work. Then the soldier's gaze dropped back to the floor and Lennox absently looked directly up into Finn Miller's lens as he took a picture of them. No recognition, even though Finn had worked at least a couple dozen recent crime scenes where Lennox had been the lead. This didn't surprise Finn, or bother him. His job was to be invisible in the slur of investigation and procedure a detective has to put behind himself once the case file is sent to the DA.

"Can you think of anybody who'd want to do this to your husband, Willa?"

"No, sir." The girl soldier flexed her wrists against the twistycuffs. Numb, she blinked away tears and confusion, trying to hold it together. Finn raised his camera. Light silvered the trace trail of moisture on her cheeks.

"And you understand your rights, as they've been read to you?"

"Yes, sir."

"Is there a lawyer you want to call?"

"Sir, I don't know any lawyers."

Lennox pretended to be sympathetic to this. "You know, I get it, I do . . ." Lennox made his play, soft, strategic. Finn had seen him do this before. His eyes shifted. He looked like he was thinking maybe he could wrap this up right here: ". . . Come home from your, what, second, third deployment? Discover the husband's hooked up with another gal . . . ?"

Flashclick.

Lennox looked up again, irritated, but Finn had already turned back to archiving the minutiae of a murder. Bloody shoe prints with a Converse tread. A bullet hole that had ripped open the drywall.

"Boom," Lennox said, gesturing. "BOOM."

Willa said nothing. She rocked, and tucked her chin, and her hair fell over her face.

"You do what you've been trained to do." Lennox shrugged. "Sure. It's war. You've got the gun. And he started it." He looked at her, sidelong. "You do what you've been trained to do."

The soldier was completely shut down, blank, emotionless until the commotion at the front door. An older man, sixties, ruddy-faced and life-worn, with two little girls that the cop monitoring access to the crime scene was unable to keep back.

"We're family," the old man was saying. "That's my daughter."

"Sir, I need you to take the kids and stand—"

"Willa?"

Chaos. The girls slipped through. Ran first to the motionless body of—

"—Daddy?"

"Carly, no—Carly—Jade—"

Flashclick.

Finn Miller often experienced time as series of still-life

vignettes captured, accumulated, camera rising and falling from his eye. Light. Speed. Frame. Focus. Brace. Shoot.

Often he wondered, did it make his days extended or compressed?

Flashclick.

Little girls stopped short by the lifeless crumple of their father veered away and found and mobbed their mother before anyone could intercept them. Raw emotions. Flummoxed cops. Lennox motioned for them to wait. Finn stood silent witness, behind his lens, to a life unraveling and a case coming together, which, in his experience, was always pretty much the same thing.

Forensic flags all over.

The guarded look that passed between the suspect and her father.

The sidearm.

The shiny black pools of blood.

And a bagged, burritoed body carried out.

Gunny Willa Ko, eyes clouded and sunken back, hands bound helpless behind her as they took her to be booked.

And her thousand-yard stare.

JOAQUIN SAID TO HIM, "Life is beautiful, huh?" He meant it to be ironic.

Finn replied, without irony, "I just take the pictures."

"Yeah, yeah, yeah. You can say that, but don't pretend there isn't a cumulative cost." The packet for the condo crime scene consisted of a hard copy folder of photos from the Long Beach murder shoot, which Finn had gone back to his studio to print— a few dozen trial-ready, well-lit, utilitarian, and successfully artless forensic eight-by-tens with a secure digital watermark, in the corner of each, unique to every forensic photographer's camera. The accompanying memory card from the Nikon Df was labeled with date, time, and location; it got separately tagged and logged by rumpled, rail-thin Joaquin, a faux-hawked crime lab clerk who also happened to be Finn's best friend. "That's why I stay in the lab," he added. Joaquin had social anxiety, to which he refused to admit; it kept him from fieldwork, except in those rare situations where the lab got stretched thin.

"The worst of this one was the alleged killer," Finn admitted. "This girl who, she's a soldier, but"—he took a moment's reflective hesitation and shook his head—"she just sat there, dude. Wrung out. No expression. While everything she'd loved swirled away in front of her."

Joaquin looked at him curiously. "What did you want her to do?"

Finn couldn't put it in words, then wasn't even sure why he had said anything about it to Joaquin, and wondered if the slow gathering of crime after crime, instead of numbing him, was rubbing him raw. "Never mind."

Joaquin said, again, "This is why I stay in the lab. But. If I could make a small suggestion? It probably didn't swirl, Finn. From the Celtic, meaning life itself."

"What?"

"It probably fell short of, you know, totality. Swirling-wise."

"Okay, stop."

"Unless you're drawing some cheap correlation to the onset of June gloom, which I fully support." Overworked, short-staffed, and underfunded—in other words, typical—the Long Beach crime lab was bare bones; anything too complicated got sent to the big boys in Los Angeles on a favored-nations basis, which seven out of ten times meant interminable delays and repeated phone calls ignored. Joaquin touch-typed codes onto an evidence database spreadsheet on the old Dell computer, booking Finn's photos into the case file, as he elaborated, as if it explained everything, "I'm talking about the endless repetition of what we on the Left Coast laughingly call weather, between April and September, morning marine layer; that gruel of gray pressing down, gloomy, day after day, cock-teasing us with the promise it will burn off in the afternoon, but, no, and suddenly it's August, and you wake up and scratch your ass and wonder, fuck, what just happened?

"*That* swirl. Where because everything gets sucked into the vortex? There's a name for it, I forget—low clouds sluicing out over the ocean and back, cycling round and round, and, the mistake is, when something comes around like that and repeats we begin to think there must be some connection with the last one, but it's just today's fog, no relation to yesterday's, or last week's, or last year's, we're just stuck in a meteorological GIF file, endlessly cycling, all four seasons in one day sometimes. And it wears on us. The illusion of continuity, of connections, of history, where what we really have is a random series of stolen moments, family, friends, distant relations, epigenetic links, and acts of violence, love, and madness strung together to make what we experience as life."

"Thank you, Mr. Happy Sunshine," Finn said, annoyed. "No, that's not what I mean at all."

As it was shift change, and Joaquin was punching out, their discussion spilled across the street and into the Palace of Justice, a cop bar famous harborwide for its inedible food and spotty service by surly waitstaff. Joaquin supped on bar mix he'd gathered from several shallow dishes, between gulps of the watery happy hour IPA Finn was half convinced was craft-brewed spillage sold on some shadowy dive bar beverage black market.

"Things are different under a microscope," Joaquin said, having reached that point in every evening where he would float a new justification for his aversion to doing fieldwork.

"Yeah, they are," Finn allowed, looking out, distracted, into the crowded bar. Arguing with Joaquin was fruitless, but Finn felt obligated to give some pushback. "There's no people under a microscope, for one thing."

"I love people. Are you kidding? I'm a people person. But. Things out there are weird and stupid and devoid of feeling, and there is no God. I mean, explain to this soldier girl who comes home from two tours of duty chasing neckbeards around the Peshawar—from *that*"—half of his thought garbled in a mouthful of nuts—"to *this*, and doesn't . . . are you listening to me?"

"No." Finn was staring, like he was poleaxed, over Joaquin's shoulder, drawn by an argument on the far end of the noisy bar. Joaquin twisted around to look and saw the homicide detective named Lennox trading angry words with a leggy dye-job redhead in a little slinky black dress and strap-heel pumps that weren't really meant to walk in.

"Ah," Joaquin said.

"Who's that?" Finn asked.

"With Lennox? Beats me. Girlfriend? Or fiancée. And don't we hope she's a ballbuster."

Finn cracked a slight smile, but found he couldn't take his eyes off the girl. "How can you be sure they're engaged?"

"Well, I guess we could pretend that fat rock he just gave her is a friendship ring. White people still wear them, I think."

Sure enough, there was a little box on the bar, and something glittering madly inside. "Since when does Detective Lennox go long with anything but his ambition?"

Joaquin laughed. "Zing."

Something the woman said got Lennox all in a twist. Their voices raised, audible but unintelligible in the raucous bar. He barked back at her, sore, his features crimped and ugly, as if a mask had been pulled away and his true soul bared; he threw a twenty at his beer and stalked out, leaving the redhead fighting tears.

"Trouble in paradise," Joaquin said, turning away, the show was over. "A betrothal no more than two brews old."

"Could it be a trick of the light and the distance?" Finn asked, serious. "The way she seems."

"The what?" Joaquin glanced at her again. She was really crying, now. "Seems?"

"Somebody should go talk to her." The way he said it surprised even Finn.

Joaquin turned back to him. "No, they shouldn't."

But Finn was already up out of his chair and halfway across the floor.

She was hunched on the last stool at the far end of the bar. Her bare legs, crossed and angled, seemed impossibly long, Finn thought, maybe because she wasn't that tall, and her eyes were green, or hazel, or brown. As he came closer, he got self-conscious, abruptly aware that what had simply been a reaction to seeing one more woman in tears now seemed, on approach, more in the neighborhood of a creepy skeeze-bar come-on by a total stranger, and the voice in his head kept murmuring: *What the fuck am I doing?* But he stepped up, didn't sit, and asked softly, "You all right?"

She looked sidelong at him, head on one hand, eyes red. She frowned. "No. Yes. I don't know."

"I'm Finn. Finn Miller."

The engagement ring was out of the box, and she was spinning it on the bar like a top. Slightly older than he was, early thirties, he guessed, she wore more makeup and mascara than she needed, and it had smeared down into Marilyn Manson moons, like a center fielder's eye-black.

"I never cry," she said.

"I don't know why. There's nothing wrong with it."

She slapped her hand down on the ring, stopping it dead. Even tear-slung, her eyes had a fierceness he didn't expect. "I hate that I cry. It's humiliating."

He offered her a cocktail napkin. She didn't take it, waiting instead for a practiced pickup line from him she clearly expected must be coming, only he didn't have one.

"Yeah, that's what it is," Finn said. "Feelings. Who needs them?" He slid onto the stool next to her and pretended not to notice the ring between them. "For instance. There's this lady scientist," he said. "Who did, like, a study. Of this very thing."

"Honestly, Finn Miller, who gives a shit?"

"With apes." Undaunted: he'd crossed some crazy line, with no intention of going back. "Bonobo apes."

Her eyes—hazel, green, who cared?—had a spark of life. "The singer, Bono?"

"—No. What? No. Not him," and he said a little louder than he meant to, "Bonobos. Apes."

"Why," she said with rising irritation, "is it that when I don't understand something, the guy thinks the solution is to SPEAK UP?"

She talked in capitals, which made him want to smile, but Finn stayed chill, didn't flinch, didn't miss a beat. Something about her had chased his nerves away. "I don't know," he said. "But they hooked all these men and women up to electrodes."

"No, they didn't."

"No, they did, I swear. I read about it on the Internet, so it's got to be true, right? She, the scientist in charge, found this footage, of bonobos, the noted species of ape, as I mentioned . . . footage of them as they mated, and then, because the accompanying sounds were, frankly, dull—bonobos don't seem to make much noise in sex, though the females give a kind of pleasure grin and make chirpy sounds so, like . . . she dubbed in some mash-ups of animated chimpanzee hooting and screeching."

She said drily: "And that made it better."

"These are *scientists*," Finn said, deadpan, "but yeah: Chimp screeching can be totally *hot* when it's the right, you know, *kind* of screeching. So then she shows the short movie she's made of monkey sex to men and to women, straight and gay. To these same subjects she also shows clips of human heterosexual sex, male and female homosexual sex, a man solo masturbating, a woman, same, a buff dude walking naked on a beach, and a well-toned woman doing calisthenics in the nude."

The redhead had turned toward him, slightly, and she'd stopped crying and a smile traced its way up from the depths. "So *he's* on a beach. But *she's* nude, so it doesn't matter where she is."

"If you keep interrupting I'll never finish," Finn told her. "The participants sat in a brown leatherette La-Z-Boy chair in this small lab at the Center for Something-Something and Mental Health, I forget, but it's a real place, this prestigious teaching hospital–type deal in, I don't know—"

"Canada, probably."

"Probably. And the genitals of the volunteers were connected to plethysmographs."

"Ouch. Well, I didn't see that coming."

"I know, right?"

"Before you said it was electrodes. Not to criticize. Which are for, what, crazy people? As if I wouldn't know that."

"What?"

"Go on. I'm enthralled."

"Hey, I didn't realize at first that you could handle the technical stuff. But now"—he smiled faintly—"it's obvious you can. The point is, it's not what you think. Like, the guys, they weren't into the chimp-on-chimp action at all. You could line up lesbian apes for, like, ever and guys were simply not responding."

"Somebody thought they would be?"

"Well . . . I did."

Then she laughed, in spite of herself. "Let me guess: guys liked the girl exercising, and, hmm, regular lesbians getting it on."

Finn frowned. "Hmm. Okay, you got the easy one. But what about the women?"

The din of the bar asserted itself as the redhead looked blankly at Finn with what were definitely green eyes, an amber-flecked green that, even though Finn knew it was probably just his projection, had grown clearer, and they took a moment to appraise him, as if they were seeing him for the first time, and she evidently decided to let Finn finish, because she asked simply, "What about them?"

"The women surprised them," Finn said. "Astonished science, as it were. The women responded to everything. Every form of contact. Didn't matter who was touching who, guy, girl, primate, the women were aroused when they saw it. They were moved."

The redhead waited warily for the punch line. Somehow knew he wasn't finished.

"Which explains why women cry for what we mistakenly think is no reason. Everything affects them," Finn said.

"Them being women."

"It's science, we objectify. So, see, it's not that there is no reason to cry. But that there are too many reasons to even count."

She stared at him, the smile still in play. "Not bad. Amazing, really, that you were able to bring that back around to where we started. Except . . . you forgot to ask me my name, Finn."

Finn got self-conscious, then looked away, into his glass. "Yeah, well, I never do shit like this."

"Shit like what?"

"This. Go for broke. Never. See a pretty woman across a room and stop thinking and just . . . walk over and say whatever." Then, hearing himself, self-conscious, "Not that the things I said were fake, or like a pickup line or anything. They were genuine." Finn faltered. "Although I guess I could be just saying that, too. From your perspective. I can see that." Now it was a disaster. "Anyway." Time to get up, mission accomplished, not press his luck. But he had to ask, "What is your name?"

"Usually you think more, is what you're saying." She ignored the question.

"Something like that. I guess."

"Is that why your friend is staring at us?"

Joaquin, on the other side of the barroom, still alone at the table where Finn had abandoned him, was taking a deliberate pull at a clearly empty beer bottle and making a meal out of pointedly *not* looking their way all of a sudden.

"Yeah. My buddy probably thinks you're going to send me packing any second. He doesn't want to miss it."

Finn had no idea what Joaquin was thinking, and the redhead was no longer smiling. She nodded, looked to be considering a lot of things, most of them having nothing to do with Finn. She tugged at the straps of her dress, uncrossed her long, pale legs. She lifted her hand like a sidewalk shark running a shell game, and they both stared at the ring, on the bar between them, its diamond throwing sparks of light as she absently turned it with her fingernail. He looked up, and found she was watching him, not the ring. She put it in her pocketbook. Drained her gin and tonic. Kept looking at him, with green eyes dusted amber, the best eyes he thought he may ever have seen, and Finn looked back at her, raw, exposed, expecting nothing.

She said: "And what'll he do if I don't?"

HIS LOFT WAS in a small concrete factory building just off Atlantic Avenue; Finn triggered only five of the elaborate octet of deadbolt locks on the steel entry door as his redhead bar pickup giggled, wobbly on the heels that made her taller than he was, the slinky dress all scrunched crooked, she seemed pretty drunk—maybe she had to be—but amazingly lucid.

"I change the order of which ones are locked and which are open," he explained, about the deadbolts. "That way a burglar can't know if he's opening or closing one."

"What are you protecting, Finn?" She'd washed her face in

the bar restroom, and hadn't bothered to reapply the war paint, so she looked younger, like a weight had come off her. Finn liked her better this way. He wondered if the artifice was for Lennox.

The door swung open.

"Cameras, lenses. Laptop and scanner, hard drives—any and all assets easily pawned by your financially challenged local meth-head." Finn flipped on lights, one by one, revealing bare floors, smog-grimed windows, and not much furniture, most of it yard sale and sidewalk salvaged. A ratty, barely functional open kitchen with a fussy convection cooktop and a refrigerator that had a slow leak. "I got broken into twice, before the locks went on."

"Bonobo apes," the redhead sang tunelessly, gliding past him. "And screeching. And Canada."

"That's right."

"Canadians are the most polite people in the known universe."

"I know. It just makes you want to slap them."

The dominant workspace was cluttered with tripods, light stands, a huge drawing table and chair, backdrop paper spooling down from a ten-foot roll along the back wall, and featured, hanging from clotheslines that crisscrossed the loft like a lazy spider's web ("What's all this?" she wondered aloud), old-school black-and-white photographs, and lurid digital color laser prints of the soldier girl murder scene that Finn had documented earlier that night. Character studies, rich in saturation and exquisitely composed: the soldier and her family, the cops, the dead man. Neither collection was anything like the photographs Finn turned in to the crime lab on contract.

"Art of the human condition," Finn quipped, self-conscious, and then realized how pretentious that sounded.

The redhead stared at them, running her hand absently through her hair. She looked moved. Transfixed. Momentarily at a loss for words. He still didn't know her name.

"I shoot crime scenes," Finn said. "For the police. That's what I do for a living."

She allowed softly he was underselling his work. And stepped close to a hard-shadow black-and-white of Willa Ko, knees pulled up to her chest, head down, back against the condo wall.

"Did she kill him?"

"I just take the pictures."

She kicked off her pumps and weaved in and out, ducking under the crisscrossing lines, graceful, maybe only pretending to be tipsy, Finn thought. Trailing her fingers, she caused the whole clothesline to shiver and sway. She frowned. "These don't look like they would be very useful for the police."

"Yeah, well. No, there's no real forensic point to them, in an evidentiary sense—but they aren't the official crime scene photos, I turned those in. These, I sort of take these at the same time . . . and in addition to . . ."

"Are you allowed to do that?"

"Um. Not—no," Finn admitted. "But I don't normally show them to just anybody. So."

"Just anyone." She smiled slightly and nodded faintly and kept moving through the suspended mosaic of Charlie Ko's murder, stopping here and there to study something, the shadows and light of the loft dappling her legs, dancing over the pivot of her hips, bending across the sturdy roll of shoulder.

A dream, Finn thought; surely he would wake up now.

Now.

Or now.

"Darkroom?"

"You're leaning against it," he said, indicating the corner large-format printer she'd put a hand on, for balance.

"I can't do anything with them, really, ethically," he said, back to the pictures, "on account of privacy laws, so they're just . . ."

". . . Beautiful," the redhead said. "Even when what's in them—"

"—Isn't. I know." She was the first person who'd ever noticed. He raised his camera from the workbench and took a series of pictures of her among the pictures, backlit, half hidden, hair aglow. Either she didn't hear the shutter or she ignored it.

"The whole idea of capturing something, isolating it from the flow of time, is strange, I guess. Right?" She turned, saw that he had the camera, and still said nothing.

"Susan Sontag says photographs don't explain, they acknowledge."

"Ooo, Sontag, he quotes. Tra-la."

"She says that photography is identified with the idea that everything in the world can be made interesting—"

"Instagram. Or Pinterest?"

"—but that entire supposedly objective purchase on the world, with its insanely unlimited comments and false insights on reality, makes everything homologous."

"Big words!"

"Disclosing the thingness of human beings, the humanness of things."

"Uh-huh. And apes?"

"Pictures don't capture anything, really. I mean, we say they do. But you can't really understand something . . . not visually, anyway, if it isn't in motion."

The redhead considered him for a moment, her expression a

language he couldn't read. "Can you stop now, with taking the pictures, Mr. Blowup? Or is that camera the only way you can get intimate with the world?"

Chastened, he put the Nikon down.

She smiled. "She's wrong. Sontag. I'm sorry. Or right and wrong, I don't know, because, okay, she's way, way smarter than I am, but . . . I think yes, you can. Understand. You just can't understand it in the same way. In a photograph, when everything is standing still, certain parts jump out at you. Distortions, even, can direct you to what's underneath, another story that's working inside of it. Not real. But true."

She steadied the print hanging closest to her. The murder suspect, soldier Willa Ko. A stark, unsettling portrait of despair. "Or sometimes, the smallest thing is all the understanding you need. You know what I mean?" Her fingertips slid across the lips of the soldier. "It's like she wants to smile."

"Or cry."

An awkward silence followed. And the redhead, as if just then becoming aware of the rest of the place, turned in circles, frowning: "Wait. There's no . . . Where do you sleep, Finn?"

Finn crossed to the kitchen, to where there was a big cartoon lever set into the stub wall on the far side of the counter island.

"You might wanna . . ." He gestured for her to move to one side, and as she did he yanked the lever and a massive Murphy bed dropped angrily down out of the main wall, slammed down to the floor to fill what remained of the loft, landing so hard and terrifying the comforter on it jumped and she gave a startled squeak. Lights dimmed automatically, and a ceiling panel slid open to reveal a skylight framing a sliver of silver moon.

"Holy shit."

"I know."

"First the locks. Then this."

Finn explained, "I didn't—It came with the loft . . . I don't know why it's all connected."

The redhead rolled her eyes. "Yes, you do." She kept smiling in wonder as she wandered to the bed and sat on it, bare legs hanging, toes turned in like a little girl. "Nothing else? No motion disco ball with the mini-mirrors, descending from the ceiling like in eighties porn?"

"Not familiar with eighties porn," Finn said.

"Liar." She fell back, tipsy, arms out, as if to make a snow angel in the rumpled duvet. "No. You cross bars to rescue boo-hoo babies." She stared up at the moon. "Okay, well, I think you should call me Riley."

An electric pause. "Because it's your name, or . . . ?"

"Would it scare you if I told you I was a hooker?"

"Riley's not really a hooker name. And last I checked, cops don't *marry* hookers, except on TV."

Call Me Riley went quiet and closed her eyes, drunk or tired. "You'd be surprised," she said emptily.

Finn crossed and sat on the edge of the mattress, politely distant. He wasn't sure how this should proceed. She'd invited herself home to his apartment, found the bed—and he was beyond rational judgment, where she was concerned—they were both all in, two consenting adults. But it was like, after a life of driving Hondas, somebody was offering him the keys to a Pagani Zonda. He felt so dizzy with the impossibility of this ever having happened, he half believed it *wasn't* happening, and was scared that he'd somehow break the spell.

"Okay, yeah, so I'm vaguely acquainted with online porn," he lied. "Strictly free stuff, mostly amateurs, of course, female friendly, because I'm sensitive, erotic with a good underlying story, usually involving clothes coming off and a natural progression leading to the viscous release. Nothing too adventurous or, you know, pandering—sensual and tasteful, normal-sized sexy bits, and a lot like healing massage, plus educational: exposing the surprising number of erotic breeze-blown love nests which can be improvised in just one tropical hotel setting."

She laughed, reached, grabbed his shirt, and, surprisingly strong, pulled him over and down onto her. "You gonna be okay with this, Finn Miller, or do you need to get your camera?" He couldn't speak. Her body was hard and soft, all curves and planes, a perfect fit. "What about the X-ray shower curtain," she went on then, as if they hadn't veered off course, "or the robot cat, or the electrodes that zoom out of the microwave and fly across the room and, by some mysterious geek math, arrive here, on the magic crash-down bed where you've cleverly arranged that I would be disarranged with plethyzizzerodes clamping—"

"—Plethysmographs."

"Whatever, clamping onto my temples and, zing, I'm a zombie. Living in Canada. Having lesbian sex with an ape while everyone takes notes, and just one more statistic, crying her eyes out."

"All that was supposed to be a surprise," Finn said.

She kissed him then. Or he kissed her. It didn't matter. It was sweet and real, even awkward, to Finn's embarrassment, and she didn't care.

Perfectly lovely, she told him after a while, with the moon and all.

2

HE HAD AWAKED, startled, naked, in a sweaty straitjacket of sheets. The redhead who called herself Riley was gone, and he took a moment thinking how the obvious thing would be to wonder, now, if the night before had been just some wild hallucination, but he knew it wasn't, and had rolled out of bed happy—no, utterly delirious—to step down hard on something very sharp and painful.

"Ow ow ow!"

Hopping, holding his punctured foot, he had found embedded in his arch the bloodied engagement ring that must have dropped on the floor next to the bed sometime during the night.

"What do you mean nothing happened?" Joaquin said skeptically after Finn insisted that nothing had. This, during the impromptu parking lot triage behind the Long Beach police station following half an hour of Finn at his loft wasting Band-Aids on the puny puncture wound that nevertheless kept slowly bleeding through them.

"We talked, I drove her home."

Joaquin had washed out of EMT training because the requisite intimacy with strangers gave him flop sweats, but he was a sure hand with minor emergencies. Finn had driven himself over and called to say he was in the parking lot, leaking all over the floor mat of his car.

"Talked." Said skeptically, as Joaquin irrigated Finn's wound with hydrogen peroxide, made a perfect staunch pad cushion, and began securing it with gauze.

"A lot. She's smart, she's . . ." Finn was a word person, but struggling suddenly for the right ones.

"Natural redhead?"

"No. I mean, how would I know?" Finn's face flushed. "Just . . . amazing." He didn't want to talk about it anymore.

"Amazing." Joaquin was mastering the skeptical spin.

"Yes. Pretty much. Stop just repeating the last thing I say."

Joaquin stared at him. Finn's face flushed again. "Dude."

"And drove her home, I swear."

It was pretty obvious Joaquin didn't remotely believe him. "Okay. And now you want me to ask around. Because you didn't get her last name."

"I'm not convinced I even got her first name, but—"

"—Riley."

"That's what she said."

Joaquin slapped a last piece of tape on the foot and started to repack the medical kit he'd brought out from the lab. "It's not what you think," Finn said, trying a different tack. "She left this thing in my car. I need to return it."

"What thing?"

Finn couldn't think of a good lie, and he wasn't going to talk about the ring. He pulled a sock up over the bandage. "A thing."

"Uh-huh." Joaquin made a face and walked Finn through a hypothetical: "So how might this go, I wonder? I mean, me asking around the station. Wandering hallways and bullpens, tapping random cops on the shoulder and, going, 'Hey, Mr. Homicide Bureau Colleague of Detective Terry Lennox'—also known, behind his back, as the Hammer, by the way, FYI," Joaquin side-tracked, then resumed, "'you know his girlfriend? Or fiancée? The hot, smart one, yeah, I think maybe her name is Riley, or not, and, welp, she and Hammer had this spat, and my friend, the sad-face forensic photographer you've seen around, he kinda swooped in and hooked up with her last night at the Palace of Justice and needs to return a thing—'"

"—I didn't hook up with her."

"Oh, right. You *drove* her home." Joaquin took a stage pause, then observed, droll: "Dude, in which case you *know* where she lives. You can just return whatever she left in your car your own self. And ask her what her last name is, directly."

Finn stared back expressionlessly, but he was busted.

"She's a cop's squeeze, Finn," Joaquin insisted, sounding worried but hard-boiled. "Walk away."

THE DESICCATED MEADOW held several huge monolithic sculptures of rusted steel, cold and stately among the dead scuffs of needle grass, and the small old man working on one of them—short-sleeved shirt and cargo shorts, arc welder throwing sparks—shoved up his face shield with one gloved hand and watched Riley park her car next to a brand-new Mercedes.

She didn't acknowledge him. She was tired and confused by all that had happened last night, and hoped he'd just keep working so she could do what she came for and be on her way.

Drought had left the broken Portuguese Bend coastal bluffs hotter and dustier than anyone could remember, but the undeveloped south Palos Verdes Peninsula had always been bleak and burned dry, in Riley McCluggage's long experience with it. Geologically unstable and therefore unbuildable, strangely beautiful, a small slice of perdition she'd escaped, and to which she always felt uneasy coming back.

At first light she'd stolen from the photographer's loft like some fallen woman, and summoned a Lyft to get to her own car, where she'd peeled off her little black dress and pulled on the jeans and a T-shirt she kept in the trunk, just in case. She wanted a shower. Her tangled hair felt like a hat.

An orchard of dead pear trees and the weed-pocked tennis court flanked the small manufactured home where Riley had grown up. Her father's big cinder-block workshop had, since she moved out, engendered a litter of smaller aluminum prefab sheds filled with the scrap steel and rebar of an angry old man's Great Art. On the ridge above the compound, foundations buckled by the shifting bentonite clay, windows boarded up, the tile roof cracked and caving, condemned remains of the old Vanderlip land-grant hacienda still glared angrily down at the world, long ruined by the massive ground failure caused by careless construction of Palos Verdes Drive back in the fifties.

She glanced briefly and indifferently at her father, the sculptor, as she disappeared into the house. The structure was strictly utilitarian, cheapest materials, aggressively low-rent. But inside was different, what little decor there was was exquisite, probably priceless, and Riley made no note of it because she'd never not known of it, had at one time been so embarrassed by it she'd made excuses why her friends couldn't come over. She went down a short, narrow hallway to the tiny back bedroom, which still faintly favored the tastes of a stubbornly conventional ten-year-old girl. Half storage, half museum, there were, taped to the pale pink wall, faded Polaroids and snapshots of a flinty, pencil-legged creature the boys had teased: *Stick your tongue out and turn sideways, you'd be a zipper!*

Track and field trophies. A withered corsage. Lots of books. A dog-eared Stanford diploma tacked to the wall like an afterthought.

She caught a glimpse of herself in the narrow mirror and thought of Finn Miller. The way he looked at her; the way he saw *her*. Shit.

What was that all about?

She shoved it away. Hers would never be a love story unless love was made a crime.

Riley pushed a moving box aside and cleared space to get at a recently installed safe. She punched the electronic keypad code and opened the door. She tugged up her T-shirt and removed a thick envelope from where she'd wedged it in the waistband of her jeans. It held cash, a thick cushion of old bills, and she put the envelope with a dozen other fat envelopes neatly aligned on the safe's top shelf, then made note of the date, time, and amount—fifteen thousand dollars—in a compact black ledger.

In the back of the safe, on the bottom, was a small black Ruger LC9 with the serial number filed off. Hitting anything farther than ten feet away with it was an iffy proposition, but the gun had kick and was reliable and slipped easily into the pocket of her jeans.

Riley returned the ledger and removed from a soft Cartier bag a lovely silver-and-gold wristwatch that she was still sliding over her wrist when a voice behind her cracked: "That's a helluva timepiece."

She straightened, startled, and then got annoyed that she'd been startled, because who else could it have been? The old man blocked the doorway, bandy-legged, regal, covered with the grit and grime from his welding. His hair was an explosion of stubby gray dreadlocks sprayed upward from a shoelace tie. Mason McCluggage, once almost a *l'enfant terrible* of the South Coast art scene, had never quite come to terms with the concept of aging out. Her father. Convinced that the only reason fame had eluded him was because the world was too ignorant and undeserving.

"Anytime you want to get your things out of this room, I could use the space."

Riley closed the safe and stood, stretching. "Why? Your new girlfriend have a kid?"

"Maybe it's two girlfriends, and I want to park the spare one I'm not using in here."

Her phone chirped with a text message she'd been expecting. She glanced at the display and told him, "I gotta go." She squeezed past him before he could react, moving down the hallway, long strides that her father didn't bother to keep up with.

"I thought you might make me some lunch."

"Can't. Sorry."

"That cop finally ask you to marry him?"

This slowed her. "How did you know?"

Mason's laugh was dry kindling. "He called for advice. I said good luck with that shit. But maybe you should jump on it. Seeing as how you're all teeth and claw. Like your mother."

This stopped her. He had to have known that it would. In the front doorway, she turned on him, eyes on fire: "And not surprisingly, Terry shares many of your finer qualities, Mason. He's even made the same keen observation about my lack of, well, a gentle disposition."

"Cops meet a lot of hard women, I guess."

Riley let the cut slide. They'd been skirmishing since she was eleven years old. "Last night I met this new guy, and he was interested in finding out who I was rather than telling me who I wasn't. Or should be. Cute and humble and warm—"

"Disney called," Mason cracked, "they want Bambi back."

"—And everything he does is, like—it's filled with life and feeling—"

"Does?"

She knew she'd said too much.

"He's an artist?" Mason scoffed. "Fuck me. Jesus H. Christ."

Riley maintained, undaunted, "And now I'm confused, Daddy. Because I thought, growing up with you, I had men and art all figured out."

Mason flinched as this hit home. "Sounds like a poofter. What's his medium?"

"The dead," Riley said, and walked out.

ONLY THE REPEATED and insistent buzzer roused Finn from fitful sleep and got him up, confused in darkness, and the loft door unlocked and yanked opened to reveal a pale and panicked Arden—"Hello, I'm still breathing"—the underfed hand model who lived downstairs. "Do you have any Benadryl?"

"Do I look like a pharmacy?"

Finn had come back to his loft from Joaquin's parking lot urgent care and tried to do some work, but couldn't concentrate and finally crashed and tossed, dreamless, on the unmade bed until dusk. It felt like somebody had plugged Finn into a wall outlet, his thoughts were caught in a Cuisinart, pulped and chaotic. His heart wanted to leap out of his chest.

Arden showed him her fingers, covered with angry red welts. "I ate shellfish. Who puts shellfish in ceviche?"

"Um . . . everybody?"

Finn stepped back and Arden swirled in, flouncy sundress and tangerine flip-flops, turning on lights, unable to stop moving until she lasered in, possessive, on the Murphy bed and made some mental calculations while her mouth motored on. "And I have a shoot tomorrow. This whole Taco Truck twitter thing is a joke. And yes, you look like a pharmacy."

Finn ducked into the bathroom and came out with a bottle of pink pills. "There are only three left."

"I saw that woman," she said, staring at the tangle of sheets and blankets that Finn worried would confess to Arden a perfume not hers.

He stayed impassive. "What woman?" His muted cell phone started to hum.

"The Clairol redhead. Slinking away at dawn, doing the walk of shame, in her little clingy black silk number." Arden looked sad suddenly, and Finn felt a tug of guilt.

"News to me." Finn even shrugged to sell it. "Maybe she was visiting the IT guy who lives upstairs."

"I'm pretty sure Jeff's into solo play," Arden said, eyes never leaving him, throwing back all three pills, dry. Finn answered his phone to avoid her probing eyes.

It was the Long Beach crime lab. Officer down, he scrawled the address on the back of a DWP bill envelope, another shooting, another job.

IT WAS A SACRED PLACE locals called Sunken City because a whole San Pedro neighborhood had, back in the twenties, fallen off the edge of the continent. Twilight, gloom, and shadows, marine layer pressing down silver spectral, and windy as hell, Riley had slid down the sandy embankment from the gap in the high chain-link fence, and scanned the well-worn paths and broken slabs that tumbled down toward the ocean like some kind of postapocalyptic dream.

"Hello?"

Every flat surface was tagged with a spectacular rambling tapestry of graffiti, most of which in turn had been recently disrupted with feral black gang markings. No moon breached the low clouds, only ambient leak from streetlights up on the bluff challenged the darkness, and it got darker as she went down. She sensed company, but saw only hardscape.

"I'm here."

A woman's shape had separated itself from the darker shadows of the headland's upheaval, she was almost turned silhouette by the last of the dying day. "It's Mallory."

Riley held the Ruger low against her thigh, gripping and re-gripping it. She crossed the broken flats of what once was side-walk, sneakers light on the concrete, not exactly scared, but a little healthy paranoia never hurt.

"It's okay," the shape called. "I'm Mallory. Charlie's friend?"

Riley recognized the voice and the dark figure resolved into a tiny woman with a helmet of black hair that framed a chalky white complexion. Mallory was strikingly attractive, Riley no-ticed, not for the first time. Upscale boho: linens, pricey flats, and dangly earrings. Twitchy and scared. "I think I was followed," Mallory said.

"I didn't see anyone."

Mallory glanced up toward the road.

"What's going on?"

"I don't know." Her expression strange, she watched Riley approach. "I thought you did."

"No. That's why I'm here."

"Charlie trusted you."

"Did he say that?"

"He said you could help us. That if anything happened to him, I should go to you. And tell you what I know."

"Tell me."

Mallory hesitated, then shook her head. "It's too late for that."

Riley felt a jolt of disquiet, then heard the footsteps coming, rapid, from behind her; Mallory's eyes went wide, but not, on later reflection, in a what-is-happening way, but more an oh-shit-here-we-go way, and Riley was already raising the Ruger as she sidestepped, crouched, and turned into the ambush. She sensed before she saw the gunman moving across the slope above her, among the rocks, low, arm outstretched. A muzzle flashed, once, twice. Riley didn't hear the gunshots, she was scrambling backward and downslope to grab Mallory with one arm and shield her, while with the other Riley fired back, off balance, nearly underhand, a random pattern of six shots placed just ahead of where she guessed the shooter would go.

He jerked awkwardly and fell into shadows.

But another muzzle fired at three o'clock, a second gunman who, Riley realized, disappointed in herself—time slowing, every-thing unfurling with hyper-clarity—must have been lying in wait for her approach and she'd failed to anticipate the possibility of it.

Snap. She was hit. It felt like an electric current drilling into her. She twisted with the pain, falling, breath lost, Mallory still in her grasp. She pulled the trigger of her gun by reflex, shooting almost upside down at the second assailant, emptying her clip, incoming bullets still sparking off the concrete slabs and rock faces, and on the ground around her from two directions.

Snap. She was hit again. This one didn't hurt. But she felt a quick tug under her rib cage and the force of it jacked her side-ways into a rock wall.

Down, tumbling, falling, mad at herself.

And in frustration, she cried out.

FINN SKATED THE TREACHEROUS DECLINE from Paseo Del Mar, twisting between fantastical earthworks from which the ruins of road, pipes, and foundations, all lathered with street art, jutted crazily. A medevac helicopter lifted out of the darkness, ro-tors churning a sand blizzard, and Finn turned his back, shielding his eyes and his camera until the chopper arced away over the water, hurrying toward Long Beach. His lanyard flapped around wildly as finally he ducked under the yellow tape to join the confusion in Sunken City.

A kaleidoscope of emergency lights, headlights, flashlights laced the Point Fermin cliffs. Cops milled, restless, more of them than usual, multiple jurisdictions, a show of force. Flares dotted the beach and the hillocks with their smoldering red fire. Soft rollers foamed up the glistening sand and fell back, ghostly, hissing. The rig lights of Terminal Island shimmered on the high tide.

Finn took his camera from his backpack and went to work.

In the backwash of the forest of portable forensic spotlights, a pale woman wringing the last out of her thirties, blunt chopped black hair a mess, blanket over her shoulders, bandage on her bloody neck and shoulder, sobbed and spoke in jagged bursts to a bald, bearded black man in civilian clothes, who Finn didn't recognize. Officer-involved shootings brought everybody out of the woodwork. A few more plainclothes cops with a full array of facial hair and Technicolor tattoos hung back like the detective's Greek chorus.

". . . we were meeting . . . I was early . . . they came out of nowhere, I couldn't see . . . the guns, my ears, I couldn't hear . . . she saved my life . . ."

Flashclick.

The chalked outline of a contorted body that had already been removed. Blood soaked the ground where it had come to rest. The geometry of broken foundations around it fresh chipped by gunfire.

Flashclick.

An empty space on a concrete landing above some stairs that

went nowhere held ragged pools of inky blood that indicated another victim had recently been lying there.

Too many empty bullet casings to count, strewn wildly, like parade candy. He switched lenses.

A long, angry smear of blood on a rusted section of railing.

Farther down, against the trunk of a spindly palm, a Hispanic male lay uncovered, thirties, sunglasses shattered but still stuck to his temple, curled back, arms wide, legs folded under him. Two small entry wounds in his chest, one under his ruptured eye. Crime technicians just getting to the body.

Some local uniforms were hunched in the shadows beyond the lights. Finn recognized faces, but didn't know names. He didn't see Lennox, which struck him as odd, but also fortunate, because Finn still worried the detective might have an inkling of what had happened with his girlfriend.

Bright glow of cigarettes in restless hands. The cops were shaken. Their mortality exposed.

"Must've popped the second guy after getting hit."

"Adrenaline kicks in. You go by instinct."

"Flatlined twice while they did CPR."

"It's a helluva thing."

Officer down. Finn's job was not to ask. He felt a weird foreboding, though; he moved and shot and cataloged the crime scene, details accruing, but this time unable to shake them, as if there were something else here he was supposed to understand.

Flashclick.

One small bloody sneaker.

A very fancy watch, its metal band broken.

Bandage wrappers, bits of bloody staunch gauze, shredded blue jeans, residue of the EMT's desperate work.

When he was finished, Finn put his camera away and stepped from the light, to climb back into the world, still confused by his uneasiness.

The black Pacific rose and rolled beneath an inky, star-starved sky.

AT THE CRIME LAB receiving desk, the graveyard-shift guy with the chin crawler, whose name Finn could never remember ("Dougg with two G's," Joaquin later mocked), quickly shuffled through the downloaded digital files from the Nikon memory card, as Finn explained to him, "I haven't printed any hard copies yet. I figured you guys'd want these right away."

"Yeah." The technician ran a hand over a rapidly expanding widow's peak and logged Finn's card into a file. "No problem, we'll do it. All fine."

"Cop gonna make it?" Finn asked.

Dougg said unconvincingly that he didn't know what Finn was talking about.

"Undercover cop who got shot. Where I just was."

Dougg, eyes limpid, tugged his wisp of beard. "Cannot confirm or deny that, Finnster. You know the drill."

The computer slide show ended on a frozen picture of the shivering black-haired survivor from the Bluff Park shooting, her face porcelain in the flash, her eyes wild with fear and confusion.

"Eyewitness?"

"I don't know. Informant, I think," Finn said, as Joaquin emerged from the back and logged off-shift on the duty board, pulling on an old Dodgers windbreaker that made him look about fourteen.

Dougg raised eyebrows at the stark image of the informant on his screen. "Hashtag: artful."

"Thanks. I guess."

"Not exactly in your job description, though, brah. Shoot and scoot, amiright?"

"I like to give the detectives something to bitch about," Finn explained.

Dougg stared blankly. Chitchat with him was a black hole. Joaquin pulled Finn away.

"Don't ever ask me to be your fucking wingman again," he told him, low, as they walked down the exit hallway. Joaquin was not happy. "Ever."

"You find her?"

"No."

They stepped out into a harsh, malodorous darkness, some kind of chilly marine event smelling of rotting fish and California crude. Finn pulled his shirt up over his nose and waited for elaboration, but Joaquin was onto something else. "Did you know there's a subReddit for Mildly Interesting Things?"

"What about her last name?" Finn pressed, stubborn.

"All these losers writing, like, 'The unseal tab on these baby wipes makes it look like the baby has a demon tail,' and, 'Someone in my house brought home a sporf.'"

"Shut up," Finn said. "Shut up about Reddit." His Fiat 500 was parked in the visitor lot, but not exactly in a legal space, and as they approached it Finn saw a sparkle of broken glass and the shattered side window. "Aw, shit."

The car had been ransacked. Joaquin went back in the station to get help, but it took twenty minutes for a dispatched black-and-white to drive the fifty yards from where it had been parked while its occupants, Anderson and Coates, had been sharing cheese fries and watching Finn do inventory in his burgled car. Lights trained on the scene, the two responding officers half-heartedly searched for clues while taking Finn's statement.

". . . Two cameras, my laptop. Four prime lenses and a 35-110 zoom . . . plus I had this little GoPro and some extra flash drives, oh, and these tripod halogen lights . . ."

"How long were you inside?"

"Maybe ten minutes," Joaquin told them. "He was delivering stuff to the lab."

Finn wandered off to check the light poles for security cameras that he had always presumed were everywhere, and weren't. Only on TV, the cops insisted. They were way too entertained by the irony of what had happened, riffing like stand-up partners at the Comedy Club.

"Looks like they used a brick," Coates deduced, kicking at a brick he located behind the back tire.

"You really shouldn't leave valuables in the car around here," Anderson, taking notes, lectured Finn.

"It's a police station! You're cops!" Joaquin snapped. "This is our fucking lot, this happened in our fucking house!"

The two cops looked at Joaquin dispassionately, almost hurt: And your point is?

3

FOR A WHILE he half hoped that he'd cross paths with her at the Palace of Justice, and kept her engagement ring in his pocket just in case, but it didn't happen. Occasionally he'd see Lennox there, drinking by himself, and Finn would imagine walking over and giving Lennox the ring, or striking up a casual conversation in which he would cleverly get the detective to tell him Riley's last name.

Instead he'd just finish his beer, slip out, unnoticed, and go home alone.

A month passed. His heart ached and he felt pretty stupid about it. A one-night stand. Nobody falls in love in one night, with a person whose name they may or may not know. In the age of Tinder and appointment sex, Finn was no saint or celibate; arguably, he was kind of a dick, as a few of the women he'd briefly dated weren't shy to point out. Bighearted, they'd admit, considerate, engaging—but unable to commit, a guy who'd bolt like a springbok at the first signs of attachment. He was a realist, he kept insisting, mostly to himself; a reasonable man resigned to the practicability that romance, like typewriters and vinyl records, was a quaint relic of a social contract breached way before his time.

Maybe Riley was, indeed, a hooker, plying his fantasy the way she might wear Catholic schoolgirl plaids—although Joaquin had tried to disabuse Finn of the idea, assuring him that working girls didn't last long giving free samples. Not that Joaquin would know.

One night, drunk on flavored vodka that Arden had left behind after another thorny Chanel-enhanced, braless-crop-top-but-patently-unsuccessful attempt to seduce him, Finn printed all the pictures he'd taken of Riley while in his loft under the spell of that one argent waxing crescent moon, gorgeous grainy low-res abstracts, her eyes looking right into his lens, fearless, nothing coy or callow in them.

If he'd misread her, his camera had missed it, too, and that, in Finn's experience, had never happened.

He felt muddled. He felt defeated.

He put away in a flat portfolio drawer all the photographs he'd taken of her, and convinced himself he was letting go.

ANOTHER MONTH BLURRED past.

A homeless man was killed in a hit-and-run.

The Sons of Samoa and the Rollin 80 Crips had a dustup in a Del Taco drive-thru that put half a dozen spectators in the hospital and took Finn three hours to document because his fancy new Nikon had a software glitch that kept fucking up the exposure.

On a hotline tip, Vice raided another San Pedro gentlemen's club suspected of human traffic in Asian female illegals, but the place was deserted when the cops arrived, a triggered sprinkler system flooding away any hopes of clues, and the department was refusing to reimburse Finn for the false alarm.

Early on a hazy, leaden-sky Tuesday morning, Finn watched Gunnery Sergeant Willa Ko, haggard in her orange prison jumpsuit, get escorted up the steps of Long Beach Superior Court through a disappointing scatter of local media and rubberneckers in what could be described only as prosecutorial grandstanding, because Finn knew she could easily have been brought in through a back door.

Outside a smaller courtroom, as one more tardy news crew hustled past, Finn met with a painfully young deputy district attorney, stress acne and a fine silk suit, who shuffled a lap-load of case folders, finally finding and spilling a packet of crime scene photographs from Sunken City into Finn's hands. "Any officer-involved shooting, we're mostly just covering our butts here, in case the two dead perps have family that decides to sue. Claim wrongful death or something. You know. It's unlikely. But."

"The cop survived?"

"Yes."

"It wasn't in the papers."

"Undercover op. Still active."

Finn watched the news crew, down the hallway, clearly freelancers, try to talk their way past the bailiff into Willa Ko's preliminary hearing, then sorted quickly through his photos from the ruins of Sunken City. When he came upon the picture of the shivering survivor in the blanket, he remembered. "Wasn't there an eyewitness?"

"She's been kinda difficult to get ahold of, went to ground, probably scared shitless," the prosecutor said. "We don't really need her. It would have been nice. But." He shrugged. "Witnesses can be unreliable. Her recollection was squishy."

Finn had stopped listening. Something in the photographs didn't track—confounded him. He kept going back and forth among a few of them, shaking his head.

"I'm assuming you've done a coroner's inquiry before," the DDA was saying, droll. "It's incredibly technical, I ask you if these are the photos you took, you say, 'Yes they are,' and we're done."

He expected Finn to laugh.

Finn said, "They're not."

"Oh, and"—the young prosecutor was already standing up, shaking out the perfect pleat in his suit pants—"we're still protecting the identity of the undercover officer, so"—he stopped, only then registering what Finn had said—"What?"

"These aren't what I shot," Finn said.

The DDA sat down. "What?"

Finn's relationship to his forensic photographs was primal: He shot them, he forgot them, but whenever he reviewed them again he remembered exactly the moment the shutter fell, like a neuron firing, more precise than a mere memory recalled because the hard evidence was in front of him, unmitigated by the fog of time and subconscious revision. Finn held up the pictures at odds for him, mystified. "These aren't my photos." He elaborated, unhelpfully. "Not all of them, anyway."

Abject panic from the DDA, "Whoawhoawhoa, what are you fucking saying?" Finn looked up at him; the prosecutor was about to hyperventilate.

"Flat exposure, the flash glare here—and here—the framing,

the focus, the contrast . . . it's all shit"—Finn shuffled the stack—"I took these . . . but not these. See? Can you see the difference in the exposure? The resolution? This one. This one, this one . . ." He sorted, agitated, through pictures that were not his: of where the wounded cop had almost bled out, the pockmarked concrete where bullets had missed, the pools of blood, the traces of paramedic triage. All wrong now.

The qualitative differences were way too subtle for the deputy. Biting sarcasm: "Sure, Finn. Must be a bitch to get the light good at a crime scene."

Finn bit back, "I'm telling you, they aren't mine."

"Man, just—"

"—No. Somebody messed with them." And then he saw one obvious, glaring difference, remembering, "There was a bracelet—no, a watch. A fancy one. Right here. I anchored my shot on it. Dutch angle, so these shadows would clear. Now it's gone. Everything else . . . It's like somebody squared the framing and Photoshopped it out. Or . . ." Finn couldn't wrap his mind around it.

"Or what?" The prosecutor was blushed furious and quiet.

Finn knew exactly what the man was thinking: In seven minutes he was due in the courtroom, but now first he'd have to call and tell his boss the crime photos were tainted, that the forensic photographer couldn't testify to what was always a routine chain-of-custody protocol, and the implication of doctoring of evidence in police custody promised a potential nuclear prosecutorial meltdown that might compromise cases and convictions going back years.

"But the watermark is from your camera. Unique to your camera."

"Which was stolen."

The DDA closed his eyes. "When?"

"Three weeks ago. Same night I took these, in fact."

"FUCK." The young prosecutor's voice ricocheted around the emptying hallway. A passing clerk glared at him. Finn mumbled an apology while the DDA collected his files and got up.

"Get out of here."

Finn said, "I can attest to all the others."

"Get the fuck out of my sight. I can't put you on the stand."

"YOU'RE SAYING IT'S SOMEBODY on the inside?" Joaquin asked, low, later, over beers at the Palace. "A bad cop. Or cops?"

"Or somebody in the crime lab." Finn was irritated that Joaquin was automatically excluding his turf.

"Yeah, yeah. Or a bad-seed teenager with too much time on his hands and, like, one of those Chinese tattoos that looks like a scribble but means Prosperity." Sarcasm.

"Teenagers." Finn wasn't amused. "Who broke into my car, and took my camera for the security code to sanctify the doctored photos?"

"Dude." Joaquin rubbed his temples. "Nobody in the lab's got the balls to do a thing like this, crims are cowards."

Finn swirled his beer in his glass pensively. "Okay, so, by process of elimination: cop."

"Or cops." Joaquin wouldn't be pinned down. "But before you go running off to Internal Affairs and make a nuisance of yourself, let me play devil's advocate on that. Why would a cop—or anybody, for that matter—want to doctor photographs of a closed case where the shooters are dead?"

"Who's to say Internal Affairs isn't in on it?" Finn said.

Joaquin rolled his eyes. "Promise me, promise me, you're not going to ask around about this."

"I wouldn't know who to ask," Finn lied.

HE SPENT MORE than an hour in the main lobby of Long Beach General, wading through the traffic jam of inpatient confusion gathered at reception, and then approached the beleaguered desk staffer, flashing his police crime scene credentials just long enough to convince her he had some kind of official standing, and combined it with a kind look that said, "Let me just get out of your hair, your job is hard enough," and was given the floor and room number of the wounded officer in question, scrawled out for him on a Post-it.

Elevator doors whispered open and Finn disembarked with a troupe of med students doing rounds under the watchful eye of a balding resident. He let the interns surge ahead of him and, consulting the Post-it, headed left down the long glass-sided corridor toward the rehab wing. San Pedro Harbor was crowded with container ships and, looming above them, the distant loading cranes hunched empty like gallows.

In the rehab wing hallway, a maze of ready gurneys, wheelchairs, and equipment disgorged from the warren of rooms, a sturdy nurse whisked out of a supply pantry and nearly mowed Finn down.

He flashed his lanyard ID again and asked his question and, already moving away, the nurse gestured and said, "Room 419, on the right. I think she's got family with her."

She? Four-eleven. Four-thirteen. Finn heard an argument

that got louder, the door to 419 banged open and a ropey old gee-zer in grimy cargo shorts and a CalArts wifebeater charged out, red-faced, smelling of liquor, steel, and fire.

"Get the fuck out of my way!"

Finn sidestepped and watched the man go. Finn thought he knew him from somewhere; he couldn't recall how or why. There was the sound of movement in the room, creak of bed-springs and metal, a weird half shuffle and grunting that drew Finn tentatively to the open door to peer inside, where a sallow, stringy young woman in Police Academy sweats had balanced precariously on the edge of the hospital bed, and was holding herself up by an overhead bar. Finn felt his stomach flip. It was the woman who called herself Riley. The one-night stand who had hijacked his heart.

She was struggling to move from the bed to a waiting wheel-chair.

Her legs were dead.

Finn blinked: Riley, Finn's Riley, who had rocked his whole world, was the cop who got shot up on the broken concrete of Sunken City.

Her hands gripped the bar and let her slender arms take her weight as she tried to find some improbable law of physics that would launch her toward her chair. Her sweatshirt rode up, re-vealing jagged purplish scars from bullets that had sawed through her spine. She lost balance, the transfer board clattered to the tile floor, the wheelchair pivoted, her legs dropped, useless, and she was left dangling, helpless, holding herself up stubbornly with her arms.

"DAMMIT!"

Her eyes found him as he began to cross from where he had been riveted in the doorway, breath held—crossed quickly and caught her in his arms and for a moment it seemed she might melt into him like in a love story. "Relax. I've got you."

But no.

"WHAT ARE YOU DOING? Stop—no—NO—" Her body jerked free of him. One hand twisted off the bar, and she swung it back tactically and clobbered Finn across the face with her elbow. He staggered, dazed, but managed to keep his arms around her, until, twisting together, her other hand lost grip of the transfer bar and Finn hinged her deadweight over one hip and dropped her into the wheelchair before he sank hard onto the floor, holding both sides of his throbbing face with his hands.

"Ow."

"WHO the fuck DO YOU THINK YOU ARE?" she barked.

"I was just trying to help."

"I DIDN'T ASK FOR ANY HELP!"

Finn brought his hands away, so she could see the hash she'd made of him: eyes red, already bruising, nose swelling, a thread of blood. They stared at each other and he waited for a recognition to dawn. "I'm sorry." She took a deep breath and calmed, visibly chagrined. "I just, I don't need, want—require—any help . . . thank you, anyway." She looked up at the bar swaying above her head, out of reach; irritated, then disconsolate. "I'm not supposed to have help. I've got to learn how to do this. By myself." She looked at him again, eyes narrowing. "Did I break your nose?" She found a tissue on the side table and offered it.

Finn stared back, still waiting for it, for the recognition, growing puzzled, wondering, hoping that maybe with all that had happened . . . with all she had been through . . . she blanked on . . . or she didn't quite . . .

"Do I know you?"

4

"It's a matter of rotation and transfer of weight. Like a golf swing, or so they tell me—which I was never much good at." Riley lined herself up next to the bed again, transfer board in place; she was intending to reverse the trip, go from chair to bed, and Finn watched, arms folded, giving her space.

After denying she knew him, she had studied him as blankly as she had the first time, in the Palace of Justice, after Lennox, when Finn had approached out of nowhere, some random guy, a nobody in a cop bar, intent on rescuing her from a tyranny of tears.

Do I know you? She might as well have hit him again.

Out in the corridor, an orderly's shoes squeaked past on waxed tile and quickly faded. *Does she?* A television jabbered in another room, indistinct. And Finn wondered, in dismay: Does she really not remember . . . or does she not want to remember?

"No," he had answered her finally. *We've never met.* He had indulged the conceit, bought his ticket, took the ride. Introduced himself, pretended they were strangers, and explained to her why he'd come.

Now Riley gripped the side rail on the chair, and her arms tensed. "Here goes nothing."

She lifted herself on her hands, like a pommel-horse gymnast—deceptively strong, triceps like ropes—but every movement that followed was ungainly, her butt dragged, her legs wouldn't cooperate, and as she swung out and pivoted to the bed her thighs got hung up, her core tilted out of center; she lurched, made a desperate stab at the overhead bar and once again was left hanging.

Finn hadn't even begun to move again, reflexively to help, when, "NO! You stay where you are."

So he let her struggle, stubborn, helpless, flopping like a gaffed fish. And eventually, through sheer force of will, she got herself onto the mattress, and, with gravity's help, arched back into the pillows, one crooked leg still bent dangling off the bed, but the bulk of her secure from sliding off. After a moment's rest, there came a muffled "Shit."

Riley levered up on an elbow, yanked on the flailed leg until it came up onto the bed, and then arranged herself into the slant of pillows, exhausted. For a moment her guard was down, her vulnerability laid bare. There were tears in her eyes, but she wasn't crying. "This is my new normal," she said softly, and seemed to measure Finn, trying to remember.

"Finn."

"Right. Finn. So listen, here's the deal: I'm not interested in your doctored photos from when I got shot, I'm not interested in who doctored them, if they did, and I'm not interested in what all that could mean. I'm sorry. You came all the way over here for nothing."

She really was a Riley, surname McCluggage, a detective recently passed and promoted to the Vice Squad where she was working on "a human-trafficking thing," she said, when the shooting occurred. He'd told her about the aborted testimony, the angry deputy DA, the photographs that weren't his, tainted evidence, the very real possibility of an in-house police or City Hall conspiracy to . . . well, what, exactly? she had pointed out. "The wristwatch I remember seeing—" he began, but she cut him short:

"I don't wear a watch, bracelets, jewelry, and never on the job, and I don't remember anything like that at the scene before or during all hell breaking loose, no." About this she was lying, Finn was sure of it; for an undercover cop, she was a lousy liar, which made them, in some strange sense, a matched pair. Was she lying about not remembering him?

"You don't care that there might be a dirty cop, that he might have—"

"—No." Again Riley cut him off. "And if you keep going down this road, you will lose your job, they will make your life hell—not just the police, but the DA, the whole fucking civic machine—because a rumor of even one doctored photograph will, in the hearts and minds of convicted felons and their representatives and the appeals courts, start to call into question every case we've tried over the past I don't even want to think about how many years. See what I'm saying?"

He went quiet. He could still feel her, in his hands, from when he caught her as she almost dropped from the transfer bar. She'd lost weight, but seemed stronger. The ripple of her ribs, the heat of her hips. Her breath on his neck. He couldn't think.

Riley waited for him, patient, eyes emptied out, but probing. "What are you thinking about?"

"I don't know."

"You're lying. It's my new superpower: I can see through the phony platitudes people toss at me, like how brave I am, all the while thinking, 'She's fucked.'" Riley angled her head, then, as if it was Finn's prompt to recant.

He sighed, frustrated, derailed. "No. That wasn't on my mind."

"Oh." If Riley was pretending not to remember him, she was doing a flawless job of selling it. Finn couldn't find anything more to say, so he just stared blankly back at her until she asked, softly, "Then why do you look at me like that?"

He couldn't tell her. He was afraid of the answer. Self-conscious, Finn broke. "I'm sorry about what's happened to you." Pushed off from the wall and murmured, "And sorry to have taken up your time."

Riley's voice stopped him at the door: "Finn." He turned. She said, "Who else takes photos for the crime lab?"

"There's a short list, I could—"

"The soldier who shot her husband—Willa Ko? You wouldn't happen to know who worked that one?"

Finn played along and said that he had done it.

"Those pictures I am interested in," she said.

"Okay." He frowned, remembering her wandering among them in his studio. And there was another awkward pause while Finn tried to understand what she was asking. "Can't you just get them from the—"

"—From the DA? They'd never share them with me, it's a homicide, I'm Vice. Or was." This sounded brittle, but she pushed hair out of her eyes, a gesture he remembered so clearly, and then she corrected herself, "Although I guess 'medical leave' is the official verdict. Subject to departmental review."

"I don't have those files anymore," Finn told her, a half-lie that she would see through, if she remembered. "I turn in the memory card from my camera. Crime lab has them." For a moment he considered offering to ask Joaquin, but if she remembered their night, she would know he had outtakes in his studio, where she'd seen them clipped to the drying lines.

He waited.

Finally, she nodded slightly. "It's just kind of touchy because I've already gone on the record saying I don't think she killed him."

"Wait. What?" Finn didn't want to leave. "Why not?"

But they were interrupted by the overwhelming promise of carnations and, a moment later, Detective Terry Lennox breezed in, treble bouquet of wilting mix-and-match gift-shop flowers in one hand and an old soft leather briefcase swinging at the end of the other. "How're we doing today, Riley Mac?"

"We're still crippled." A hug, a kiss. Like siblings, Finn thought. "But we enjoy flowers." The detective cut his eyes toward Finn, but ignored him for the time being.

"That's Finn Miller," Riley said.

Obligated now, Lennox glanced again and frowned and Finn elaborated, "I work with the crime lab."

"I thought you looked familiar."

"Forensic photography."

"Sure. I've seen you. What's going on with your face?"

"Uh. Allergies." Lennox was a good enough detective to be troubled by Finn's presence in Riley's room, out of nowhere, and Finn saw and sought to defuse it. "I just came by"—he dug in his pocket—"to return this"—the engagement ring.

He held it up, but Riley gave no indication she wanted to take it from him, so Finn placed it on the bedside table next to her cell phone. She didn't look at it, she just watched him, as if wary. She knows, he thought. She knows.

"About a month back," Finn explained to Lennox, breezy, making it up as he went along, "outside the Palace of Justice, I saw it drop on the sidewalk when she was getting into an Uber. I asked around, but nobody could tell me who she was." This last part he said to Riley, searching her face for the tell.

She didn't give him anything.

"Riles was working undercover," Lennox said. "Transferred in from L.A."

"Hunh, okay. Anyway. I kept at it and"—he shrugged at Lennox, like how random was this?—"finally somebody at the station sent me over here."

Lennox seemed assuaged, but still annoyed Finn hadn't taken care of his business and left long ago. "Well done. Thanks."

"Pleasure." Finn grinned at Lennox, then faced Riley, who remained unmoved, unchanged, unreadable. Finn's heart sank. Without his camera, without his cloak of invisibility, he was exposed. "So I'm gonna"—he gestured at nothing and walked to the door. "Good luck with that new normal."

Riley said, "Yeah."

Finn cleared the doorway, but did not continue down the corridor. Instead, he lingered to eavesdrop on the brittle argument that he correctly guessed might follow his leaving.

"How do you lose the ring and not tell me?" Lennox said.

"How did you not even notice I wasn't wearing it?" A chilly silence and a change of subject: "Did you ask him?"

"What?"

"Did you talk to the captain, Terry?"

"I did, yes."

Finn drifted to the other side of the corridor, tucking himself in the open doorway of an unoccupied room, where he could look across and see Lennox open the leather satchel and remove some documents.

"What did he say when you told him I know she didn't do it?" Riley asked him.

Lennox shuffled the papers, a stall, evasive. "He's put you in for a commendation. OIS Committee has cleared you in the use of deadly force. City Council voted to cover everything union medical won't. It's all good, Riles." But there was something else, and he couched it all casual: "They just need you to sign a few waivers and releases concerning the assignment of fault."

Lennox swung the rolling bedside tray over and in front of her, trying to queue up the sheaf of disclaimers. He had a pen ready, but she must have refused him.

"Fault?"

"Culpability. From your end."

"What are you talking about?" Lennox balked, but Riley decoded it. "They want me to agree not to sue them?"

"That's the gist of it."

She faltered. "Why would I sue them?"

"It's just, you know . . . they need to cover their asses. Standard operating procedure. Bureaucratic bullshit."

She repeated her question. "Why would I sue them, Terry?"

Lennox opened his hands emptily. He had to have known there would be pushback.

"What aren't you telling me?"

"City attorney wanted to come himself," Lennox said, lowering his voice, speaking so quietly Finn could barely make him out. "I thought it might be easier hearing it from me. Look, I know what you're going to say and—"

"No."

"Riley."

"I can't do that. I won't. It's insulting."

"Riles—"

She cut him off. "And what about Willa Ko? Did you or did you not communicate to the captain that I know for a fact she didn't kill her husband?" The ensuing silence stretched as Lennox seemed to be debating what to say next. "And did you ask him to put me back on the case?"

Lennox slipped his hands in his pockets and jingled some keys and leaned again the edge of a chair back and sighed. "You know for a fact."

"Yes."

"No, baby. It's a feeling you have, and all the evidence says you're wrong."

"What about the casings?"

"What about them?"

"Did you even check?" Finn felt sure he hadn't.

"We don't need them. We don't need ballistics—"

"You don't have fucking ballistics, from what I remember." She didn't let him respond. "Her dad shot Charlie Ko, Terry. She's taking the fall for her father. Willa had given her gun to her dad."

"According to Charlie."

"Yes. Her husband, my informant."

"Who is dead. Making it kinda hard to go to him for corroboration."

"My word's not good enough for you?"

"Don't twist this."

"What does Mallory say?"

"She's kinda gone off the grid. But we're still—"

"You guys just don't know where to look. She's probably scared shitless. Put me back on the case. I'll find her, I'll find a second source, I can prove that—"

"The case is closed. We got our guy. Or girl, as it were."

"Why the fuck won't you listen to me?"

"Shhh, baby girl, c'mon, focus on getting yourself better."

"I'm not your baby. I'm not your girl. I'm a full-fucking-grown woman, I killed two knuckleheads who tried to kill me, I've got a shattered spine to show for it—don't act like you're gonna be my big macho manly protector, because you are way too fucking late."

"This is crazy" was all Finn heard Lennox say.

"No, what's crazy is you're going to convict the WRONG PERSON." She threw the waivers. They separated, fluttered around Lennox like giant snowflakes, and settled to the floor. "And I'm not signing those. It's insulting. I'm a cop, Terry. I knew the risks going in. Why would I sue the city and jeopardize my whole career?"

Lennox hadn't moved from the foot of the bed, he took a deep breath and put his hand on her leg, her lower body all Finn could see of her from where he watched; the gesture was meant to be intimate, Lennox probably forgetting, Finn thought, that Riley couldn't feel it anymore. "You don't have a career, baby," he said softly. "You gotta come to terms with that's not gonna happen."

"And why is that?"

"Cops need legs," he said.

Finn's heart broke for her.

Riley must've just stared at Lennox, devastated, and even from the hallway Finn could imagine the expression, he'd seen it once before: She was not going to cry. He saw her hand reach and fumble for the control in the blankets, heard the lowering of her hospital bed, and the curling of her upper body fetal, turned toward the wall. "I'm tired."

Her legs Finn could see: twined, loose, like lifeless tendrils.

For a long time there was just the dull churning hum of the rehab ward: machines, footsteps, soft discourse of nurses at their station, the murmur of muted televisions.

Lennox looked like he didn't know what to do. Riley didn't move. Finn watched until Lennox started to pick up the scattered legal documents, hard on his haunches, head down. Finn found he no longer cared how this might end, and he quietly walked away.

5

THERE WERE YOUTUBE VIDEOS to show him "How to Pick a Door Lock," and he watched the best of them on his desktop several times in succession while arranging his old reflex camera and lenses—the ones his grandfather had given him before he passed—into a backpack. And just before midnight he stood at the front entrance of an upscale condominium building, pressing call buttons randomly until somebody buzzed him in.

He had never done anything like this before. Still reeling from seeing Riley broken, and awed by the grit she showed in the face of it, he had convinced himself that denying him was, for Riley, the simplest act of self-preservation—with everything else that had happened, a soap opera with rancorous would-be fiancé and coworker Terry Lennox was the last thing she probably wanted, or needed.

The alternative explanation was too grim to contemplate: that he hadn't meant anything, that he been just a blip on the grid, a one-off drunken assignation that, in the tsunami back-wash of her catastrophic injury, didn't even warrant a backward glance.

Finn loitered out front and slipped through the secure entrance with someone who lived in the building, catching up with and holding the door for her and her angry scrap of a dog after she unlocked it, then veered away from the elevator, took the stairs up to the top floor, and moved directly to a familiar door crisscrossed with yellow police tape and sealed. Without removing the official barrier, he gently pried away one end of the crime scene seal the way Joaquin had once explained to him was why cops sealing things was bullshit, and then, using the technique he had just learned from the Internet, picked the deadbolt lock in about ninety seconds flat.

The apartment door yawned; he stooped, stepped through the tape, and inside. Long, faint shadows fell dark on darker shadow gaps fanned across the room from vertical blinds on the west-facing windows. Blocky blue tape outlined where the body had lain. The little forensic flags still marked where evidence had been gathered or noted: the body's position, bloody shoe prints, handprints, bullet hole through the arm of a chair, a shat-tered corner of tile, impact craters low in the concrete wall from which the shattered, useless slug fragments had been removed. Finn made a preliminary pass without his camera, moving just as he had before, same footwork, like an odd dance, slowly re-membering as if by instinct the positions from which he origi-nally took his photographs. Then he took his old camera from his backpack and began shooting new photographs because the outtakes back in his studio would not be enough for her.

Flashclick.

The room reeled under bursts of light that tore at the abiding darkness.

Flashclick.

The condominium still held the dead, he felt it, and tried not to think about all the transgressions he was committing by being there, against the law, against his own long-held rules of survival.

He was out of his comfort zone. It felt amazing.

There was only the soft squeak of Finn's sneakers on the floor, the hush of his measured breathing, the slip-shuffle of the old Pentax doing its thing.

WATER WAS a miracle.

Submerged in it, she could almost believe that nothing had happened to her spine, the hard rehab weeks since the shooting dissolved in the slick streaming forward motion, practically weightless, gliding and crashing onward, body lithe, turning, arms thrusting her through the water, steady, paced, swimming laps of the hospital pool and blowing off steam from her dustup with Lennox.

Water sounds banged off the walls, the pool's fractious surface shimmered with broken light. She loved the loneliness. No one wanting to know how she was feeling, what she was thinking, how she was coping. Her empty wheelchair waited at the far end of the pool, like an insult.

The patronizing sympathy was the worst of it. People wanting so badly to know but afraid to ask what it felt like, if she was angry, or suicidal, or just depressed, but it was all about them, not her, projecting their worst fears on her, dipping their toes into her tragedy, and drawing them safely out again, horrified, unable to really comprehend how you adapt because you have to adapt; how you accept your new normal because there is no other option. Reality has quaked. You don't think about it. You stumble forward and bring along what you can.

The chair. The legs. Ineluctable.

None of it was how they imagined it might be.

One life died, another was born.

Her breathing broke rhythm and she swallowed water and was forced to pull up, treading, coughing.

And everything from that past life, from who she was, and what she had done? Up for grabs. She imagined that her legs were still scissoring below her. Phantom limbs she couldn't feel and yet her mind still conjured the cool currents shivering her ghost feet and toes.

Like Finn Miller.

That was another life, wasn't it? The moonlight that fell through the studio skylight. Where she early morning stood there barefoot in the wrinkled cocktail shift she'd slipped back on, the cold grain of the hardwood floor beneath her, and watching Finn sleep, wandering on legs she no longer had among the clotheslines of photographs, ghosted lunar pale, and the way her body felt, then, it wasn't the sex, it was something else she'd never—new, it was like—a little scary—an unfamiliar sense of arriving, an odd quiet at the center.

She remembered studying the photos. Seeing what she hadn't seen a few hours before. Or, rather, not seeing what a good detective should have seen right away.

She had unclipped the photo of Willa's gun from the line and held it up next to a photo of Charlie's body, just to be sure.

Without waking Finn, she had left the loft, unsure what she

should say, unwilling to confront what she had done (was it betrayal or escape?), distracting herself, as she always did, with the work at hand. She was in property lockup as the sun rose, rooting through an open bin containing puzzle pieces from the Charlie Ko murder. A sleepy graveyard-shift property watch officer had stood behind her with the key, asking what she was looking for.

Bullet casings, she told him. She took up Willa's bagged service weapon from the bin. "Where are the bullet casings?" she had asked aloud. The suspect allegedly fired the gun twice. The clerk didn't know what she was talking about, and mm-hmmed mostly for show. He'd been told the recovered slug fragments were so degraded it wasn't feasible to pull a conclusive rifling. Nobody'd mentioned casings.

She had asked and he had shown her Finn's official crime scene photos on a flat-screen monitor at the front desk; Riley clicked through them quickly, knowing they would confirm what she already knew from his studio.

When Riley walked into the interview room at Sybil Brand jail, Willa was waiting, with one of her little girls on her lap and her anxious, gray-faced father sitting opposite and watching distractedly as the younger girl on his lap played Angry Birds on an off-brand smartphone.

Willa's public defender had stood and mumbled a greeting and motioned for Willa's dad to take his granddaughters and go see what was holding up bail. The old man threw an uneasy look at Riley and collected the girls. The phone spilled from the younger girl's hand and skittered to Riley's feet, where she picked it up and handed it back, and Willa Ko said, "What do you say?" And the older girl had answered for her sister, "Thank you, ma'am."

Riley only had a couple questions. She had promised the public defender it wouldn't take long.

Willa said without prompting that she had not killed her husband, Charlie.

Riley said, okay, that wasn't one of my questions, but go ahead and finish your thought.

Willa had measured her, then. Ever the soldier. She said, I've been with Charlie since high school. He was the most beautiful boy and I couldn't believe it when he asked me out. He wasn't perfect. I know that. And I was really mad at him. But we have the two little ones to think about.

If you didn't shoot him, who did? Riley asked.

The public defender told Willa that she didn't have to speculate, and she nodded but said to Riley that she didn't know.

How old?

Carly's six, Jade's four.

Charlie was a good father.

He sure wanted to be.

"Want" and "was" are two different things.

I was away for a long time. Men can't . . . really deal with loneliness, I don't think.

Sort of like how women can't deal with betrayal?

Willa frowned.

Riley asked her question: What did you do with the bullet casings that were ejected from your gun when you shot him?

Willa looked at her public defender, and he nodded, and she looked at Riley and just shrugged, noncommittal.

And if you didn't shoot him, why did you hide the gun?

Willa explained that they'd agreed to meet after she got done with work. They were trying to figure things out. The door was open when she arrived, and she walked in and found Charlie on the floor. There was no emotion in her voice when she said she'd seen what dead looks like and Charlie was, but she had put her head down to his heart anyway, to listen, because, she said, it was Charlie and she was hoping somehow she was wrong and then Willa's voice trailed off and after a moment she said that that was when she got his blood on her.

Where was the gun?

On the floor, she had said, right there. She heard a police radio coming down the hallway. She realized what it would look like, and so she took the gun and hid it.

That was why she tested positive for GSR, her lawyer said.

Riley asked the question she came to ask: You didn't see the casings on the floor? You didn't pick them up when you picked up the gun?

For a moment Willa had held Riley's gaze. The public defender told Riley his client had already answered the question, and Riley said not really, and Willa had said, no, ma'am, why would a soldier think of that?

Which was when Riley had known for certain that Charlie Ko hadn't been killed by his wife.

The world went dark with a faint echoing click.

The complete blackout yanked Riley back to the rehab pool where all of the lights, in-pool and overhead, everything had plunged into darkness, slowly relieved only by a feeble green bleed from an EXIT sign tucked around the corner where the doors were. Riley could hear the soft splash of her arms treading water, but she couldn't see her hands causing it.

"Hey!"

Nobody answered her. At first, she thought a janitor or an

orderly must have inadvertently flipped a switch thinking the pool was empty.

"I'm still in here! Hello?"

She was disoriented, couldn't see to the sides of the pool, but told herself that if she swam slowly in any direction, eventually she'd find one.

It didn't calm her. She made her choice. And moving through the water, she thought she heard the faint click of footsteps on the deck tile. She stopped and heard nothing but the lap of water on the sides. She let a silence gather, waiting. Sensing someone there, waiting. Her arms were fatigued; she wouldn't be able to tread water much longer. Keeping her arms under the surface, she began moving again, drifting really, trying to make as little noise as possible, straining to hear the soft footfall she was certain had resumed, but with no way of knowing whether she was swimming right toward it.

FINN HAD FINISHED his photo shoot, had put his camera into his backpack, and was hurrying away from the apartment when the elevator door gaped and caused him to duck into the stairwell to avoid being seen by whoever was coming out. He waited for the footsteps to pass, then cracked the door and watched a hulking white man walk down the corridor like he owned the place. High-wall haircut and a windbreaker, under it the bulge of a short-barreled nonregulation gun that Finn knew some of the local blues liked to carry off-duty. A cop? The weapon was out as soon as the new arrival saw that the crime scene seal had been breached. The big man had a key, pushed the door open, and listened for a long time, before he disappeared inside.

While a voice in Finn's head kept worrying, *Walk away, walk away*, he reemerged from the stairwell and crept back to the apartment and peered inside. Against all better judgment he wanted to know why someone else was, at this late hour, creeping the scene of a months-old murder.

The living room was empty. He thought he heard a soft noise, deeper in the apartment, then nothing. He waited. But got impatient and went in again.

It was as if the big man had vanished. What was he looking for? Riley would want to know. What had Finn missed? There was no one in the kitchen, the hallway to the bedrooms was dark and deserted. Finn listened: nothing. A television, faint, muffled, from the floor below. A hollow clearing of throat.

He moved, again, soundless, deeper in. Deciding the big man had to be in the master bedroom, Finn convinced himself he would just go far enough to get a glimpse of the man, see what he was doing, and then get the hell out of there.

But he saw no one in the bedroom, and heard the flushing of a toilet behind him too late and the bathroom door at the head of the hallway swung open and Finn, panicked, darted into the darkness of the master suite without considering that in so doing, he was trapping himself, because now the big armed man controlled the egress.

"Hey, now."

Finn heard the hallway light switch flipped, but nothing happened, the power had been turned off. The heavy man began to move toward where he must have seen Finn's shadow slip, and Finn, pulse skittering, pressed himself against the wall just inside the open doorway, holding his breath, understanding now that he was doomed, listening to the interlocutor's relentless advance.

"Yo. I could just park out here until it's light."

He could, but Finn was pretty sure an armed man wouldn't. He struggled to think, his chest so tight his shoulders ached. He pulled his camera from the backpack and held it in one claw hand, finger frozen on the shutter button.

Finn had no plan. But the man's big shoe found a squeaky toy in the darkness, it momentarily startled both of them, caused High-wall Hair to look down, and by the time he lifted his eyes Finn had lurched out of the bedroom with eyes closed and the Pentax held high like a talisman, a camera flash all he had to offer in his own defense.

FOOM.

Blinded, the big man threw one arm up and ducked, swung his other arm and gun hand out wildly at the afterimage of who-ever was trying to get around him, so Finn set off another flash. The gun cracked against something fairly soft and hollow (Finn's head) and the big man tapped the trigger and the gun went off, blowing a huge hole in the wall (first passing through the flutter of Finn's shirt, nearly drilling him as he recoiled from the blow), a muzzle flash glimpsing a gypsum dust storm as, through it, Finn made his harrowing escape: pivoting, camera coming up again, pure instinct now:

Flashclickflashclickflashclick.

The big man tangled legs and stumbled. Finn, shoulder down, bouncing off man and wall, willed himself clear, blood smeared on the side of his face from the scrape of the gun; he blundered to the end of the hallway, out through the apartment, scattering evidence flags in his wake, snapped the police tape like he was crossing a crazed race finish line, out into the build-ing corridor, to the stairwell doorway and down.

As the fire door winged shut behind him, Finn could hear a big cop's angry roar of disappointment, and the dry crackle of the police tape still flapping in disarray.

RILEY GROPED FOR THE EDGE COPING, found it, splashing a bit inelegant, frustrated and tired. She steadied herself and located the faint silvered outline of her chair. At the other end of the pool. Miles away.

And now again she heard them: slow, careful footsteps on the tile deck. The room's acoustics deceived, she still couldn't tell where. Getting louder, coming closer? *This* side. She knew not to call out to it. She felt an unfamiliar panic rise wrought by her new helplessness. *Fuck fuck fuck.* She didn't like it; tried to push it away, *no no no.* Went very still, silently pushed away from the coping and, helicoptering her arms under the water, began to swim back across the pool.

So vulnerable. Drowning in blackness. Her eyes everywhere, and nowhere. The water no comfort now. How far to the other side? Nothing but shadows on shadows.

A hand stabbed down from behind her and grabbed roughly at her arm. She stifled a scream and tried to twist away—

"—Riley?" Lennox.

"Oh, God, it's you . . ." Now she could see his worried face.

"Me. Yeah. Why are you swimming in the dark?"

"The lights went out." She thought it through, heart still racing, but the fear gone. "Probably on a timer. Is it late?"

"I went to your room, they said you were down here." Riley, still treading water, stared up at him, and he squatted down and rocked back on his heels. "I came to apologize for earlier." His features were softened and made even more handsome by the dim light. Had she ever wanted him? She couldn't remember. She'd wanted to be wanted. Had even that changed? "When you asked about . . ." Lennox thought for a moment, and started again. "Captain has said from the beginning he'll consider bringing you back. But it's going to be a desk job, Riley. Feel-good departmental PR."

"No."

"Filing and phoning. I know. That's not who you are, baby. You've always been go-go-go."

Riley held the edge of the pool and pushed her wet hair all the way back on her head. "They don't ever come out and tell you that you're crippled, like in a TV show, did you know that? Doctors hedge; it's day by day, current status, letting you believe that maybe what's happened will heal. They leave everything in flux, words measured, anything possible, but really they just don't want to admit they can't fix you. And meanwhile you make the necessary adjustments and accommodations. We're prisoners of the one-way trip of time."

"Your smarts never take a break," Lennox said fondly.

"My whole life I've wanted to be a cop." It came out hollow. "What am I supposed to do now?"

Lennox shrugged, and smiled, easy, kind. "Marry me. Raise a family. I mean, hey, you wouldn't have wanted to work once we had kids, anyway."

This is what happened, Riley thought. She pushed off, turned in the water, irritated, and started to sidestroke to where her chair was parked. Lennox stood and followed, pacing her along the side of the pool, misunderstanding everything. "And if you can't have kids, we'll adopt." Getting no reaction, he tried "Riles,

I'm so sorry." And when that didn't work, he said, "I'm sorry you got shot, I'm sorry you have to deal with—hell, I'd give you my legs if I could, but—and I'm sorry we have to talk about this now, but you keep pushing things, you know? And somebody's got to say it, it's time, and I love you—but you've got to stop pretending that things aren't different now."

"Things."

"You know. Don't play dumb."

"Maybe things were never what you thought."

She watched his expression change as he slowly understood what she might be telling him.

At the pool's end was a hydraulic lift with a sling seat that Riley sat in, pulled a lever, and it raised her up out of the water to the deck, where her chair waited. She made the lift arm pivot, and then, dripping wet, executed the shift and transfer into her seat, still clumsy, but defiant, now, and too pissed off to care how it looked.

"You make assumptions. You assume the world will bend to your inclination."

Lennox sighed. He had recently perfected a whole language of sighs. But he was still dodging and weaving around her emotions like the good-looking, calculating jamook she'd always known. Riley tried to wheel herself away, but Lennox grabbed the handles of the chair and she couldn't go anywhere. Her wet hands skidded on the wheel tread.

"Let go."

"No."

"Let. Go."

Muscling the chair around, Lennox got her facing him and sank to his knees, right in front of her.

"Never." He seemed to think this was his manly moment; it was, she realized sadly, how his head worked. But Riley was crying, and hating that she was crying, trying to scrape the tears away with the sides of her hands, as Lennox made his plea. "We're going to get through this together. Okay? I promise. You're the only girl I've ever wanted, since the first time I saw you. Back on the track. At Peninsula High."

She let the "girl" pass, and reminded him, "Throwing up after the fucking eight hundred, which I never wanted to run but Coach Walter made me, promising me he'd give me the three hundred hurdles, which he never fucking did."

"Who brought you a towel? My towel. It never smelled right again."

Riley couldn't help but smile a little. They'd known each other for so long, had their moments, she softened and considered that maybe they could find new common ground, if he would just listen.

No. What were the odds?

Lennox's hands found her hips. She lowered her head. Their foreheads touched.

"I want my job back."

"You're tired." Lennox attempted a soothing voice that wasn't convincing at all. "You're frustrated. Why don't we sleep on this and then—"

"You mean dream, not sleep. And I'm done with dreams." She felt him tense up. Gently she disengaged, held him away by the shoulders and looked into his eyes and said, "I want my job back, Terry. So I can prove Willa Ko is innocent."

Lennox said nothing. And Riley's frail smile died.

———

SHE JOLTED AWAKE, as if she'd been shot again—or dreaming about it—heart speeding, sweating, trembling, she fumbled for the bed's control, raised up, and saw, covering the entirety of the opposite wall, a mosaic of photographs: dozens of old-school chemical-print color eight-by-tens matched overlapping in a tiled, wall-spanning study of the Willa Ko condo murder scene, assembled from Finn's late-night reshoot.

In sum, it was breathtaking: lurid, striking, beautiful, ambivalent, and cruel. Every nuance of the crime peeled back, the palpable sense of the violence done there, overcast with sadness, and loss.

Finn Miller was asleep in the big chair across the room. A glaze of oatmeal light seeped from the windows, cast by another June morning's marine layer draped low across the harbor.

Riley angled forward, drew the covers aside, lifted her transfer board from beside the bed, set it in place, and slid competently over into her wheelchair. With every repetition she was better at it.

She rolled her chair close to the wall of photos. Studying it, holding her breath, transfixed by the ambition of it. Her fingers traced the outline where Charlie's body had been, the tile floor painted with dark pools of dried flaking blood, the forensic flags, the frenzied spatter and drywall impacts, the jagged bullet hole in the overturned chair.

It was like she was in the room, but better, because the stillness of it, the immutability of Finn's timeless tableau, allowed her to find distance, think, reflect.

She studied the wall for a long time, rolling back and forth. Then she pivoted her chair away, glided to where Finn was scrunched up sleeping, and sat, studying him, confounded. Sleeping, he looked painfully young, almost helpless. Why this man? She didn't find him all that attractive, so how was it possible she was attracted to him? Who was he, this new normal, before she was even caused to have one?

Surely a misstep.

She reached and gently touched the huge new ugly bruise on the side of his head. His eyes fluttered open and her heartbeat skipped. *Fuck.*

Finn's voice was dry and growly. "Oh, hi." He sat up awkwardly, surfacing, self-conscious. "Hi. Hi, I—"

"Yeah, that's enough times with the 'hi,' okay?"

"Right. Okay. So—"

"—The wall? I noticed."

"Yeah."

"It's something."

Finn blushed, Finn rambled, "Well you said you needed the crime scene photos from the Ko murder and I don't have backup because everything got stolen so I went back to the condo and, because my memory for how I shoot things is pretty photographic, no pun intended—"

"That's not—" Riley started to interrupt.

"At first I was just going to re-create what I did for the crime lab—"

"—a pun, though. Is it?"

"And then I thought, Heck, maybe if I just did a close composite of the whole space you could get a clear idea of—"

"Amazing and useless," she said over him. "Very David Hockney, though."

"What?" He looked at his wall, frowned. "No. Hockney's not

the only artist who—" then caught himself. "I used an old Pentax film camera. I had to get this guy I know—who's not a guy, actually, I guess now—but she's got a portrait studio and a darkroom and we printed all these, I forgot how long it takes, they're still a little damp."

"Did I need to know all that, Finn Miller?"

"No. Right."

But couldn't resist noting, "I see you're not a big fan of the golden ratio."

He was caught short. "No. Wait. How do you know about—"

"Too provincial for you?"

"Yeah. Well, no. I mean. It's just, I think every composition has its own unique, organic logic. If you start to apply some artificial rule—"

"Was it Susan Sontag who said that the knowledge we get from still photography is always going to be sentimental? Cynical or humanist. Do you agree with her?"

"Sontag?" Finn stared, with an expression that seemed to ask, *Is she fucking with me?*

No, she was acutely aware that he had done this for her, and her voice shifted gentle. "You're collecting head wounds."

He touched the bruise. "Yeah . . . ignoring that some chick sucker-punched me first, last night this yeti-like personage walked into the condo while I was there—"

"Wait. How did *you* get in?" She didn't wait for an answer. "Don't tell me. The condo was sealed." She closed her eyes in frustration. "Finn, that's illegal, it's a felony, if you get caught."

Finn shrugged it off, digging in his backpack for a proof sheet, jacked. "I kinda blinded him and ran, but he caught me with a lucky punch." He showed her the strips of blown-out, overexposed images. "But when I triggered the flash, I also took pictures of him, so—see? There—" Sure enough, tiny photographs of the big man from the condo, Dutch-angled, flash-washed, that would have been comic if he hadn't come so close to shooting Finn.

"Oh, no."

"What?"

"Don Mexico."

"You know him? I think he's a cop."

"Oh, yeah." Riley tried to guess what business Mexico could have had in going there. "Cop and a half."

Finn seemed not to have processed it yet from the way he said, almost thrilled, "He tried to kill me."

Riley stared at Finn, worried, for the first time understanding the full measure of what he had done. He took the proof sheet back and met her gaze and she looked away, face flushed, at the wall of photos from the crime scene, but she wasn't really seeing anything, she was momentarily overwhelmed.

"What."

"Nothing."

"Can I ask you," Finn said, then, "why would a cop want to go back there after, what, six, eight weeks? And—"

Riley talked over him, "You need to get out of here, Finn," rolling backward, away, "and you need to take me with you." At the closet, she pivoted the chair and started stuffing her few spare clothes and belongings into an overnight bag.

"Wait, what? Why?" He watched her, completely confused. "I'm . . . Slow down for a sec. What does this—"

"Take the pictures down," she told him, and when he didn't start moving, repeated, louder, "Finn. TAKE THE PICTURES OFF THE WALL."

He did, then, grabbed and stripped, leaving a couple corners and bits of tape.

"We can't let them figure out it was you—"

"Who's they?"

"Mexico. Whoever. Just hurry."

He held up the thick messy stack of rumpled photo prints. "What should I do with these?"

Riley threw him the duffel and started to wheel out the door. "In the bag. LET'S GO."

"Slow down—wait . . ." It took Finn another moment to get the sheaf of photos from his mosaic stuffed into the duffel, and he had to run to catch up with her as she sped down the corridor. "How would he figure out who I am, he barely saw me."

"I DON'T KNOW. He's a cop. Maybe he's seen you before at a crime scene? It doesn't really matter." They shot past the floor station, where a desk nurse absently watched them go. "And if Mexico finds you here, sees those pictures, connects you with me? All hell's gonna break loose."

"He already tried to *kill* me. What other hell could there be? And anyway, I want to hear him explain what *he* was doing in that condo middle of the night this long after the shooting."

"No, you don't. You were in a court-sealed crime scene, Finn. He's a cop, he can make up a reason. You've got no defense."

"Why don't we call your fiancé and have him give us some protection?"

"And tell him what? That his number two went back to an active-case crime scene to look around?"

Finn was quiet.

"We can't prove anything, except that you broke in. And if

Mexico IS dirty?" She let the comment hang. "You're the one with all the theories about doctored photos and bad cops on the inside."

Finn became defensive, "Okay, but." He didn't, however, have any defense to fall back on.

"And Terry Lennox's not my fiancé, he's—"

"—none of my business, I know. I was—"

"—Don't." They arrived at the elevators, and Riley punched the call button.

Ding.

The elevator doors gaped, Riley backed herself in, and Finn followed. "Where are we going?"

Riley said, "Where do you live?" as if she didn't know.

Did she?

Ding.

A second elevator arrived, its doors whispering apart to deliver a relatively upbeat Detective Terry Lennox, in no real rush. He had another excessive offering under his arm, a plush stuffed *Fifty Shades of Grey* teddy bear he got from God only knew where. Little pink handcuffs and a blindfold over the button eyes; Terry couldn't help himself, Riley thought sadly, and if he'd turned the other way he would have seen her, seen her leaving with Finn Miller, but Lennox strode off toward Riley's rehab wing, checking his reflection in the big windows, clearly liking what he saw there, and oblivious to the elevator doors closing behind him, and her escape.

6

FURTHER ELEVATOR ADVENTURES upon arriving at Finn's building: The ancient utility lift doors were open, but the car itself was stuck four feet off the lobby. There was a repair guy from Otis beneath it, bitching under his breath and hammering on something so filthy it was shedding grime like dandruff.

"Gonna be at least the end of the day, sorry, kids," he mumbled to Finn and Riley after they had stared at him for long enough. "I'm waiting on this master control dealio my trainee's bringing down from Camarillo, but there's a Sig Alert on the 101 at Topanga. Traffic's backed up all the way to Oxnard."

Finn and Riley swapped vexed looks, and moments later Finn was carrying her up the stairwell, already sweating when they got to the first landing.

"You can stop if you need to rest."

"I'm fine," Finn insisted grimly. "You're not that heavy."

They both knew he was lying. By the time they summited

the second floor, Finn's legs were wobbly, and as he gathered himself for the final ascent, the nearest loft door opened and Arden came bustling out, dolled up for an audition. She locked up, turned, saw Finn with Riley in his arms, and stopped dead, all dagger eyes.

What could Finn say? "How's the rash?"

Arden answered icily, "I made you lemon cake." She wheeled, fumbled with her lock, and went back into her flat, slamming the door.

"Is that your girlfriend?"

"No," Finn said too quickly, and kept climbing.

"She's gorgeous," Riley added.

Sure enough, lemon cake was in a Tupperware placed by the door to Finn's third-floor entry. "Arden thinks lemon is a comfort food," Finn said. He faced up to the skein of locks, Riley sagging in his aching arms; he needed his keys but also to not drop her, which was physically impossible. His legs started to shake.

"Here"—at least her voice was light—and reaching down into his pocket, she said, "Let me . . ." She found the keys.

Finn started to give her instructions, forgetting for the moment that she would already have heard his disclaimer: "There's a pattern. To how they open. You gotta do it in exactly the right order. Let me—let me just—catch my breath—and I can tell you—"

But Riley got the right order, first time, and before Finn could calculate the ripple of that obvious confession, the unlocked door swung open and they were staggering inside.

"I'm a good guesser," Riley deflected, then, as if she could read his spinning mind. "I even used to teach SAT prep. When they didn't dock you for guessing."

"Where do you want to—"

"—Wherever. Just so I can sit without tipping over." And then, gesturing, "There, there's good—"

He put her in the drafting chair. It was his most expensive piece of furniture, spine-friendly ergonomic, with soft rollers and a lever that she used to lower herself as Finn shrugged off his backpack and, exhausted, said, "I'll go down and get your chair and duffel."

"No rush." Using her hands, she spun and pushed off from the drawing table, rolled tilt-a-whirl to the kitchen counter, where she pushed off again, ping-ponging around the room—"I like this thing"—until she was back among the unofficial photographs from Charlie's murder, which he'd left clipped and hanging from the lines all this time and which, now that he thought about it, must have been why she had wanted to be brought to his place.

"Hey. Are all these from the Charlie Ko shooting?" she said, not really a question, but without guile, and again he couldn't read her, whether she was jerking him around or truly thought she was seeing them for the first time. She went carefully from photo to photo for a while, then asked: "Would it be possible to print these in black-and-white? And can you reprint the others . . . the ones you took last night?"

"Sure. No. The others are film, I'd have to go back to the darkroom." He couldn't quite bring himself to ask the one question he wanted answered.

She nodded, distracted. "That's okay, we'll use what we have of those." A quiet loomed, and after a while Riley glanced over her shoulder and looked at him. "What?"

Finn took the easy way out. "And the cop Mexico?"

Riley shrugged. "Finn, I figure I have about twenty-four hours until the full wrath and weight of Long Beach PD comes down on us, or me, in the form of cease and desist, conduct unbecoming, suspension from active duty, mandatory Internal Affairs inquiry, psychological evaluation, and dismissal with cause for obstruction of and interference in an active investigation. That's what I'm focused on. Whatever that fat squirrel is up to is the least of my worries." Riley returned to the photographs. "*This* is what I needed: the pictures you took on the day, AND the pictures from last night. Do you have a loupe?"

Finn did indeed.

"Sweet. Oh, but first can you get my phone out of my bag?"

HE ANSWERED ON THE FIRST RING, an angry "Where are you?"

Riley said, simply, "Safe. I wanted you to know, so you wouldn't worry. Or harass the nurses."

From the guilty pause that followed, she knew that he had. "Riley what the fuck-all are you doing?"

"Solving your murder, Terry," she said. "Since you don't seem fucking interested."

And before he could respond she'd hung up on him.

Had he been speaking from her empty room? She wondered if he'd notice the bits of tape and photo paper from Finn's mosaic on the big facing wall. For a detective, Lennox was easily blinded by his emotions, but she was fairly certain he'd find the engagement ring Finn had put on the side table and Riley had forgotten and left behind still untouched, and maybe he'd finally understand that the shooting had taken more than just her legs.

RILEY HANDED THE PHONE back to Finn. "Take the battery out, hit the phone with something, a hammer, if you've got one, break it into pieces and throw it in the trash." She was settled again in her wheelchair, Finn having sherpa'd it up from the lobby with her duffel; a selection of Finn's new photographs of the Charlie Ko condo crime scene were already tacked along the length of the longest loft wall at just the right height for her, while his big printer spat out black-and-whites of the unofficial photos from his original crime scene shoot. Finn watched her roll along the span of images, his photo loupe in her lap.

"I could download and scan everything to my desktop," he said, as he resumed tacking up another set, parallel to the first, for her perusal, "better resolution, infinite zoom . . ."

Riley shook her head. "I like how I can move through them." She leaned into one photograph and then another, using the loupe to enlarge the odd detail. "Look at this hand. The way the fingers curl, like he's hiding something." She parked in front of a wide shot of Willa's father, Albert, frozen in the act of trying to collect his granddaughters from their father's lifeless corpse.

Next to it, closer view, Albert has lured the girls away, he's holding their hands. There's no sorrow in his expression. His eyes almost black.

"He's glad Charlie's dead." Riley noticed. "Absolutely no remorse."

Finn had his doubts. "Pictures can lie."

"Sontag says photographs don't explain, they acknowledge."

"More Sontag?"

"Yes."

"You mocking me?"

"I don't know what you're talking about." She looked over at him innocently.

Finn pointed his chin at the picture of Albert. "That's just a fragment in time."

"Okay, but look." Finn couldn't, because Riley had the loupe; she gestured anyway from a close-up of Willa looking off-frame left to a different close-up of Albert, seemingly looking right back at her, connecting them by inference. "Look at her eyes, look at his body language: Like, he knows what she's done, he doesn't much like it, but she's going, 'Please don't stop me.'" She sat back. "A silent communication, daughter to father. She's totally falling on the grenade for him."

Finn frowned. "Dad shot Charlie?"

Riley caught him staring at her in a way that left him feeling exposed. "What."

"Um." Finn didn't quite agree with her theory, but, "Can we scroll back and talk about why someone inside the department, one of your brothers or sisters in blue, doctored the pictures of where you got shot?"

In Finn's pocket, because he'd neglected to terminate it, Riley's phone hummed. Lennox was calling back. Riley shot Finn a scolding look and he sheepishly handed the phone to her, unwilling, he tried to explain, not exactly truthfully, to be a party to her domestic hurricane. But instead of answering, she pried the battery out, dropped the phone on the floor, and rolled over it, back and forth, until it cracked and was ruined.

"Maybe there's no connection," she said. "Maybe it's two

separate and unique events, my shooting, Charlie's killing, connected only by the variable that is you."

Finn couldn't decide if she believed that or just wanted *him* to believe it. He felt the throb of his eye swelling, the whole side of his face ached; a trip to the bathroom had disclosed a lurid bruise, leaching down purple and yellow.

Riley resumed where she had been interrupted. "You're the photographer, picture this: Charlie Ko, a sweet, hapless guy, first-generation Korean-American whose wife became a warrior, so he, left behind, maybe feeling the challenge to his masculinity, developed a weakness for softer girls and hard drugs. Picture him side-lit, deep shadows, sinfully easy on the eyes, an eggplant-colored silk suit he can't afford on Willa's salary, showing off the perfect orthodontia his parents spent a fortune on, gliding through the glittery ripples of hotties and hipsters at an upscale waterfront club."

Finn shook his head, stubborn. "I want to hear about Sunken City."

"He found both," Riley continued about Charlie, ignoring Finn's question though she seemed pleased that he wasn't giving up on it, "in a bad little rich girl named Mallory Koenig, while his wife, our Willa, femme-patriot, was chasing Islamofacists around the Fertile Crescent, a zillion miles away."

"Mallory? The witness from—"

Impatient: "Yeah. Pale waif, five-four on her tiptoes, probably can't remember her natural hair color, perky silicone implants. That kind of heroin chic that went out of style in the nineties, gift-wrapped in linen or whatever, spike heels and a Hermès Baccara clutch."

"She seems nice," Finn said, dry.

"Backseat blow jobs, sexy kisser—*lots* of tongue—and just like that Charlie was all tangled up in this nickel-dime neighborhood drug ring I had stumbled on while trolling for bigger fish."

"Undercover."

"It was casual, he didn't even know at first that what she had him doing was dealing. She'd slip a night's supply of white powder and pills from her purse into his pocket, and while Mallory danced with the skinny-jean hipster neckbeards, not holding, blameless, out on the main floor, Charlie was over in some dark corner selling eight balls or Molly to horny bros and party people."

"If you knew all this," Finn said, resigned to let her spin out her tale, "why didn't you just bust them a long time ago?"

"I needed a snitch. Mallory, Charlie, they're chum bait. You put them in jail and two more losers show up waving their hand, ready to step in. I was chasing this shadow, Mallory's supplier—he calls himself Mr. Rogers—from the old kids' TV show? Because what with the Mexican cartels and the Vietnamese syndicate and the Mongols biker gang, the southland narco-economy getting so damn crowded a man's got to diversify his neighborhood, Mr. Rogers has moved way past the party drugs into trafficking in human beings. Guatemalan black-market babies, contract sweat labor for the rag trade and high tech, underage girls for Fullerton pimps or Asian hostess clubs, and indentured domestic servants for certain Orange County elite."

She took a breath. "Charlie had no idea what he'd stepped into, and when finally he did, discovered he couldn't get the stink off."

Her color rose, her voice took on a different tone; Finn saw the pure cop in Riley, passionate, unrelenting. The job was at her core, fundamental; legs had nothing to do with it, Lennox was so wrong.

"I got super close," she said. "Twice we raided pop-up hostess clubs on Charlie's call and found them empty. Girls gone, but with the K-pop still playing, cigarettes smoldering, ice not even melted in the drinks."

"Somebody tipped them off?" Finn now saw where it all looped back to the bad cop.

"Maybe." Riley maneuvered herself under a print still clipped to a line, reached high, snagged it with two fingers and plucked it free. "Willa came home and everything went sideways." It was a photograph of Gunny Ko, after the crime, in a nakedly candid moment Finn had stolen from her: tucked in on herself, hands bound, small against the condo wall.

"Couple of months ago, I watched as Willa—no makeup, hair pulled back, combat fatigues, decidedly unglamorous—came out of the belly of a plane having mustered out from another so-called advisory tour in Kabul. Mobbed by her girls. But looking across the tarmac at Charlie, who hung back, already slouching his retreat, because he'd been fucking Mallory Koenig blind just two hours earlier in the backseat of her car."

Riley's voice grew husky. "They argued right there in the parking lot. Willa, ballistic. Kids wide-eyed and quiet, in the car with Albert. The wild of it is, Charlie wanted her back. He owned what he'd done. He was just weak."

"What did Willa want?"

Riley stared at the picture in her hands. "Well, he was beautiful, wasn't he? Exotic. He treated her, when he was with her, like an empress. I mean, yes, okay, Charlie worked her, too. But is that not too reductive? So elegant, and gentle, even in the face of her fury, he never touched her in anger. Loved her as completely as he completely betrayed her."

When she looked up at Finn, Riley's eyes were filling with those annoying tears he knew she hated. "And I let it unfold. Because I needed my goddamn informant." She thumbed at the corner of one eye. "And what can you say to a girl, anyway, guy like that, she feels like she's won the lottery when she's with him and he's not too high?"

FINN WAS QUIET for a while. He watched as Riley moved again among the pictures, collecting a few selects and then rearranging them in a new order, illustrative of her theory of the crime as she told it. "So. Now picture Willa's kids, at the playground, on the climbing structure the day after Mom got back. Albert is watching them, protective, but with one jaded eye always on his daughter and Charlie, who were off to one side, on a bench, deep in marital crisis, Charlie doing almost all the talking, believably contrite, pleading his case. Willa in tears. And Albert seething."

It was her version of Mason's sculpting, and Finn understood where Riley was going with this. "How did her dad get ahold of her gun?"

"Charlie told me Willa gave it to her dad, for protection. She smuggled it off base because she was worried that Charlie's drug dealing would blow back on her family. She'd just spent three years watching innocent Afghans get caught in crossfire. It wasn't going to happen on her watch."

Finn was not convinced. "And you believe her father killed Charlie why?"

"Didn't want them back together. Albert's old-school."

"Racist."

"No. Well, I'm sure there's some of that, but no. A morals-and-standards thing. He's ex-military himself, his wife was this ballsy federal agent who got killed back in '99, Ensenada, I think, a shootout with the Arellano Cartel. Willa is Albert's everything. And Charlie Ko was messing with his daughter's heart."

Finn imagined it: Charlie and Albert, condo living room, big blowout argument, Albert has the gun, pulls the trigger—Finn looked at the photograph of Charlie, dead on the floor, all bled out. "Is this how you always roll? Like, flash judgments that cherry-pick whatever evidence you need to prove your point?"

"I didn't roll at all until recently." Riley's eyes flickered impatience, stung. "And you took the pictures."

"Yeah, but what if they never actually looked at each other the way you say? Or looked, but didn't really see?" Finn gestured between single stills of Willa and her dad. "Maybe I just caught them at the exact instant where their gazes crossed. Willa's looking to her children, Albert's turning to talk to a cop just out of frame. But the eye-lines match, out of context. You see what you want to see."

Finn waited for the argument, but Riley seemed willing to consider that she had it wrong. For a while she didn't say anything, and moved the pictures around again, and tacked up, off to the side, a wide-angle Finn had taken of the entire tableau: Albert, Willa, cops, kids, body. "Is that how you remember it?"

"Like you said, I just take the pictures. I don't try to understand them."

Riley faced him. "I don't believe that." But when Finn chose not to respond, she didn't pursue it. "Well, in any case, Willa Ko didn't kill her husband."

"How can you be so certain?"

"Bullet casings," Riley said. Finn, who was not a cop, didn't have the slightest idea what she was talking about. "Gun with a clip, like Willa's, the empty casings eject," she explained. "We find them afterward, scattered around the crime scene, unless the shooter remembers to pick them up."

"Okay."

"They aren't in any of your pictures from the scene, official or otherwise."

Finn was confused. "So Willa took them."

"No. I asked her. She said she didn't. I implied we had already found them, and she wanted me to believe that, yes, she'd left them there."

"Because she thinks her father committed the crime."

Riley just nodded.

"Okay." Finn pretended to think about this, but hadn't let go of his original question. The mystery in which he was most interested was Riley. "So what were you doing out in Sunken City the night you got shot? And why did those pictures get doctored?"

But Riley had pivoted away, turned her back to Finn, to stare at the new mosaic of photographs she'd tacked to the wall. "Who's the detective here, Finn?" she said, then answered for him, "Me, I'm the detective."

Finn saw no reason to dispute it.

"I'LL NEED A NEW PHONE. One of those throwaway ones, where you buy a chunk of time."

"I'm, what, your assistant now?"

She didn't take the bait. "You've got that friend who can get us in the crime lab, yes?"

Finn hedged, "Yeah. But—"

"—Forget about Mexico." Riley's shoulders stiffened. "He didn't doctor your photos." She was motionless. She didn't elaborate, she didn't turn.

"SHE WANTS TO SEE what Forensics found in the victim's pockets."

"What's going on with your eye?"

Finn mumbled something about whacking himself with the camera and Joaquin shot him a doubting look, but Finn gave back nothing as his friend led him down the narrow aisles of old wire-front lockers, looking for a number scrawled on a Post-it. The property room was cramped, never intended to hold so much detritus of misbehavior, and smelled foul, the overhead lights old-school fluorescents, hideous blue-white tubes that cast everything in a glaring bleak hue of shame.

"Everyone in the lab's making bets on how many weeks it'll be before Lennox skins and guts you for stealing his woman," Joaquin said under his breath.

"She doesn't belong to him," Finn schooled him. "People aren't property."

"I took the under on two."

Finn cut a dark look in Joaquin's direction and Riley's voice came thin and filtered through the cell phone Finn held out in front of them in his hand like a *virgula divina*: "What?"

"Nothing," Finn assured her.

She was with them via FaceTime on the tiny screen, and he was dowsing for her, still kind of puzzled and pleasantly annoyed by how easily she was able to convince him to do things he would never have done before he met her. "Why does your friend keep whispering?"

"You clear this with Homicide?" Joaquin said.

"Why would we need to?" Riley countered from the phone. "We're just looking. Not going to mess with anything."

Joaquin shot Finn another dubious sidelong look that Finn ignored, but that Riley was somehow able to read.

"What."

"Nothing," Finn and Joaquin both said, too quickly, as Joaquin stopped short and keyed open a cache filled with the physical evidence collected at the site of Charlie Ko's murder. Bagged and tagged and sealed and carefully labeled, case number on everything. From his pocket Joaquin pulled on a pair of latex gloves, just in case, and Finn lifted and aimed the phone so Riley could see, streaming back to the desktop computer in Finn's loft, the items Joaquin retrieved from the locker. Keys, wallet, credit card, loose change, lip balm, a couple of crumpled receipts. A small bulging brown crime lab envelope that Joaquin squeezed open to show the two empty brass bullet casings inside.

Riley laughed. "Magic," she said to Finn.

Finn understood that these had not been in evidence the last time Riley visited. "Not really helpful, though," he pointed out.

"No," Riley said, then explained, "The night he got killed, Charlie left me a voice mail. Said he had something important to tell. That's why I was in Sunken City to meet Mallory, I thought she knew what . . ." Her voice went thin, and Finn could hear how difficult it was for Riley to talk about the shooting, still.

"I took her picture," Finn said, and thought it useless until Riley asked where it was. "One of the flat drawers," Finn told her, unable to remember which one.

"I had hoped she knew what Charlie wanted to tell me."

"She was the bait," Finn said. "They used her to get you out there."

The video feed was quiet, which told Finn that Riley had long ago come to the same conclusion. He zoomed his phone camera in on the bin as Joaquin rummaged through what remained. "Anything else of interest?"

But the chat window was empty; Riley had disappeared from frame, and all Finn and Joaquin could see on the phone was a slice of Finn's loft kitchen, a short run of the photographs hung from clothesline, a blank stretch of wall and ceiling.

"Riley? You still there?"

They heard her voice, hollow with the loft's naked echo, tinny through the phone, but couldn't decipher it. They waited, and for a long time she didn't say anything. There was a dull rumbling that Finn guessed was Riley rolling around his loft in her chair. Joaquin made a face. Finn tried to ignore him.

"What are you seeing?"

"It's not what I'm seeing, it's what I'm not seeing," she said, still out of frame, but her words clear.

Finn and Joaquin stared at the empty feed.

"I'm not sure I follow."

"His phone, Finn." Riley came back into frame. "A player like Charlie never goes anywhere without his phone."

"True dat," Joaquin quipped. "Nobody ever goes anywhere without their phones."

"And it's the first thing Homicide would have looked for. If it's not there in Property, they didn't find it." Riley let this settle. "So where is it?"

7

CONCENTRATE. She was looking but not seeing. Finn's photos reeled before her in a wall-mounted slide show:

—Charlie, dead.

—Willa, inconsolable.

—Albert and the little girls, bursting in.

—Puzzled faces reeling toward their dad.

—Cops and Albert gently pulling them away.

—Carly, sobbing in her mother's arms. Jade, lost, fists clenched, clutching a dark object—

—*There.*

Riley swung her chair around sharply, and rolled to Finn's photo cabinets because she'd misplaced the loupe. One of the many consequences of the chair and the legs was a tendency for things in her lap to disappear; she couldn't feel them go, and, once gone, she couldn't search all the dark nooks and hiding places where things tend to tuck away.

She discovered archived in the top wide flat drawer a collection of hundreds of square-format, black-and-white chemical-print photographs from the middle of the last century: a Los Angeles captured almost accidentally, as if by a blind man, not Finn—grainy, under- and overexposed, in and out of focus, a plurality featuring some part of a haunted-eyed, sad-lovely young woman apparently resigned that she was never going to be correctly centered in the frame.

In the next drawer down she found a spare loupe on top of a newer sheaf of freshly printed ink-jet eight-by-tens: crisp moonlit pictures Finn had taken of her on their one-night stand. The pictures were stunning, and she was so stunning in them that at first she didn't recognize herself, thought it was some art model Finn had hired to pose and felt a stab of jealousy.

But they were of her, and seen through his very biased lens, well, Riley had never thought of herself as pretty, and certainly not at all vulnerable, and yet Finn's eye had captured both.

Time stopped. For a moment she was frozen by a complicated flood of conflicting emotions. Like a thief, Riley drew the photos out of the drawer and went through them slowly, deliberately, studying each one, trying to reconcile this stranger with the one she saw in the mirror every morning, handling them cautiously, as if afraid she might break them, or break the spell they cast, just by touching them.

And after a while she gathered herself, put the pictures back the way she found them, took the loupe, and closed the drawer.

She rolled directly back to a single photograph, still hanging from the line, of Willa's little girls in the bardo between Charlie's body, Albert, and their mother. Riley tugged it free and placed the loupe over one of Jade's grainy, underexposed little fists. And saw quite clearly that the four-year-old's fingers were wrapped around a cell phone.

"MURDERS, DIRTY COPS, sleeping with their girlfriends." Joaquin put all Charlie's personal items back in the bin, securing the door, turning the key in the lock. Finn had already hung up and slipped his cell phone into his pocket. "I hope you know what you're doing," Joaquin said.

In fact, Finn did not know what he was doing, and moreover didn't even have a pithy reply, so he just started walking back up the aisle, and his friend followed him, rambling because Joaquin didn't like the quiet:

"I met this chick once. Did you ever meet Gracie? She lived in that duplex I sublet on Fourth Street for a while with three Jet-Blue stewardesses who may or may not have been polyamorous, but definitely not with me—anyway, Gracie went out with this Signal Hill cop for a while, he was divorced. And his ex-wife, also a cop, in Bell Gardens, used to stalk them when they went out, like, not even trying to conceal the fact, and if Gracie brought it up her boyfriend, the Signal Hill cop, would tell her to 'just ignore the bitch'—his words, not mine. And I mean seriously stalking. Late-night phone calls with just breathing on the other end, a dead opossum in a bag on the front porch, showing up at IHOP in her Bell Gardens black-and-white to stare at them through the parking lot window. She broke it off, finally. Gracie, I mean. And reads in the *Times*, six weeks later, that her former boyfriend cop had been found in his bathtub, drowned, and the ex-wife arrested on suspicion of offing him."

Finn had stopped short, but not because of Joaquin's

parable—a small detail that Joaquin missed, continuing, oblivious, "I know, right? So I'm just saying—"

Joaquin nearly collided with Finn, but Finn deftly slipped aside of him, took a few strides back the way they'd come, and peered into another property bin, where a Nikon Df camera was prominent among a cache of stolen items.

He was sure of it. "That's mine. That's my Nikon."

Joaquin checked the booking tag, annoyed. "Nah, dude, this is from a burglary happened six months ago."

"I'm telling you, J, it's my camera: There's the fucking nick on the lens from the first week I had it, and—look, see?—some gaffer tape on the underside that I put there to help me grip it."

After a pointedly doubtful eye roll, Joaquin unlocked the bin and checked the camera: nick, tape. "Shit. What's your camera doing in a B-and-E bin?"

Finn could think of a couple reasons, but decided not to share them. "Who logged it in?"

Joaquin checked the tag again and this time frowned. "Lennox," he said. "Detective T. L. Lennox."

THE SKEIN OF MORNING MARINE LAYER seemed about to burn off, the sun an egg smear already leaking hard down on the concrete crawl of greater Long Beach, and Riley. She was waiting in her wheelchair on the curb outside his loft building when Finn drove past looking for parking. He was so surprised to see her that he failed to stop, and had to make a hard U-turn at the next intersection and come back. The elevator, she said, was working again.

Finn didn't tell her about the camera he'd found in property lockup with her fiancé's name on the booking slip, but Riley asked about the old-format photos she'd found in his flat drawers while looking for another loupe. The frangible timbre of her voice made him think she'd also seen the pictures he'd taken of her, and while she didn't say anything about them, he worried that she'd think he was some kind of stalker.

"I got them at a yard sale," he said, about the old photos.

"Why?"

"They were taken with a Rolleiflex. One of those cameras you look down through the top." Riley was waiting for a punch line; there wasn't one. "I know. They're crazy, but. So many of the same woman. I don't know. Something about them. Like somebody took them without looking, and yet they *see*."

"They're true," Riley said.

"Yeah, I guess." He was surprised she got it.

Assuming that they were going to the Huntington Beach address for Willa Ko's father that Riley had acquired from DMV, Finn swung right onto Ocean View, intending to angle inland, but Riley said she needed to take a detour up into Palos Verdes, so they crossed under the 110 and curled out toward the ocean.

It was quiet in the car. The palisade drive was like a California coastal cliché: Kodachrome brown-and-green bluffs above pleated cliffs, the roiling slate ocean confettied with ivory sails. Finn rarely came up here. South of where the big estates began, where very rich people lived and where Finn was sure she couldn't possibly have grown up, this cop who was nothing like any cop he'd ever met before had him leave the paved road and take a ragged dirt driveway deep into an area that backed into the Portuguese Bend Reserve, condemned and restricted because of the threat of massive landslides.

At the end of this drive, at the foot of a ruined manor house and a dead orchard, there was an ugly compound of manufactured structures to one side of which rose enormous, odd, geometric sculptures rusted red-brown by time and weather.

"Mason Mac," Finn said, amazed.

Riley looked at him icily. "How do you know that?"

The Fiat, too light for the gravel apron, fishtailed to a halt in front of a piss-yellow prefab home tentatively resting on cinderblock risers. "I've seen some of these pieces in art books," Finn said. "I'm a sucker for the guys who never got their due."

"He got as much as he deserved," Riley said, and then she fell quiet.

"What are we doing here?" And then it hit him: Riley McCluggage, Riley Mac, Mason Mac—

A gnarled fist rapped so hard on Riley's window that she flinched. An old man's face was behind hers, squinting in at them, and Finn saw in his piercing eyes the uncanny semblance.

"Hell's bells, it's the girl volcano," Mason Mac mumbled. He had several Band-Aids casually covering tiny puncture wounds on one side of his head.

"I'm not getting out," Riley told Finn, rolling down her window, and then, to her father, "Daddy, this is Finn, he's going to get something from my room."

"He the bone smoker?"

Finn said, "What?"

Riley shut her eyes, and Finn pushed his door open and climbed out from behind the wheel to look over the top of his car at her father. "I'm a fan of your work."

"Fuck you," Mason said.

Undaunted, Finn: "You were friends with Sam Francis."

"Sure. Taught me the whole business of trading in wives when they get too much mileage on them."

"And James Turrell."

"Said he'd help me slip the draft," Mason said, trending gloomy. "Instead, he went to jail, never served, and became rich and famous. I got drafted, shipped to Quang Tri, came back hooked on heroin and never made diddly-squat."

"It's the pink room," Riley said to Finn, cutting the history course short because, as she would explain to him much later, it always ended with a bitter rant. "There's a safe. You know the key code. You don't like it, but you know it. Bring me everything inside."

I know the combination? Finn didn't want to ask; she had that look, and clearly did not want her father to know what the combination was.

"It's not pink anymore," Mason warned him, as Finn headed inside.

The tiny house had been gutted, and half rewrapped with panels of tin from an old roadside sign that, if Finn was right in how he quickly mentally rearranged the tiled confusion, had once been a billboard advertisement for Ojai Pixie tangerines. The furniture was handmade, sensuous shapes of bent maple and steel highly brushed. The floor was bamboo, but unfinished where it joined the walls. You could see right down to the crawl space, and smell the dry rot and musty soil.

Finn found Riley's room, and it had indeed been repainted in a violent, unruly Abstract Expressionist sawtooth of black and white. Boxes and belongings were heaped in a corner, but the safe in the closet was exposed, bolted down, the flooring around it chipped and splintered where someone had recently tried to remove it.

Finn knelt down and stared at the keypad.

You know the code, she'd said. How was that even possible?

"I BUILT A RAMP to the front door."

There wasn't one.

"It looked like shit, so I tore it out."

"Oh. Well. Thought that counts, right?"

"I can build another one. If you're going to be coming out here more." His voice was thin, he'd aged since her shooting, she thought, and mused how that must really piss him off.

The question her father wouldn't ask lingered.

"It's okay," she said. "I doubt my chair will fit through the front door, anyway."

"Yeah, that's why I moved you out of your apartment."

"You what?"

"I put everything in storage," he said, and off her look of incredulity, "Second floor of a walk-up duplex, you weren't ever going up there again."

She groped for words. "You didn't ask?" But of course he didn't, the question was pointless. "Where did you think I was going to live?"

Her father shrugged. "I figured you'd either change your mind about the cop or bunk with your new fag"—meaning Finn—"until we found you a place you could roll into."

"Jesus, Daddy."

Mason nodded and looked out at his sculpture field, but Riley could see the moisture that was suddenly making his eyes shine. "I never wanted you to be a cop."

"I know."

"You could be anything you set your mind to."

"And I am," she said.

"Is it because I'm a failure?" he asked. He always said it almost like he was proud.

Riley didn't care to answer this question anymore.

"Your fiancé called again," Mason said, as if it just occurred to him, but she knew he'd been saving it. "He claims you're in some kind of denial about what's happened to you."

"Meaning my legs? Or that I never actually agreed that I'd marry him?"

"I dunno. Either or, I guess."

Riley said, "He's wrong. About both." Mason didn't argue it. Or didn't care. She said, "I know I'm changed. Same dreams, different stuff to deal with."

"Shit to shovel."

"Yeah, whatever."

"That new f-stop boy toy with this shiner, for instance," Mason said, nodding at the open door of the house.

"Well, maybe, sure, okay." Riley wondered what was taking Finn so long.

Her father turtled his head down and regarded her then through the open car window with a look that defied any words, an understanding and, weirdly, acceptance of her that, when it surfaced, she always found thrilling. But then, as it always would, the moment passed, it became about him. "I did the best I could." He said this defensively, but there was some pride in it, too.

"I know."

"An ex-junkie wifeless narcissist art dog knows fuck-all about a brainy little girl. Christ on a cracker, Riley. What the hell." She hated him, she loved him. She couldn't imagine it being otherwise. Mason peeled off one of the Band-Aids and tried to stick it on again, but his face, all sweaty, wouldn't have it back. "Got too close to heaven again," Mason said, about his wounds, grand. "Lah-dee-dah."

Same as it ever was, Riley thought.

FINN STARED AT the safe's keypad, blank, stumped, feeling the seconds tick past. How would he know what her code was? And why wouldn't he like it?

He stood up, irritated, suddenly wearied of whatever artful lark this was for her, and the way they couldn't, neither one of them, and wouldn't, talk about the one thing they should have sorted out by now (life was all about finding the proper proportions, wasn't it?), and needed desperately to address before proceeding (or was he being too provincial?), and he turned to go back out and just ask her for the goddamned combination when the riddle's answer dawned on him, and he couldn't help but smile.

He crouched back down and pressed six numbers: 1 6 1 8 0 3: the golden ratio of formal composition.

The safe door beeped, clicked, unlatched, and gaped open.

"STEPS," SHE SAW, fought back tears.

Finn had found a parking space right in front of the post-and-beam Seal Beach cottage that dated back to the thirties, original lap siding thick with white paint and blue trim and a drought-ruined little brown lawn from which a wide wooden stairway rose up to a low, covered porch.

Seven steps to the front door. Finn was beside her, "I'll carry you up."

"No."

Dusk was dropping, blue-gray and ambiguous, the line between sky and sea obscured, a soft mist rolling in off the channel, muting everything. They'd been tense and quiet again on the drive from Mason's, Riley in her own thoughts and Finn trying to sort out what he'd discovered in the safe, and why she'd trusted him to see it. The fat envelopes of what Finn could feel was cash, and which looked suspiciously like bribes, were in a plastic grocery bag Finn had found in the kitchen. He brought the ledger book she asked for, and which Riley had glanced through and then dropped at her feet with the money and the empty Cartier bag, without reaction, despite what they implied.

If she was dirty, was it a slow bleed from her undercover role, the by-product of flying too close to the source? She wasn't sharing anything with him, suddenly, and he wondered once more where he stood with her. Perhaps she was just using him because there was no one else, or because he was the easy option. Or maybe they were approximating the ugly, fitful, Gordian tangle of a real relationship, lovers becoming friends.

He had pulled Riley's wheelchair from the hatchback, set it up on the sidewalk; she swung out of the car and into it smoothly and had started up the walk as Finn closed the door . . . and then . . . she'd stopped.

Steps.

"It's not a big deal—"

Riley snapped, "NO." She angrily wiped at her eyes, pissed about the porch, and, Finn thought, her new penchant for tears, or maybe even her dependency on him, when the front door opened and a sturdy barefoot woman in leggings and a Lakers three-peat sweatshirt peered out at them.

Riley said her name and number and showed her badge. "Is Albert home?" Willa Ko's littlest girl peered out from behind the barefoot woman's hips.

The woman said, "Not home, no," her accent thick with clicks and vowels Finn knew by heart from his childhood.

"Could we—"

"—no, not home, sorry." She gestured the little girl back into the house, "Jade, go," and was about to close the door when Finn launched into what must have sounded to Riley like beautiful French gibberish but was, in fact, his passable pidgin Basque— polite, warm, simple—and the woman responded, formal, suddenly shy. Finn understood enough of it. She was the housekeeper. She didn't know where Mr. Albert was. Finn took his time, searching for words he hadn't spoken in years, gesturing to Riley, gesturing to Jade. The housekeeper smiled at Riley, showing gold crowns and mismatched laminates, nodded to Finn, and went inside, leaving the door open, and Jade playing peek-a-boo around it.

Riley's look expressed a certain amazement. "What did you tell her?"

"I said you were a hero policewoman who was trying to prove that Willa was innocent and they shot you in the back to try and shut you up."

"Oh." Then, "In what language?"

"Basque," Finn said. "My grandfather was a portrait photographer who immigrated here after World War Two."

Riley just stared at him. "Basque."

Finn shrugged. "A lot of immigrants came to Long Beach on account of the port. And, lucky for you, the Basque love subversives."

"Is that what I am?"

The housekeeper returned, trailing Jade's older sister, blunt-cut hair, six going on twenty-one, super-serious. Reaching into the pocket of her sweatshirt, the Basque housekeeper showed Riley a phone.

"That's Daddy's," the older girl said gravely. Riley asked, and she said her name was Carly. "With a *y*."

Riley turned the phone on. Someone had been keeping it charged. The Basque woman spoke to Finn again, low, animated, and he could understand only a fraction of it; Riley had Carly's full attention, and Finn was intent on watching them both.

"She likes to listen to his voice on it," Carly explained, meaning Jade, who had crept out to the top of the steps and squatted with her arms around her knees, a tiny curl of girl, to glare down at them from under her bangs. Carly said, "Jade found it under the chair where Daddy was dead."

Finn flashed back on the scene as he had shot it: cops confronting Albert at the door, the girls running to their father. Adults tried to stop them, Carly was caught but Jade had twisted away, resisting, low, letting her stubborn legs go limp, flopping down on her knees where she would have been eye-level with the overturned chair, and reached under with the perfect-sized hand to gather her father's phone.

"Daddy's still alive on it," Jade said.

"He's not," argued Carly.

Riley scrolled screens to find the message application; Carly, impatient, crowded in, took the phone away, and deftly pulled up Charlie's voice message:

"Hey, this is Charlie, leave me a message, I'll get right back to you."

Jade echoed, "Right back to you."

"Are there messages people left for him?" Riley asked.

"I can't read the names," said Carly.

But she clicked through to the voice mail archive, handed the phone back to Riley, and let Riley play the last message that Charlie had received, the day he died. Its incoming call ID read: ALBERT ZAPPACOSTA.

A voice broke, low: "I want you to stop."

"Grampy," Jade said.

"Just . . . stop. Get out of our lives, you've done enough damage, it's time to let my daughter heal." There was a whistling static of hesitation. "You don't deserve her. If you weren't the father of my grandkids you'd've been dead by my own two hands long ago. I'm—"

Riley cut it off before it went too far. There was an uneasy silence.

Carly said, "Grampa Z. was always mad at Daddy."

Finn waited for Riley to look up at him, her hunch confirmed. But she just stared at the screen, lost in thought, and scrolled back one message. No more than ten minutes before Albert's call, there was another one. The screen ID said: WILLA.

Her voice was fragile, there was street noise behind it, "Okay, I'm on my way over. I should be there by oh-sixteen-hun—um, sorry—four, or ten after, at the latest." They heard her unhappy sigh. "I can't believe you're doing this to me again." Another, longer pause, and then, barely audible, "Charlie, if this turns out to be another one of your epic fails . . . oh, golly, I'm gonna kill you."

The message ended there. Jade and Carly were motionless, caught up in the spell of their mother's voice. Riley finally looked at Finn. He shrugged, completely confounded now.

Circles within circles.

8

A WAXING GIBBOUS MOON hung in a pale blue cloudless morning framed by the skylight.

Riley stared up at it, alone in Finn's bed.

Sunrise angled through the big front windows like a surprise party, a welcome disruption of the ceaseless summer dirge of marine layer, casting from what remained of the line-hung photographs a gap-toothed crazy quilt of square shadows across the studio floor. Like a map of her life. There was a faint smell of baked dust and photo developer. The scuffle of blankets under one of his worktables revealed that Finn had slept fitfully there. Presently he was up, slouched in Riley's wheelchair, watching for her slow awakening. He had been watching for a while, as if hopeful she would feel the weight of his gaze and look over.

She didn't.

On their return from Albert Zappacosta's house with Chinese takeout last night, Finn had been called to a hit-and-run out in Bixby Knolls, multiple victims, multiple crime scenes, so Riley was left alone with the accumulating contradictions roiling the Charlie Ko murder, along with her doubts and her new normal and the lukewarm orange-peel chicken that she ate with a fork. The phone evidence of Albert's threats against Charlie Ko had been trumped by Willa's call minutes earlier; Riley began to think that Finn was right about his pictures, they were telling a story she wanted told, and by rearranging them she could contrive at least a couple of other versions equally convincing and patently false.

Frustrated, she started to reassemble the full mosaic of the crime scene Finn had hastily removed from her hospital room, hoping that she could start all over. But after tacking up the lower rows of its foundation, she realized she wouldn't, from her chair, be able reach high enough to finish.

Tears erupted, unchecked. She was alone for the first time since the shooting and no one would see her cry. At first she was worried that Finn would walk in and see her pitiable deliquescence, but then thought, would that be such a bad thing?

She turned off the lights and gave in, sat sobbing until she was all wrung out. It didn't really make her feel any better, and finally she banged into the bathroom, washed her face, rolled to the hidden latch in the kitchen, and lowered the Murphy bed.

Finn came shuffling in after midnight, and she pretended to be asleep. Her back turned to the room, she could see his reflection in the big windows when he flicked on the bathroom light and its soft illumination threw wild shadows on the walls.

She watched Finn shrug off his backpack and cross to her, and for a moment she tensed, worried he was going to join her in bed. She'd pulled off all her clothes and left them clumped on the floor where she could reach them. But he just gently rearranged the sheet over her, and then the duvet, unnecessarily, because her body's thermostat was all out of whack and—hot, cold, clammy, night sweats followed by chills—she'd tugged it off for a reason.

She smelled a faint sour of beer on his breath.

She heard him get blankets from a closet, toss them down beneath the desk, and then in the windows' reflection saw him stop and notice the wall of pictures. Finn's shadow reflection drifted across the loft to pick up the sheaf of remaining dog-eared photographs from where she'd dropped them, and she watched him spend the next half hour completing her crime scene tableau, worrying the damaged puzzle pieces as best he could and working in a hazy half-darkness that eventually lulled her to sleep.

Now the oily odor of freshly ground coffee reached her because Finn was in the kitchen, striped with that rare June morning sunlight, measuring out some dark roast. Riley twisted around to face him, wondering if he was pretending not to notice her watching, or whether he was really so intent on his French press that all else fell away. She doubted it was the coffee.

The French press looked like it had never been used. And she'd already remarked yesterday on the dozens of discarded Starbucks cups in the big studio wastebasket, belying a habit fueled more by convenience than precision. She lifted and wormed herself backward the way she'd practiced because there wouldn't always be an electric bed, to sit up propped on pillows against the wall and run a hand through her tangled hair. She needed a shower, wondered how that would work, here, when, so far, all her showers since the shooting had been facilitated by nurses and female attendants in the big wheelchair-friendly hospital room stalls.

How long can you go without a shower, in a new normal?

All Finn had was a claw-foot tub with a circular curtain and an overhead spout.

Eventually Finn looked up and met her eyes. Riley gave nothing away. And Finn, well, she could tell from how he couldn't hold her gaze that he was still pretty much at sea where she was concerned, and she had to admit that she enjoyed his unmooring, and her part in it.

She said, "What." There was a challenge in it.

He hesitated. She could almost feel him working up his courage. "So are we just going to pretend we never knew each other in your new normal? Is that the plan?" Even adrift, he was resolute, indefatigable, and it wasn't the proud obstinance of Terry Lennox, it was something else. A mystery. And Riley did love solving them.

There were so many possible answers to his question, some of them even honest, but she said, almost believing it, "I don't know what you're talking about."

Finn stared back at her. He was right, Riley thought, about her being a lousy liar. The front doorbell buzzed.

"I'm still trying to decide how much of the past I want to bring into the future," Riley said.

Locks snapped and the door was opened by Arden, who, tellingly, also knew the correct sequence. She was pissed, saw only Finn at first, and went at him. "We are friends. Whatever else has happened, or could, potentially, happen, someday, circumstances providing—you're the person I can come to and know won't judge me for not necessarily making the best decisions and maybe you're probably thinking and I don't blame you it gets a little one-sided, but I took care of you when you had the mumps, don't forget, and the thing with the weird bugs in your crisper, I solved that, so—yeah, we're friends, that's undebatable. And the thing is friends don't keep secrets from—"

Arden was a good five steps inside the loft and two steps past Finn, who'd come around the kitchen island too late to cut her off, when she registered: (a) Riley's wheelchair, (b) women's clothing piled on the floor, and (c) Riley in bed, wearing only the sheet and a sleepy smile. "Oh."

"Hi, I'm Riley."

"Arden." Riley watched as tumblers in Arden's brain spun.

"Riley's that cop who got shot," Finn explained.

Riley added, "Finn's been helping me with a case."

Arden blushed, then, and looked at Finn almost abashed, and blurted out, "I'm sorry."

"For what?"

Finn was pretty slow on the uptake, Riley thought, and as Arden started to retreat out the open door, it was Riley who stopped her: "Arden?"

Riley could see the heartbreak in Arden's brave smile. There was nothing to be done about it, but this was somebody she already had decided she could grow to like, and a friend she didn't want Finn to lose.

"I've got kind of a situation here maybe you'd be willing to help me with," Riley said. Arden said nothing, stayed in the doorway, her expression guarded. Riley knew she needed to get this just right. "Finn being Finn," Riley said, "our partnership, if you want to call it that, doesn't include certain . . . personal, intimate, not necessarily crime-related exigencies."

"Finn being Finn," Arden agreed.

"One example: my stuff, which you can see is piled where I thought I could get to it, but I'm not so sure. Another is personal hygiene, which, in my current condition, still as new to me as anyone, requires a certain amount of assistance that Finn—"

"—being Finn," Arden was warming to it.

"—exactly—and his shower, which looks, honestly, not just insurmountable for me but, like, also probably a breeding ground for biological weapons yet undiscovered. More immediately, there's just getting my pants back on."

"His shower." Arden rolled her eyes as if there was no need to say anything more.

"I could get the jeans off okay last night when I went to sleep," Riley allowed, "but they're a bitch to get back on and, well . . ." She glanced to Finn and let her voice trail off and watched Arden begin to understand that Riley had never meant to be her rival.

Nodding, Arden said, "He's all thumbs," and Riley wondered, a little jealously, which surprised her, if Arden had some personal knowledge of it.

"I'm not," Finn protested.

Arden came back in, pulled the door closed, and ignored him, picking up clothes after she wheeled Riley's chair to the bed and asking, "You want to get clean or get dressed or both?"

WILLA KO WAS unnecessarily prevaricating. Thinking, Riley guessed, she could find a gap between guilty and innocent and somehow squeeze through it.

Which would be what?

"I never said I shot him, ma'am."

The good soldier wore the requisite jail jumpsuit, and her public defender, Aaron, or Baron, Riley hadn't paid attention when he mumbled his name, had shown up in some unfortunate dad jorts and a polo shirt, hair all scrunched flat on one side where he'd evidently been napping hard, not that long ago, telltale pink of a nascent sunburn, not expecting a call from Riley asking him to bring his client in for another talk.

She had arranged to have Willa brought from the women's jail to the Long Beach Police Department where Riley was fairly certain weekend staff would allow some leeway on her duty status. Even on a Saturday, it wasn't hard to coordinate all the moving parts of her fishing expedition, but it was afternoon by the time, showered and dressed, she made Finn wait in his car in the parking lot and rolled alone through the lobby, down the familiar corridors, enjoying the shouts and greetings of the short-staffed weekend watch she encountered.

The public defender nursed a frozen coffee drink and looked to be ruing his lost leisure as Riley, who made it clear to him beforehand that she was only moonlighting this case, tried to guide his client toward an uncomfortable truth.

"No," Riley admitted, "you just said it in a way that suggests you could be lying, so that you'd be arrested and arraigned."

"I pled not guilty."

"Jeffrey Dahmer pled not guilty." Riley pushed herself up straighter in her chair, folded her hands together. "And said he didn't do it. Sergeant, we found Charlie's phone. There's a threat from your dad on it, made not more than thirty minutes before Charlie was killed."

Willa said nothing. No reaction. No emotion.

"Here's what I think you think happened," Riley said: "Your

dad had your gun. He saw Charlie was trying to pull you back into his circle of hell, went to warn him off, they argued, it got confusing . . . you came home too late and found Charlie dead. Girls gone. Dad? The math of it was easy. Blood on you, cops showing up. You hid the gun, made sure your prints were all over it—hid it where anybody could and would find it." Willa said nothing, but there were tears running down her face. "You're taking the fall for your father."

Willa looked guilty of something for the first time.

Riley watched the public defender shift uncomfortably. "If you found his phone, and it's been in the hands of others, I doubt it's admissible," he pointed out.

"And anyway," Willa offered, abruptly defiant, "it's got my voice on it, too."

Her attorney frowned. "Excuse me?"

"You heard my message, right?" Willa was staring at Riley, resolute. "I called him before my father did. Right? You heard what I said I'd do to him."

"Can I have a moment with my client?" Aaron or Baron asked, really confused now, but neither Riley nor Willa was paying any attention to him.

"I heard it," Riley said.

"Okay, then."

"Are you saying you killed your husband?"

"Do not answer that," her lawyer said, and Willa didn't, but Riley wasn't expecting her to lie about it.

"Your phone message," Riley said, "changes nothing. Different context, Sergeant. Different inflection—I heard that, too. *If he was lying,* you said in your message. Which Charlie wasn't, was he? Just weak."

Willa shook her head. "Ma'am, I said what I said."

"I discount the threat. Figure of speech. Or . . . are you confessing to me now? You can't have it both ways." Riley knew that was exactly what Willa wanted.

Willa clammed up.

THE METRO BLUE LINE ran from Long Beach to downtown Los Angeles, but Finn got off midway, where the blue and green lines crossed, a crazy-ass terminal that seemed to hang suspended between the ribbons of elevated traffic ramps connecting the Harbor and the Century Freeways.

Traffic rumbled and hissed above and below and to either side of the platform, arteries thick with chrome and rubber and steel that pulsed past in spasms. The swath of perfect cornflower-blue sky only intensified the surreality of what Finn was doing.

Riley's sack of cash-fat envelopes was on his lap, along with the journals she had stacked together and fastened with rubber bands. The handoff was scheduled for 10:14, but the green line came in early, and when the passengers straggled off Finn didn't see anyone who matched the description Riley had given him.

She didn't explain the money, and he didn't ask. It had become part of their understanding now that she would tell him what she wanted to tell him, and what she didn't want to talk about he wouldn't press for. Finn had never been good at asking questions, anyway; his camera lens usually did it, or provided him with the answers he needed. Words were generally unreliable, in his experience, easily spoken, too often imprecise, usually fraught with misdirection.

"She described you perfect, right down to how you turn your right foot in when you get a little anxious."

A black man in saggy pants and a spotless white T-shirt sat down on the other end of Finn's bench and let his huge hands hang off his knees. Finn hadn't seen him get off the train, and wondered if maybe he had been waiting, watching for a while from somewhere below. He didn't look like a cop, he was lanky and soft in the wrong places, bald with a full-on James Harden beard, but something about him betrayed a veiled menace. Finn had a fleeting thought that he had seen this man before, but couldn't remember where, or when.

"You got something for me from Riley Mac?"

Finn held up the bag and the journals. The man made no move to take them.

"How's she doing?"

"She says to tell you she's okay."

"Right." The man nodded, staring out at the freeways. "Fuck those guys," he said after a while, and it sounded sad. "It was a helluva thing."

Finn glanced at the platform clock. "I've got to get back to her."

"You're the picture man."

"Yeah."

"You know what's in the sack?"

"I could make a pretty good guess, yeah."

"Don't." The man stood, hitched his pants, but they fell low again, and he held them up on one side. "Just leave that shit there and forget about it, okay?" He looked at Finn with quiet eyes. Emphasis on "forget."

Finn nodded, put the sack on top of the journals, and walked back down the suspended staircase to the blue line platform, where a southbound train was just pulling in.

"HOW CAN YOU THINK Albert will be better raising your kids, if he was the one who pulled the trigger?"

Willa, petulant, replied that Riley didn't know anything about her father, or raising kids. Both were true; Riley felt her case going sideways again. The Möbius tangle of cross-intentions and misunderstanding that Willa and her father had created kept looping back on itself.

The public defender said, "Are we done?"

Willa wasn't, though. "You've killed somebody," she said, and stared at Riley, intent. The shootings were not something Riley wanted to get into, but Willa took her silence as an opening to continue, dismissive: "So you know what I'm talking about."

Riley tried to deflect, "Your little girls—"

"Ma'am, I've been gone so long and so many times they don't even know me," Willa said, without rancor. "And you of all people should understand about how the triggers I've pulled and the lives I've watched bleed out—how that changes you and what that might have done to my soul."

Riley didn't. She hadn't experienced it in that way. But before she could say anything, Terry Lennox had opened the door and come in, hot.

"What is going on here?"

The public defender shot up out of his chair, startled.

"We're done," Riley said simply, because there was no point

in pressing Willa any further. Even if Riley got something more than vague threats on a phone to offer him, Lennox would never be able to see beyond the narrow window of his personal and institutional bias; this was his case, he had everything he needed to win it.

She pushed away from the table and rolled past her presumptive fiancé without even looking at him, out the door, into the corridor, and she was almost to the security door when Lennox caught up with her.

"Riley—hold up—hold up!—What the hell do you think you're doing?"

"Don't worry. Your ass is covered, Terry. I didn't record anything, I didn't misrepresent my status on the case. Congratulations on your big bust."

"That's not—"

"I don't know what's more discouraging," she said, fiery, pushing her chair faster, hoping that Lennox would have to break into a run, "the fact that you didn't want me in Homicide before I got shot, or the fact that now that I'm crippled you want to pretend that it's all about that."

The desk officer saw her coming and buzzed her through. But she had to slow for Lennox to open and hold the door. "That's not—" His indignation was already starting to splinter with the usual tumult Riley knew she caused for him. She stopped, turned her chair to face him down. He made a point of calming himself. "Look, you're a doer, Riles, not a thinker."

"What?"

"That's a compliment."

"Is it?"

"Go-go-go. You know? That's you. And it's what I love about you. Hell, a year ago you were applying for the SWAT team. I mean. Homicide is slow, it's cerebral, you'd be bored stiff—"

"I don't see a lot of deep mental activity going on in Homicide right now, Terry. Just saying. Or you wouldn't be letting Gunnery Sergeant Willa Ko take a fall for a killing she didn't commit."

Twice Lennox started to say something, then thought better of it and stopped. Riley just waited; watched him go through the half a dozen mental calisthenics he needed to prevent himself from saying something to her he'd regret. They'd known each other forever, it had always been the same. She wondered if he had always just assumed that she would change into the woman he wanted her to be, needed her to be, or was it just his foolish pride (and hers?) that had kept him from giving up. Finally, sighing and mumbling as part of an exasperated exhaling of breath, he surrendered:

"What do you want from me?"

MALLORY, Finn finally remembered, was the name of Charlie's girlfriend.

Windows rolled down to embrace the last rays of sun before it sank into a gathering chill of four-o'clock haze, Finn had the Fiat wedged into what wasn't really a precinct parking space, and was idly fiddling with Charlie's phone while he waited for Riley, flipping through the messages, the contact list, the text messages, keen to test what Riley had told him about how sometimes it's not what you see, but what you don't see.

And what he wasn't seeing was the name of Charlie's girl-friend, Mallory, in any of those lists and archives.

He flipped back and forth between the screens. No contact information for anyone named Mallory. No call history. No text thread. Where's the girlfriend? It wasn't credible that Charlie wouldn't have her queued up somewhere, easy to access.

Maybe, Finn considered, she was listed only by her last name, though, considering Charlie, and all the Charlie-like guys Finn had ever known, women—girls—were never allowed the formal importance that accrues from a family name.

Nickname?

Maybe Charlie had Mallory under some kind of alias so that Willa couldn't Tiger Woods him. Or maybe there was another, secret dedicated phone they used to talk to each other exclusively.

Or, he realized, a different, dedicated app.

On his hunch, Finn backtracked to the main page, sorted through the app icons. There were several screens of them. At least two dozen games, alone.

And a German chat app called Sicher. Which was . . . eccentric, for Charlie Ko, to say the least. And which Finn opened to discover had but a single contact name, with scores and scores of secure messages to and from a "King Friday."

Not Mallory, surely. Was this the guy Riley was undercover trying to get closer to? "King Friday" rattled around his brain, seeking purchase. He was sure he knew it from somewhere. Who's the detective now? Finn thought, pleased with himself. Me. I am.

Dates, times, pickup, delivery.

Drug deals? Some other criminal enterprise?

The last message Charlie received from King Friday read:

we need to talk about u leaving

THEY USED THE CAPTAIN'S OFFICE, because it was quiet and private and unused on weekends. It looked civil. Anyone glancing in through the glass would have assumed, perhaps because they'd heard something about it from Lennox, or from someone who'd heard him bitching about it in an unguarded moment, that maybe Riley was finally coming to terms with her condition, and with Lennox.

In fact, they had been slowly spiraling out of each other's orbit since the day they met, were now more estranged than not, and all that held them together was the photographic evidence Riley was showing him, copied and chronicled on Riley's phone, including Finn's candid-camera shots of Don Mexico from their close encounter in the condo.

"Anybody could have tampered with your informant's phone over the past several weeks," Lennox said. "This is not evidence that will hold up."

"I know that. But maybe Mexico went back to the—"

"And camera boy broke into court-sealed condo. I should be filing a warrant."

"Did Mexico go there on your orders?"

"No, but there are about a thousand legitimate reasons for him to go back to an active-case crime scene."

Riley shook her head. "Mexico went to the condo looking for

Charlie's phone. Had to be. There's a dirty cop in our department, it comes from more than one source. Taking payoffs. Contract killings. Protecting this human-trafficking network. Why did you think they took me off book?"

Lennox said, "I made a call, Riley Mac. They told me they had shut you down six weeks before the shooting."

Riley was quiet. Trust was one thing they always had.

"That they hadn't heard from you since. That you might have gone into business for yourself."

"Tell me this, Terry, what's the protocol for protecting your cover in the event you stumble across the possibility of an inside source, but have no way to know his reach, or his rank?"

Lennox closed his eyes and squeezed the bridge of his nose with a pained expression.

"I can't prove anything, if that's what I'm hearing in your tone. Putting me on inactive has made it impossible for me to prove."

"Well, what are you asking me to do?"

"Gee. I dunno, Terry. I guess that depends upon how comfortable you are having one of your detectives on some very bad guy's payroll."

"How can I be sure," he said carefully, "that it's only the one cop?"

She hesitated, another ugly Terry truth dawning on her. "What does that mean?"

Lennox dodged her question. "And if I accuse my decorated investigator, Don Mexico, and you're wrong . . . he'll have my badge, he'll have my job, which he's been after since day one—and I can basically kiss my whole career goodbye."

Riley stared at Lennox, expressionless. "Bummer."

Frustrated, Lennox stood up. "What's happened to us?"

"Nothing. I don't know. Maybe you having to ask what happened is what's happened."

"You don't mean that," he said. She could see in his eyes that he was realizing: *She does.* His next move was too predictable, "Look, if you're afraid that I'm not going to stick with you—help you get fixed—"

"I'm not broken," she said, "I'm just changed."

Lennox wasn't hearing her. "If I do this for you," he said sullenly, "will you stop with all the getting-your-job-back nonsense and reconsider what I'm—"

"—For me?" Riley cut him off. "I don't want you to do this for me. Do it because he's a criminal, Terry—do it because he covered up a murder, almost two—do it because he's on the fucking dole, working for a monster—" Her eyes were on fire. "You wonder about me? Who are you? Who the fuck are you?" She wheeled and stormed out.

FINN THUMBED HIS TEXT onto the glowing Sicher app screen:

> i found this phone and all ur texts—
>
> whats it worth to u?

Whatever vague worry he might have felt about what he was about to do got trumped by the thrill of doing it. The safe remove of digital communication had suckered him in.

He pressed Send and looked up to see Riley come out of the station's side entrance, powering herself around the switchbacks of the wheelchair access ramp toward where he was waiting, through the twilight mist halos of parking lot halogens, leaving Lennox holding the door in her wake, his body language strangely impotent, like he didn't know whether to chase after her or what. The anxious moment where Finn wondered if they'd patched things up passed, and as she got closer he could see that Riley was pretty steamed. Finn thought if he were Lennox he'd let her cool down a bit, too. He slipped Charlie's phone in his pocket, deciding not to tell her just yet what he'd done, in case his amateur sleuthing put him on the wrong side of a Riley typhoon.

He clambered out to help her transfer into the car. "How'd it go?"

Riley said nothing, and used him like a valet: ignored the transfer board that he'd gone to get from the back hatch, and, as the door warning dinged like a timer, using only the handhold inside the door, violently muscled herself out of the wheelchair and into the passenger seat as if she'd been doing it this way all her life, and then lifted her useless legs in after.

While Finn collapsed her chair and slid it in the back cargo space, she slammed the door shut, the dings ceased, and she waited impatiently for him to drive her away.

"That good, huh?"

He punched the clutch and shifted into reverse. The station side door had closed, and Lennox was back inside his safe haven.

"You want to talk about it?" Finn asked, after driving for a while.

"No."

But later, on the 405 South, tires ticking over the concrete expansion gaps and the cityscape flooded woolly with the fog's dream glow, she said, "I've been wrong about everything," and left it at that.

9

RILEY'S ANGER hadn't abated much as she rolled along the shiny hardwood in front of the ball-return racks at Seal Beach Penny Lanes, interrupting the happy hour bowlers and intent on Albert Zappacosta, who was down on his knees, inflating a gutter guard for a rowdy party of little kids.

Albert looked unhappy to see her. "You upset the girls yesterday."

"Really? What will they think when they find out you let their mom confess to killing their dad?"

Riley said it softly, and no one but Albert heard her; he scowled, rose stiffly on old-man legs, and hurried off behind the scorers' tables, to short stairs that split the spare-ball shelves and led up to the shoe desk and concession, stairs where Riley couldn't follow him.

"Hey," she said, irritated, "don't do that." She raised her voice so that now everyone could hear, kids and their mothers and the early-bird leagues, and a pro giving a lesson. "Really? So is this you running away, Albert? Running from a cripple in a wheelchair?"

Albert sagged and slowed. Everyone was watching him, and Finn was waiting at the entrance, blocking his escape. Like a parade balloon deflating, Albert broke down. Quietly sobbing, making them wait until he pulled himself together, they went into the tiny, grimy coffee shop, Finn and Albert opposite each other in a booth, Riley at the end, wheelchair tucked under.

"She loved him." He brooded on Riley, ignored Finn. "After everything that K-town loser did. Willa still wanted him back."

"And she thinks you couldn't abide that happening?" Riley said without conviction.

"Is that what you think?"

"What we think isn't the issue," Finn said.

Riley shot him a warning look. This was her interview. Finn folded his hands and sat back, chastened.

"Okay, sure, I did it. I did it, gladly."

"Did what?"

He flapped his hands.

"You think she did it," Riley disagreed.

"He was an unfaithful meat sack and a user and I shot him dead."

"Willa loved him," Riley said. "And you love her. So, no, you didn't. But you're both responsible for this clusterfuck because you both actually believed the other capable of shooting Charlie Ko. Don't lie to me, Albert."

The silence that followed was broken by the clattering of pins falling. Albert stalled. "They let cops be in wheelchairs now?"

"How many cops do you know?"

"Thousands. If you count TV."

Riley smiled a little. "It's part of a new cost-saving program, putting wheels directly on the detective instead of buying squad cars."

Finn laughed out loud and Riley shot him another warning look. Albert measured his words. "I got no concept of Willa's life over there, you know?" Albert said. "Me, I never left the goddamn base. If my wife—Willa's mom—was alive . . ." He stopped himself. His hands trembled. "The things these kids have got to do to survive. The lives she's watched blown away." He looked away, at nothing. "My wife would've known what to say. I can't help her with that. I don't know who she is anymore."

"You do. She's still in there." Finn knew as Riley said it she could have been talking about herself.

"Well she didn't see him clear enough. Charlie goddamn Ko. No, she was two thousand miles away. Didn't see him step out on her. Didn't see him squire that treacherous lady-bitch. Didn't see him scared, curtains pulled, crybaby, going on and on about how hard it was going to be to get out from under it all. People pulling him all directions."

Finn watched Riley's eyes narrow as she listened to this and realized, "*You* gave *him* the gun."

"Willa came back from her third tour," Albert rambled, on a tangent, "I told her not to go back to him." He blew out air. "It wasn't just the racial thing, either, that they're from two different worlds, I mean—you could see he wasn't a person she could count on. They don't have the same values we do." Albert let that suffice, as if the weak disclaimer *But, hey, I'm not a racist* was implicit. "The hair, the clothes, the guy was so stuck on himself . . ." Albert stopped and took a breather and stared at Riley blankly, as if transported somewhere else, perhaps a moment in time where he thought it all could have gone a better way. Riley waited. "So I went to see him, yeah. Night he was killed. I brought the girls. Could have been to make sure I wouldn't . . . you know . . ." Albert reset himself, then. "To talk to him, to make sure he would try to make a go of it. That this wasn't just another one if his . . ." Again his voice trailed off as he seemed to rerun events through his head. "He swore it wasn't. He said he was gonna change things and get out."

"Out of what?"

"I gave him her gun, I did that. He kept saying how the drug stuff was the tip of a much bigger, more dangerous iceberg. How it wasn't going to be easy shaking everyone off his back." Albert looked from Riley to Finn. "Charlie was freaked out. His drug dealer, the big, big boss, whatever, I wasn't sure. His goddamn girlfriend."

"He was scared of his girlfriend?"

"I guess they have a cop on their payroll, too, you probably know about that. But now I think back on it, Charlie just kept saying he was afraid of her, he was afraid of *her*."

"The dealer or the girlfriend?"

Albert couldn't say. "I told him he needed Willa's gun way more than I did. I had it on me, I gave it to him and—"

Finn interrupted, "You were lugging a gun around when you were looking after the little girls?"

"I was an ordnance specialist"—Albert sniffed—"and Willa was worried Charlie's friends would come after her family, so, yeah, I went around packing. I have a permit."

"Finn," Riley cautioned.

Albert plowed on. "I took the kids for froyo and left their dad alone in the condo. Said he wanted time to figure stuff out." Then he added, "I know that sounds like a mistake, but he wasn't suicidal or anything. He was clear as I'd seen him in a while, and he was sober. I just . . ." Albert's guilt overcame him. "Help me out here, Detective. I'll confess I killed him if it'll spring her."

"I know. It won't," Riley said. "She made a mess of this by hiding that gun, and compounded it by thinking you pulled the trigger." Riley started to push away from the table, but Albert wasn't finished:

"Those little ones shouldn't grow up without their mom. I had to raise Willa. I'm useless. Hell, everything I touch."

Riley may have wanted to say something, but Finn beat her to it. "She thinks you did good enough that she's trusted you with her children. What does that tell you?"

Finn felt Riley staring at him curiously. Albert sat back in the booth, sad, and jangled his hands loose on the tabletop.

"Well, are you cops gonna get the one who did it, then?" Albert asked.

"That's not always how it works," Riley said, a little bitterly, Finn thought. "We get the one we can best prove did it. And hope to God that does the trick."

"IT NEVER OCCURRED to me that Charlie would have any direct contact with Mallory's supplier," Riley said, more to herself than Finn. "I just hoped he could help me get another step closer."

Finn knew that he needed to tell her about the text message he'd sent out into the void, but he didn't fully appreciate the monumental stupidity of not telling her right away. His ego had chosen an inopportune time to assert itself; everything that had transpired between them was so ragged, ungainly, and out of focus that one more badly framed and underexposed act of will-fulness was inevitable, if ill-advised.

He was deep into second and third thoughts about it when they arrived at the front door of his loft building, and as he held the door for her he was weighing ways to broach the subject without pissing her off.

"From the way Mallory treated him, I figured Charlie for a foot soldier. A malleable boy toy," she added ruefully. "I'm so clueless about relationships sometimes."

Finn had his own opinion on this, but didn't want to get into it. "The big boss killed Charlie, or had him killed, because Charlie wanted out?"

"Read between the lines, isn't that what Albert is telling us?"

"I don't know, it seems pretty thin," Finn said. "I mean, he sent minions to take you out, why expose himself by doing Charlie directly?"

Riley looked cross and shut him down. "Don't play detective, and I won't take pictures." She was hurrying ahead through the lobby to the elevator, wheel treads squeaking, when the phone in Finn's pocket, Charlie's phone, trilled a text message alert that he hoped Riley couldn't hear. She stopped, punched the button, angled sideways, and looked back at him curiously. He didn't react right away, but knew his hand had been forced.

As the elevator arrived, Finn casually took Charlie's phone from his pocket, glanced at the incoming text, and tried to throw up a smoke screen. "Unless Albert's lying."

His diversion failed. "How is it you're getting a text on Charlie's phone," Riley asked, backing in, "two months after he went in the ground?"

The doors didn't close. Finn avoided her stare and tried to shift subjects. "So I guess we can conclude, from your safe's combination, that you are a fan of the golden ratio?"

"Finn. Charlie's phone. The text?"

He took an oblique angle in on it. "You know how you said, about people and their phones, always having them? Well, I thought, right, and a guy with a girlfriend is gonna have her on speed dial. So I messed around while I was waiting in the car for you and *your* boyfriend"—no reaction from Riley—"and I couldn't find *anything* for Mallory in the normal places on Charlie's phone, but there was this strange German chat app with a slew of messages from just a single source: King Friday. And I'm like, That's weird. So I took a flyer and sent my own text out to see if anyone responded and thought if someone did I would tell you and if not—"

He pushed the third-floor button. The doors slid shut.

"—Lightning-in-a-bottle kind of thing."

"You what?" Riley, like a scolding schoolteacher, reached and snatched the phone out of his hand—

"Hey."

—and read the message:

who r u

She swiftly scrolled through the previous King Friday texts, not so much reading as absorbing them. "King Friday was the puppet ruler in *Mister Rogers' Neighborhood*," she said. She looked up at Finn. Her expression could pretty much be summed up as: *Oh, fuck.* "You've texted Charlie's killer."

Still trying to downplay it, Finn pretended he had already

made that connection. "Mr. Rogers is King Friday, okay, yeah, that's pretty much what I was thinking, but . . ." He trailed off. "So this is good, right? Set a trap?"

Riley was staring at him, her mind churning. "He can track the phone and find us."

"Well, find me, if you want to get technical—and we've been in motion all day, so." Finn got defensive. "Look, I'm sorry, but at least give me some props for—"

She laughed. "Props? You want fucking props?"

Finn knew enough not to say anything more. Riley shook her head, less angry than he expected her to be. "I keep forgetting that you're not a cop." She was growing calmer, and colder, which Finn found odd. Then he remembered what Lennox had said: She thrived on threat.

"The bad news is you're in over your head," she said. "The good news is you're with me."

Third floor, the doors gaped while Riley was digging into her purse for her own phone, and Finn got a brief glimpse of the gun in it and felt a jolt of adrenaline and his mouth dried out.

"Nobody's going to find anybody," Finn said, with less conviction than he wanted, mostly trying to convince himself, "until we respond and . . ." He was looking down the hallway to his loft door, where, for some reason, Charlie's girlfriend Mallory was rising up from where she'd been sitting, surely waiting for them. She looked small and strung-out. Pale without makeup, twitchy and helpless and scared, same as she'd been the night of the Sunken City shooting.

"Hi." She looked past Finn, at Riley. "I didn't know where else to go."

"How did you know to go here?" Riley asked, and Finn realized she already knew the answer and what he'd read as fear in Mallory's face was a calculation altogether different. Lennox's voice mail message bled thin from Riley's phone until she hung up.

"Somebody texted me," Mallory said, as she pulled a big .44 from her Longchamp bag and aimed it rock-steady at Riley.

For some reason he couldn't even later explain, Finn reached back and punched the CLOSE DOOR button as he stepped out of the elevator, into the line of fire, raising one hand halfway, like a kid in class. "That was me."

The elevator doors snapped shut on Riley as she said Finn's name. She was safe inside. But Mallory came faster than Finn thought her capable of moving, swift, assured, and she pressed the gun barrel against his head so he could feel its perfect circle stamp into the skin of his temple.

She yelled at the elevator doors, "I will kill him, Detective. You have five seconds."

10

FINN CLOSED HIS EYES, dizzy with panic, smelled gun oil and Mallory's perfume, heard the whistle of her breathing, his thoughts swirling, circling back weeks to that first night and a crying girl in a slinky dress, and apes, Canadians, the moon in the skylight, and the frozen ticks of time, photographs, that had set all this in motion.

"Four."

He felt like he might throw up.

IN THE ELEVATOR, Riley was staring at the control panel, thinking, Who am I kidding? She was wheelchair-bound, Mallory had a hostage. Every rational instinct said, *Push the DOWN button and call for backup, now. Get help. Cops need legs.*

Mallory's voice cut through, muffled. "Three."

But what about Finn?

"Two."

Riley drew her gun from her bag, slipped the safety, primed the chamber, punched the DOOR OPEN button and aimed out, two-handed.

The doors split. The corridor was empty. Finn's loft door was wide open, lights on inside.

"We're in here," Mallory called out.

In her career, in her life, Riley had never felt so exposed. She tried to keep her gun level with one hand and push herself forward with the other, but it all got clumsy wobbly with her chair pulling hard to the right and the wheel rubber squeaking, giving her approach away. *Who am I kidding?*

Mallory's mocking siren call lured her on. "Weren't you paid to protect everybody? Charlie delivered cash to you twice a month, and for that you were supposed to guarantee—"

"—I can protect you from Rogers," Riley said, talking over her. She gave up the protocol of unsupported engagement, put the gun in her lap, and closed the distance to Finn's doorway in one coasting thrust, stopping the chair just out of view.

"Rogers? You have no idea."

"Try me."

"HOW'S THAT WHEELCHAIR working for you?"

Mallory had walked backward into Finn's loft, pulling him with her, thrashing with her free hand at the lines hung with photographs, tearing them down, prints scattering. "I bet it sucks, trying to work those wheels and hold a gun at the same time." The Murphy bed was tucked away, giving her a lot of room to work with, Finn noticed, and no way for Riley to enter except through the open door. Mallory whispered, practically giddy, to Finn that all the stupid bitch was doing was stalling the ineluctable endgame, which, well, who could blame her?

Finn felt an eerie calm. Was he past fear, or just so scared it no longer registered? His mind was blank, his body on autopilot, everything in front of him playing out like a streaming video, remote, unreal.

"Was it Rogers who killed Charlie? Couldn't have been Mexico, he would've known not to pick up the casings." Riley's voice sounded thin, and already defeated. "You must've been there. You got him to give you the gun."

Mallory separated herself from Finn. Reached back and threw open the curtains on a big arching window of mullioned, beveled glass that faced, across a narrow alley, another loft building, which is why Finn generally kept the draperies closed.

Black eyes intent on the empty doorway, Mallory said to Riley, "You turned Charlie against me."

Behind her, through the window, in the facing flat of the building opposite, Finn could see a lumpy shadow resolve into Detective Don Mexico and stand tall, bracing a sniper rifle with a scope lens that refracted Finn's loft light, and a bright red sighting laser rose to fix its pinpoint on Finn's heart, its beam frayed into a hundred threads of silky traces as it passed through the bevel panes.

"No," Riley's voice replied. "That was someone else."

"WILLA?" Mallory spat the word like an obscenity.

"Love tends to unravel things."

"Love. You think I was in love with him?"

Riley watched a splintered laser-sighting beam dust the wall across from her, opposite Finn's loft doorway. She reevaluated her options, and confirmed that they were few. "I didn't presume to judge. That was between you and him. You and Charlie," Riley clarified. "On my end, it was always about getting to Mr. Rogers.

"Charlie gave you up. He thought it was his ticket out."

"Charlie was a disappointment."

Riley pulled her cell from her bag again, dialed 911, and let the call connect but didn't risk talking. Instead she put the phone down on the floor so that the operator could listen in and trace it. She felt her pulse, it was steady. The only fear she had was for Finn, the sweet, hapless dope who had stepped in front of a gun for her.

"So dark up on those cliffs," Mallory complained. "Dark, and the contract men made a hash of it, but I chose to let you live because I thought there was no way you'd connect the dots, that'd you'd go away and things could get back to . . . you know."

"Normal," Riley said.

"Besides, I don't like having to be the triggerman," Mallory admitted.

There was a moment's stillness that Riley knew meant nothing.

"C'mon in, Detective," Mallory said, impatient. "It's not like you're going to sneak up on me."

FINN WAS FROZEN in the middle of the loft, arms tingling, swallowing metallic bile and with Mexico's sight still pinned on his heart when Riley rolled through the front door, gun raised.

He hoped she couldn't see the fear in his eyes; he could read nothing in hers, but they fell to the dot on his chest and the flat line of her mouth softened. He grasped for something, anything, to put between himself and this terrible new unstable, slip-sliding terminus.

Mallory raised her .44 in two hands, and aimed it at Riley. "Put the gun down."

"Let Finn go."

Mallory shook her head. "How would that ever work?"

Riley's forward momentum took her to the kitchen counter, where she stopped herself, put her gun flat on the counter, and pivoted, open hands spread out to either side. Mallory, still cautious, respectful, distrustful, took another step backward into the empty space beyond Finn, finding even more separation, while still using him as a shield.

"Wave the shooter off," Riley said. "I don't know who he is, I don't care. If you finger Rogers for Charlie's murder, we can make a deal. Maybe you're a victim, here, too, Mallory. At the very least you could skate having to serve hard time."

Mallory laughed. "Yeah, but, see, here's the thing—" She let the sentence hang, milking it for all the drama she could. "Rogers is me, Detective. I'm who you were looking for all along."

Stunned, Finn had to run Mallory's confession through his head twice before it landed. But Riley just shook her head, calm, and said, "I don't believe it," in a way that again made Finn realize she'd already figured it out before Mallory had even spoken the words.

Mallory looked aggrieved. The red dot slid from Finn to Riley.

"It's all me, Detective," Mallory bragged. "My Charlie. My cop. My world. And I decide who lives and dies in it."

———

RILEY KNEW she'd run out of time. "You're going to have your cop do this?"

"Why not? He'll be the first responder," Mallory said. "I was never here."

Riley nodded. "Okay, but Charlie—that was for love, right? Killing him for dumping you? You were the triggerman on him, couldn't have been anyone but you gets that close, and shoots him with his own gun."

"I fucked up with the casings."

"You did. But love makes us do stupid things." She looked right at Finn when she said it.

"Love. Love is a lie," Mallory spat out acidly, as Riley's hand found the cartoon lever for the Murphy bed and jammed it down. The big window was shattered by gunfire and Finn and Mallory disappeared under the falling bedframe as bullets from the shooter's semiautomatic ripped through it.

Sweeping her gun from the counter with her other hand, Riley fumbled for the grip and put four rounds into the breaker panel beside the door, plunging Finn's loft into darkness. The shooter raked the room with pattern fire. But Riley had set her brake, yanked hard on the other wheel, and upended her chair. Bullets punched through the sling seat as she crashed out onto the floor, twisting her upper body as she fell, her gun held out at arm's length in one hand while the other cushioned her landing, carefully locating and aiming at the muzzle flashes bursting from the building across the alley and then tapping the trigger with her finger in quick succession the way she'd been trained until her clip was empty and there was just the ringing in her ears and the desperate silence and a delayed flood of useless adrenaline that caused her hands to shake and a cold sweat to overtake her.

"Finn?"

A milky light cast in the open doorway from the building corridor held particles of dust and plaster and fabric, and smoke eddied in it, lazy and diaphanous.

"Finn?"

She heard Finn crawl out from under the bed. "Yeah. Yes. Here."

"You hurt?"

"No."

Riley couldn't go to him. Couldn't even get herself up to a sitting position without a lot of wrangling that she was too spent to attempt just now. Sirens wailed outside, approaching. A faint voice of 911 bled questioning from Riley's phone, still active out on the landing.

"Did I forget to say 'duck'?" Riley asked Finn, wry.

He didn't say anything. She heard him moving, though, then saw the dull glow of his smartphone screen take his shadow to the work desks, then a brighter beam cut through the darkness, from a flashlight in Finn's hand. It found Mallory knocked senseless, crumpled half under the Murphy bed. It swept across and found Riley where she was sprawled on the floor near the kitchen, in the scatter of photographs, hand up to shade her eyes, squinting in the glare.

"Hey."

"Hey."

Finn shifted the beam away from her, to the shattered window, which glittered like diamonds on the floor, and then across to the facing apartment, where the cop named Mexico was disarranged awkwardly on the floor in front of the gaping window of that vacant loft space, his semiautomatic rifle just beyond one outstretched hand, black blood already pooling under him from a wild scatter of holes Riley had put in him.

It was a crime scene. And as Riley watched, Finn picked up a camera and went to work.

FLASHCLICK.

The empty loft and its bloody contents resolved itself and found some welcome coherence in his viewfinder. He saw everything in terms of light and composition, stripped of any connection to him, any emotion he might have struggled with. He was a camera.

By the time the first responders to Riley's 911 arrived on the scene, Finn was already in the building across the alley, photographing Mexico and his ambush staging area.

Body. Gun. Casings. Blood.

Through the broken window he could look back into and witness a scene he'd seen play out hundreds of times, surreal now in his own personal space. Cops and crime technicians in throwaway booties and latex gloves. The yellow evidence flags. Riley, in her damaged chair, was talking to Lennox and another Long Beach detective. She was wrapped in a reflective thermal blanket, ruddy scuff marks swelling on the side of her face where she fell.

EMTs worked on Mallory, who was unmarked but concussed, sitting up, mute, a bandage holding an ice pack to the back of her head, hands twisty-cuffed in front of her, eyes fixed and unfocused.

As she spoke with Lennox, Riley's eyes found Finn's. He felt his heartbeat shuffle the way it had when he first saw her, and not for the first or last time wondered how he'd ever found the courage to cross the bar.

11

"So you and her, this is gonna be a thing?"

"I don't know."

Joaquin had the forlorn look of a tween whose single parent was starting to date and which, considering Joaquin's lush new pelt of hipster neckbeard, seemed, to Finn, disingenuous at best.

"It's a fluid situation. Don't worry, you and me, we're still good."

"I'm not worried." Joaquin grazed on beer nuts and looked around the Palace grumpily.

Finn said, "Maybe this is the summer you learn to surf. Doesn't Diana, the blood-spatter crim, have that whole posse of *femmes* who shred?"

"I looked it up," Joaquin said, and Finn, for a moment, had no idea what he was talking about. "When upper-level large-scale air flow along the complex topography of the Southern

California coastline comes onshore by way of the Channel Islands, it gets turned around inland by the mountains that ring the basin and causes an obdurate counterclockwise circulating low-pressure vortex, accompanied by a southerly shift in coastal winds."

"Oh," Finn said. "We're back to that?"

"A soul-crushing increase in the marine layer. And a thickening of the coastal stratus. A schizophrenic spin cycle of gray and gloom, followed by fleeting wanton late-day sunshine, reset and repeat."

"It usually clears up after the Fourth."

"It can happen anytime between April and September, or drag on continuous from April to September, but peaks in June, yes."

"I'm gonna talk to Lennox about my camera," Finn said, eager to change the subject. "Should I be worried he'll try to kill me?"

"You're not worth the hassle," Joaquin said. "All that paperwork and mandatory incident review by the police commission. Plus there are at least half a dozen single women at City Hall that I know of who would gladly magic the Lennox baby wand."

"The what?"

"But," Joaquin continued, returning deftly to his theme, "here's the thing to remember, Finn: It turns counterclockwise."

Finn asked, "What does?" He knew, though.

"The eddy. It's why it always feels so melancholy, dude. Nostalgia. Our substitute for regional history. What is it Gatsby says? 'Boats against the current, borne back ceaselessly into the past'?"

"I didn't like Gatsby."

"You never read it."

"I did," Finn said. "In tenth grade. But you know me and mysteries."

Joaquin nodded, sardonic. "I thought I did."

"CHAIN OF CUSTODY works pretty well, but to say that it leads to justice, or truth, is a lie that we, collectively, in law enforcement, kinda just let slide."

They were alone in the Homicide bull pen. No witnesses. Finn watched Lennox flick his Clayton Kershaw bobblehead paperweight to make it shake.

"Truth and justice are two different things. And neither is absolute." For example, Lennox explained, casual, not apologetic, it was patently unfair, yes, but Finn's former Nikon Df was going to stay behind the wire mesh in property until the investigations into the Charlie Ko murder and the Sunken City shooting were completed. The Internal Affairs inquiry alone, the detective noted, could take many months.

Finn said, "You broke into my car, stole my camera and my laptop, and doctored my photographs."

He expected an explosion of denial. Lennox just tilted his head as if to say: *So?* "I doctored the crime scene," Lennox clarified. "I used your camera to take new pictures of it."

"Why?"

Lennox didn't answer for a while, but when he did, he first jumped way back to when Riley had left him in her angry wake, following their Willa Ko interview dustup, after which he had gone up into his office to sit with his gnawing discomfort that she could be right about everything. "I was like, what the fuck?" he explained to Finn. Lennox was a man for whom life had always run like a rotary engine, steady, smooth, no maintenance required. Homicide had always been his destiny; his dad was a cop, his uncle, his brother. And Riley, he said, had always been the one he'd marry. Since the moment he set eyes on her in the third grade. Life was locked in.

But it was after formally proposing to her at the Palace, he admitted, that something had snapped. Before her shooting. And then she spun out of his orbit, started to dissect him whenever they were together, "like she was looking for something she wasn't seeing." And, later, like she was seeing through him, he said, or past him, or worse. "For whatever it was I didn't have. It felt pretty shitty." But Lennox wasn't a complainer, and she was the one.

"Always," he insisted.

"Did she know that?" Finn asked, but Lennox wasn't listening.

Hard copies of the forensic crime scene photos from the Charlie Ko killing were on his desk, he said, along with the small envelope containing the bullet casings that had been in the evidence bin but not, as Riley had pointed out to him, in the photographs Finn had taken.

He had flipped through his murder book for a while, the notes and the statements and the timelines all a blur.

Finally he pulled up the day's duty log on his computer and saw that Mexico had checked in. He gathered together the photos and the casings and walked out into the Homicide bull pen but didn't find the big detective at his desk, so he asked the new girl, from bunko, with the lesbian haircut whose fucking name he could never remember—Poplowski's partner—where Mexico was and she said Donnie got a call and took off.

Jenson. Jennings? Something with a *J*, he was pretty sure. "Unless that was her first name."

Finn just listened.

Anyway, Lennox had returned to his own office, then, tired, but relieved, he told Finn. He decided he'd talk with Mexico as soon as the detective came back to the station, but this would give him time to prepare, so he could do it carefully, because he still didn't quite believe Mexico was on the dole. "For one thing, a cop would never kill Charlie in the condo, he'd have been way smarter than that, even Mexico." But a discussion would have taken place, Lennox wanted to be able to tell Riley that he'd tried.

"And then the call came in about the shooting."

"At your loft, yeah."

Finn waited. Lennox had talked himself in a circle, Finn's question still unanswered.

"The Cartier watch at the Sunken City scene was hot," Lennox said. "It raised certain questions about how Riley got it that I didn't want asked. So I contrived to disappear it from where she got shot."

"You thought she was the bad cop."

"Was, wasn't, I figured it was best not to expose her to closer scrutiny," Lennox hedged.

Finn thought about this for a few moments. "Tampering with evidence is a felony."

"So is receiving stolen property," Lenox countered, "accepting bribes, protecting criminals, obstruction of justice, accessory to the distribution of controlled substances, and the trafficking of people. Just for starters."

"You really believed she'd done all that?" Lennox said nothing. "You didn't trust her."

Finn thought, He still doesn't.

Lennox said, "The job of being a modern cop has a lot of moving parts."

"She was undercover."

"Was she?"

Finn wasn't sure how to take this, didn't know enough about Riley's cop life before he entered it to make a judgment on what she'd done, or what rules she may have broken. He remembered the man he'd met on the green line platform. Partner? Partner in crime? It wouldn't have surprised him if she'd broken all the rules, and unlike Lennox, he assumed that her reasons for doing so would be sound. No. *Airtight*.

Lennox looked so uncomfortable Finn felt sorry for him. But he understood something else, suddenly, and allowed himself a slow grin. "This is how cops try to say I love you."

"I'm not giving her up to you."

"I don't know her very well, but I'm pretty sure she's not something that can be taken or given," Finn pointed out.

Lennox bristled. "You know what I mean. She . . ." He thought better of whatever he was going to say, and announced instead, "We have history, me and her. You can't erase that."

"Depends on who wrote it," Finn observed.

Lennox looked away. "Well, she did what she did, I did what I did. Eventually IA will come ask you questions about both of us. You gonna make a big deal out of it?"

Finn shrugged, ingenuous. "Out of what?"

WILLA SAT with her public defender in the interview room, civilian clothes, nervous, waiting with an expression that a disinterested observer might have thought heartbreaking if she didn't already know that this was going to turn out okay. A faint reflection of Riley stared back at Riley in the one-way mirror window glass, seeming to watch Riley as Riley watched the door open and Willa's little girls charge in. They attacked their mom with ebullient hugs and frog kisses while Albert hung back in the doorway, smiling at his family reunited.

Riley said, "It's easy," and turned her chair away from the one-way window to face the observation room. "You make me a Homicide cop. I sign the waiver."

The room, in this case, consisted of the district attorney, the city attorney, and Homicide lead detective Terry Lennox.

"The doctored photos, the ones that cast a cloud over my shooting, the activities of Sergeant Mexico, and the sanctity of forensic evidence used to indict and convict God only knows how many other criminal cases . . . it all goes away. Win-win. Cast the late Detective Don Mexico as a heel or a hero, I don't care."

"I'm good with that, actually," the city attorney said.

Lennox said, "I bet you are," and affected his neutral, good-cop expression, which Riley knew well from many hours she'd watched him work witness interviews and suspect interrogations. It veiled his righteous rage. "But what if she's not—and I'm on the record saying she is not—capable of handling the physical demands of a job she just took like a hostage?"

Riley said, "She's right here, Terry. If you need to talk to her."

"He makes a good point," the DA told the city attorney, but the latter wasn't impressed.

"And this undercover operation she ran," Lennox continued. "Nobody downtown even seems to know much about it. No oversight."

Riley and the city attorney traded blank looks. He was African-American, in a smart linen suit, and if Finn had been in the room with them he might not have even recognized the man to whom, on the metro platform between Harbor and Century, he had given Riley's journals and collection of envelopes filled with bribes. "She caught a killer. She bailed out both of your ivory asses," the city attorney said. "Saved us ten years of appellate nightmares, and about a gajillion dollars in potential cop-malpractice civil settlements. Could be bipedal locomotion for cops is overrated."

The DA squirmed. "Look, could we—"

"—Finn Miller can be my legs," Riley said.

Lennox squeezed his eyes shut like he felt a headache coming on. The DA found some dirt under his thumbnail. The city attorney opened his briefcase.

"And I've still got hands," she continued drily. "Which means I can manage a firm grip on a venti soy macchiato and a cronut just like all the other bros in the bull pen."

The city attorney murmured, "Maybe better," amused. He slid some waivers in front of Riley and had her sign them before Lennox and the DA could delay it any longer.

"Sweet. Welcome back, Detective." He parked the documents, snapped his briefcase shut, and ushered the grim, unhappy district attorney away.

Lennox let the door close and lingered behind while Riley looked one more time with satisfaction into the interview room, now empty of Willa and her family.

"Happy now?"

"I don't know. I'm still in a wheelchair, Terry." She looked up at him and dug in the pocket of her jeans for the engagement ring she'd been keeping there, and thinking about, for days now, ever since the hospital had returned it to her. She held it out for Lennox. "You should have this," she said. "It's beautiful. Save it for someone who deserves it."

His swagger took the hit. "You can hang on to it awhile longer if you want," he said, low, a little husky. "Things keep changing. You know. Circle of life."

She laughed. "*Lion King*, Terry?"

Lennox flushed red. She flipped the ring on the table, between them, and it landed flat and skittered.

Lennox stared at it, and then said to her, his voice hard, "Do you know what you're gonna get? You're gonna get all the worst cases, the shit, the ones that make no sense, the ones that can't be solved. One after the fucking other. Piling up on your desk. By the time you come up for your six-month review, you won't be able to see over them."

"Is that supposed to scare me?"

With malice, Lennox said, "Yes."

"I earned this. I paid for it."

He took the ring and shoved his hands in his pockets. "Have it your way." He started to go, but paused, not looking back, offering her just the back of his head, and the razor burn from another cheap haircut. "You're on your own now." He walked out.

Through the door that he left open, she could hear the thrum of life in the building: bodies slurring by, police business, normal. Riley took a deep breath and wheeled herself out into it.

FINN MILLER WAS waiting for her. Slouched against the corridor wall, backpack lumped at his feet. He'd watched the lawyers leave, then Lennox storm out. It made sense to him, somehow, that Riley would be the last one out of the room, and it was all he could do not to smile. All these unanswered questions hung between them, swirling, like Joaquin kept saying, trapped between the islands of their past and the rocky ridges up ahead; or maybe just framed and frozen in time, to be archived, understood or ignored, mysteries. He didn't care. There was so much time.

"What's it like outside?" she asked him.

"Oh, you know."

She swerved past without looking up, as if denying that he was there, or maybe still unwilling to accept the possibility that he could be there, would be there for her, but nevertheless expecting he would shrug on his camera bag and catch up with her, walk beside her, keep pace with her as best he could, so that they could make their way together.

ACKNOWLEDGMENTS

Despite many factual touchstones, I don't pretend to be a stickler for police procedure, so any technical errata or liberties taken in the unfolding crime stories of the eddy are all mine. Similarly, the Los Angeles, Long Beach, and San Diego of my fiction are constructs of my imagination: not meant to be documentary, but aspiring to be true. That said, I was helped with granular details of an assistant U.S. attorney by the fine screenwriter and former federal prosecutor Barbara Curry. Teal Sherer generously shared with me her life with wheelchairs, spinal injury, and paraplegia. Erich Anderson provided key psychological and historical insight into San Diego, as well as an early read that helped convince me I wasn't crazy to pursue this triptych. Michael Convertino was mostly responsible the glorious bonobo diversion, Scott Shepherd an invaluable sounding board for '50s L.A. noir, and Susan Sontag's essays "On Photography" was an inspiration for the work of Finn Miller. I am, as always, deeply indebted to all the other usual suspects, including my fabulous agent, Victoria Sanders, the editorial genius of Benee Knauer, David Rosenthal, and all the excellent people at Blue Rider Press.

utt 3-16-17

ST 5-18-17

AL 7-20-17

ET 9-21-17

ST-9-9-21 DISCARD

ET 9-21-17 kp